FURY OVER TEXAS

Look for these exciting Western series from bestselling authors William W. Johnstone and J.A. Johnstone

The Mountain Man
Luke Jensen: Bounty Hunter
Brannigan's Land
The Jensen Brand
Smoke Jensen: The Early Years
Preacher and MacCallister
Fort Misery
The Fighting O'Neils
Perley Gates
MacCoole and Boone
Guns of the Vigilantes
Shotgun Johnny
The Chuckwagon Trail
The Jackals
The Slash and Pecos Westerns
The Texas Moonshiners
Stoneface Finnegan Westerns
Ben Savage: Saloon Ranger
The Buck Trammel Westerns
The Death and Texas Westerns
The Hunter Buchanon Westerns
Will Tanner: U.S. Deputy Marshal
Old Cowboys Never Die
Go West, Young Man

Published by Kensington Publishing Corp.

FURY OVER TEXAS

WILLIAM W. JOHNSTONE
AND J.A. JOHNSTONE

PINNACLE BOOKS
Kensington Publishing Corp.
kensingtonbooks.com

PINNACLE BOOKS are published by

Kensington Publishing Corp.
900 Third Avenue
New York, NY 10022

PUBLISHER'S NOTE: Following the death of William W. Johnstone, the Johnstone family is working with a carefully selected writer to organize and complete Mr. Johnstone's outlines and many unfinished manuscripts to create additional novels in all of his series, like The Last Gunfighter, Mountain Man, and Eagles, among others. This novel was inspired by Mr. Johnstone's superb storytelling.

All Kensington titles, imprints, and distributed lines are available at special quantity discounts for bulk purchases for sales promotion, premiums, fundraising, and educational or institutional use.

Special book excerpts or customized printings can also be created to fit specific needs. For details, write or phone the office of the Kensington Sales Manager: Kensington Publishing Corp., 900 Third Avenue, New York, NY 10022. Attn. Sales Department. Phone: 1-800-221-2647.

First Pinnacle Trade Paperback Edition: July 2026

ISBN: 978-0-7860-5233-2

ISBN: 978-0-7860-5234-9 (ebook)

10 9 8 7 6 5 4 3 2 1

Printed in the United States of America

The authorized representative in the EU for product safety and compliance
is eucomply OU, Parnu mnt 139b-14, Apt 123
Tallinn, Berlin 11317, hello@eucompliancepartner.com.

FURY OVER TEXAS

Chapter 1

Pine Lick, East Texas
Late summer 1888

Whiskey pulled the wet bandana from his back pocket and patted his sweaty face. He leaned back in the wooden chair as far as he could go without toppling over, hoping to catch a stray breeze wafting through the open door.

The humidity set his joints to hurting something fierce. He considered grabbing the bottle in the sheriff's bottom drawer just to take the edge off. Instead, he got up and walked over to the table just big enough to hold the washbasin. He dipped his head in the lukewarm water, using his cupped hand to pour some of it across the back of his neck.

"Why don't you bring some of that water over here, *boy*."

The man in the cell looked like a hundred pounds of melting lard wearing filthy clothes.

"I ain't your boy, and if you wanna keep talking like that, I'm happy to open that cell door and make you forget all about the heat." Whiskey dunked his bandana in the water and draped it around his neck. Whatever bit of cooling it brought couldn't compare to the heat of his anger.

"I'm happy to take my chances," the man said with a lopsided grin on his bearded face. His fingers gripped the iron bars, twisting them as if he could pull them apart. He was a scoundrel Whiskey had caught in Maxel's General Store the night before. The man, a stranger to the town, had first beat up Pap Maxel's teenage daughter as she was closing shop, before helping himself to three burlap sacks' worth of goods. Luckily, Whiskey had been making his rounds and heard the commotion. When he spied through the window Miss Lana on the floor doubled over in pain, the top of her dress nearly torn right off, he kicked in the door and had a go at the would-be thief. His knuckles still hurt, but it was a good kind of hurt. The kind that meant a job well done.

Quicker than a jackrabbit, Whiskey grabbed the shovel handle he kept by his desk and cracked it against the man's fingers. The prisoner flew back from the bars, howling like a whipped dog. He jammed his hands under his armpits.

"You broke my damn fingers, you no-good rat!"

Whiskey settled back in the creaking chair and leaned the shovel handle against his desk. "Well then, if you're a praying man, you might want to get down on your knees and give a little thanks to the Lord that your fingers are all I broke. Now sit down and shut your mouth before I really get angry."

Moaning in agony, the man said, "I need a doctor."

"How about I get a seamstress to sew that mouth of yours up? After what you did to Miss Lana, there's plenty women in town who would volunteer for the privilege. And some of them aren't as nice as me."

The prisoner shut up for a while, but more so because he set to whimpering in pain than from Whiskey's threat.

Whiskey heard the ring of familiar spurs as he was popping his knuckles, hoping it would release some of the pain.

"Morning, boss," he said as the sheriff strolled in.

"Whiskey."

The sheriff removed his tan Stetson and wiped his brow with the sleeve of his shirt. He spotted their prisoner and turned to his deputy.

"He broke into Maxel's and put a beating to Miss Lana."

"She okay?"

"She'll be hurting some the next couple of days." Whiskey tapped the side of his head. "How long this will take to heal is anyone's guess."

The prisoner, sitting on the unpadded bunk, lifted his swollen and bleeding fingers so the sheriff could see.

"Your houseboy did this to me!" A trail of snot went from his nose to the fibers of his overgrown mustache and into his mouth. "I want a doctor and to press charges!"

The sheriff pulled up a chair beside Whiskey. "What'd he do?"

"Called me *boy*."

"Like he did just now?"

Whiskey made it a point not to look into the cell, lest his ire get the better of him again.

"Mmm-hmm."

The sheriff addressed the prisoner. "You say that again to my deputy and I'll come in there and finish what he started." He sauntered to the cell and stared hard at the man's hands. "Claws like that won't be much good for stealing . . . or hitting on defenseless women. Might be, in the end, ol' Whiskey did you a favor. He just might have saved your neck from a future hanging."

They eyed each other for a while, before the prisoner broke first and went back to his suffering.

"What's your name?" the sheriff asked him.

"That's none of your business," the man said with his back to him.

"I'm about to make it mine in five seconds." The sheriff took the key to the cell out of his pocket and brandished his pistol. When the man turned around, his eyes went wide.

"All right! Fine! Name's Kelly."

"Kelly what?"

"Kelly Marsden."

The sheriff grinned. "Your momma named you Kelly? No wonder you have a hair up your rear." His laughter clearly irritated the man, who once again turned away from him to nurse his hand.

"You look tired," the sheriff said to Whiskey. "Go on home. I've got it from here. I'll see if there are any warrants for ol' Kelly."

Whiskey slowly extracted himself from the uncomfortable chair and tucked the wet bandana in his back pocket. "I'll make a round first before hitting the hay."

It was going on eight o'clock and the town was just coming alive, seeing as it was a Sunday. Pretty soon the sounds of church bells would fill the air.

"You had to babysit this plug-ugly fella all night. I've got morning rounds. Get some sleep. You earned it."

The sheriff was a quarter of a century younger than Whiskey, but the deputy always deferred to him, and for very good reason. He'd known the man since he was knee high to a grasshopper and respected the hell out of his father.

"Thank you, boss. Much appreciated."

Whiskey had gotten no more than one foot out the door when the sound of beating hooves stopped him in his tracks. He spied a young man on a blood bay headed straight for the sheriff's office.

"Company's coming."

The sheriff was beside Whiskey just as the rider dismounted, holding tightly on to the reins. The boy was covered in sweat and out of breath.

"You the sheriff?" he asked. The towheaded rider looked to be no more than ten or eleven.

"Pretty sure I am," the sheriff said as he tapped the star on his vest.

"You need to come to the reservoir quick! There's been a murder!"

"Just slow down, son."

The boy's chest heaved mightily, and his mouth opened and closed like a catfish on land. It looked as if tears had carved a path through the dirt on his face.

"Now, what's your name?" the sheriff asked calmly.

"Arch . . . Archibald Gibbons."

"Okay, Archibald. Who's been murdered?"

The boy's upper lip trembled. "My pa."

Sheriff Armstrong's spine stiffened.

"Did you see who did it?" In a way, he hoped the child was not witness to his father's murder, but rather having found the body after the fact. It would make his job more difficult finding the murderer, but it would be less of a blight on the child's mind.

"I don't know. A man. He came to the edge of the lake and started yelling his head off. My pa yelled back, and they started fighting, us in the water, and him on land. Then out of nowhere, he shot my pa dead!"

Whiskey looked to the sheriff. "My bed can wait."

"All right, then." He asked the kid, "You in shape to take us there?"

"Yes, sir."

"Then lead the way."

Whiskey and the sheriff mounted their horses, a pair of paints from the same breeder, and put the spurs to them as they followed the boy to the scene of the crime. Whiskey knew that even though the Lord took the seventh day off to rest, misguided men were always busy at their dirty work.

The hard run to Lake Stanton just a few miles away cooled the sweat on Sheriff Mack Armstrong's face and neck. Sure, there were better reasons to get out of that stifling office, but murder wasn't a new or rare occurrence in Pine Lick. Ever since the lumber boom, folks from every point on the compass had been coming to the growing town in search of the almighty dollar.

Situated just south of the over 30 million acres of Piney Woods, Pine Lick was a perfect location to take advantage of the country's increasing need for lumber. The railroad hadn't made it there yet, so the cut trees traveled by river to the sawmill in town, where they were processed before heading farther south along the Angelina River.

With the economic boom came a never-ending stream of bad actors. One of the previous sheriffs had been shot down while having his supper at the Sawdust Saloon. He never had a chance to see who hated him enough to take his life. After him was another short-lived sheriff, who went by the name of Bushwack Bill. Old Bill had had his horse shot out from under him by a gang of bank thieves. They took off with the loot, while Bill suffocated under his horse's deadweight.

Then came Mack's father, Branch, who had maintained law

and order while keeping this side of the grass. He'd retired his tin star to fill his time building the modest family farm. He saw what Pine Lick was itching to become, and decided he'd rather live out the rest of his life in relative peace and hard work while his body could still stand it. The last thing he'd wanted Mack to become was anything even remotely related to law enforcement.

Mack figured he wasn't the first son to go against his father's wishes, and was damn sure he wouldn't be the last.

"Getting close," he said to Whiskey. His deputy slipped his Colt revolver from its holster.

Riding alongside the worried kid, he said, "Fall back behind us and stay there."

The kid did as he was told.

The paints dug into the grass and soil, hugging up the rise to the lip of the lake. Sheriff Armstrong gave the dam a quick look, as he always did, just to make sure there were no signs of leakage. Hastily constructed years ago, the dam's worsening condition kept him up plenty of nights.

For the moment, that wasn't his top concern.

The man lying in the grass beside a canoe with his arms stretched above his head was front and center. A large man wearing worn overalls standing beside the body saw them and waved them over. He was dripping wet and holding his moth-eaten hat in his thick, callused hands.

"I seen what happened and swam across. Thought maybe I could help, but he was already gone."

Armstrong and Whiskey's heads were on a swivel.

"Good man, Bear. Did you see who shot him?"

Michael "Bear" O'Hanlon nodded his head. His wiry black beard brushed against his chest. "My eyes may not be what they once were, but I swear it was that fancy fella who's building the lodge over yonder."

"Cheever?" Whiskey asked.

"Yep. That'd be him."

Armstrong dismounted and checked the man's pulse. He saw the neat hole in his throat and motioned with his head to Whiskey to make sure the boy didn't come any closer.

"You see Cheever shoot this man?"

"I sure enough did. What with all the shouting going back and forth, it was hard not to."

The sheriff nodded at his deputy. "Stay here with the boy and Bear. I'll find Cheever."

"Maybe it'd be wiser if I went with you. He did just shoot a man."

Armstrong's stomach coiled with disgust. "Yes, an unarmed man in a boat with a young boy. Cheever's a gutless coward. I'll be fine."

Buzzards had already started circling in the leaden sky. "Bear, make sure that body isn't touched."

The big man looked up and said, "Can do, Sheriff."

The Arcadian Men's Retreat was just a hundred yards from the scene of the crime. The main house had been completed, the fresh smell of wood from Pine Lick's own sawmills riding what warm, moist breeze was about. Half a dozen smaller bungalows were in various states of construction, most of them complete. Since it was a Sunday, the working crew had the day off. The sheriff had heard that there were plans to build a dozen more, granted, if the opening was a success.

Armstrong tied up his horse at the hitching post and pushed his way inside the main house. The heat of anger burned red on the back of his neck. He flexed his fingers and balled them into fists.

"Cheever! Where the hell are you?"

After a slight pause came a reply. "In the study, Sheriff."

Striding through the vestibule, Armstrong opened a door to an empty room. He'd yet to pay a visit to the lodge house and had no idea where the study was located.

"I'm not in the mood for hide-and-seek," he said. "Why don't you just come to me with your hands over your head."

"If you insist."

Cheever sounded as if Armstrong's presence was an inconvenience. Armstrong pulled his Colt out of its holster, ready to see the wealthy snob catch a bullet if needed.

Tony Cheever had arrived at Pine Lick a year prior, leaving his home in Chicago "to tame the South," as he'd been overheard by many within earshot, and add whatever level of sophistication was possible. His goal was to build a men's retreat catering exclusively to the wealthy. Hunting, fishing, a chance to get away from the hustle and bustle in the fledgling cities of the Midwest and Northeast, were the advertised main attractions, though anyone with half a brain knew there would be a lot of power brokering going on over expensive scotch and cigars. Cheever was going to charge astronomical fees to enjoy the very things the citizens of Pine Lick did every day of their lives for free.

But to do so, he had to make the lake and neighboring land a rare and exclusive commodity. To that end, he'd been buying up what he could and making a general nuisance of himself to anyone who dared trespass. One thing Cheever did not do was share. Not for nothing anyway.

Cheever emerged from an open doorway on the left side of the oak-paneled hall. He wore a white three-piece suit, his jet-black hair slicked back on his head, a pencil mustache plastered on his lip. His hands were half-raised in clear defiance of Armstrong's order.

"To what do I owe the honor?"

"I'm taking you in, so if you'll oblige, I'd like you to turn around and put your hands behind your back."

He arched an eyebrow. "Taking me in. What for? Is it a crime to read a book on a Sunday morning? I admit it wasn't the Bible, but that shouldn't be an offense to anyone but the local preachers around these parts."

Armstrong stepped closer. Cheever did not turn around or put his hands at his back.

"I'm happy to do this the hard way."

"I'd like to know what I'm being arrested for, if that's too much to ask."

Not punching Cheever in the face was just about too much for Armstrong to ask of himself. Instead, he grabbed the man by his upper arms, wheeled him around, and pushed him against the wall.

"You're too smart to play this dumb. I'm taking you in for murdering a man at the lake."

Cheever grunted as Armstrong slapped the cuffs on him, driving his knee into his back, but managed to keep his composure.

"Murdering a man at the lake? That's patently ridiculous."

Armstrong turned him around so they could see eye to eye.

"I have two witnesses. You care to change your statement?"

Cheever's eyes went dead and cold. "I've never murdered anyone in my life. You sure you want to go through with this? My lawyers can make your life very unpleasant."

Armstrong had heard that Cheever had amassed his fortune from being a card sharp who bounced from city to city, adding to his coffers at every stop. Looking at the man's blank, unreadable face, he understood all the stories told about him. His was a poker face that told no tales.

"I'll take my chances," Armstrong said, roughly leading him out of the lodge house.

Armstrong was hot and angry and in need of some kind of release. When Cheever stopped at the doorstep and was about to open his mouth, the sheriff walked through him as if he were cigar smoke hanging in the air. Cheever went down like a sack of flour. With his hands cuffed behind his back, his face smacked off the wooden porch with a satisfying crunch, followed by a spate of yowling that would bring the chickens on home.

For the first time that day, Sheriff Armstrong smiled.

Chapter 2

The rain came down in sheets so thick, it was hard for Branch Armstrong to see the barn from the field. The humidity had been rising all day, and Branch knew sooner or later the skies had to pop. He guided his sorrel, Gypsy, back home at a slow trot.

As he passed the unassuming house he'd built with his own two hands over a decade ago, he spotted his wife, Kate, standing outside the open door, letting the rain wash over her. She waved when she saw him before tilting her head back and smiling into the storm.

There was a time during the Civil War when he thought he'd never see Kate again. Not when Fort Fisher, where he was stationed, was being pounded by cannon fire from invading ships in the harbor, and especially not when he was captured by the Union soldiers and sent to the Elmira Prison Camp in New York, a state he'd never had any intention of visiting.

Those were bleak days, and try as he might to put them behind him, there were some things that he knew would never go away.

His slight limp was a constant reminder of one particular night that both saved him and troubled him. Frostbite had led to him losing three toes that night. It was a minor nuisance compared to the lost limbs and disfigurements so many other men suffered, which is why he never complained, not even to his wife.

The town of Pine Lick attracted people from every walk of life. Prosperity had a way of doing that. There were quite a few Civil War veterans in town, from both sides of the war, looking to make the last half of their lives more tolerable. He knew them by their missing legs and arms, or in some cases, the vacant glaze that would fall over their eyes from time to time.

It had been a dry summer and more than just the crops had suffered. A day like today was a long overdue gift from above. During his Sunday sermon, last week and today, Reverend Smiley had said a special prayer, asking God Himself if He might send a few rain clouds Pine Lick's way. He'd beseeched the Lord with a loud voice and song. It had reminded Armstrong of the rain dances he'd heard tale of Indians conducting when the land was dry and dusty, crops wilted, and wild game skinny and ragged.

Armstrong had been a churchgoing man because his wife insisted on it. He had to admit, there was a kind of comfort to those Sunday mornings, even when the church was hotter than a bonfire or colder than the deep end of a well. Something about the ritual, the familiarity of it, had a way of settling his soul. Reverend Smiley's sermons, long-winded and meandering on his good days, were something Armstrong could do without.

This rain, this is what made him feel closer to God.

"So long as it doesn't peter out," he said to Gypsy as the entered the barn. He patted her neck, dismounted, and went about unsaddling her before walking her to her stall and making sure she had plenty of food and water.

Kate had gone back into the house. He found her dripping wet next to their wood-burning stove. Branch came up behind her and pulled her close. Kissing the raindrops from her neck, he let his hands wander.

"Aren't you frisky?" she said, dropping the spoon into the pot of stew.

"You can't go getting yourself soaked to the skin and not expect a reaction."

"The house is so hot, I couldn't resist."

Branch turned his wife around and looked deep into her chestnut eyes. She may not be the young filly who bedeviled his brain with her looks and curves, quick laugh and even quicker wit. But to Branch, she was even more beautiful than when they'd courted. Knowing exactly what was under those clothes had him riled up and anxious. With their son grown and out of the house, their marital relations had never been better.

"I can't resist, either," he whispered in her ear.

They stripped off by the stove, some part of the back of Branch's mind thinking it was best to leave the clothes in a heap right there. Maybe the stove would dry them some.

He carried her to the bed, where they made love. After, they lay together. Branch rested his head on his wife's chest, listening to her heartbeat go from a wild gallop to a slow and steady lope.

The sound of rain pattering the roof lulled them into an easy but brief sleep.

After a while, Kate shifted, waking Branch up. "The stew's going to burn."

"Just add a little more water," Branch replied sleepily.

She got up and put on her robe, a threadbare thing that her mother had given her when they'd married almost thirty years ago. Branch had promised her many times to buy her a new one, but she'd flatly refused. Kate was a sentimental woman, as well as frugal as a banker. As long as it fit—she'd put on a few pounds, but not nearly enough to come close to bursting the seams—and covered what it needed to cover, what was the sense of replacing it?

"You coming back to bed?"

"No, and you're getting up as well. We need more wood."

He reached out for her. She playfully slapped his hand away. "Sakes. I keep waiting for you to settle down a bit. *We're* not young anymore."

"You make me feel young. Besides, we're just making up time lost to the war and raising that son of ours."

Kate grinned. "Oh, I think we've more than made up for it."

Branch had just swung his legs out of bed to put on his overalls when there was a pounding at the door. Kate's face clouded with concern. It wasn't often people came calling, much less practically breaking down their door.

With no time to fiddle with clothes, Branch grabbed his Schofield from the holster hung over a peg in the wall and motioned for his wife to get as far from the door as possible.

Pine Lick was a town on the rise, thanks to the constantly buzzing sawmills and lumber trade. There wasn't an empty lot in all of Main Street. That also made it an attraction for a never-ending stream of unsavory characters looking to make a quick buck and cause a lot of trouble in doing so. Branch put his finger to his lips. Kate took their hunting rifle off the wall.

The pounding continued.

"Yeah!" Branch shouted.

There was no answer.

The pounding became more urgent.

"Who is it?"

Now fully aggravated, Branch whisked the door open and raised his pistol. A blast of rain pelted his naked flesh.

The short man standing in the doorway looked more relieved

than worried. The deep lines in his rawhide face tilted up just a bit when he smiled. He had a thick cigar tucked into the corner of his mouth.

"Is this the way you have come to greet your guests?" he said, exhaling a plume of smoke.

Branch exhaled and lowered his pistol. "Why in hell didn't you answer me, Otto? I thought you were trying to bust my door with all that hammering."

"I could not hear you," Otto said. "Your door is thick, and my ears are not those of a young man."

"Well, come in before the whole place floods."

Otto was a Kickapoo Indian, who had traveled anywhere that was not a reservation. He'd settled in Pine Lick five years ago, taking up land abutting Branch's. In that time, Otto, whose Indian name he said had been something that translated to Gliding Otter, had become a good friend and handy neighbor. His long, braided gray hair hung wetly down the center of his back.

Branch knew that people talked behind his back, wondering why he associated himself with an Indian, and, when he'd been sheriff, selecting a Black man as his deputy. What they didn't know was that he'd seen enough division between men during the Civil War. Atrocities that would forever haunt him had also changed his way of thinking. He didn't care about the color of a person's skin or where they were from. All that mattered was that they were good, fine people.

Otto certainly fell into that category.

Something had to be wrong because Otto was not one to go slamming on doors.

"What has you all fired up that you scared me out of my underwear?"

When Otto spied Kate, sans rifle, he removed his moth-eaten

hat and gave a slight bow. "Sorry to be a bother, Miss Kate." He also tamped out his cigar on the bottom of his boot, fully aware that Kate was not a fan of the smell of cigars or cigarettes.

"You're never a bother. You just gave us a start."

Otto eyed Branch up and down. "I do not believe I am the reason for your lack of underwear."

"Hold on." Branch went to fetch his clothes.

"What seems to be the problem?" Kate asked their usually reserved neighbor.

"There is trouble in town. Men from an outfit in Arkansas are tearing up the Sawdust Saloon. And I hear the jail is already full with a thief and Mr. Cheever."

Branch emerged from the bedroom fully clothed and slipping on his holster. "Cheever? What did he do, other than be a pain in the rear?"

Water dripped from Otto onto the wood floor. "They say he killed a man just for fishing."

"He's a nasty piece of work, but I never took him for a killer. Strange. How many men from this outfit?"

Otto tilted his head in thought. "I think ten or twelve. No, ten. That little Timmy told me when I was going into town for a drink. I think they will need some help."

Though it had been a couple of years since Branch Armstrong had been sheriff, he knew he could never fully retire until his son removed his star. Mack was young and smart and strong, not to mention pretty handy with a gun, but still, Branch worried about him. With the exception of his own time keeping the town safe, sheriffs in Pine Lick didn't have a firm grip on longevity, most of them ending up in a pine box or crippled.

Branch kissed Kate on the cheek. "Be back soon."

"It doesn't sound like it."

"You know how much I love your stew." To Otto, he said, "You armed?"

"Always."

Tugging on his oilskin, Branch ran to the barn. Gypsy would not be happy going out again, but such was the life of a horse.

And, it appeared, retired lawmen.

Chapter 3

Sheriff Mack Armstrong got word about the goings on at the Sawdust Saloon from several frightened patrons as they poured in the jail's doors. With everyone talking over one another, he was a dog's hair close to firing his pistol into the ceiling to get them to settle down.

Cheever looked amused at the chaos, while Kelly the would-be thief begged for someone to get him a doctor. The townsfolk paid him no mind.

"I'll head on over," Armstrong said once he got the lay of the situation. "Can one of you rustle up Whiskey for me?"

Young Timmy Cuthbert, who shouldn't have been within spitting distance of the Sawdust, volunteered and darted out into the pouring rain.

It wasn't the first time a company of cowpunchers had stormed into town looking to raise some hell while spending their hard-earned money. He was reasonably sure he couldn't count as high as the number of rabble-rousers who had besieged Pine Lick over the years. Success, like a cow pie, attracted flies.

This particular crew appeared to be a little heavy-handed. Some towns in the county didn't have a bona fide lawman on the payroll. This outfit most likely thought Pine Lick was just like the others.

"How many?" Whiskey said when he walked into the crowded jail. His soaked shirt was buttoned wrong, and he was still adjusting his belt. Little Timmy must have roused him from his cot.

"I counted ten," said Fingers, the piano player at the Sawdust. He wore a black bowler hat and always kept his hands in his pockets when he wasn't playing. Fingers was the first to hightail it out of any skirmish, lest his ten moneymakers get damaged in a fight.

"Okay, I want everyone to go home. Whiskey and I will take care of it."

"Just two against ten?" Fingers said.

"You want me to deputize you?" the sheriff asked.

"I was just saying," the piano player replied with his head down.

"And I thank you for pointing out the obvious. Now if you'll please."

Armstrong and Whiskey parted the packed crowd and stepped into the muddy street. The Sawdust was just a couple of blocks away.

Sam Redmond, the town barber, called them over. He stood under the awning to the post office. Sunday was his day of rest. He was a regular at the Sawdust when he wasn't cutting hair or shaving faces.

"I hear half of 'em went on over to Belle Dupree's. And Butch got the wrong end of a rifle stock."

Butch Nathans owned the Sawdust and was the sole bartender. He was as broad as a barn and mean as a grizzly when the occasion called for sterner measures. Armstrong had been counting on Butch's help.

"How hurt is he?"

Sam slicked the remaining raindrops off his bald head. "He was out cold when I hightailed it out of there."

"We'll head to the Sawdust first. I want to make sure Butch is okay. I'm sure the ladies at Belle's will keep the rest preoccupied until we get there."

The sheriff gave Whiskey a nod and they were back in the muddy streets and pouring rain. The humidity only seemed to be getting worse. It was hard to tell where his sweat ended and the rainwater began.

Shops and restaurants of all kinds lined both sides of Main Street. They passed the butcher shop and bakery, with a dressmaker to their right, next to the always-busy carpentry/furniture store. Sheriff Armstrong took note of Wilson's Drug Store and the new pane of glass in the front window. Someone had thrown a rock through it two weeks ago and made off with a bushel of the chemicals Wilbur Wilson used to make his medications and tinctures. The massive stone structure of the Second Federal Bank was cold and quiet. The shops were closed up for the night, their windows dark and mysterious. There were a few people walking into the Palace Hotel down the road, most likely calling it a day.

There were livery stables on both ends of the road, where he was sure the troublemakers had put up their horses for the night. He'd make it a point to visit each when they were done, to make sure the horses were kept from their owners.

They were not fifteen feet from the double swinging doors to the Sawdust Saloon when two riders came hell-bent for leather at them. Armstrong went for his Colt. So did Whiskey.

It wasn't until they got closer and reined their horses in that Sheriff Armstrong realized they were friend, not foe.

"Pa? What are you doing here?"

Mack's father tied his horse to the hitching post and slipped his rifle out of the holder on the horse's side.

"Otto said you might need a hand."

Mack was of two minds. On the one hand, he wanted to remind his father that he was the sheriff now and he didn't need civilians getting in the way. On the other, he appreciated the help in evening out the odds. Because of this mental storm, all he could do was nod.

Otto had a six-shooter in each hand and an unlit cheroot in his mouth. The Indian had helped his father when needed in the past. He was a crack shot, even though he looked ready to be put out to pasture.

Sheriff Mack Armstrong made sure he was the first in the door, with Whiskey practically alongside him. The saloon was a mess. Chairs and tables had been thrown about, many of them broken. Glasses were smashed and bottles of booze leaked their contents on the sawdust-covered floor. He spotted Butch face down at the end of the bar. Blood seeped from a cut on his forehead.

Four strange men sat at a round table playing cards, paying them no mind.

"Well, at least we're even," Armstrong whispered to his deputy.

The Sawdust had a second floor with rooms to rent. Whiskey cast his eyes along the balcony. "For the moment, any others are sleeping it off."

Armstrong was pretty sure the rest were at Belle's. These four either cared more about cards than a roll in the hay, or they were too drunk to make the walk up the hill.

And Belle had Tiny Ed to keep the men in line. Armstrong had never met a larger man, and neither had his father. Tiny Ed was taciturn by nature, but the sheer sight of the size of the man was enough to stop most people in their tracks if they were up to no good. If it came to a fight, a trail of broken bones led from Tiny Ed's fists to the prairies of Texas.

The sheriff kept his gun trained on the men. "Hate to put a damper on your fun."

Three of the men gave him a side-eye, their gazes taking the newcomers in. The one that had his back to them turned around and tipped his hat. Dried rivers of mud creased his face and beard. Still holding his cards close to his chest, he said, "Can I help you?"

"Where's the rest of your crew?"

The cowboy tilted his head. "Oh, out and about, I guess. I'm not their momma."

Sheriff Armstrong slipped his finger on the trigger. None of the men appeared to be drunk, which robbed him of an advantage. Knocking drunks over the head and dragging them to the jail or a wagon headed out of town was simple stuff.

"I need you to put your cards down real slow and raise your hands."

"We can cut you in if you like, Marshal. You and the old fella. The other two'll have to watch. We don't play with those kinds."

Armstrong's blood simmered.

"It's time for you to go. You wore out your welcome quicker than most. And leave the money on the table. We'll call that the fine you pay for getting this place back to respectability."

The man turned away from him, checked his cards, and placed a bet. The other three took his cue and ignored them.

"Maybe they are like me and do not hear so good," Otto said.

"No, they hear plenty good," Branch Armstrong said. He'd come across men like this before. In his experience, confrontations never ended without an exchange of lead. As usual, when there was danger with his son near, he offered a quick prayer to let a bullet find him instead. He picked up a broken stool and smashed it on the ground. "Hey! That wasn't a request."

With that, all four men pushed their chairs back and spun to face them. Their slickers spattered mud in every direction.

Guns were drawn.

Before anyone could pull a trigger, a massive gust of wind pummeled the Sawdust. The saloon doors swung open, blowing an almost-supernatural sheeting of rain into the saloon.

It pelted the backs of the sheriff and his men. A minor inconvenience.

It nearly blinded the cowboys with grit and dust whisked up from the saloon's dirty floors.

The Armstrong men, Otto, and Whiskey took advantage of the distraction and barreled toward the stunned cowboys. Each wrapped their arms around the cowboys' waists and drove them hard to the ground.

Sheriff Armstrong made sure to take the man he thought to be the leader. He mashed the cowpuncher's wrist with his knee hard enough for him to release his pistol. They struggled, but a few quick jabs to the cardplaying cowboy's nose stopped him right quick.

A shot cut through the tussle. One of the cowboys wailed.

Armstrong looked over to see Otto putting his pistol back in its holster. "He did not want to release his weapon."

There was blood on the floor and a hole in the man's hand.

The sheriff looked over at his father, who had just choked a cowboy until he passed out.

Whiskey, straddling his captive, breathed heavily as he looked at the flapping doors. "I guess we have to thank a lady for making sure we all got home tonight."

"A lady?" the sheriff said. "I don't see no lady."

"You cain't see Mother Nature. But sure enough, she brought the cavalry tonight."

Chapter 4

The covered wagon had set up a ways from the raging river. The rain had been an unwelcome companion for over a day now. The only silver lining, as far as Slip was concerned, was that there hadn't been any lightning accompanying the soaker. When he was a teen, he'd seen a man fried like a potato dropped in a fire, and he'd had a healthy fear of those celestial sparks ever since.

"You see anyone around?" he asked the old man who was busy surveying the area with his spyglass.

"No, but that don't mean they aren't."

"Probably just some homesteaders taking a spell from the storm."

The old man collapsed the spyglass and stuffed it in his coat pocket. "Probably so."

Sitting atop their horses, they stayed perfectly still behind a tall bush, watching and waiting.

"I'm wet and I'm starving," Slip opined. "Sitting here ain't getting us anywhere."

He had a point. If they were going to lose precious time, they might as well do it productively.

"Hell, maybe they're the type that found Jesus and will be happy to help a couple of strangers. Only way to know is to head on over."

The old man's horse nickered. He wasn't worried about the folks in the wagon hearing it on account of the durn blasted noise the rain made. It would be easy to saunter over there and ask for some Christian kindness without rousing suspicion.

It would also be easy for Slip to send their situation sideways. He was young and passionate and driven. He also had that dark, hardened thing inside his heart, which sometimes made him reckless and brash. What had happened in West Virginia had planted a seed of growing concern in the old man. Maybe he should have left Slip back home. Then again, the boy's mind was made up; and if he wasn't here to keep Slip in line, the boy would most likely be on the wrong side of a rope about now.

"You stay behind me," the old man said as he urged his horse around the bush.

"Whatever you say. I'm just hoping there are some biscuits in there. A bottle of rye wouldn't be too much to ask for, would it?"

The old man didn't reply. He kept his eyes on the wagon and surrounding area. He didn't want to be surprised by anyone who might be out and about.

Just a few feet from the wagon, the rain got worse, if that was even possible. It beat against the canvas. The old man suspected it must sound like being surrounded by a thousand drunk Indian drummers inside that wagon. It might be better to stay out in the rain.

But the allure of there being some dry food was enough to drive him on. He looked back to make sure Slip was still behind him.

When he got within kicking distance, he put his boot to the side of the wagon. A light flared inside. He squinted through the rain to make out how many people were inside the covered wagon. It was too hard to tell.

The back flap kicked open. A gray-haired man poked his head

out and spotted the old man and Slip. He held an old rifle. There was no shake to his grip.

"Yes?" he said testily.

The old man tipped his cap. What seemed like a bucket of water spilled onto his horse and saddle. "Sorry to disturb you. My companion and I were just wondering if you had anything to eat that you could spare. Between this storm and a run of bad luck, we're kind of desperate at the moment."

The rifle swung toward Slip when he pulled up alongside the old man.

"Howdy," Slip said, mustering up his best smile.

"I don't have anything you'd want," the man said.

"We're not picky," the old man said, tilting his head to get a better look inside the wagon. He spotted an older woman before the man shifted his position and blocked his sight line.

"Man won't live long in Texas if he is picky. But that's not my concern."

"Even a bit of jerky would do us just fine," Slip said.

The man shook his head and readjusted his grip on the rifle. "I told you, I don't have a thing to share."

Keeping his tone friendly, the old man said, "That big wagon of yours. Surely, there has to be something for a pair of fellow travelers. Heck, even a place to just sit and dry for a spell would be a gift from on high."

There was a click when the rifle's hammer was pulled back.

"The only thing I have for you is advice. And that's to get moving."

"That's not very Christian of you," the old man replied with a heavy shake of his head.

"I'm not Christian. Now, if you'll please."

The old man knew there was no way of changing this buzzard's mind. If the roles were reversed, he'd be the same way. Trust was in short supply out in the wilds, especially when you had a woman along.

With the rain pounding down on the wagon, the old man didn't hear Slip dismount and run at the old-timer. Slip grabbed the rifle barrel and wrenched it from the man's hands. Before he could stop him, Slip hit the man with the stock and crawled inside the wagon. The woman immediately yelled bloody murder.

The old man tied his horse to the wagon wheel as fast as he could, with the rain making everything too slick to handle, and jumped into the wagon. Slip's back was to him. A woman with gray hair spun up in a bun held her shaking hands before her terrified face. Her screams were close to drowning out the cacophony of the storm.

"What in the hell do you think you're doing?" the old man shouted as he grabbed Slip's arm and spun him around.

"Getting what they should have given us. Look!"

At the woman's feet was a cast-iron skillet, half-full with biscuits. An open jar of honey sat atop an overturned crate.

The old man did a quick check on the unconscious geezer. Blood trickled from the split skin on the side of his forehead.

Slip whipped his arm from the old man's grasp and picked up the skillet of biscuits.

"Will you shut your mouth?" he said to the woman. "All that caterwauling will set my appetite back."

"Put the food down and let's go," the old man said.

With his mouth full of dry biscuit, Slip pulled out his pistol and said, "Well, we might as well take the whole kit and caboodle now."

He pointed the pistol at the frantic woman's forehead and spit crumbs at her face when he ordered her to shut up again.

Things were getting out of hand in a hurry. There were plenty of lawmen all over Texas. The old man was well aware that even though the state had been far from tamed, leaving a trail of bodies was a good way to get them killed. They'd had to look over their backs ever since Slip's incidents in West Virginia and Missouri. They were too close to blow everything all to hell now.

A split second before Slip pulled the trigger, the old man chopped at his arm so the shot went through the canvas top of the wagon.

"What'd you do that for?" Slip asked, his eyes wild, while bits of biscuit peppered his lips and decorated his shirt.

"Keeping you from making a mistake you'll regret."

The errant shot had tamped the woman's screams to hurried whimpering. She cowered against a wooden chest, with her eyes fixed on her sleeping husband.

"Well, we can't just leave them here. They've seen us."

"Which would not have been a problem if you'd done what I told you," the old man said, feeling his impatience rise like the morning sun. If Slip hadn't been family, he'd have left him months ago to fend for himself.

Slip had always had a wild streak in him, and an anger that came out in peculiar ways. The old man thought a little hardship on the trail might have knocked some of the stuffing out of him by now. That was a miscalculation that worried him more and more.

Helping himself to another biscuit, Slip said, "So, what are we gonna do? Hold hands while we travel together and sing songs?"

The old man removed his hat and pinched the bridge of his nose. He was in no mood or condition to be making decisions like this. What he wanted to do was grab the bedroll he spied beside the unconscious man and have a long, dry sleep. That wasn't in the cards.

What bothered him was that Slip had a point. Surely, the couple would report them to the nearest authority. Sure, they could wave guns in their faces and make them swear on their children's lives and God almighty not to breathe a word of what happened to a solitary soul. The promise would wear off once he and Slip rode away. It was human nature to renege on a promise made out of fear. He'd seen it plenty of times in the war. It wasn't a double cross so much as, he guessed, setting the balance of things right. One couldn't commit acts of evil and expect to die in grace.

Slip snapped his fingers, stopping the old man's mind from wandering. "I know what. Come over here and help me hold her down."

The woman's eyes sprang wide open. She tried desperately to scramble out of the wagon.

"Oh, no you don't," Slip grunted as he grabbed her by the ankle and pulled her back. He straddled her waist and took out the big bowie knife that had been his father's. The woman twisted and turned, struggling to get out from under him. He adjusted his knees to pin her arms to her side. Slip grabbed her roughly by the chin.

The old man had a notion to knock Slip sideways.

"They can't describe us to the law if they can't talk," Slip said, angling the tip of the knife at the woman's open mouth. "If you don't help me hold her head still, I might take off more than I should."

The thought of cutting the woman's tongue out sickened the old man.

Then again, at least the momentary pain would fade away in time, and she and her husband would live. What life without a tongue would be like was anyone's guess. It all depended on how one took to the situation. Plenty of soldiers had lost parts of themselves on the battlefield. Some went back to their homes and farmed, built families, thrived. Others fell into a bottle or put a gun to the side of their heads.

"Damn you, Slip."

The younger man paled, as if the words had wounded him somehow.

"It's the only way," Slip replied, turning his head away so he didn't need to see the look in the old man's eyes.

It wasn't the only way, but Slip's irrational actions had forced them into a corner yet again.

After a short while, the old man placed his rough hands on either side of the woman's head. He spoke to the woman, trying to soothe her fears, though he saw it was pointless.

Slip propped her mouth open with a chunk of wood he'd found in the wagon. The bowie knife slid between her teeth and Slip got to sawing.

Chapter 5

Reverend Jake Smiley stood in the center of the aisle and stared up at the ceiling with a scowl. Heavy drops of rainwater came through a hole in the roof, plinking into the washbasin Matilda had brought in. She watched each drop splash into the basin, her hands wrestling at her stomach.

"I just thought, how are we going to carry the basin out to dump it when it's full?" she said. "It'll be too heavy for us."

Her husband shook his head. "If the rain keeps up, we're not going to have to worry about that, dear. We just need to make sure we're not here when the roof crashes in."

As if the poorly constructed First Baptist Church understood the reverend's words, the timbered eaves cracked and groaned as another gust of wind growled around them. Outside, in the nearby barn, the horses whinnied with growing panic.

"I'll get us a couple of buckets so we can lighten the load," Reverend Smiley said. "I'll check on the horses while I'm there. Kill two birds with one stone." The church groaned. "And speaking of killing, I suggest you wait in the narthex, get out from under that roof. We have the Sorensen funeral on Tuesday. I don't want you to steal his thunder."

Matilda couldn't help grinning at the awful joke. "Go get those buckets."

She followed him as far as the narthex. The rain resoaked the reverend to his undergarments in three strides. He ran to the barn, almost losing his footing in a soaked cow patty. He kept his balance, managing to skate through it the way he did Elmer's Pond when it was frozen over during his younger years.

He and Matilda owned two horses and a mule. They were understandably agitated. He couldn't imagine any living creature not being affected by this hellish weather. He gave them extra feed, grabbed two milking pails, and headed back to the church. Along the way, the wind ripped this hat from his head and sent it off into the distance.

When he strode through the door, he saw that Matilda wasn't alone. Their good friends and parishioners, Roger and Anna Abercrombie, flanked his wife, all eyes on the leaking roof.

"I'll take one of them," Roger said as he grabbed the pail's handle. The men scooped water out of the big basin and tossed them outside.

Matilda and Anna clasped hands, closed their eyes, and prayed.

A few times, the entire church sounded as if it were about to pull from its foundation and tumble away like the reverend's hat. Jake and Roger ran up and down the aisle, doing their best to lessen the basin's burden.

Reverend Smiley wondered if all this was for naught. It seemed that no matter what they did, in the end, the only thing left of the church would be that rainwater-filled basin.

They had gotten almost half the water out when more people came out in the storm to congregate.

"You shouldn't be here," he said to them. "It's not safe."

"We come to see if we can help," Elmer Mizner, the local

blacksmith, said. He'd lost his wife to consumption the year before and had turned to Jesus in his despair—that, and the bottle. The man always had a haze of whiskey about him.

"All we can do now is pray," Matilda Smiley said.

Jake Smiley was exhausted and anxious. "I agree. But we should pray somewhere safer."

If the church collapsed, they would be buried under the crushing weight of soaked timber. The wind howled and rain sluiced through the open double doors.

"This is the cornerstone of our faith," Matilda said, addressing the crowd of seven wet and fretful folks who had gathered around. "This is where we talk to God every Sunday. This is where we offer our prayers. If we want God to hear us, it must be here. If we show our faith in God, He will reward us."

Jake Smiley wanted nothing more than to question his wife's logic. Prayers could be offered anywhere.

But there was that word: "faith."

In order not to lose his standing in the church, Smiley tamped down his fear, not to mention the potential humiliation of being upstaged by his wife.

"Let's all hold hands while I lead us in prayer," he said.

So he prayed, a plea for mercy, a promise of obedience, and thanks for all that had been given to them. He prayed until his voice was hoarse and he wanted a drink of more than just spatters of rain. The storm kicked up in intensity and the church moaned as Jesus had when He was whipped and scorned before His Crucifixion.

Several more people gathered and joined the prayer circle. Smiley was positive they had come for comfort from the storm, not to pray the building would remain in one piece. The more voices, the better their chances to be heard by the Lord over the raging storm.

At one point, Matilda started singing. She was a right songbird, who led the choir every Sunday. It wasn't much of a choir, consisting of five elderly women with voices as thin as bed linen. But Matilda always shined.

Some of the others began to sing along with Matilda until the reverend found his prayers trailing off so he could listen to her beautiful voice.

"Amazing Grace" flowed into "A Mighty Fortress Is Our God." Abner McCutchin risked darting into the center of the church to gather an armful of hymnals.

It took some time before Reverend Smiley realized the worst of the storm had passed. The rain had whittled down to a light drizzle and the winds appeared to have blown themselves out.

His wife and parishioners raised their arms and praised the Lord for delivering their beloved First Baptist Church from certain ruin.

Jake Smiley gave an amen, then walked out the door to inspect the damage. A few tiles on the roof would need to be replaced, but that was all that he could see.

Matilda startled him when she grabbed his arm. "Isn't it wonderful? I just knew that if we prayed hard enough, God would hear us."

He patted her hand. "We have that voice of yours to thank."

She rejoined the parishioners while he walked on unsteady legs to their modest house. Pulling the third floorboard from his side of the bed, he snatched up the bottle of whiskey with a shaking hand, yanked the top open with his teeth, then took a deep drink.

He sat hunched forward, taking deep breaths between long sips of the fiery liquid.

He'd never told Matilda about how his entire family had been killed in a tornado back in New Orleans. He was just a young one then. The sky went black and what sounded like the roaring of a thousand wild beasts filled the air.

Before they could run for the root cellar, the tornado smashed through the center of their home. Smiley still couldn't remember what happened between the moment he cried for his parents and waking up dazed in the cornfield about fifty yards from the house.

It took a while to gain his senses. When he finally stood up and started walking, calling out for his parents, brother, and sisters, he saw that the house was no longer there, aside from some odd shattered planks of wood.

Worst of all, his family was nowhere to be seen.

It would be days before their bodies were discovered, scattered in all directions, left broken and twisted like rag dolls. His mother's body was found folded in a cornfield a mile away.

If not for Matilda, he would have run for the nearest shelter today.

If this was a test of his faith, he had failed. For he hadn't had faith that the same God who had taken his family from him would spare the rickety church. His faith was in his wife, and he knew that was blasphemy.

Half the bottle was gone before he realized it. He tucked it back in its hiding place and lit his pipe to dampen the smell.

Better to check the animals again. He wasn't in a right mind to give comfort or celebrate the majesty of the Lord above at the moment.

The rain pounded on the roof with such relentless fury, Mayor Eli Tibbs paced the thin-carpeted floor until he practically wore a hole in it.

"Maybe you should sit down and have a brandy," his wife, Eleanor, said. Despite the cloying heat and humidity, she was wrapped in a wool shawl, her pale face and dark circles under her eyes belying the illness that had left her housebound for the past two years.

"If I start with one, I won't stop until the bottle is finished," he replied more testily than he wanted to.

Eleanor slumped into her padded chair by the empty fireplace. "It was just a suggestion."

Tibbs's worried demeanor melted. He walked over to her and cupped her chin in his palm. "I'm sorry, Ellie. I didn't mean to snap at you."

In turn, she caressed his beefy hand. "It's all right, darling. I've just never seen you so distressed by a storm before. Is something else bothering you?"

Tibbs didn't care one whit about the storm. It was the unending tapping of the rain that was vexing him.

No, his worries were, at the moment, centered on the conniving interloper Tony Cheever. Doing business with the man made him want to take a scalding hot bath, and that was before the dang fool had gone and murdered a man for trespassing on his precious property. If Tibbs didn't need the Arcadian to succeed so badly, he would have thrown Cheever in the jail himself.

Keeping his problems to himself, he said to his wife, "Just the usual things that come with running a boomtown. Nothing to worry yourself about."

"I've grown too weary to worry about myself. It's you I'm more concerned about."

"Well, we need to find you a diversion, because I'm fine. I've never been better."

She looked at him skeptically. "You have put on a few pounds. That and the stress aren't good for your heart."

Tibbs thumped his chest with his fist. "My heart has no intention of giving out anytime soon. In fact, I have so much to do, I may never die. You know how much I deplore unfinished business."

That brought a wan smile to his wife's pale, thin lips. "That, I do. At least stop your pacing. Just watching you is wearing me out."

"Sorry. Yes, I'll have a seat. And maybe one brandy won't hurt."

Eli Tibbs went to his liquor shelf and poured some amber brandy into a snifter. He brought it back to his desk, took a seat and a sip. It felt good going down. Too good. He tried to keep his mind off Cheever, but it was difficult.

He'll go down and drag me with him, he thought.

Selling his soul for money was one thing. Helping a man get away with murder was another.

With two more years left of his term, Tibbs needed to sock away as much money as possible to make his grand plan come true. According to the doctors, Eleanor's condition would only worsen in this Texas climate. It was suggested they pick up stakes and settle in San Diego. To that end, Tibbs had schemed, bargained, and negotiated like a whirling dervish, building the nest egg that would provide their new home and allow him to live out the rest of their days with his sole focus on taking care of his wife.

He spoke of this to no one, not even Eleanor. Tibbs knew what people said about him behind his back. He was all those things, and for a very good reason. None of their opinions mattered. He needed to get Eleanor well.

Thunder rumbled. Tibbs looked across the room and saw that his wife had fallen asleep in her chair.

"Two more years," he whispered so she couldn't hear. "Just hold on and things will get better."

Chapter 6

The din at the sawmill seemed louder than ever. The sun seemed to add a little extra pep to the men bustling about like ants.

Pat McManus focused on his work, drowning out the steady explosion of noise from the steam engines powering the high-pitched and deadly saw blades, the constant thump and thud of logs hitting conveyor belts, and the shouting of workers. At least he liked to think he was able to distance himself and put all that racket in the background. His wife reminded him daily that eight years on the job was making him deaf. Some men would have been concerned at such a prospect. For Pat, known as Bull by his friends and co-workers (both because of his near-legendary strength and stubbornness), he looked forward to blessed silence in his later years.

Though working at the sawmill was a good way to cut those later years short. They had just lost Franklin Washington last week when he was crushed between two mammoth logs. And Hosmer Guilfoyle had lost his hand when he got careless operating one of the heavy saws a month before that. They'd managed to stop him from bleeding to death, but the ensuing infection took him to an early grave not long after. He'd only been twenty years old.

Bull's current position as a lumber grader was much safer than most. His job was to inspect the timber for quality and to sort it. Luckily, his eyes were still good, and he had a knack for spotting the tiniest defects, which was part of the reason the lumber produced by the Smits and Knoop Sawmill was in high demand and fetched a pretty penny.

He only wished more of that money flowed to him the way the lumber floated down the Angelina River to the sawmill, before it made its final journey down the Neches River and finally to the port city of Beaumont.

Henrik Smits and Jens Knoop were the richest men in town by a long shot. They'd been generous when it came to helping the town thrive and grow, and were known to do charitable acts of kindness every now and then, if only to keep their names in good standing in the local paper and on the lips of men and women throughout Pine Lick. Bull had worked for a succession of scoundrels and thieves all his adult life. At least his soul didn't feel tainted when he worked for Smits and Knoop.

"Your back!" someone shouted.

A man hurried by with a load of long wood planks on his shoulder. As he made a turn toward his destination, the planks swept toward Bull's head. He ducked just in time. If he hadn't, he'd surely be on the ground, dazed or concussed.

What alarmed him was the fact that he'd barely heard the man's urgent warning. It was more like a muffled bark from a dog locked away in a distant barn.

Rubbing his head on the spot where the planks would have connected, Bull shook it off and went about his business. Falling behind was out of the question. Though this did prove his point that the workers at Smits and Knoop should be paid far more than their current wages when they were literally putting life and limb on the line every day. There had been talk of forming a union, but that was quickly squashed. The men who worked at the sawmill came from all over the country. No one wanted to leave Texas with their tail between their legs.

"Hey, Bull! Didja hear about Seamus Doyle?"

The man with the Irish brogue, and covered in sawdust, tapped Bull on the shoulder to get his attention.

"What?" Bull said.

Tommy Crawford put one finger to his left nostril, turned his head, and snorted out a great ball of snot and wood shavings. He was a right fine sawyer, but a pest on his best days.

"Poor Seamus and his family were flooded out of their house. They managed to get out just before the damn thing collapsed. You know he has a wife and three wee ones. There's not a thing left for them. I'm hoping you can donate a little something, you know, to help them get back on their feet."

Crawford was carrying a small burlap bag. He opened it to show Bull how much he'd collected so far.

"At the rate you're going, Doyle will be richer than he was before. Maybe all of us should lose our houses."

"It's important we all stick together, Bull."

By "we," he meant the Irish. The workers of Smits and Knoop were just about split down the middle between Irish and German immigrants, with a smattering of other European nationalities, Mexicans, and freed slaves.

Tommy Crawford was always the first to come holding the collection plate. Bull suspected the man skimmed a little for himself. It would be simple to do, since no one was exactly doing the accounting on his charity work. But Crawford was right, the Irish took care of their own. He reached into his pocket and handed over a few coins.

"Where is Doyle now?"

"Hook in hand, rolling logs as usual. The wife and kids are staying with neighbors for now. Thanks, Bull. This will surely help."

"Too bad he won't be able to afford the lumber we produce. Maybe if he could, his next house would stay upright."

Crawford shook his head. "Right you are. Right you are. Well, thank you, Bull. You're a man of fine upbringing." He clapped Bull on the back.

"What I am is a man with a job to do, and you're getting in the way of doing just that."

Bull went back to inspecting the lumber as it trundled past him, putting the annoying Crawford and sad state of affairs of the Doyles quickly out of his mind.

When there was another tap on his back, he whirled around with a scowl on his face. "What now?"

He was surprised to see Sheriff Armstrong. The young man took a step back.

"Catch you on a bad day, Bull?" A small smile played on his lips.

"Sorry, Sheriff. I thought you were Crawford coming to pester me again."

"He already got me. I'm a dollar lighter. Shame what happened to Doyle's house."

"Well, I'm sure Crawford assured you a place in heaven for your charity."

"As a matter of fact, he did. That's not what I came here to ask you about. I heard from Belle Dupree that you were at her place."

Bull looked around furtively and motioned for the lawman to follow him to a more private space between stacks of lumber already prepared and ready for a long trip down the Neches.

Sheriff Armstrong put a reassuring hand on Bull's shoulder. "No need to worry. I'm not here to broadcast your personal life."

"It's getting so a man can't have a personal life in Pine Lick anymore. Too many damn people." Bull had been married to his wife, Maureen, since he was just eighteen and they were setting off for America from their home in Limerick, Ireland. They were the first of their large families to depart the Emerald Isle, leaving behind quite successful pig farms. Maureen hated the stink of the pigs, as did Bull. Both felt there had to be a better way to make a life, and what better place to do it than a land bursting with opportunity.

Maureen had never been able to bear children, which was a bitter disappointment, but something Bull had learned to live with. As she got older and beyond childbearing years, his wife had turned more and more to her Catholic faith. Without there being a chance for procreation, there was, in her mind, no point of "carrying on," as she liked to call their lovemaking. In her despair, Maureen had dedicated her life to Christ, leaving little room for Bull. He never complained to her. He just accepted it as the ways of a woman who would spend her life grieving for what never could be.

He loved her dearly, but he was still a man—a man with needs that had to be fulfilled at Belle's a few times a year. The shame he felt immediately afterward stayed with him for weeks, sometimes months, until his primitive urges took control again.

The sheriff asking him about his dalliance last night brought color to his cheeks. The back of his neck burned. This was the last thing he wanted to talk about.

"That's the price of prosperity. I just want to ask you about the cowboys that came by Belle's that night. They did a number on the Sawdust and Butch Nathans, to boot. We have half of them in the jail right now. The others must have caught wind about what happened and slipped out." Sheriff Armstrong removed his hat and wiped his sweaty forehead with his shirtsleeve. "I swear the storm only made the humidity worse. Anyhow, what I wanted to ask is if you saw those men, or maybe overheard them talk about where they were headed."

Bull relaxed, but only a bit. "I heard a commotion, a lot of whooping and hollering, but I was, ah, not in a position to pay much attention."

Just saying it out loud made him want to punch himself for being so weak. As Maureen reminded him constantly, humankind was weak. It was only the strength of Jesus Who kept them all from collapsing into the fiery pits of hell.

Truth be told, Bull would rather a hot day in hell than continue this conversation.

Sheriff Armstrong was perceptive enough to sense his discomfort and broke eye contact, pretending to inspect the stacks of lumber. "So, you didn't hear any of them say anything specific?"

"No. Just grown men acting like children on the last day of school."

The sheriff slapped a log. "Okay, thank you for your time. I suspect they're long gone by now anyway. As long as they don't come back to Pine Lick, I'm fine with that."

Before he could walk away, Bull said, "You promise you'll keep this to yourself?"

He wasn't worried about Belle Dupree or Tiny Ed keeping his secret. In his eye, they could be trusted more than most priests. Locking away shameful secrets was their stock and trade.

"This is the last you'll hear of it. Take care now."

Again, Bull went back to his work, but he was shaken. His dirty business was now in the sheriff's head. Who knows how many others were aware of it?

"So help me God, if Maureen finds out about this."

For the first time in all his years at Smits and Knoop, his mind wasn't on his work.

When the steam whistle blared, signaling yet another work injury and stopping everything for the moment, he was grateful for the interruption.

Chapter 7

Despite Otto's insistence, Branch Armstrong preferred to head to town alone. He wanted to check on the gaggle of prisoners in lockup and, truth be told, see if his son needed any help. That jail cell had been built for two. It was now accommodation for six. He was sure the prisoners were getting downright ornery on account of the overcrowding. The chamber pot alone would be an issue.

Armstrong knew from experience. There had been plenty of times when he was sheriff when there was no room at the inn, so to speak. He'd asked the mayor for the funds to add another cell. The town was growing, and so were the problems. He'd been turned down flat every time. Now there was a new mayor, but this one seemed more full of himself and corrupt than the one before. Mack said he did his best to steer clear of the man. It was better for his blood pressure.

Armstrong rode his horse, Gypsy, at a slow trot, taking the time to appreciate the sun and blue sky. It was still hot as blazes, but that was better than getting soaked to the bone. The ground was wet and muddy, making for difficult traveling. Gypsy stumbled a few times, sparking worries that she would snap an ankle. He'd hate to lose such a good horse. He slowed down, realizing there was no rush. Best to take it slow.

What most concerned him was Tony Cheever. That oily snake was not to be trusted. They may have thought they had him for murder, but Branch Armstrong worried the interloper would find a way to free his neck from the noose. Thoughts of Cheever paying for his crime, and the Arcadian being left to rot so the townsfolk could enjoy the pristine land, had him thinking it was all too good to be true.

Sure enough, when he walked into the jail, Cheever was nowhere to be found.

His son, Mack, was oiling his pistols, ignoring the yammering coming from the crammed prisoners.

"Looks like the cell's a little lighter today," Branch said.

A dark pall fell over Mack's face. "Lawyer sprang him just an hour ago. Mayor Tibbs was with him. His face was so red, I thought he was gonna pop like an oversized tomato with a stick of dynamite stuck in it."

Branch's back molars pressed tightly against one another. "They give a reason?"

"Plenty. Got so I couldn't keep track. It all boiled down to Cheever being an upstanding citizen, meaning a man with money and means. Also, how can we trust the testimony of a young boy who probably, in the mayor's words, just learned to wipe himself last Tuesday, and a crazy fella like Bear O'Hanlon? Bear, by the way, is nowhere to be found. I have Whiskey out looking for him now, but I'm not holding out too much hope."

"Get that mayor back!" one of the cowboys they had captured in the Sawdust shouted. "We want to get sprung, too! You can't keep us in here for just having a little fun."

The others started talking over one another, demanding they be set free.

Mack turned to face the cell. "You're right. Normally, I'd make you pay for the damages, apologize to the man you brained, and run your sorry behinds out of town. But the moment you pulled a gun on the law, well, that's another story. Now shut up and sit down. You're giving me a headache."

The men continued to jaw at Mack, hands squeezing the iron bars and faces pressed between them as if they thought they could wriggle through.

Branch Armstrong squared his hands on his hips and shot them a look that would drop a charging buffalo. Silence mercifully filled the jail.

Mack gave his father an almost-imperceptible nod to thank him. Armstrong's son was young and smart and tough, but he lacked the hard-life experience that had forged Branch's spirit. He was just glad he was still able to help out every now and then. There would come a day when Mack would no longer need his assistance, or he would no longer be able to give it.

"I almost forgot the most important part," Mack said. "Cheever is set to open his little resort or retreat or whatever the heck he calls it tomorrow. He has guests coming from as far as New York City and Chicago. Big money from big cities. Just what we need." He lowered his voice. "I'm sure some of that money is going to find its way into Tibbs's pockets."

"I wouldn't bet against it." Branch shook his head and stared out the window. A warm wind blew through the jail, bringing no relief from the cloying heat.

Mack held up a finger. "And before you say it, yes, I plan to pay him a social call when I know his guests are around. He may think he's gotten away with murder, but I'm not finished with him by a long shot."

Branch smiled. "Well, you let me know if you need company."

"I got Whiskey. We'll be all right. I'm sure you have plenty of other things at the farm to keep you busy."

That was true. Branch had been up and working since four in the morning. He was on his second wind now and in need of a distraction that didn't involve tending to animals or the property. Truth be told, he was tired of wallowing in the mud. Even more so, he missed being the sheriff, being relevant.

"You know me," he said to his son. "Sitting still isn't my strong suit. Your mother wanted me to tell you to stop by for dinner. She's making chicken fried steak."

Mack patted his stomach. "You can tell her I'll be there, unless something comes up. Usually quiet on Tuesdays."

Armstrong thought he heard a muffled rumbling. He knew his son often skipped meals and wasn't taking proper care of himself, what with working all hours of the day and night. It was part of the reason why Branch had been put out to pasture. Being a sheriff in a booming town was a young man's game. But you could only burn the candle at both ends for so long. Pine Lick had grown beyond a two-lawmen operation. Not that Mayor Tibbs would open the coffers to add a deputy or two. It was why Branch and Otto pitched in every now and again.

Not to mention, Armstrong wanted to see his son retire someday, alive and well.

"That'll make her happy. See you tonight." Before he left, he snapped his fingers and turned around. "I forgot to ask. The boy who saw Cheever shoot his father."

"Archibald Gibbons. Hates to be called Archie."

"Who's looking after him? Is there any way to get family to come here?"

Mack Armstrong shook his head. "His mother died last year. He said the grippe took her. He has no brothers or sisters left. The poor kid's busted up. Luckily, Gloria Amaryllis agreed to take him in for now."

"I can think of a lot of far worse places to be."

"She took an instant shine to him, and I think, when he isn't crying or shutting himself off from everyone, the feeling is mutual."

Gloria Amaryllis was a widowed schoolteacher, who was just about one of the prettiest women in all of Pine Lick. With her red hair, full lips, and body with curves that would give a man whiplash, the men of the town wondered how any lad managed to pay attention to their schooling. She was also one of the most educated people around, having gone to private schools in New England before she married a man with big dreams that landed her in Texas seven years ago. Her Christian kindness was well known by all, to boot. Armstrong would have asked her to take in the boy as well, if he'd still been sheriff. His son also held a torch for the older woman, so it was no surprise that he'd found a way to enlist her help.

"Well, good call, son. I'm sure she's doting on him as we speak. Probably just what he needs about now." The former sheriff pointed at the silent men in the cell, his countenance going from kind to ornery in a flash. "You all best stay like that or I'll be back. You don't want me to come back."

Several of the men cast their eyes at the floor. Mack shook his head and grinned.

Walking outside felt like entering the hot, wet vapors coming off a warm spring. Branch had spent some time in Yellowstone when he'd tried his hand at cowboying after the war and ended up for a short spell in Wyoming. With the hopes that some time free on the open range would heal the mental wounds he'd suffered during the war and his short captivity by the Union, he'd left Kate with a promise to be back in several months. Branch discovered that America was a wide, untamed, beautiful land. One worth fighting for. But not fighting with one another.

He recalled those hot springs and geysers that would scald man or beast to death if they were too close when one erupted. He and the other hands thought the place was dangerous, though it did possess a breathtaking beauty that was hard to deny.

Despite the heat, Armstrong was still feeling anxious. There was no sense hanging around with his son. He was a grown man. The last thing he needed was his father meddling in his affairs and making him feel like a child.

"Howdy, Sheriff!" a voice called from across the street.

Armstrong spotted Vito LoPresti, the town's lone chandler. The Italian transplant spoke with a heavy accent, but tried very hard to speak like an American. "How're things? You keeping busy?"

"Alwaysa busy. Some-a-times too busy."

"That's good. Keeps you out of trouble," Armstrong joked. LoPresti's idea of a wild time was having a single glass of beer on his birthday. Running into the jovial man did remind him that he needed to visit his shop soon and buy some candles for the house.

After unhitching Gypsy, he had to wait while several coaches hurried down the mucky street. It felt as if everyone who didn't work at the sawmill was out and about, folks raising their faces to the sky to savor the sun. Pine Lick needed some drying out. For a while, crops suffered from a drought that saw several brush fires threatening to wipe the town off the map—if not for the hard work of every man, woman, and child to douse the flames. Now they'd been getting drenching rain off and on, which was clearly more than the soil could handle.

He decided now was a good time to visit Tony Cheever's Arcadian, see how things were doing, since it was set to open. Cheever had moved to Pine Lick during Armstrong's last year as sheriff. They'd been introduced by Mayor Tibbs during a big to-do dinner at the mayor's house. Armstrong had taken an instant disliking to the Chicago swindler. He had a strong inclination that the feeling was mutual.

During the early days of the Arcadian Men's Retreat's construction, Cheever had barged into Armstrong's office hell-bent for leather, screaming about someone stealing supplies from his site. He demanded Armstrong find and apprehend the culprit by the end of the day, adding that he should have expected this to happen on account of the unclean rabble that made up the town. Armstrong was quick to point out that he and his family were part of that so-called rabble. A staring contest ensued, with Cheever breaking the gaze first like a skittish cat.

It turned out the construction materials had been dragged into the brush, most likely by a bear. Armstrong detected food stains on the bag that contained workman's tools. When he politely pointed it out, Cheever made no apologies. They'd been on shaky ground ever since.

The retreat's grounds were a beehive of activity, with men bustling about putting the finishing touches on the cottages. The smell of fresh paint rode the humid breeze. There was a chorus of hammering and sawing. Several men were adding planks to a dock set on the man-made Lake Stanton, named after the man who had constructed the Stanton Dam some thirty years earlier. Somewhere a dog howled.

"His senses are probably on overload," Armstrong said to Gypsy, whose own ears twitched as they got closer.

Armstrong guided Gypsy to the hill leading to the top of the Stanton Dam. He checked for any leaks, just as he'd done almost daily as sheriff, at least for the past five years or so after an engineer who'd been brought in to consult at the sawmill saw the old dam and warned everyone at a town hall that it was unsafe. The aging structure needed a lot of costly work if it was to retain any sort of integrity.

The dam held back the man-made Lake Stanton, a reservoir of water that was just under two miles long, a mile and a half wide, and a hair over eighty feet at its deepest. The engineer told Armstrong that he estimated Lake Stanton to total over 20 million tons of water. It was a number too large for Armstrong or just about anyone in the town to fully comprehend. Suffice to say, it was a hell of a lot of water. How the Stanton Dam held it all back was a marvel to him.

Whenever he came by the dam, he thought of the phrase "ignorance is bliss." Before the engineer had come and laid out the true size of the lake and the myriad problems with the dam, Armstrong had barely given it all a second thought. Now there were times when it kept him up at night. He wished it had never been built, though it was key for providing extra power to the sawmill, which was the lifeblood of the town.

A warning system had been put in place by the Smits and Knoop Company, which had agreed to fund the repairs. It wasn't entirely altruistic on the part of the sawmill company. If the dam was damaged or gave away altogether, the floodwaters would be catastrophic for the town *and* the sawmill.

A guard shack had been put in place and manned twenty-four hours a day. If there were signs that the dam was in danger of collapsing, the guard would get on his horse and race to Pine Lick, ringing a heavy bell and warning people to evacuate to higher ground.

Mayor Tibbs scoffed that anything was wrong with the dam. He claimed the engineer was simply looking for a new boondoggle in order to line his own pockets. After several false alarms, resulting in a wild panic in the streets, the mayor put a stop to the warning system. The citizens of Pine Lick were relieved, feeling that the false alarms were far worse than thinking about the minute chance of the dam being breached. Besides, the engineer was from the Northeast. Not someone to be trusted.

Some work was done on the spillways, but not much else. The longer it remained standing with no clear and present danger, the more interest was lost in keeping up with the necessary repairs.

The engineer left town, and most folks had more pressing things on their minds.

Branch Armstrong was not most folks. He'd had a deep discussion with the engineer, a man named Ventarola, over dinner at the restaurant at the Palace Hotel one night. The man had been amiable, highly intelligent, and, most of all, a straight shooter.

"You wear that star to protect the people of this town, correct?" Ventarola asked between bites of steak.

"I do."

"Then do what you can to protect them from that dam, and their pigheaded ignorance. You know, a fish rots from the head on down, and in the case of Pine Lick, unfortunately, that head is on your illustrious mayor's neck. Maybe you can convince him to change his mind, either by promising the carrot or prodding with the stick. Your call. Until that time, keep an eye on the dam, especially during and after storms. Can you promise me that?"

"I'll try my best with Tibbs, but he and I don't exactly see eye to eye. I can promise you I'll check on that dam."

Ventarola wiped his face with a linen napkin. "Well, that's all I can ask for now. If the mayor comes to his senses, or even if you have any questions, here's where to find me." He handed Armstrong a business card with his name and contact details finely embossed on the front. It was the first business card he'd ever received.

Now several years later, he still had that card at home, tucked away in a drawer. He wondered if Ventarola was even still alive. The man had a prodigious belly and was overly fond of food and wine. He hoped to never have to reach out to the man.

The dam looked to be just fine today, which relieved the nagging pressure that always sat on Branch's shoulders when he rode by Lake Stanton.

Armstrong turned to the main house and spotted Cheever talking to a man who had a set of plans spread out between his hands. Cheever's mouth was in constant motion, and judging by the worker's face, Branch assumed nothing good was coming out of it. He jabbed his index finger repeatedly at the long sheet of paper.

Armstrong dismounted and tied his horse up to a low-hanging tree branch. He slowly made his way toward Cheever, who hadn't noticed him yet. He was too engrossed in chewing the worker out. Cheever dismissed the worker with a curt flick of his hand. The man looked grateful for it to be over.

"Did I catch you at a bad time?" Armstrong asked.

Cheever's usual air of arrogance faltered for just the briefest moment. "When you're opening any property, there is no such thing as a good time."

Armstrong removed his hat to dab at the sweat on his head and back of his neck with the bandana he always kept in his pocket. "Well, I didn't mean to disturb you. Just curious as to how things were getting along. Heard you were open for business this week."

There was a long, uncomfortable pause as Cheever narrowed his eyes and studied Armstrong, most likely wondering if it was possible his son hadn't told him about the shooting.

For his part, Armstrong played it cool. He looked around the place as if he didn't have a care in the world.

"I have to admit, it looks awfully cozy. I'll bet it'll cost a pretty penny to hang your hat in one of those cottages."

"Pennies don't factor into the equation. Is there something I can help you with? I have more things to do than there's time in the day."

That was Cheever. Always on the offensive, always quick to dismiss. The man was in a perpetual state of being put out, unless he was in the company of someone with money or influence, or, better yet, both. Armstrong had heard that Cheever tried cozying up to Smits and Knoop, but was soundly rebuffed. They may have been wealthy businessmen, but they were also exceedingly practical.

Henrik Smits worked six days a week and was often the first man at the sawmill and the last to leave. His partner, Jens Knoop, was the definition of "austere." He had a cabin built close to the sawmill property, on the other side of the Angelina River. He preferred to walk everywhere because he didn't want to be bothered with the cost and time of owning a horse, much less a carriage.

"Nope. I guess I was just curious. Old habits die hard. I still like to do my rounds of the town."

"Yes, well, thank you for coming. If you'll excuse me."

Armstrong turned as if to leave, took two steps, and spun on his heel. "Oh, one more thing."

Cheever was waving a trio of men to come to him. "And what is that?"

"I may not be sheriff anymore, but this is still my town. No one, and I mean *no one*, gets away with murder."

Cheever's eyes burned first with shock, then anger. His lips pulled into a grim, pale line.

"You left that young boy an orphan. Probably scarred him for life. Could be he'll grow up and come for you one day. He wouldn't be the first." Armstrong wagged a callused finger at the murderer. "But, I'm gonna put my money on you not being around for that day to happen, which in a way is a shame to rob a boy of his due."

"Are you threatening me?" Cheever said, seething.

"No, sir. Only promising. Your day will come. I reckon sooner rather than later. Oh, but not to worry. I'm sure nothing will stand in the way of your grand opening."

"You can't talk to me like that." The man was practically trembling with anger. It was a wonder to Armstrong how men who had committed horrendous deeds could be filled with so much righteous fury. It made delivering justice to them all the sweeter.

"It's a free country, as far as I remember. Not like your pal Mayor Tibbs can do anything to me now that I'm not on his payroll."

Now Cheever smirked. "You may not be, but I know someone who is."

The urge to punch Cheever square in the face was practically a force of nature. Armstrong took a slow, steady breath and maintained his composure. "I wouldn't do that if I were you. It would most certainly be bad for your health."

A man carrying two buckets of paint walked between them with his eyes on the ground, clearly avoiding getting trapped by Cheever. The interruption shattered the tension between Armstrong and Cheever.

"You take care of yourself," Armstrong said, turning his back to Cheever and heading for his horse. He could feel the man's hardened gaze at his back.

Cheever would rest his head that night filled with dread, and that was a very good thing.

Branch Armstrong spun Gypsy around and tipped his hat to the murderer before heading home.

"Always keep them guessing, and always leave them afraid," he said to his horse. "Sooner or later, he'll trip himself up. And we'll be there to snatch him."

Chapter 8

The trek from New York to Texas was taking its toll on the old man. It wasn't so much the traveling as it was the unbearable heat in this part of Texas. And much more than that, it was having to live with his decision to allow Slip to come along with him. Yes, the boy had a stake in what they had set out to do. And yes, that incident back home had necessitated Slip's need to skedaddle.

What the old man should have done was tucked him away somewhere in Pennsylvania or New Jersey. Anyplace where no one had ever heard the name of Slip Bragg, and that was plenty of places. The old man should have brought enough money to allow the impetuous boy to start a new life, free and clear from his troubles.

Who am I kidding? His troubles always find him sooner or later, when he isn't making new ones, the old man thought.

No, it was always going to be the two of them on this road to vengeance. Maybe that was the penance he had to pay for embarking on such a journey. If the man who had murdered his brother finally paid for his sin, so be it. He'd face any price to right that wrong.

They were close now. He could practically smell it in the warm, damp air today.

Too close to allow Slip to throw it all to hell.

"I'll just be five minutes," Slip said as they rode past a tucked-away farmhouse. The boy had his eyes on a large chicken coop in the distance. "How hard can it be to grab me a chicken, and maybe some eggs?"

"Very hard if that farmer has a gun. A man doesn't appreciate thieves trespassing on his property. Can't say I'd blame him."

Slip patted his holstered pistol. "Yeah, well, I have a gun, too."

"A gun you aren't gonna need to use because you're leaving those damn chickens alone. Now come on."

The old man put his heels to his horse and moved ahead of Slip.

"But I'm starving!"

"There's plenty of jerky and biscuits in your saddlebag. Fill your mouth up with them, because I'm tired of hearing you speak."

Slip reluctantly followed him. He reached into one of his saddlebags and took out a hardened biscuit. The old man turned around and saw him take a crumbling bite with a sour look on his face.

It wasn't the chicken that Slip wanted. No, it was the mischief he missed. The chance to mix things up with a total stranger, to entertain the darkness that dwelled within him.

That business with the old folks in the wagon weighed heavily on the old man. He'd found it hard to sleep ever since. Nights were spent keeping an eye on Slip, who slept sound as a dead man.

The question that vexed him day and night was the matter of what came after they accomplished their mission? Slip had only gotten wilder, meaner, more uncontrollable. In that sense, the old man had failed the boy. Lessons he taught, whether by word or action, fell on deaf ears. Or maybe it was a matter of Slip not having the ability to comprehend. It wasn't that he was dim-witted so much as touched in the head in such a way that only the bad things seemed to seep into his consciousness.

Like this trip, Slip is my burden. No sense worrying over it now. Not when we're almost there.

At least the godforsaken rain had stopped. Though getting dry in this blasted weather, even with the sun out, was darn near impossible. The old man knew this spot of sun was just a tease. His bones forecast the weather, especially storms, with a degree of accuracy that his friends and family said bordered on the supernatural. And those bones were telling him more bad weather was on its way. All the more reason not to stop to steal some chickens and double-time it to a town called Pine Lick.

He'd had it on good authority that the man he was searching for was there. Not only that, he was a lawman, which would make him easy to find.

"I hope they have a cathouse at this town," Slip suddenly came out with after being silent for a long stretch. "I can't remember the last time I had a woman. That sure would be nice."

"Just keep your mind on what we're out here for," the old man replied irritably. "Don't you mind messing with women. You haven't got a penny to your name, and it's not like I'm going to subsidize you."

The old man remembered at least one of the last times Slip had been intimate with a woman. The girl, a visiting cousin to Slip's neighbor, had ended up with two black eyes and fractured ribs for having the poor sense to wander off with him. Luckily for Slip, her family was not well regarded, so their collective cry of abuse didn't amount to much. They could not compete with the wealthier Bragg family line, which also boasted its share of war heroes and politicians.

But people talked. And strange looks were given. Whispered warnings to steer clear of the wild, violent boy were hard to ignore.

"What if I said I won't help you if you won't help me?" Slip asked.

The old man stopped his horse, pulled out his pistol and aimed for Slip's heart. "If you think I need your help, you're sorely mistaken. I don't know if you've gotten it through your thick head or not, but you're on the run, son. And while you've been running, you've only made matters worse. You're here so I can protect you. I've just about given up getting you on the straight and narrow. If you think I'm going to give you money to beat up some old hooker or worse, well you might as well ride off by yourself. I'll give you a week before you're dead or waiting for the noose."

They stared at each other for a while, the old man showing that he meant every word he said. If Slip wanted to threaten him, he was free to go.

For his part, Slip scratched at his sweaty neck and looked as if he was running his options through his head. After a spell, he said, "No need to get so mad. It's only human to want a woman every now and then. Can you blame me?"

I can blame you for plenty, the old man thought.

Disgusted, the old man spurred his horse on. He heard Slip once again close behind. For a moment, he had hoped the boy would choose to go solo and meet whatever unpleasant fate awaited him. As welcome as that would be, a part of him still thought the boy would come in handy when it came to facing the sheriff. Lord only knew what they were going to walk into. The odds of one man against a lawman, and who knows how many allies, were not in his favor. Someone as wild and unpredictable as Slip could tip the scales.

* * *

They rode until the heat of the morning gave way to an afternoon so stifling, the old man wondered who would give out first, them or their horses. His own was laboring, so he led it to a creek he'd heard burbling to their right. As the horses pushed their way through the brush, they came across a campsite. Four one-man tents circled around a fire pit. Ropes were tied between a pair of trees with wet garments hanging on them.

The men of the camp weren't far. As the old man and Slip's horses dipped their heads to drink, he spotted four burly men quietly fishing on the bank twenty or so yards away. Four heads covered in great, bushy beards turned their way. They didn't look happy to have their camp disturbed.

The old man raised a hand. "Afternoon," he said amiably. "Didn't mean to disturb you. We just have a couple of horses that don't cotton to the heat. Happy to move on to another spot if you think it'll stop the fish from biting."

One of the men set his pole down, while the other three went about their business, though one, larger than all the others and hairy as a wild man, kept flicking his gaze their way. His hand slipped to the leather sheath strapped to his leg.

The man who approached them wore clothes that were riddled with holes and had probably last been washed when Johnson was president. He was tall and angular, with small hands that looked as if they belonged on another man.

"You have any tobacco?" the man asked with a surprisingly high-pitched voice.

"Nope," Slip was quick to reply. He looked anxious to leave. The old man breathed a sigh of relief. Even Slip wouldn't try anything foolish with this group.

"That's too bad. We'd be happy to trade some nice sunfish or crappie for a smoke. What we had was ruined by all that durn rain because someone left it outside their tent. Ain't that right, Bear?" he shouted over his shoulder.

The hairy man, who certainly fit his name, waved him off. "Quit your griping."

"That sounds like a deal too good to pass up," the old man said. He reached into his jacket's inner pocket for his pouch of tobacco and tossed it to the burly man.

"Much obliged. Does four fish sound like a good bargain?"

The man lumbered to the creek and fiddled with a line, pulling up a string of freshly caught fish.

"That'll be just fine."

"That's the last of our tobacco," Slip whispered. "Why'd you give it to him?"

The old man ignored him. The man came back with four fish, which he promptly wrapped in a cloth.

"I was wondering if you could throw one more item into the mix," the old man said.

The man looked wary. The old man grinned.

"It's actually free. Just looking for information. We're headed to a town called Pine Lick. We don't have a map, and I want to make sure we're on the right path. Have you heard of it?"

The bearded man nodded. "Sure have. My brother works at the sawmill there. I plan to visit him once we've had our fill here."

"Well, that's a good bit of luck for us. How far you figure it is from here?"

"Oh, about thirty miles, give or take a few. Just keep heading south until you come to the Angelina River. Then follow that all the way to Pine Lick. Hard to miss it."

Slip perked up. "They got girls?"

The man chuckled. "Name me a town worth its salt that don't. When you get there, just ask for Belle Dupree. Ooo-weee. She's a sweet but tough thing all the way from Louisiana. Everyone knows

Belle's place and can point the way. Young buck like you, I'm sure what's in your britches will find it all on its own."

The old man forced a laugh. "Well, thank you for the fish and directions. Much obliged. And good luck with the fishing, though by the looks of it, you don't need my luck."

The man gave them a wave and joined his friends, showing them the pouch of tobacco.

The horses had slaked their thirst.

Thirty miles.

Oh yes, the old man could feel it in his aching bones.

He tossed the fish to Slip. "Better than a measly chicken. And if I hear one more word about women, you're going to regret it. Understand?"

Slip nodded, though the old man wasn't certain he fully comprehended his threat.

No matter.

Just thirty more miles. If it wasn't hotter than Hades, he'd push his horse, but a dead horse out in the middle of nowhere would set him back.

They'd be in Pine Lick well before nightfall tomorrow if they kept a steady but agreeable pace.

A long-overdue debt needed to be paid, even if it meant unleashing hell on the unsuspecting town.

With narrowed eyes, Bear O'Hanlon watched the two men ride away. He didn't like the look of them one bit.

His fishing buddy, Chuck, flashed the pouch of tobacco. "We'll have us a good night now."

"They say they were heading for Pine Lick?" Bear asked.

"That, they did," Chuck said as he pulled his fishing pole from the ground.

"They say what for?"

"Nope. None of my business anyway."

The last place Bear wanted to be was in Pine Lick. Being dragged into the whole affair of Cheever murdering that man was not on his dance card.

But there was something about those two . . .

Chapter 9

Gloria Amaryllis patted her face and neck dry with powder. It wasn't easy trying to look presentable in this weather. No sooner had she gotten up from her vanity and walked out of the room than fresh beads of sweat dotted her fair skin.

"Are you done with your breakfast?"

Young Archibald Gibbons sat at her small kitchen table, a plate of half-eaten bacon and eggs on his plate. He looked lost in thought, his mouth turned down and an inconsolable, faraway look in his eyes. One hand gripped his fork upright, but there didn't seem to be any inclination to use it to eat.

"I'm not very hungry," he said without looking at her.

She rested a loving hand on his bony shoulder. "That's all right, dear. You had something and that'll do just fine. Now, why don't you wash your hands and face and we'll walk to school."

Archibald slumped off his chair and headed for the washbasin in his room.

With a lump in her throat and an ache in her heart, Gloria watched him go. The boy was in so much pain. He woke up several times a night screaming in terror. It was all she could do to calm him down. Dark circles hung under his eyes.

Haunted.

The boy was haunted. He never spoke about his father or what he saw. He didn't have to. It was written all over his face, the way he walked, his loss of appetite.

She would give anything to take away that hurt, but she knew only time and some loving care could ease the nightmare that held him in its grip. In this often cruel and uncaring world, children lost the ones they loved, saw things they should never have seen, more often than was acceptable to a Christian heart. All children reacted in their own ways. Gloria kept telling herself that Archibald was handling this in his own way. Her job was to be there for him until he returned to some sense of normalcy.

And there was the question of where Archibald was ultimately going to live. There was an orphanage two counties over that was run by St. Luke's Catholic Church, and it had a fair reputation. That was a possibility. But he was in no condition to be thrust into that kind of environment. The longer he stayed, would she be able to part from him?

So many worries.

At the moment, she couldn't spare any time to ponder them. She had to get to school before her students.

"You ready, Archibald?"

The young boy walked timidly to her, freshly scrubbed and dour. She held out her hand and kept it in the air between them until he took it.

"Right. Off we go."

The air outside was even more stifling than in her small house tucked just off the main street. Even though it was early, the sounds of hard labor at the sawmill filled the heavy air.

"At least the dampness will keep the sawdust in the air to a minimum," she said to Archibald. He looked up at her briefly with a look of utter incomprehension.

Many people were already out and about, flitting from one shop to the next. Daisy's Eatery was especially full with sawmill laborers who didn't start until the eight a.m. shift. The smell of fresh-baked biscuits wafted out of the open door as they passed.

Archibald stopped suddenly. He looked into Daisy's window with hungry eyes.

"Would you like to come here for breakfast tomorrow?" Gloria asked.

His head bobbed as he took in a lungful of the enticing aroma.

"Good. It's been a long time since a fellow took me out to eat."

That got a tiny smile.

The schoolhouse was located a half mile from the center of town. It was beautifully constructed (how could it not be in a town known for its fine lumber?) and had plenty of tended space for the children to play at recess. The only drawback was its proximity to the sawmill. There were times she practically had to shout to be heard over the daily ruckus.

"Good morning, Mrs. Amaryllis. Is that the young Archie Gibbons I've heard about?"

Reverend Smiley was dressed in his usual black suit and hat, which he tipped. The sides of his clean-shaven face were awash with rivulets of sweat.

"He prefers Archibald," she said to him with a wide grin to ensure he knew she didn't mean offense.

"Ah, my apologies. It's nice to meet you." He went to shake the boy's hand, but Archibald kept his at his side. The reverend chuckled and wiped his palm on his pants. "It's just as well I keep my sweat to myself. Heading off to school?"

Gloria waited to see if the boy would so much as raise his eyes to the reverend. "Yes," she said finally. "It's his first day. It will be more of a chance for Archibald to sit in and observe. He'll be my assistant today, won't you?"

He gave a barely perceptible nod. He tightened his grip on her hand, an obvious cue that he wanted to move on.

Before that could happen, the sheriff spotted them and sauntered over. He looked as if he hadn't slept in days.

"Howdy, Reverend. Mrs. Amaryllis." He squatted so he was eye to eye with the boy. "Good to see you, Archibald. You getting along with Mrs. Amaryllis?"

Archibald had no problem looking Sheriff Armstrong in the eye. "Yes."

"I just knew it. You're in very good hands. Heading off to school?"

"Uh-huh."

"Good. Learn as much as you can so maybe one day you can run this here town."

"I'd rather be a sheriff. Do you think I could be one?" Archibald replied, shocking everyone.

Sheriff Armstrong patted his shoulder. "Stick to learning and fill that brain and you might have second thoughts."

A sudden coldness washed over the boy's features. "No, I want to be a man of the law."

There was no need to say why. They understood. And Gloria was sure they all privately hoped he would change his mind as he got older and there was a good deal of distance from the terror he'd experienced.

The sheriff was quick to change the subject. He stood up and said to the reverend, "I hear your church was saved by the power of prayer."

Smiley rolled his eyes. "Word gets out fast around here."

"Not as fast as it used to, but it still makes its rounds," Mack Armstrong said.

"Well, I'm not going to discount the power of prayer. The construction of the church itself might have had something to do with it as well. Though it's going to need repairs, and soon. I'm not sure how well it would do if another storm like that comes along."

"Word is that you might have a full house on Sunday," the sheriff said. "Pass the collection plate for those repairs. I'm sure you'll have what you need in no time. Plenty of men around will donate their time, including myself and, I'm sure, my father. I can talk to the sawmill about getting you some discounted lumber."

"That would be very fine. Thank you, Sheriff. If you all don't mind, I have to pick up something for my wife at Wilson's. Good day."

He tipped his hat and hurried down the street.

"That was a very nice offer," Gloria said to the sheriff.

"My deputy tells me another storm is brewing. How he knows is anyone's guess. He has a knack for some things. Hopefully, we can get that work done before it hits town . . . if it does at all. Lord knows I could use some time to dry out. Not that it's going to happen today."

Gloria let go of the boy's hand and said to him, "Wait here just a moment. I need to speak to the sheriff in private."

He followed her a few paces ahead. In a soft voice, she asked him, "Is it true that the man who murdered Archibald's father was set free?"

Mack Armstrong put his hand on his hips and looked about at the folks milling around. "The reverend was right, word really does get around fast."

"So, what I've been hearing is true."

"Unfortunately." He looked pained to confirm it.

"What are we coming to when a murderer is allowed to walk free?" She hugged herself and shivered as if they were standing in the midst of a snowstorm.

"He's free for now. We'll see what eventually becomes of him. Rest assured, I'm not done with him yet."

"That gives me some comfort." Gloria checked her watch and gasped. "It's getting late. I better be off."

"I could walk with you, if you like. This way I do my rounds, *and* have fine company for a change." He looked back at Archibald and winked. To Gloria's surprise, his face lit up.

Gloria knew the young sheriff was smitten with her. It had been written all over his face the first time they'd met. Although she had to admit that he was quite the eligible bachelor, her being almost ten years his senior precluded any sort of romance. She didn't want to give him any aspirations, but it was nice to have a man of the law accompany them to the schoolhouse when there was a known killer about. She didn't know much about Tony Cheever, which made him a mystery—and now a threat to any decent man, woman, or child.

"If you don't mind walking very fast, that would be much appreciated."

"This will be the best part of my day," the sheriff said. He offered Gloria his arm, which she readily took. He smiled at her and blushed. She felt heat bloom on her own cheeks. It felt good being escorted by the handsome young sheriff. And if she was willing to be honest with herself, it also felt a tad right.

The trio hustled down the street, narrowly avoiding innumerable puddles of mud.

Gloria kept casting her eyes to the sky, wondering where in all that blue, the deputy could find a storm.

Chapter 10

Otto may have lived on the outskirts of Pine Lick for years, but wandering was in his blood. When the rain had stopped an hour or so before dawn, he'd saddled up his horse and gone riding. He saw the sky turn from black to a dazzling pink before it became blue and cloudless. Birds that had cowered in their nests came out, just like him, to greet the new day.

It was hot, but nothing he couldn't withstand. At his age, he was grateful to still be walking among the living. Heat, cold, blustering winds, they were all opportunities to feel something. It was better than the alternative.

If he believed the things he heard the white religious men say, and there were times when their words weighed on him, he would spend an eternity in hell for the things he'd done in life. The killing alone sealed his fate, though there was time to ask for forgiveness and have his sins absolved.

And therein lay the problem. Otto was not sorry about the men he'd killed. In every case, as far as his reckoning, they had all deserved to die by his hand. An Indian living in this wild, tumultuous century had to be prepared to fight to the death if he wanted to live. Otto had fought plenty. Most of those times, the battle came to him. He was not a seeker of war with the white man, or any man for that matter. Otto simply wanted to be left alone. The massacre of his tribe had left him cut off from his world, left to find his own way in a world that despised him.

Oh yes, he had softened over the years. Spending so much time in one place could do that to a man. Befriending Branch Armstrong had healed some of his brokenness. Because in Armstrong, he sensed a kindred soul. He was a man with a past that haunted him as well, though he'd been wise enough to find a good woman and raise a child to keep the nightmares at bay.

On a day like today, Otto feared his inevitable death most of all.

Best to enjoy it as much as he could. For him, that meant riding his horse wherever the winds took him and enjoying what nature had to offer. He rode for hours, not worried about where he was headed or how he would find his way back. The smell of sweetgrass and pine filled his lungs.

By midmorning, he found a stream and led his horse to drink and eat some oats he'd brought along. Otto sat under the shade of a tree and smoked a cigar, puffing out great rings, which floated into the dewy leaves above him.

"It is a fine day for a cigar," he said to his horse, who had cast a strange look at him when he lit the cigar. "I would offer you one, but I am afraid you would not feel the same joy."

The horse, as always, remained an animal of very few words.

Otto recalled the time he'd spotted Branch Armstrong jawing with his own horse when he thought he was alone. It was very gratifying to see that he had rubbed off on the white man.

Between puffs of his cigar, he dozed. He and the horse both needed the rest if they were going to head back during the growing heat of the day.

The sound of voices disturbed his slumber.

Two men on horseback. Their words, still too faint to decipher, carried on the wisp of a moist breeze.

Otto put his now unlit cigar in his pocket and crept to his horse. He removed his Winchester from the scabbard and hid behind a tree, listening.

A man like Otto could never be too careful. He'd lost count of the number of times strangers had appeared seemingly out of nowhere with cruel intentions on their minds.

He spotted the pair heading his way, their rides going at a long trot. One was older than the other. He had the look of a man who had seen his share of hard times. The younger one, now that they were closer, had the eyes of a rabid wolf.

They would have passed Otto, had not his horse whinnied, no doubt spooked by the mere presence of the wolf-eyed man. There was no sense hiding now. Otto relit his cigar and stepped out from behind the tree with his rifle pointed at the ground. He wanted to appear to be someone who had no inclination that someone was nearby. To help with the charade, he tugged at his pants, as if he'd just made water on the tree.

When he came within the sight of the two riders, he managed to look surprised.

"Ho. I did not hear you coming."

"Easy there, old-timer," the one with the wolf eyes said. "Try not to shoot yourself."

Otto looked down at the gun, as if he hadn't been aware he'd been holding it. "You see any rabbits? I thought this would be a good hunting spot."

"Nah, we ain't seen any rabbits. You'd be better off with a fishing pole." The young one pointed at the stream.

"What was that?" Otto cupped a hand to his ear.

"No rabbits," the older one said. "Better off catching them at dusk."

Otto gave him a confused nod. He'd learned long ago to make

it so folks underestimated him. It was the main reason he'd managed to survive as long as he had.

The potential drawback was if these men decided to take advantage of him. Maybe try to steal his horse or rough him up. That's when the killing would begin, and more sins added to the fire and brimstone that awaited him.

"You wouldn't happen to know the town of Pine Lick, would you?"

Pausing a moment as if to think, Otto said, "Yes." He didn't need to be a wise old Indian to know these men could not be trusted.

"Can you point us in the right direction? We're new here."

Otto mumbled some directions and landmarks. They would lead the men far west of the town.

The older one looked at him with a degree of skepticism.

Otto added, "I hear there is much to occupy a man's time at Pine Lick. Good food. Good liquor."

"Any good women?" the wolf-eyed man asked with a lascivious grin.

"I hear."

The older man looked sharply at the younger one, wiping the grin from his face.

"Well, good luck to you."

They rode past him as if he was an afterthought, though the one with the wolf eyes gave him one last look that slid on over to his horse before thinking twice and turning his back on him.

The strangers were no more than a dozen paces away when Wolf Eyes said, "I can't wait to see you put it to that son of a biscuit eater. If that old-timer is right, we'll be there before we know it."

"Just remember to hold your water. This is my show. You're here to watch."

"I hear you. I hear you."

They spoke so openly because Otto had gotten them thinking he was hard of hearing and feeble. He listened to every word.

"Sometimes I think *you* think you do, but I'm not sure. Get this deep into your head. Armstrong is mine. You are not to interfere. If you so much as try to indulge the sickness in your brain, I will put you in the ground *before* I'm done with what I came to do. Understand?"

Wolf Eyes hung his head. After a spell, he said, "I understand."

After that, they spoke no more, and then were out of earshot.

Otto mounted his horse and headed back to Pine Lick. He wasn't sure which Armstrong the men were talking about, but that wasn't a big concern. With the directions he gave them, he had plenty of time not only to warn father and son, but to be prepared for their arrival.

He could try to take the duo on himself and make sure they never made it to town. As much as Otto liked to think he was still a young man, he conceded that the passage of time and hard living had slowed him just enough to admit he wasn't up to the task of being outnumbered. Both men looked dangerous in their own way. If Otto tried and failed, there would be no one to alert the Armstrongs.

The rumble of thunder far off in the distance rattled at his back. He turned to see the start of gray clouds on the horizon.

The nice day had come to an end.

Whiskey sat at the bar at the Sawdust Saloon nursing a glass of buttermilk. Despite his nickname, the sheriff's deputy hadn't had a drop of alcohol in years.

The shack he called a home was too cloyingly hot for rest. So he'd ridden back to town, hoping things would be cooler in the saloon. It was, but only by a few degrees. Not enough to stop him from feeling like he was sitting in warm bathwater.

"You want something to eat?" Butch Nathans, the owner/ bartender, asked. He had a knot on his head and a black eye from his tussle with the rowdy cowpokes.

"Too hot to eat."

"I can't see how you can drink that stuff. It's probably curdling in your gut as we speak." Nathans eyed a mug to make sure it didn't have any spots before setting it on the shelf behind him.

"Better than what you got there," Whiskey replied, angling his chin to the lineup of rotgut that lined the back of the bar. "That'll cut a hole clear through you."

"It might, but at least you'd have some fun along the way."

"Too dang hot for fun."

Nathans leaned against the bar. "It's too hot for anything. If I had my druthers, I'd close up and jump in the Angelina. Just stay in that cool water until sundown."

"You own the joint. What's stopping you?"

Rubbing his thumb against his fingers, Nathan replied, "That'll be five cents."

Whiskey thrust his hand in his pocket and gave the bartender a knowing nod. "Cain't say holding back your freedom for a plug nickel is worth it."

"Ah, but those nickels add up, especially when it's two bits for a pint of whiskey and you have a town full of thirsty workers."

The sheriff's deputy slid the nickel across the bar and Nathans rang up the sale in the big metal cash register.

Both men turned, muscles coiled, when the saloon doors banged open. Thankfully, instead of trouble, it was only Otto. Whiskey held up his half-drunk glass of buttermilk. "Someone sounds in desperate need of some of that firewater."

Otto marched to the bar. Up close, Whiskey saw the concern on the old Indian's face. His flesh was shiny with sweat.

"Where is the sheriff?"

Whiskey set his glass down and got up from the stool. It didn't take a smart man to sense trouble.

"Last I saw, he was making his rounds. Why do you ask?"

Otto flicked his fingers at Nathans. The bartender poured him a shot of bourbon.

"I was out ridin' this morning. Came across two men asking for directions to Pine Lick. I did not like the look of them, so I gave them the way to Tuftstown. As they were leaving, I heard them say they were looking for Armstrong. It did not sound like they were coming to pay a social call."

"Did they say which Armstrong?" Whiskey's hand absently went to his holstered gun.

"They did not."

"If they headed off for Tuftstown, they won't be here until nightfall, or more likely tomorrow if they hunker down for the night. You can describe them to Mack and Branch?"

Otto knocked back the drink. "Yes. I was almost as close to them as you are to me."

"Good. Maybe it'll ring a bell for them. I'll find the sheriff. You want to go to Mr. Branch's farm and bring him here?"

"To the saloon?"

Whiskey set his hat on his head. "No privacy at that jail for the moment. Here is as good a place as any, I suppose." He rapped his knuckles on the bar. "Anyone in that room of yours upstairs, Butch?"

"Not at the moment."

"You think we could use it for a spell?"

Nathans lifted a case of whiskey off the floor and settled it onto the bar. "Can't see why not." He tapped a key on the register. There was a loud ring, and the drawer popped open. He fished a key out of one of the money slots and tossed it to Whiskey. "Guess I don't have to tell you to give it back when you're done."

The sheriff's deputy dropped the key in his shirt pocket. "Much obliged. Let's go, Otto."

Each man unhitched their horse and headed in different directions.

Whiskey felt trouble coming the same way he did that storm.

He'd worked with the senior Armstrong for some years. He'd always felt the postwar transplant had something in his past he'd been spending a lifetime seeking atonement for. What that was, the man would never so much as hint at. But it was there. Maybe now, it was coming to find him.

Chapter 11

Branch Armstrong sat across from Otto and tried to conjure up a picture of the men his friend described. Kate stood behind him with her hand on his shoulder in silent assurance.

"I can't think of anyone that comes to mind," Armstrong said after a while. "There are plenty of men I've arrested or run out of Pine Lick over the years. Most of them were two-bit drifters who weren't around long enough to make an impression."

He'd been sheriff for almost a decade. He'd lost count of the number of men, and sometimes women, who would have a grudge against him because of the star on his chest.

"So, you think maybe they are coming here for Mack?" Otto asked.

At this, Kate Armstrong stiffened. It had been hard enough seeing her husband work a profession that usually ended in a funeral. She'd never cottoned to her son taking the reins. Let another woman suffer the constant anxiety. Surely, she had done more than her bit.

"If that's the case," she said, "you have to stop them, Branch."

Clouds had been scudding through the sky for the past hour. It had gotten so dark inside the cabin, Armstrong got up and lit a couple of lanterns. Otto pulled out a cigar and asked Kate, "Mind if I smoke? It helps to settle my nerves."

To both men's surprise, she said, "Go right on ahead. I might join you if it'll help calm me down."

"There's no need to borrow worry," Armstrong said. He took his gun belt off the peg on the wall and secured it around his waist. "Let's meet at the Sawdust and talk it out with Mack. We don't know, for sure, what these men are after."

Lighting his cigar, Otto said, "They are a bad wind, for sure."

Kate paced the kitchen. "Let me come with you."

"I think it's best you stay here."

Her nostrils flared. "Don't give me that line that this is man's work. This is my husband and my son we're talking about. If you think you're going to leave me out of the discussion, you're sorely mistaken."

Branch Armstrong held up his hands in surrender. "I'm all for keeping the peace."

"Good. No sense dawdling."

Kate was out the door, heading to the horse corral.

Hidden amid a cloud of gray smoke, Otto said, "I wouldn't want to be those men if they come across your missus."

They rode hard into town. The moment they walked into the mostly empty Sawdust, Nathans called out to them, "The sheriff and deputy are upstairs."

"Thank you kindly," Otto said.

The trio took the stairs, two at a time. Branch Armstrong opened the door to the tiny room. Mack and Whiskey sat on the only chairs, with a small round table between them. Both of their hands went to their guns when Branch swung the door open.

"Good grief, Pop, that's a good way to get your head blown off," Sheriff Mack Armstrong said, rising from his chair. "Especially after learning about the men Otto came across."

"Well, at least you would have shot me and not your mother."

"Please take my seat, Mrs. Armstrong," Whiskey said, angling the chair toward her.

"I don't think I could sit if I tried," she said.

Otto sat on the edge of the bed, tamping his cigar out, since they were in close quarters. He stuffed the stogie in his shirt pocket for later.

"Describe the men to Mack," Branch said to Otto.

When the old Indian was finished, Mack paced at the end of the bed for a moment, deep in thought. "I mean, they sound like a lot of the folks who blow in and out of town."

"I think if you had come across the younger one, you would remember him," Otto said. "He has the look of a rabid dog in need of putting down. A man like that exists only to cause harm. I have seen two others with that same look in their eyes. One I sent on his journey to the spirit world. The other murdered a great number of my people and disappeared. I regret never being able to find him. No, if you had come across him, those eyes would have been burned in your brain. I could see that he even made the man he was with very nervous."

"I can't say I've met anyone quite like that," Mack said.

"You've only been sheriff for a little over a year," his mother said. She had her hands tucked in her back pockets. Kate was one of the few women in Pine Lick who preferred waist overalls to dresses. "I doubt you'd forget someone like that in so short a time. Branch, that leaves you."

Branch Armstrong pulled the curtain aside to peer out the window. The street was busy with horse-and-buggy traffic. The skies had turned to slate, and a gust of wind blew a woman's hat clear off her head. He turned to them and shrugged. "It could be anyone. Like I said before, I've tussled with too many men to rightly count. And things weren't exactly a bed of roses before then. Hey, Otto, did they mention knowing anything about the Armstrong they were after being the sheriff?"

"They did not." Otto had put his feet up and relaxed on the bed. Branch had seen what Otto slept on. The ratty bed above the bar must have felt like lying on a cloud in comparison.

"Okay, so we're pretty much in the dark. But to be safe, we have to assume they know more about us, or me, than we do about them." Branch pointed at his wife. "Which means we need to keep you safe. Just in case."

Kate squared her hands on her hips. "Oh, no you don't. You're not going to hide me away like some helpless creature."

Branch Armstrong smiled. "No. I'm going to hide you away so there's one less thing worrying my mind while I deal with whatever trouble these men are bringing with them. Seeing as I've rousted more than my share of bad hombres, I'm going to guess that it's me they're after. If they know the town I'm in, they might know where I live as well." Before his wife could protest, he held up a finger. "And that's final. Distractions can get a man killed. I fully intend to be around long after tomorrow. Can you understand that?"

His wife took a deep breath while staring into his eyes. He saw a hundred rebuttals swirling in her brain. To his relief, her face softened and her shoulders sagged just enough for him to know he'd gotten through to her. "Fine. It doesn't mean I like it."

"Thank you. You don't have to like a thing in order to make it right. Mack, you think you can talk to Sam Snodgrass over at the Palace Hotel about setting a room aside for your mother?"

The young sheriff wiped the sweat off his face with a towel that had been neatly folded beside a basin and jug of water. Even with the window wide open, the air in the cramped room had become stifling. "I sure can. And I can promise it won't cost a red cent."

"We should pay the man for his hospitality," Kate said.

Her son waved his hand. "He owes me a couple of favors. Everyone who checks in to the Palace isn't a member of high society. I'm sure Dad did his share of hotel cleanup during his time."

Armstrong nodded, recalling some of the more rambunctious guests who sometimes had to be strong-armed off the premises. There was the one couple who fought like bobcats that he'd had the misfortune of getting between. Snodgrass had rushed to the jailhouse, telling Armstrong through hurried breaths that the husband and wife's fiery antics were disrupting the entire hotel. Armstrong went right over, finding them yelling inches away from each other's faces in the middle of the lobby. The woman had swung at her husband, but walloped Branch instead. The punch united the couple as they turned on him, shouting that he had no right getting in their business. He'd had one heck of a shiner the next day. For such a small lady, she packed one hell of a punch. Once they'd realized he was the sheriff and settled down, he'd pulled her husband aside and suggested he run for the hills and never look back.

"I have one more favor to ask, son. From tonight until tomorrow, I'd like to park myself in the jail. If these men come to town without knowing where I am, they'll ask around. Most people will think a stranger is looking for the sheriff and send them there. And, Otto, it would be nice if you could walk about the town, keeping an eye out for them."

Mack looked as if he was about to protest being evicted from his own place of business. He cocked his head and asked, "What about me and Whiskey?"

"Just go about your regular business. This might all be for nothing and we'll feel pretty foolish later. But I'd rather feel foolish than be caught off guard. The one thing that concerns me is that Otto says they're bad men. I haven't known him to be wrong."

"Darn straight."

"In *that* regard," Branch Armstrong finished, casting a half smile in Otto's direction. "Now let's get the heck out of this room before we melt into the floorboards."

Chapter 12

"I'd like to speak to Miss Belle Dupree," Tony Cheever said to the brothel's mountain of a bodyguard. His bulk filled the doorway. Behind him, the parlor was brightly lit. Men and women talked and laughed in high voices. It was just after dusk, and business was picking up.

"You an' every guy in Texas," Tiny Ed said. "She ain't for sale. If you want a soiled dove, we got the best you'll find north of New Orleans."

Cheever thought that was an interesting way to refer to the women who sold their bodies. Maybe there was a bit of a poet hiding within the lumbering giant.

"Ah, no, I'm here more to speak to her about a business proposal."

"She don't need no business proposals."

Before Tiny Ed could shut him out, Cheever stuck his foot in the door. It was a risky move because he was sure Tiny Ed could smash it to a pulp with ease.

"One moment. You are aware of who I am?"

With his deep-set eyes, Tiny Ed's gaze bore into Cheever. "Yeah. So what?"

"As one of the wealthiest entrepreneurs in Pine Lick, I would think Miss Dupree would be interested in what I have to say. But the only way to do so is to be spared a moment with her."

"Move," Tiny Ed commanded as he looked down at Cheever's foot. Cheever pulled it back and the door slammed shut.

A rush of wind howled at Cheever's back, lifting the flaps of his coat. It was still hot as blazes, even with the sun down. He always wore suits, no matter the weather. Clothes may not have made the man, but a fine wardrobe was a smart way to create a positive first impression.

That seemed to be lost on Tiny Ed.

Cheever hadn't heard a lock being thrown on the other side of the door. He was tempted to open it and look for Belle Dupree himself.

It was a fleeting thought, replaced by images of what the bouncer would do to him if he trespassed.

Just as he was about to turn and head back to his buggy, the door opened.

"You got two minutes. Follow me."

The parlor was wallpapered with burgundy floral prints. There was a small bar, with men and women sitting side by side, being served by a woman wearing a black corset. Plush chairs and couches were everywhere, all populated by couples either drinking or starting negotiations. No one gave him so much as a glance, not even the "soiled doves."

The women were of varying ages, sizes, and complexions. All the more to appeal to a wide clientele, Cheever thought. He'd frequented other brothels in the past and had found a drab and depressing sameness in the painted ladies on offer. Even in Chicago, there had been paltry choices for those with varied tastes.

Not so here—in Pine Lick of all places. It showed that Belle Dupree was a shrewd businesswoman.

He stayed close to Tiny Ed, his nostrils flaring at the overpowering aroma of perfumes and powders.

The bouncer led him down a narrow hall and rapped his knuckles three times on a closed door.

"Entrez, s'il vous plaît."

Tiny Ed stepped aside so Cheever could get past him. Belle Dupree sat behind a massive oak desk. The only things on it were a large leatherbound ledger and a lockbox. She looked to be north of forty, but aging gracefully, though it was hard to tell under all the makeup. The madam wore a gold satin dress with a plunging neckline designed to highlight the string of pearls around her neck.

"Please take a seat," she said with a slight French accent. Cheever had lived in Paris for four years when he was a younger man. He knew a fake French accent when he heard it. He supposed there had to be a certain degree of mystique to run the kind of business Belle Dupree did. "How can I help you, Mr. Cheever? If you're ashamed to ask for pleasure, rest assured there's no need to feel that way within these four walls."

Cheever fidgeted in the hard-backed chair. "Of that, I have no doubt. And yes, I have come seeking your professional help, but not for myself."

Belle Dupree's face remained impassive.

"As you know, I've built an exclusive retreat for men of a certain, ah, *caliber*."

"Yes, I've heard all about the Arcadian. I also hear you're having your grand opening tomorrow."

"Correct. Now, I've done everything I can to provide various forms of entertainment and relaxation for my esteemed guests. Ordinary men would want for nothing during their stay at the Arcadian. However, these are not ordinary men. Not in the slightest."

She held up a hand to stop him. "And you want my girls to be at their beck and call. *Est-ce exact?*"

Cheever reddened. He'd always had difficulty discussing carnal matters. It was a weakness that vexed him, to no end.

"Yes, something like that," he replied. His throat had gone dry.

The madam sat back in her plump velvet chair. "Well, sure, *mon cher*. Bring them around whenever they have that itch that my girls can scratch like no other."

Tapping his fingers nervously against his leg, Cheever said, "I was thinking your, um, *girls* would come to the Arcadian instead. It would not do for my guests to make the journey to your bordello. The experience I aim to provide at the Arcadian is centered upon one word: 'convenience.'"

Without hesitation, Dupree said, "No."

Cheever was taken aback. "I would pay over the standard asking price."

"Still, no."

"May I ask why?"

"Protection." She opened a drawer and plucked out a silver cigarette case. Without offering one to him, she extracted a slender cigarette, lit it, and blew a cloud of smoke over his head. "You know why my girls are so loyal to me? One, because I treat them well. Better than they'll get anywhere else in the state of Texas, or any other state as far as I'm concerned. Two, I keep them safe. Well, Tiny Ed and I keep them safe. We can't do that if they're over at your little boys' club."

Before Cheever could respond, the building shook from a rumble of thunder. Dupree leaned over to shift the heavy drape aside from the window. Light flicked at the edge of the glass pane. "Looks like the rain's not done with us yet." She shook her head. "Bad weather is bad for business."

"Name your price," Cheever said, not caring about the weather's impact on Dupree's illicit business.

That got her attention. Belle lit a fresh cigarette with the dying one and paused for a moment. "How many girls are you talking about?"

"That would be hard to say. It would vary with my clientele's needs."

"What nights would you need them?"

"Again, I'm in the business of catering to the whims of the men who pay a significant amount of money to escape the trappings of their very busy lives. I would need your ladies available at a moment's notice."

Belle Dupree shook her head. "I can't be at the beck and call of you and your guests. I have a business to run right here. Now, if you were to specify a certain night for entertaining at the Arcadian and were willing to make it financially worth my shutting down for a few hours, we might have a deal. But unless you can find an exact copy of Tiny Ed and myself so we can be in two places at once, I'm afraid the answer is still no."

Cheever stared at the madam, flabbergasted. A madam turning down a lucrative payday because she didn't want to send her soiled doves to his finely appointed retreat was beyond him.

"Maybe you should take some time to think this over," he said, recovering from his surprise.

"I've taken all the time I need. Maybe you should consider *my* proposal, *oui?*" Her hand disappeared under the desk. A small bell rang outside her office. The door opened seconds later, Tiny Ed once again filling the open space. "Believe you me, you get enough men up there, those roosters will come for the hens if they have to walk fifty country miles on their bare knees. When they do, we'll be happy to have them."

"I'll say it one more time—" Cheever said with some iron in his voice. He wasn't a man who was told no.

She cut him off. "Actually, you won't." A flick of her wrist had Tiny Ed's meaty hands on Cheever's shoulders. It felt as if his bones were being crushed in a vise. He was lifted off the chair. "Besides, I don't get into business with murderers."

As he was being escorted out the door, Cheever turned to her as best he could and said, "That is slander! I have not been tried or convicted of such a thing!"

Belle Dupree smiled wide with her painted red lips. "You're new here, Mr. Cheever. When you're in the crosshairs of Sheriff Armstrong, both father and son, your days as a free man are numbered. Maybe I'll buy the Arcadian when you're gone and expand my business. Then those rich city boys won't have to leave their comfy rooms to get a little of what they need."

His anger rising, Cheever spat, "The Arcadian will never be left in the hands of a tramp like you!"

Dupree chuckled. She then said to Tiny Ed, "*Quelle merde.* Would you mind throwing out the trash?"

Cheever was lifted off his feet as if he weighed no more than a bag of flour. Tiny Ed carried him down the corridor. One of the working girls saw him, got up from her chair, and opened the front door.

Next thing he knew, Cheever was airborne, at least until he landed on his side in a mud puddle.

The urge to threaten Tiny Ed died in his throat when lightning flashed and he saw the dead look in the man's eyes. He instead scrambled to his feet, just as the light drizzle turned to rain.

As he climbed onto his buggy, he thought he heard Belle Dupree's laughter before the bouncer slammed the door.

Chapter 13

The men crammed in the cell were mercifully quiet while they ate. Branch Armstrong had just tucked his wife safely out of the way, and he and Otto had gone back to his farm to see if anyone was lying in wait. It was a miserable gray day. Armstrong's oilskin duster kept most of him dry, at least until the sheets of rain got so thick, he could hardly see the Indian, even though he was riding not more than five feet away from him.

They stopped at Daisy's for some stew and biscuits to bring back to the jail for themselves and their prisoners.

Even in terrible weather, the sounds of the big blades and bulky steam motors still emanated from the Smits and Knoop Sawmill.

"Where's the sheriff?" one of the cowboys asked between bites of biscuit.

"None of your business," Armstrong said.

The man looked like he was about to say something else, but thought better of it. His beard was so full of crumbs, Armstrong knew from experience he would wake up with mice feasting amid his wiry hairs if he didn't wipe them off.

Otto opened the door to a thick curtain of rain pounding the wooden planks outside. Water splashed into the jailhouse, carried by a hot wind.

"This weather will buy us more time," Otto said as he closed the door and fished a cigar out of his pocket. "Can't see even a crazy man traveling in a storm like this."

"A lot of crazy men working right now." Armstrong pointed in the direction of the sawmill.

Storms like this were a surprising boon to the sawmill. With the water surging in the Angelina River, they could transport lumber quicker than on a dry, sunny day. Might as well make the most of the gift from Mother Nature.

"Work is not the same as traveling through hard country," Otto replied. He scraped a match against the adobe wall and fired up his cigar. "Not good to risk your horse."

"Unless you're crazy," Armstrong said, putting his boots up on the desk that bore the scars of a decade's worth of his bootheels.

Otto pointed the lit end of the cigar at him. "I said one is crazy. The other is just bad."

"Comforting."

"Hey, wagon burner, you pass the peace pipe?" the thief named Kelly blurted out.

Armstrong shot a look at his friend and held his tongue.

Otto turned to the man, then studied his cigar for a moment. "It is a big cigar. I cannot see why not."

He approached the bars, holding the cigar out.

The thief was shocked at first.

"It is good," Otto encouraged the man. "I get them from a Mexican who passes through each spring."

"Don't mind if I do," Kelly said, moving toward the bars to accept the proffered stogie.

When he was close enough, Otto pressed the glowing end into

the top of the man's hand. He shrieked and whipped his hand back so he could cradle it under his arm.

"I never burned no wagons," Otto mumbled as he turned away from the wounded man.

Armstrong got to his feet, assuming he'd have to command the thief, who was cursing at the top of his lungs, to shut his mouth—voluntarily or by force.

Just then, a wraith slipped into the jailhouse trailing a gallon of rainwater. The small and impossibly thin figure was Ella Schmidt, who worked the telegraph at the post office.

"Oh, hi, Sheriff," she said when she closed her umbrella. "I didn't expect to see you here."

"Just minding the store for a spell."

Ella had been an old woman when Armstrong first came to Pine Lick. She may have been older now, but she had the energy of a pup. The thief stopped his yowling when he saw her. Armstrong had to give the man credit for having at least a smidgen of manners.

"I just got word from Louisiana that they are getting hit with one heck of a storm," Ella said. "Other operators south of there are starting to see it, too. Looks like it might be headed this way. I'm not saying to spread the word just yet, but I wanted y'all to be prepared just in case."

Otto pointed out the open doorway. "It appears to already be here."

"From what I hear, this storm is just a babe compared to what folks are dealing with down in Louisiana."

"Bad storms are just a way of life down there," Armstrong said. Because Pine Lick provided a bulk of its lumber to the ports in Louisiana, there was constant chatter between both sides of the border. From everything he'd heard, living on the Gulf of Mexico had its share of beauty and sheer ugliness. Pine Lick wasn't perfect, but he didn't have to fret over tropical storms several times a year.

"Thank you kindly, Ella," Armstrong said. "You want me to walk you back to the post office?"

"Only if you could carry a roof over me to keep me dry. That umbrella of mine has seen better days."

"I wish I had one to give you. Come on back anytime if you get an update." He went for his duster. "That reminds me. I should go check on the Stanton Reservoir."

Otto plucked the duster out of his hand and put it back on the peg in the wall. "I am sure Mack is going to do that. We cannot have you out there, alone."

Ella looked at Armstrong and Otto quizzically. When neither was forthcoming, she said, "Far be it for me to pry. If I don't come back, assume no news is good news."

She put up her shoddy umbrella and zipped out of the jailhouse, almost as fast as a jackrabbit.

Branch Armstrong reluctantly sat back down. When Kelly started to grumble again, he said, "You have another hand, and my friend here has plenty of cigars."

Silence, except for the pounding of the rain, prevailed.

Almost at the same time that Ella Schmidt was warning his father about the storm, Mack Armstrong and Whiskey, soaked to the bone, had just come upon the reservoir. It had visibly risen since the day before. There didn't seem to be any leaks, but it was hard to tell in the driving rain.

"It looks fine to me," Whiskey practically shouted to be heard over the rain.

Mack dared to look into the sky and was pelted by the downpour for his effort. "If it keeps up like this, we should plan to stop by later."

"Should we draw straws?"

Mack looked at his deputy with mild surprise. Whiskey rarely made jokes, and when he did, he was so deadpan, it was hard to tell if what he'd said was serious or not. The little gleam in the man's eyes confirmed he was joshing.

They turned their horses to leave. The main lodge of the Arcadian was flooded with gaslight. Mack counted four carriages out front.

"At least the storm is raining on Cheever's picnic," Mack said. "There's our silver lining."

"I'd like to see that son of a biscuit eater come out here and take a shot at me. We wouldn't have no need for hauling him into jail and calling on the judge. I'd pay the undertaker out of my own pocket to have him boxed up."

The fact that Cheever was allowed to open his men's resort and live as if nothing had happened chapped both men. They would like nothing more than for Cheever to give them an excuse to arrest him again or, as Whiskey said, step on out to the hereafter.

"It's too bad Bear up and disappeared," Whiskey said. "If the weather was better, I'd set out looking for him in his usual haunts."

"Unfortunately, it'll take more than the word of just Bear and a little boy to put Cheever away. Money speaks louder than eyewitness testimony."

Whiskey's horse slipped for a moment as they took to the slight hill leading away from the reservoir and the Arcadian.

"I think we all need to dry off for a spell," Whiskey said. "Some coffee will do my joints good."

"I'm with you on that. If anyone is coming for me or my father, I doubt they'll brave this storm. And even if they do make it to Pine Lick and find out we're all at the jailhouse, they've lost the element of surprise. Four against two are pretty good odds."

"Or we can hope the good Lord washes them away in this storm," Whiskey said as he put his heels to his horse.

Chapter 14

One thought kept the misery from being overwhelming.

Rain and warm weather were better than snow and bitter cold.

The old man kept his head low so the rainwater sluiced off his hat and onto his horse's neck. Slip had been silent for miles, lost in his private grumbling about traveling in weather not fit for man or beast.

At any other time in their journey, the old man would have found a dry place to hole up for the night. But they were too close to stop now. There was an itch in his veins that only grew worse if he wasn't moving.

That damn Indian's directions took them to the wrong town, making them lose precious time they needed to make up. If he saw that Indian again, he'd make him pay.

They hugged the swelling banks of the Angelina. The brown water was roiling with whitecaps now, and loud as a flock of roosters at dawn. He eyed those waters warily from time to time. Having never learned to swim, the old man tried to stay as far away from bodies of water as he could.

In this case, he was happy to make an exception.

He turned back to see if Slip was still behind him. With the wall of rain and the roaring river, he'd lost all sense of the boy's presence.

Slip was there, all right, with his face scrunched up in disgust. When he caught the old man's gaze, he looked down to avoid any reprobation, even if it wasn't done in words.

Sure, Slip was cowed now. When they finally found Armstrong, the old man knew things with the wild boy would be different. Concern about how Slip would comport himself weighed down on the old man as much as the pounding rain.

Times like this, he almost wished he were a churchgoing man. He'd seen prayer give comfort to many people in his life, including his parents, who were devout Lutherans. Not that the prayers, in his opinion, were ever heard or did a lick of good in the end. But at least for the moment of the praying itself, there was a sense of calm, that things would turn out as God intended them to, which most assumed meant would be for the better.

If the old man prayed now, he would pray that they came upon Pine Lick soon, and that Armstrong would be easy to find. Then the hard part would be over.

The rest would be a relief. Not just to him and Slip, but to many others back home in New York.

He held his free hand out, capturing a small puddle of rain in his leather-gloved palm. It made him think of rushing out during that first snowstorm every winter when he was a young boy, eager to collect snowflakes before they hit the ground. He remembered the morning he'd spied the falling snow outside his window when he awoke in the morning. Without a care in the world, he ran out of the house with no shoes or jacket on, eager to feel the cold, wet flakes on his skin.

He shuddered in his saddle at another memory. That of the day he'd found his brother, Henry, lying dead in the snow—soft white flakes touching upon his cooling face. His eyes were wide open, in shock or pain—there would never be a way to know. The wind blowing off the Chemung River could freeze a man's soul to his bones.

His blood had turned to ice that night.

For over two decades, he performed his duty as caregiver for his brother's widow, poor Amanda, whose heart never fully recovered, and their four children. He buried his mother and father, shells of what they once had been. He watched Amanda die slowly, somehow surviving the passing of three of her children from pneumonia in three consecutive years. She had become a living ghost, barely inhabiting her home, rarely speaking, sometimes not moving for days.

When mercy finally came and they put her in the ground, the old man found that the fires of vengeance still burned as hot as they had that frozen winter night. He could no longer wait to do what had to be done.

Taking his wayward nephew, Slip, was never in question. The boy had heard him talk of his daddy, and how a low-down Confederate prisoner had taken his life during a rare escape from Elmira Prison Camp. The boy had no recollection of his father, but he did know violence. That mean streak was both the reason they had to leave New York, and how he could come in handy during the long ride to Texas.

If the old man wasn't fortunate to catch Armstrong alone, he knew Slip would take great pleasure in removing any distractions. He just hoped the boy wouldn't overstep his bounds and rob him of what was rightfully his.

As the old man's thoughts churned, Slip pulled up alongside him.

"Lookit there."

He pointed to a horse tied under a great, leafy tree. Sitting in the mud, with his back against the tree, was a man dressed for the weather in a long coat and wide-brimmed hat. One of his legs was stretched out before him. It was bent at a funny angle from the knee down.

The man looked up when they got close enough for the constant barrage of rain to lessen as they edged under the tree cover.

"I thought I was the only crazy person out in this weather," the man said with a note of hope in his voice. His face was as pale as the underside of a brook trout. He grimaced when he tried to shift a bit to look at them head-on. "Had myself a little accident. Beulah over there ain't as nimble as she used to be. We went down, and she landed on my leg. It's all busted up."

"Can you stand up?" the old man asked him.

"Not without a lot of help, I suppose. I tried to get back up on old Beulah, but the pain stopped me cold."

"That leg don't look so good," Slip said with a trace of a smile. The wounded man didn't seem to notice.

"I'd sure appreciate it if you two wouldn't mind riding into town and asking the sheriff to come on out here with a wagon." Pain hit the man so hard, his body went rigid and he shut his eyes and mouth up tight. His face went from pale to waxen in an instant. The old man was sure that if they were to cut his pants and reveal the leg, it would be a sorry sight indeed.

"When you say 'town,' do you mean Pine Lick?" the old man asked.

"Sure enough," the man said after a ragged exhale.

"How far are we from it?" Slip asked.

The man pointed with a shaky finger. "Just a couple of miles that way. You can't miss it. Sheriff's office is just a block into the town proper."

The old man felt a thrill run through him. "We can do that for you. What would your name be, son? Might be good for the sheriff to know who he's coming out in this godawful storm for."

"Russell. Russell Laychek."

"Russell Laychek," the old man repeated. "I'll be sure to tell him. Is there anything you need before we head off?"

He rested his hand on his busted leg. "It's getting so I can't feel my foot. Maybe ask him to bring the doc, too. Sheriff Armstrong will know what to do."

At the mention of Armstrong's name, the old man had to stop himself from grinning from ear to ear. He'd heard rumor that the man he was after had become a lawman, but that was from a drunken petty thief who had been run out of Pine Lick months ago. They'd met by sheer accident at a saloon back in New York.

But the old man had known it had not been an accident. Divine Providence had shown him the way to exorcise the demons that had beset him and his family since the night of that escape at Elmira. And now here was this man confirming what had driven him to travel for more miles than he could count.

The end was near.

"I'm sure he will," he replied, struggling to keep his tone friendly. "You just hang in there. We'll be back in the time it takes to skin a hare."

Slip pulled his horse closer, removed the Henry from its scabbard, and leaned over to tap the bottom of the man's boot ever so lightly. It produced a keen howl that would have made a wolf blush. The man breathed heavily, his face a rictus of agony.

"Why did you go and do that?" he asked pitiably.

"Just wanted to see how much it hurt. You know, even if they fix it best they can, that leg will never be right again."

"What did you say?"

Slip nodded. "Yep, that kind of injury makes a man lame for life. Now, if old Beulah over there were to break her leg even half as bad as that, what would you do?"

The man looked to his horse, then back to Slip. "I . . . I don't understand."

"Sure you do. Any man who owns a horse knows that if they

become lame, you put them out of their pain and suffering. Just pull the trigger . . . and BAM!"

When the wounded man jumped, Slip cackled.

Then Slip pointed his Henry at the horse and pulled the trigger. The bullet caught Beulah right between the eyes. She barely even made a sound. One second she was standing, the next she was in a heap beside her owner.

"What in the hell did you go and do that for?" the man shouted, suddenly forgetting his agony. "Why you son of a . . ."

He reached for his pistol, but his body was all twisted and stiff.

Slip shifted the rifle to the man and shot him in the neck.

The man's eyes rolled into the back of his head as a geyser of blood erupted from the hole in his neck. His shaking hands clutched the grievous wound as his body jittered. Blood flowed between his fingers, mingling with the rain as it stained his shirt.

His bad leg kicked once and his hands fell away. Slip continued laughing as the top half of his body dropped into the mud.

The old man watched it all with impatience.

"Are you done now?" he asked his nephew.

"Way I see it, we couldn't leave a witness. Especially someone who knows Armstrong."

For the first time in their lives together, the old man said, "You did good, son. Now let's go finish the job."

Puffed up by the simple words of encouragement, Slip secured his rifle and happily followed the old man as they rode beside the river into Pine Lick.

Chapter 15

Kate Armstrong thought she'd be used to situations like this by now. Her husband had chosen a dangerous profession and had, by will and wits, managed to survive his time as sheriff. Their son, Mack, was an apple that hadn't fallen far from that tree. She trusted his abilities and instincts implicitly.

But no matter how good you were, there was always someone—if not better, at least more cunning, driven, or just plain lucky in their pursuits—waiting around the corner.

She sat by the window in her room at the Palace Hotel nursing a glass of bourbon. She would rather be at the bar in the Sawdust, surrounded by so many others like her, drinking their troubles away. That would be improper, especially for the current sheriff's mother. So, there she was, feeling as if she was locked away, watching the seconds pass, along with the heavy raindrops outside her window.

It would be better if she could have waited things out at home. At least there, she had things to do that would keep her hands and mind occupied.

The room was nice and all; of that, she had no complaints. It was the lack of anything to do other than fixate on her worries that was driving her up the wall.

A hard gust of wind rattled the windowpane. The rain pelted the thin glass hard enough to cause her to wonder if it would break to pieces.

Kate finished the bourbon in one large swallow.

Sam Snodgrass, the hotel manager, had been nice enough to send someone up with a bottle when she'd checked in, on her son's request. For that, she silently thanked them both as she poured another glass.

She sat on the end of the bed, felt restless, then got up and sat back in the chair by the window overlooking Main Street. The few folks out and about were rushing to find shelter. An umbrella that had been blown inside out by the wind rolled down the street like a tumbleweed.

After a few more sips, she slammed the glass down. "That's it."

Kate got up and went down to the lobby. She needed a distraction, to be around other people.

She got what she was looking for when Gloria Amaryllis, the teacher, came bustling in the front door with a young boy in tow.

That must be the orphaned boy Branch told me about, Kate thought.

Mack had never come outright and said it, but she knew he carried a little torch for the older woman. Now, Kate would prefer he tied his heart to a woman closer to his age, if not younger, so they could fill her house with grandchildren. He could have his pick of the Pine Lick litter, but the heart wanted what the heart wanted. This was her chance to get to know the woman a little better and find out why her son was so smitten. She was pretty enough, but a strong marriage took more than looks.

They were soaked to the bone. Rainwater dripped off their clothes, forming instant puddles in the lobby. The boy's clothes were caked in mud. The front-desk clerk saw this and was about to say something when Kate shot him a look that stayed his tongue.

"Why, Mrs. Amaryllis, are you all right?" Kate asked, striding across the lobby.

The teacher did her best to smile. "Just a little worse for wear. The storm is really picking up."

"Someone looks like they've been making mud pies," Kate said to the boy. He averted her gaze and stared at his soiled shoes.

"Wouldn't you know it! A gust of wind not only took my umbrella from my hand, it also sent poor Archibald here sprawling into the mud. I need to fatten him up a little more. I believe my umbrella landed somewhere in Nacogdoches."

Kate crouched down to get a better look at the shy boy. His cheeks and forehead were smeared in mud, and it looked like he'd been crying.

"Well, let's get you dry and Archibald cleaned up." She turned to the front-desk clerk. "Please send some fresh towels to my room and draw some bathwater."

"Oh, please, you don't need to do that. We'll just dry off a bit here until the wind and rain have settled down some."

"Nonsense," Kate said. "You drink bourbon?"

Gloria blushed a bit and leaned closer to Kate. "I have a nip every now and then."

"Good. The fire it brings will help dry you off." She turned her head and said, "I'll also need another glass and some milk as well."

"Yes, Mrs. Armstrong."

Archibald mumbled, "I like milk."

"And you can drink as much as you want." Kate took the teacher by the elbow. "Now let's go on up to my room and wait this thing out."

Gloria looked confused. "You're staying at the hotel?"

"It's a long story. I'll tell you all about it once you're a little drier."

* * *

Henrik Smits removed his glasses so he could polish them up a bit. His eyes were starting to get bleary from reading through the pile of ledgers on his desk. There was never a dull moment at the sawmill. For that, he never once complained. A widower going on ten years now, with no children, he devoted his entire life to his successful business.

His partner, Jens Knoop, had left the sawmill offices an hour ago to check on his house. It was on the other side of the Angelina River and close to the shore. The raging waters had been rising precipitously over the past couple of hours. He'd told Jens not to build there, but his old friend liked to fish in the little free time he had and wanted to be as close to the water as possible. It was a modest house, with an immodest propensity to flood during even the most minor of storms.

Smits's own home was on a high hill on the outskirts of town. He had no worries about being flooded.

The wind howled outside, trying to find any small crack so it could creep into the office. It would have to try harder than that, for the building was sturdily made.

There was a knock at the door.

"Come in."

Pat "Bull" McManus opened the door and waited at the threshold, dripping wet. He looked like a drowned possum.

"I'd tell you to take a seat, but considering your condition," Smits said as he settled his glasses on one of the open ledgers.

"I wouldn't think of it," Bull replied with a hint of an Irish brogue.

"But please do come in. A little rainwater won't harm the floor."

"Thank you, Mr. Smits. I just wanted to let you know that we just fished two men out of the river."

Smits went stiff with alarm. "Are they all right?" Injuries were a sad fact of working at the sawmill, though Smits and Knoop did all they could to make safety improvements. Saying men were *fished* out of the lake usually meant they had perished. He dreaded having to give families the news. Promising to take care of them financially did little to lessen the shock and pain.

"They're a mite banged up and waterlogged, but they should be fine. I had them brought to the doctor just to be safe."

Exhaling with relief, Smits asked, "Who were they and what happened to them?"

Bull wrung his sopping hat in his hands. "It was Flaherty and Dominguez, sir. As far as I can tell, a log broke loose and swept their legs out from under them, pitching them into the river. They must have been dazed, because neither attempted to swim to shore. Fortunately, Peter Railsback spotted them and himself dove in after them. I sent him to the doctor as well, as he'd swallowed a great bit of water and was complaining of tightness in his chest."

We're not out of the woods yet, Smits thought. For all they knew, Railsback was dying of a heart attack in the doctor's office right this minute. Railsback was a hardworking man who was stronger than any two men combined. He was also going on forty and a regular at the Sawdust. Smits had heard that Railsback could drink any man or woman in Pine Lick under the table, and had proven his prowess just about every week.

"Have you sent anyone to tell their families?"

"Yes, sir. Except for Railsback. He doesn't have any that I know of."

A more tyrannical boss would have been relieved at knowing there was no next of kin to break the news to, should the man perish from his heroic act. It still worried Smits that such a good worker, and a good man by all accounts, should suffer, especially after saving two lives. He got up from behind his desk and looked out the window, with his hands clasped behind his back.

The storm was getting hellacious. To continue in such conditions would be to endanger even more lives.

"Let everyone know we're calling it a day," he said to Bull.

"That's a wise decision, sir. It's not just the rain. The wind is blowing mighty fierce."

"Make sure everyone knows to batten down every moving part of the sawmill. We'll have to ride this out and hope for clearer skies tomorrow. A storm bellowing like this will burn itself out quick."

Bull had a grave but relieved look on his face. "I'll do just that. Thank you, sir."

He bounded out of the office before Smits could tear his gaze away from the window.

The Angelina looked angrier than Moses when he came down from the mountain to find his people slipping back into paganism. Flaherty and Dominguez were very lucky men. He prayed that Railsback would be just as fortunate.

He also offered up a prayer that the storm would abate sooner rather than later. If the river kept rising at its current rate, there could be serious damage to the sawmill.

And not just the sawmill.

Most of the town proper had been built in the basin of land around it. If things got worse, it could be catastrophic for Pine Lick.

Smits grabbed his pipe and tamped some tobacco into it. Smoking settled his nerves. He'd make sure everyone left the premises safe and sound. Only then would he go down to his buggy and head to his house well above even the highest waterline.

Ella Schmidt read the incoming telegraph with rising dread. She hoped she had gotten it wrong, but when it repeated itself, her heart jumped.

Turning to Clifford Mintel, the postmaster and her boss, she said, "There's a hurricane headed right for us."

Mintel had been rifling through envelopes. He stopped suddenly. "Did you say a hurricane?"

"Yes," she replied in a shaky voice.

"But we don't get hurricanes in Pine Lick."

"Well, we do now."

"Are you sure?" He came around the counter so he could stand over her.

"As sure as the people reporting it. And it sounds like it's very big. Every town it's touched has gone silent."

He wiped the sweat from his brow with his ink-stained hand. "We have to let folks know."

"We have to let the mayor know first," she reminded him. There was a system put in place in case of emergencies that would impact the town. Ella Schmidt might have been the only one to remember it, since it had never been used before.

"Right. Right," Mintel said, his eyes roving to the window and the scene of driving rain and wind outside. He didn't make a move toward his slicker hanging on the coat-tree not five feet from Ella's workspace.

"I'll go," Ella said with noted exasperation. Mintel was a good man, but he was soft and lazy.

"No, Ella, I'll go."

There was a long silence, and still he hadn't made a move to grab his slicker.

Fed up and knowing that time wasn't on their side, Ella pushed her chair back and got to her feet. Still damp from her trip to the sheriff's office, she didn't bother with her own jacket. "I'll go see the mayor. You might want to spread the word to the other businesses."

He didn't offer to make the trek to the mayor's house, which was about half a mile from the post office. On a nice day, it was a short and pleasant walk. On a day like today, it would feel like ages getting there and back.

Ella scooted out of the post office as fast as her thin legs would carry her. She knew if she stayed there one more minute, she might say something to Mintel she'd regret.

Folks liked to think the Wild West was tamed by cowboys and

rough-and-tumble men. She knew better. Any woman who bore a child knew they were far more resilient than the men who had put the baby in there in the first place.

The wind and rain battered her head-on as she trudged down the street. She wished she had a horse at this moment, and considered commandeering one of the ones tied up to the various hitching posts. Most of them were just outside the Sawdust. The men inside cared about drinking and cards, not the well-being of their horses. It was a shame.

In no time, she was wetter than if she'd taken a dive in the pond out by the schoolhouse. A few times, heavy gusts of wind stopped her in her tracks. One of those times, she lost her balance and spun on her heels. Her hip banging into a wooden cask beside Maxel's General Store was the only thing that kept her upright.

She hoped Clifford Mintel felt deep shame for letting an old woman set out on a day like this. Sure, she could have goaded him into alerting the mayor, but there wasn't time to waste. This moment was also just one of countless incidents in her life where she felt it her duty to prove that women were just as capable, or more so, than men.

Speaking of men, she hoped Mayor Eli Tibbs was not in his cups, as was his wont on most afternoons. Pine Lick needed a clear-thinking leader if a hurricane was truly on its doorstep. Not that Tibbs was much of a leader. The man cared more about the almighty dollar than the people of the town. Nevertheless, he was, at this moment, Pine Lick's figurehead.

Fighting against the wind that seemed dead set on pushing her all the way back to the post office, Ella lowered her head and concentrated on keeping her feet on the ground.

Out of the corner of her eye, she spotted light spilling out of the jailhouse windows. She could always detour there and let the former sheriff grab his horse and ride to Tibbs's place. Branch Armstrong, being the gentleman he was, would more than likely bring her back to the dry confines of the post office before heading to the mayor.

Once again, there was that stubborn streak in her.

"A little wind and water won't kill you," she said into the biting wind as an act of defiance.

No sooner had she said it when a shard of clapboard, picked up and flung by the storm, came straight for Ella.

On account of her keeping her eyes on the ground, she never saw the runaway shard of wood. It hit her square in the forehead with enough force to split the bone of her skull in two.

All Ella felt was a sharp thump, and then nothing at all.

Her body pitched forward, landing face-first into a puddle of mud.

The hurricane had taken its first life. Only a few residents of Pine Lick would ever know that a hurricane was screaming their way. It was too late to prepare anyway.

Many more would perish before it was over.

Chapter 16

Mack Armstrong and Whiskey had tucked their hats in their saddlebags to prevent them from blowing clear off to Arkansas. The intensity of the storm had kept on building as they made their way back to town.

Not far from the jailhouse and a hot cup of coffee, there was a small shape lying in the middle of the road.

Mack reined in his horse and jumped off when he realized the shape was a person. Falling to his knees, he pried the person out of the sucking mud. The rain washed the face clean in seconds.

"It's Ella Schmidt!" he shouted to Whiskey, who held on to the reins of both horses.

"Is she dead?"

One look at her graying eyes told Mack all he needed to know, but he checked for a pulse on the side of her neck just to be sure. "She's gone."

"Let's get her out of this rain."

It was a short walk to the jail. Mack pushed the door in with his boot, as his hands were cradling the waterlogged corpse.

His father leapt from his chair. "Mack! What happened?"

"I don't know. Whiskey and I found her in the middle of the road not far from here."

Otto cleared Whiskey's desk so Mack could set her down. The old woman was so small, she almost fit perfectly.

Branch and Whiskey grabbed two lit kerosene lamps and brought them over to Ella's body. Branch's limp was more pronounced than usual because of the bad weather swelling his damaged feet. Ella's forehead was caved in, the skin split in an angry fissure. Mack thought he saw the white of bone beneath the thin layer of pulp.

"Somebody done killed her," Whiskey said, running his nervous hand over his mouth and chin, over and over.

"Did you see anyone else around?" Branch asked as he leaned closer to inspect the wound.

"Not a soul out there but me and Whiskey. And if there was someone, we can forget about tracking them in all that mud and running water."

"Where exactly did you find her?"

"Just a little past Maxel's," Mack said, chinning in the direction north of the jailhouse.

The former sheriff found a blanket and covered it over Ella's body. He rested a hand on her shoulder. "What were you even doing out there, Ella?"

The prisoners had been quiet as church mice ever since Mack had walked in with the corpse. A barrage of wind gusts pounded the jail. The front door slammed hard enough to split the wood. Everyone jumped, startled by the sudden noise.

Finally one of the cowboys said, "If she ain't been killed by a person, you can bet this storm had something to do with it."

"Nobody asked for your opinion," Mack said gruffly.

"I've been on my share of cattle drives, and I've seen men picked off by storms quicker than by any Apache raid," he continued, despite one of his compadres whispering for him to shut his mouth.

Branch Armstrong said to Otto, "You mind fetching the undertaker?"

"I do not." Otto set his cigar on the windowsill and headed out into the storm.

"Normally, I'd say this was a clear case of murder," Mack said, "but Ella didn't have an enemy in the world. There'd be no reason to take her life." He shivered despite the cloying warmth.

"I tend to agree with you," his father said. "When you think murder, you have to think motive. I can't think of a single one, unless she came into money we don't know about."

Whiskey stood over the covered body and made the sign of the cross. "Knowing Miss Ella, if she did have money, she'd just about give it all away trying to help folks."

The roof of the jailhouse made an alarming groan as the building was buffeted by an intense lick of wind. All eyes went to the ceiling. The collective breath of prisoners and lawmen paused until all realized the roof was holding steady.

The man who had attempted to rob Maxel's and beaten his daughter griped, "Hey, I don't think it's safe to be here. I have rights."

His bunkmates stepped away from him, their eyes on the current and former sheriffs.

"I suppose you'd like me to set you free," Mack said.

Kelly's eyes flicked back and forth between Mack and Branch. He licked his lips and tapped his boot, suddenly regretting opening his mouth. "I'm just saying, while I'm in custody, the law has to provide for my personal safety."

Mack sauntered over to the cell, relieved for the distraction from Ella's death. "The storm is affecting all of Pine Lick. Where do you suppose I should bring you, huh?" He snapped his fingers. "I know.

How about a deep, deep hole in the ground? I'll be happy to dig one for you. I got a shovel right out back, as a matter of fact."

The men engaged in a staring contest for a few moments before Kelly looked away.

They were interrupted by the entrance of Woodrow Paulson, the town's only undertaker. He was wetter than a largemouth bass, his black suit dripping all over the floor. He looked none too pleased to be called out of his dry office.

"Is that her?" he asked, pointing at Ella's covered body.

Otto took his cigar from the windowsill and gave it a few puffs to bring it back to life. "What gave you that idea?"

Paulson shot Otto a look of mild irritation. He lifted the corner of the blanket to uncover Ella's face. First he checked the side of her neck, then reached under the blanket to probe her wrist. "Yep, she's gone."

"We already knew that," Mack said.

Woodrow Paulson was a man fit for his job. He preferred his own company, which was fine with the townsfolk. An odd man on his best days, he always seemed to Mack to be someone dropped from the sky with rudimentary knowledge about the ways of ordinary men.

What he did know was death and dealing with its aftermath. He clearly enjoyed his job, which worried everyone who knew him.

The undertaker's eyes grew wide when he focused on the indentation of her skull.

"What do you suppose did that?" Whiskey asked.

With a shake of his head, Paulson said, "Something heavy. Something blunt. What it was or who did it would be for you folks to figure out." He covered her back up. "It's funny. Ella was at least twenty-five years older than me, but I never thought I'd live to see the day when she passed on."

"You're not the only one who felt that way," Branch Armstrong said. "Ella had more life in her than most children."

"Where was she found?"

"Out there, in the middle of the road," Whiskey said. He had his thumbs hooked in the pockets of his pants and was clearly unnerved by having her body on his desk. Mack was pretty sure his deputy would pitch that desk out the back door after the storm settled.

All were silent for a few seconds, and then Paulson said, "I'll get my wagon and remove the body. There'll be a lot of shocked people in Pine Lick when word gets out."

Before he could leave, Mack took him by the crook of his arm and said, "I'd appreciate it if word didn't get out just yet."

Paulson gave a grave nod. "Of course. You let me know when news of her demise should be made public."

He slipped from Mack's grasp and was out the door.

"You mind showing me exactly where you found her?" Branch asked.

"I was just going back out there myself. See if there's anything we missed. Come on, Whiskey."

His deputy, who hadn't taken his eyes off Ella's corpse, was happy to oblige.

"You mind sticking around here to keep an eye on things?" Mack asked Otto. The Indian's long hair was matted to his back and shoulders.

"I can."

He took a seat facing the cell.

As the three lawmen left the prison, a steady drip of rain fell from a tiny hole in the ceiling. Otto eyed the leak while he smoked his cigar.

"Anyone want a puff?" he asked the prisoners.

They replied with silence.

"I thought not."

Chapter 17

Tony Cheever was in desperate need of a drink. Five of his six guests were in the main parlor playing a high-stakes game of poker. Forced inside by the storm, the men grumbled about the weather and the timing of their trip to the Arcadian.

To keep them happy, Cheever had supplied them with the finest cigars in his collection and imported single malt scotch. That seemed to keep them satisfied . . . for now. With the way they were draining the scotch, they'd soon be too drunk to even know there was a storm raging outside.

It would have been even better with the presence of some of Belle Dupree's soiled doves, but that, for now, was a dead end. Quitting was not in his vocabulary. He would meet with the madam again and she would eventually acquiesce to his business proposal.

What worried Cheever more at the moment was the havoc the storm was wreaking on the main house itself, as well as the bungalows. The paint had hardly been dry on two of them. He dreaded seeing what they looked like now.

What sounded like a thousand cats scratching at the wood of the house set Cheever's nerves on edge. Out of the corner of his eye, he spotted the branch of a tree rake against a window. It was a miracle the glass hadn't broken. He groaned, imagining the damage to the building.

He reminded himself that was a worry for tomorrow. He was not going outside to assess the repairs that would be needed. Not now when it seemed like every drop of rain on the planet was coming down in thick sheets, and the angry winds of the pantheon of Greek gods were howling.

Just past the swaying trees, he could spot the edge of Lake Stanton. He thought back to the man he'd shot for trespassing. The intent was to send a clear message to the town that the grounds of the Arcadian were forbidden to those who could not afford to be there.

He'd only intended to scare the man off. Unfortunately, his gun-handling skills left a lot to be desired. What was supposed to be a warning shot over the man's head drifted a little farther south than he thought it would. Cheever had been momentarily stunned when he saw the spurt of blood and the man collapse onto his back in the canoe.

The boy began screaming right away and Cheever ran for the main house.

In the darkest days of his past, he had paid men to murder for him. Now he had a true sense for what it was like to take a life. He told himself it was probably a just thing for the table to turn on him.

Once he overcame the shock of it all, he felt an odd, alien thrill. As a man who built his fortune on being in control, what greater power was there than being the arbiter between life and death?

Other men would feel remorse, wrestling with a guilty conscience.

Not Cheever.

He had lawyers the likes of which the Podunks of Texas had never seen. There was little concern that he would pay for his poor shooting. The whole thing was both a success—for no one in Pine Lick other than the sheriff and his deputy had set foot on the grounds of the Arcadian since the shooting—and an irritant, since he knew he'd have to go through all the legal shenanigans at one point in time.

"I wouldn't be surprised if this is just the front end of a hurricane," the lone man not playing poker said to Cheever's right. Cheever had been so lost in thought, he hadn't noticed him. The man smoked his pipe, quietly looking out one of the great windows, deep in thought.

"A hurricane?" Cheever said doubtfully. "Yes, I admit, it's a bad storm. But Pine Lick is not in a region that gets anything like a hurricane."

The man was Armand Gloucester, founder of a string of manufacturing plants in central New Jersey. He was older than the other guests by a handful of years, with a well-trimmed salt-and-pepper beard and the broad figure of a man who had toiled under hard labor during his formative years. He'd outlived two wives and fathered seven children, all but one of them perishing for one awful reason or another.

"Have you ever seen an actual hurricane?" Gloucester said.

Cheever eyed a two-by-four tumbling, end over end, on the front lawn. "I can't say that I have."

"I lived for several years in Florida when my second wife fell ill. We were told the climate there would do wonders for her health. What we encountered was heat that made it difficult to breathe, much less function, and storms that were the stuff of nightmares. We suffered through three hurricanes, each one worse than the one before. The town's foundation was demolished. Lives were lost."

Gloucester relit his pipe and gave a few puffs. The rain beat against the windows like a hive of mad bees desperate to get inside.

"Hurricanes are not something to take lightly, Mr. Cheever." He turned to look down the hall, through the open doors to the men sitting around the card table. "Judging by your proximity to the lake and reservoir, I'd hazard a guess that you don't have a storm cellar."

The wealthy man's piercing gaze and tone instantly made Cheever feel like a child being calmly reprimanded by his father for not having finished his chores.

"I was told there was no need for one," Cheever replied stiffly.

In actuality, no one had ever said such a thing. It was also a question he'd never asked the architect or builders. That they hadn't brought it up themselves was an indictment on them. He had a good mind to take them to task, once the storm settled down.

"What would you then say is the sturdiest structure on the Arcadian grounds?"

Cheever swept his hand across the room. "I would say you're standing in it."

Gloucester tapped the end of his pipe against his lower lip. "I see," he replied, seemingly unconvinced. "When I arrived, I took a quick stroll around to get the blood flowing in my legs. I noticed that dam over there. In my opinion, it looked to be a bit shoddy. My father was an engineer and for a while I thought of joining in the family business. I assisted him with the construction of a similar dam to the one you have here. One thing I learned, constructing a dam may seem like a lot of work, but *maintaining* one makes it pale in comparison. Now, with all this rain . . ."

Cheever shook his head. "You needn't worry about the dam. Because of where the buildings are situated, we're not in any danger, even if it were to somehow completely give way. Which, I might add, is not going to happen."

The guest gave him *that* look again, which made Cheever feel small and insignificant.

"I'm not concerned about my well-being, Mr. Cheever. But I do understand the town of Pine Lick would be right in the path of those waters, should they escape their bounds." He tapped his pipe against the windowpane. "It's the people down there that concern me. I noticed there's no observation post."

"'Observation post'?"

"Yes. For a warning system, should anything happen to the dam."

There had been one. But the workers needed lumber one afternoon and Cheever didn't want them to waste any time going to town, so he told them to dismantle the unused post.

"I've been told that was the responsibility of the sawmill company. They had their own engineer inspect the dam and I assume he deemed it fit, because the sawmill hasn't posted anyone here since before I arrived."

Gloucester shook his head and pinched the bridge of his nose.

In dire need of changing the subject, Cheever said, "I noticed you don't seem to be a scotch man. Can I interest you in some rye?"

Gloucester turned to him with a skeptical look. "Cheap rye will do me just fine. I don't suppose you have anything like that. I began my drinking education alongside hard men and haven't seen a need to spend top dollar on something that may taste better, but has the same end results."

Cheever was pretty sure a bottle of that swill the construction workers liked to nip from should be around somewhere. "I understand. I'm sure I can find one that suits your tastes."

"If you can, by all means. I'll take it right here." Gloucester settled into a padded velvet chair by the window. Cheever moved a side table next to it and placed an ashtray on top.

There was no sense asking him if he wanted to join the men at poker.

If the man preferred to spend his time staring at a storm and fretting over a damn dam, so be it. He'd already paid for his visit. Though Cheever was sure he would not be a returning customer.

He just hoped the man didn't kill the Arcadian's chances of future guests within his inner circle.

Thunder rattled the chandelier above their heads.

Gloucester's eyes roved to the ceiling.

"Strongest structure on the grounds you say."

Chapter 18

The old man and Slip pushed the horses as hard as they could, desperate to make town and get out of the hellacious storm. At first, the old man's only concern had been finding Armstrong and exacting revenge.

Now, with the wind gusts almost sweeping him off his saddle, he needed a place to shelter for the night.

Slip was bellowing nonstop. Even though he rode right next to the old man, he couldn't be heard above the howling winds and constant beating of the rain.

That was one silver lining.

The other was seeing the sign for Pine Lick.

Not far past the sign was the first inkling of a town proper. They came upon a church with a small cemetery out back. The old man read the sign out front as they ambled past.

ST. PETER'S CATHOLIC CHURCH. ALL ARE WELCOME!
SUNDAY MASS AT 9AM.

Not one to care much for Catholics, the old man's spirit was lifted. After decades of longing and months of travel, they were finally here. It almost felt to him as if the hand of God had been holding him steady and guiding him to this moment.

And the storm was the work of the devil, trying his darndest to keep him from his destiny.

Well, Old Scratch could spit in this wind.

They were here, and sooner or later, the storm would peter out.

The old man chuckled.

Peter out. He looked back at the placard for St. Peter's and gave the church a salute.

A piece of airborne flotsam came at the duo. They jerked the reins and moved their horses just in time to avoid taking it to the face.

"We're gonna get ourselves killed out here!" Slip shouted. He looked terrified, which was a rare expression for the boy. For someone beset with so many dark thoughts and deeds, fear was certainly a stranger.

When the old man looked over at him with a serene smile on his face, Slip went from scared to confused.

"Looks like a livery just up ahead. We'll settle our rides and ask the proprietor to point us to the saloon. That sound good to you?"

Now Slip was shocked. It was the first time during their entire trip that the old man had spoken to him of anything resembling rest and catering to a man's needs and vices.

A blast of wind hit them sideways. Slip latched on to the pommel to keep upright. "Well, what are we waiting for?" He put his spurs to his horse and took off ahead of the old man.

Sure enough, they came upon the Lady B Livery.

The man who answered the door looked none too happy to have to poke his head out in a storm like this. He was even older than the old man, with a gray handlebar mustache that did its best to hide the fact that the man had lost all his teeth, probably around the time Lincoln was freeing the slaves.

"We appreciate the inconvenience," the old man said, handing the owner a wad of bills.

"Name's James Winston," the livery owner said with wide eyes. "Let's get those horses dry and fed."

There weren't many other horses in the stable. The old man assumed most people with good sense were home, riding out the storm.

"You fellas are new to Pine Lick," Winston said. "I'm good with faces. What brings you to town on such a miserable day? Can't be for the scenery."

"We have jobs at the sawmill. Wanted to get here early just to get to know the town a bit," the old man replied. "Don't think we'll do much exploring today."

"I suppose you won't." Winston opened the top of a barrel, then reached inside and brought out a half-empty bottle of whiskey. He saw the look the men gave him and said, "My wife is a teetotaler, but I ain't. I keep the peace by keeping my spirits out here. You boys look like you could use a nip."

Slip grabbed the proffered bottle. "Don't mind if I do." He guzzled the whiskey like a man fresh from the desert who had come upon a watering hole.

"That's enough," the old man said, swiping it from his nephew's hand and mouth. "Where's your manners?"

Slip wiped his mouth with his sleeve. "That's good stuff, mister. Can you point us to the saloon?"

The old man took a modest sip and gave the bottle back.

"Sure thing," Winston said. "It's just down that road apiece. The Sawdust Saloon. You can't miss it. I suppose the doors are open even in this weather. Say, you must be from somewhere back East. You talk like my wife's cousin. He's from New York."

"Thank you kindly," the old man said, concerned that the livery owner had pegged them for New Yorkers. Not that he could have known who they were and what they'd come for. It was just paranoia, now that he was so close. "We haven't stayed anywhere long enough to set down roots. I guess you could say we're from just about everywhere. We'll come back tomorrow to check on the horses."

"Take your time. I would say to stay dry, but that seems impossible."

The wind blew the door back in their faces when the old man and Slip made to leave. In the short amount of time they'd been in the stable, the storm had gotten even more intense. They had to carry their hats and lean into the wind, cutting through it like a pair of knives as they slowly made their way to the saloon.

A cat darted out from under the boardwalk along the shops. A lick of wind seemed to pick it up from its tail and send it sailing, end over end, until it rolled out of sight. Slip laughed as if it was the funniest thing he'd ever seen. The old man slapped his shoulder and shouted against the wind for him to shut his trap.

They dodged things flying through the air that shouldn't have been off the ground.

Luckily, it wasn't a far walk to the saloon. It was a miracle they made it there without incident. They'd already been soaked to the marrow, so the rain wasn't the issue. It was the wind that had the old man concerned.

Inside was brightly lit. There was a long, scarred bar to the right, and a dozen round tables with chairs to the left. A man sat at the piano sipping from a mug of beer, but not playing. The old man counted seven patrons, each appearing to be there alone. He supposed these were folks who had no one to go home to during the storm.

"Afternoon, fellas," the bartender said. He had a knot on his head a man could hang his coat on. "I'm fixin' to close up soon, but there's time for a drink or two if you like."

They made their way to the bar and took a pair of seats at the end. The other patrons barely looked at them. All eyes were at the rattling windows.

Throwing some coins on the bar, the old man ordered two shots of bourbon.

The wind rattled the saloon. It creaked and complained mightily. The rafters sounded as if they were having a hard time staying in place.

After pouring the shots, the bartender called over to the man by the piano. "Fingers, why don't you play something to drown out all that racket?"

Fingers set his beer down atop his piano. "I'll try, but you'd need a marching band to top that."

"After that shot, you can have one more beer. And that's all she wrote," the old man whispered to Slip. He didn't need or want the young man drunk and even more reckless.

"Two beers?"

"How about no beers?"

Slip's shoulders slumped. "Fine. One beer."

"You shouldn't even need that after guzzling that man's whiskey."

Slip knocked back his shot and slammed the glass on the bar top. "Been a long time since we had a proper drink. You can't blame me for that."

The old man turned away, thinking of the many other things he could blame on Slip.

There was a loud crash outside. One of the men got up and went to the window.

"The big winda over at Casey's just broke!"

That was followed by a heavy thump on the saloon's roof. The old man felt the impact right through his boots.

"I might be closing a little sooner," the bartender told them. "So drink up while you can."

He immediately started moving the bottles of booze on the shelf behind him under the bar for safekeeping.

Two men doffed their hats and hurried out of the saloon. The man at the window whistled. "Well, there go some fine hats. Jeezaloo, the wind almost knocked them flat! I ain't never seen a guster like this."

Tapping the side of his shot glass, the old man contemplated where they would hunker down. A town like this surely had places to stay. But the day was still relatively young, despite the slate skies. A hotel would have a lot of prying eyes. At least here in the saloon, the drunks wouldn't recall them, and bartenders were famous for keeping their noses out of things.

Slip glanced nervously at the window. "We sure are lucky we got here when we did. I'd hate to be riding right now."

"We'd probably be knocked off our horses in no time."

The old man motioned for another round of shots, which the bartender quickly refilled. The piano player banged away on the keys, hammering out a joyful tune that was in direct contrast to the storm outside and the feelings of everyone inside.

When the bartender was done stowing away the liquor, he eyed the grandfather clock beside the staircase. He nodded at the piano player, who abruptly stopped playing.

"Okay, gents, I think it's best everyone gets on home so I can do the same."

"Wait, here comes someone!" the man who was still at the window exclaimed.

The door opened, ushering in a heavy breeze soaked with rainwater. A young man in a dripping suit ran to the bar. He was dressed like a waiter and had the look of someone straight from the farm.

"Heya, Butch. Any chance I can get four bottles of whiskey, two rye, and two bourbons? Mr. Snodgrass said you can put it on his tab. He'll stop by tomorrow to settle it, if the town is still around."

His joke fell flat.

Butch, the bartender, barely concealed his annoyance. "Let me get a crate. Be right back."

"That Mr. Snodgrass sounds like a thirsty fella," Slip said. The old man wanted to swat him. There was no need for Slip to call attention to them.

The man slicked the rain from his dark hair. "Oh, it's not for him. Guests at the Palace have nothing better to do than drink while they wait out the storm. I'm not even sure this will be enough, but it's what I was told to ask for."

Before Slip could say anything else, the old man kicked him in the leg under the bar and out of sight.

Butch came back with a wooden crate and quickly slipped eight bottles of booze into it. "Tell Snodgrass I said good luck. I'm closing up in just a bit, so you'll be the only game in town if people want to drink."

The hotel employee looked over the bottles. "Oh, I almost forgot. We need one bottle of Old Crow."

"Let me look."

"That's a special order by Mrs. Armstrong."

The old man's ears perked up.

Butch found the bottle of Old Crow. "Mrs. Armstrong? Why would she be staying in the Palace?"

The waiter shrugged. "Beats me. I'm just the guy fool enough to go out in this weather to get booze I'm not allowed to drink so that other people can have fun."

"Well, keep your head low out there," Butch said as he pushed the crate across the bar.

"I sure will. I wouldn't be surprised to see a flying steer at this point!"

He hurried back out into the storm, the bottles clinking against one another.

The old man slapped his hand on the bar and asked, "Where's the Palace? We'll need someplace to bed down for the night. And a place to drink."

"Just two blocks down the road on the right. Just be aware, they charge more for their booze than I do."

"Good to know." He turned to Slip. "Let's go so this man can get home."

He barely noticed the raging storm when they stepped outside. Fighting the wind every step of the way, the old man and Slip made their way to the Palace Hotel and Mrs. Armstrong.

Chapter 19

From his kitchen window, Reverend Jake Smiley watched half of the roof of the First Baptist Church sheer off in a spray of wood and tiles. His wife, Matilda, had been on her knees on the hardwood floor for the past thirty minutes, deep in prayer.

He wanted to tell her, "Look what good all that praying has done us!"

With most of the roof gone, the interior of the church was exposed to the furious storm. The water damage alone would wipe it out, right down to the foundation. He would have to go back to preaching out in the open or under a tent. Smiley thought he'd left that world behind for good.

Or they would leave Pine Lick and he would find another church. There was no lack of towns in need of the Lord's messenger.

That would be a shame because they both felt a strong connection to the town. So much good work had been done here. Pine Lick had grown considerably in the five years they had been here and would only continue to grow. He imagined a day when the church would be standing-room-only every Sunday.

Now there would be nowhere to stand.

Matilda didn't even open her eyes at the horrendous sound of the church being torn asunder.

She's not praying for the church, Smiley thought. *She's praying for the well-being of the people of the town. That's what I should be doing.*

He was too busy fighting the panic that had seized his chest and threatened to drive him stark raving mad. Their house wasn't half as sturdy as the church. When it shuddered and rocked and groaned, Reverend Smiley went deeper and deeper into himself, mired in his childhood fear that had never been exorcised.

He went back to their bedroom and snuck another sip of the fiery liquid he kept hidden from Matilda. Surely, she had to smell it on his breath by now.

Not that she had paid him any mind since she went to her knees.

They had spent less than a year in Kansas when he was between churches a decade earlier. It turned out, he couldn't stand living in a place beset by tornadoes. His preoccupation with the whirling winds of death and destruction became such a distraction, he could hardly focus on his parish. Too many days had been spent with both of them deep in prayer, asking God for the winds of hell to bypass their town.

At least we had a storm cellar in Kansas, he thought. What he wouldn't give for one now.

He gingerly set his fingers on his wife's shoulder. "Tilly, the church is just about gone."

Her lips stopped moving and she opened her eyes to look up at him. "Then we need to thank God that no one was inside it when it happened."

Smiley loved her with every ounce of his being. A more perfect woman to betroth a man of the cloth could not be found.

He also envied her faith, her conviction.

Because right now, he was miles away from thanking God for their blessings.

"Anyone want to get a card game going?"

"That's a great idea, Bonnie," Belle Dupree said to her top earner. "*Mesdames*, let's fill our glasses and break out the cards."

Having been born and raised in New Orleans, the madam knew a hurricane when she saw one coming. Hell, she'd smelled it on the wind first thing in the morning. She'd instructed Tiny Ed to board up all the windows, with the help of her girls. There would be no entertaining gentlemen today.

Not that it stopped men from knocking on the door, even when the storm started to get hellacious. Tiny Ed did not open the door. He simply barked at whoever was on the other side to go away.

Now they were all hunkered down in the parlor, with lit candles and oil lamps keeping the darkness at bay. The big house shuddered from time to time, and a few of the girls couldn't help but gasp, their wide eyes looking above to make sure there was still a roof over their heads.

There were six soiled doves in all. Dupree asked Tiny Ed to move two tables together while she poured drinks. Aside from the blustering wind, the steady staccato of rain made it sound like the house was beset upon by a Gatling gun. It was wearing on everyone's nerves. She needed to get these girls tipsy and distracted.

"Have a seat. Join us," Dupree said to her bouncer.

He sat on a hard-backed chair with his meaty arms crossed over his chest. "I don't like playing cards."

"At least have a drink, *mon cher*."

His gaze turned to one of the boarded windows when a gust tried to make its way inside. "Maybe when the storm is over."

She wished he would change his mind. Tiny Ed wasn't afraid of anybody. Since the storm had picked up, he'd been visibly tense.

The girls fed off his unease, and that could make for a long day and night.

"Drink up, ladies. We might as well enjoy ourselves." She said this without any trace of the French accent she affected for her clients. There was no sense maintaining that charade in here, with her girls and Tiny Ed, the closest thing she had to a family.

There were titters as glasses clinked. Dupree was quick to refill them, figuring the overriding tension in the room would lessen after some more rounds. They played a few hands of faro. At first, when the house quaked, the girls would get to looking like frightened does and lose track of the game.

After three rounds of quality booze, their nerves had begun to settle.

Normally, Dupree forbid her girls to drink in the house. Even when the parade of randy men came to visit and asked them to drink with them, Tiny Ed would pour colored water in their glasses.

Tonight was a necessary exception.

None of them had ever been in a hurricane before, including Tiny Ed. Fear of the unknown was often times the worst kind of fear.

Hurricanes and tropical storms had been a natural part of life for Belle Dupree. She never thought she'd see one here in Pine Lick, but life had a way of surprising you. She chuckled as she placed a bet, wondering how the young Belle, born Gertrude Falmouth, would react if she could see what she'd grow up to become. Gertrude went to church on Sundays and thought she would meet a good man, marry, and have a passel of children by this age. Her parents died when she was twelve and she was sent to a horrid orphanage. It was there, and her need to get as far away from it as humanly possible, where all her childish dreams died.

The world was a tough place for a lone young girl on the cusp of becoming a woman. She did what she had to do to survive. And when she achieved a measure of success, she made it her mission to provide a safe haven for other lost and lonely women in need. Belle Dupree's soiled doves were cared for like no others, and they returned her efforts to provide them a way of life with their loyalty.

The house suddenly rumbled. For a terrifying moment, the madam thought the structure was about to become unmoored from its foundation.

Bonnie and Ivy laughed with abandon, causing the others to join in.

Tiny Ed looked at them as if they'd all gone insane.

Good, laugh in the face of nature's wrath, Dupree thought. They would get through this, even if the house did not. *Best to cut them off now. When this is over, Pine Lick is going to be in a sorry state. Folks will need help. Some of them look down on us. Well, we'll see to changing their opinion when we're there to help pick up the pieces.*

That was one thing she'd learned in New Orleans. When disaster struck, everyone worked together to spit in its eye and continue on, whether you were a preacher, teacher, beggar, or thief.

Pine Lick would soon find out there was more to Belle Dupree and her working girls than anyone thought.

Pat "Bull" McManus regretted building his cabin by the Angelina.

It had been a pretty spot and within walking distance to the sawmill. His wife, Maureen, had fallen in love with it, from the water burbling against the rocks at the river's edge, to the loblolly pine, dogwood, and sycamore trees that provided shade from the punishing Texas summers. Just like Jens Knoop, his boss at the sawmill, Bull loved to fish. The cabin provided quick and easy access to his pastime.

Bull now counted seven fallen trees, with the latest one clipping the edge of the cabin's roof, but sparing it from structural damage.

The remaining trees that surrounded the cabin swayed dangerously, threatening to snap or become uprooted at any moment.

Maureen had screeched like a banshee when the tree hit the house. Her eyes were wet with tears as she paced about the room.

"Have a seat by the fire," Bull said.

"I'll not sit until this storm is over, Pat."

He checked outside the window for the twentieth time in the past hour. The now-brown waters of the Angelina were rising fast, inching closer and closer to the cabin. He tried to estimate how long they had until they were washed out by the flood, and figured if the storm didn't dissipate, they had maybe an hour or two.

However, if it got worse, they'd be counting the minutes.

Always prepared, Bull had packed their essentials and kept them in two suitcases by the front door. If they had to abandon the cabin, they could be at the small barn and in their wagon in no time. They would still stand to lose much, but at least the things Maureen held sacred would live to see another day.

Something heavy knocked against the cabin. Maureen gasped.

"If you're going to react like that every time something gets flung at the house, you'll be worn to a nub," he said.

Maureen dabbed at her eyes with the handkerchief she'd always kept stuffed in her sleeve by her wrist.

"I can't help it. I just keep waiting for the walls and roof to cave in."

"It won't do you no good worrying about something that hasn't and may never happen." He pointed at the raging Angelina. "That's what you should worry about. If it keeps swelling, we'll find this place in Louisiana before we know it."

Bull didn't want to admit to himself that he shared his wife's same fear about the house being blown apart. In the end, though, whether it was wind or water, they would have to make their escape and pray they weren't knocked senseless by one of the many objects being thrown about by the storm.

"I wonder how old Jens's house is holding up," he said.

Jens Knoop's house was on the other side of the river and had been built closer to the bank. If the sawmill owner was smart, which he was, he had moved himself to the sawmill to ride things out. He had the money to replace anything that was lost.

"I pray he's safe, but I'm more concerned about us at the moment."

The cabin made a sound Bull had never heard before. He looked all about, waiting to see a rent in the structure itself. When the sound passed and nothing untoward had happened, he ushered Maureen to the fireplace.

"You best keep nice and dry for now, because if we have to leave, it might be a while before you feel that way again."

Maureen pushed her fist to her mouth and stared into the fire with the eyes of a frightened cat. Bull rubbed the back of her shoulders and kissed her neck.

"We'll find our way through this. We always have. Remember the sea when we came here from Ireland? Such a thing we'd never seen. We just had to hope the captain knew what he was doing. Och, how our stomachs turned. You know, I still haven't gotten the smell of all that sick out of my mind all these years later."

Maureen turned to face him. "Everyone got sick, but you. That's how I knew we'd make it. Because I was with you, and nothing can break you." She hugged him close and wept.

As he calmed her down, he noticed the first finger of water poking beneath the door. Extricating himself from her embrace, he hurried to the window.

The Angelina was close enough to shake hands . . . violently!

The wind hadn't died down one bit. The air was rife with projectiles that could hurt or even kill them. It reminded him of the stories of Indians on the warpath, their arrows blocking out the sun.

Hurrying into the kitchen, he found a wooden bucket and gave it to Maureen. "Here, put this on your head."

"What on earth for?"

"To protect your skull, my dear." She followed his gaze to the water pooling by the door. "When I open that door, I need you to stay close to me and keep that on your head, even once we get in the wagon."

He wished he had buckets for his own head and their horse's. Who was to say their horse wouldn't be brought down by a stray branch or whatever else had been plucked and thrown about?

The second he touched the doorknob, the door blasted open, nearly knocking him down. He grabbed the two suitcases and said, "Stick to my back!"

Bowing his head, Bull trudged toward the barn. He felt Maureen's hand clutching the back of his belt. Outside, the wind howled like the lamentations of an angry god. It brought a shiver down his spine.

The ground had turned to a sucking mud pile, trying its best to capture their feet and legs and never let go. Running was out of the question. He'd had to stop twice and help pluck his wife from the mire. She looked ridiculous with the bucket on her head, but at least a part of her was protected. The second time he had to tug her out of the mud, something solid and sharp hit him in the small of his back.

Back when he'd been a recalcitrant teenager in Limerick, he'd been stabbed in the arm by Timothy Deevey for trying to nick a few pounds from him. It hadn't been fatal, naturally, but it had hurt like blazes and bled like a stuck pig.

That's exactly what he felt now.

His body wanted him to take a knee and catch his breath. But his brain shouted at him to keep moving.

They made it to the barn and were riding into the storm a minute later. He felt a growing warmth at his backside. There was no time to stop the bleeding. Maureen clung to his arm. He could hear her reciting the Lord's Prayer, over and over.

Whipping his horse to beat the devil, Bull McManus drove them away from the wild Angelina and deeper into the trees, hoping God would hear Maureen's prayers.

Chapter 20

The search for whoever or whatever had killed Ella Schmidt didn't last long. The wind was getting too strong to stand against. The gusts and the rain were quickly wiping away any evidence that might have been left behind.

When Whiskey took a blow to his lower leg from a piece of what looked like a wagon, Branch Armstrong began to lean toward the imprisoned cowpoke's theory that poor Ella had been struck by something propelled by the gale force winds.

"We have to get back inside before we end up like Ella," he said to his son and Whiskey.

The deputy was on one knee, his hands grasping where he'd been clobbered.

"You okay to walk?" Mack Armstrong said.

"I'm ready to run, just to get away from here."

And run they did. All three staggered for a moment when an especially meaty gust nearly knocked them down flat. Rain and mud sprayed their faces, momentarily blinding them. It was an effort to walk the last fifty feet or so to the jail.

When they made it back inside, they saw that Ella's body was gone.

"The dead collector came here quick," Otto said, puffing on the remnants of his cigar. "Did you find anything?"

The men were dripping wet and disheveled. "Not a thing," Mack Armstrong replied.

"I did not think you would. I also think it is too late to go anywhere without risking our lives."

Otto threw a fresh log on the fire in the cast-iron stove. He gazed out the rattling window, watching debris whiz past.

"I should probably head to the Palace to be with your mother," Branch said. "It's clear no one is coming out in this weather to find either of us."

Whiskey had rolled up his pants to examine the damage to his leg. The dark flesh had already started to purple, and in the midst of the raised welt was a red gash that leaked blood down his leg and into his boots. "You mind handing me that bottle behind you?" he asked Mack.

The deputy pulled the cork out with his teeth and splashed the brown liquor on the wound, wincing in pain.

"You should see the doc when this blows over," Branch said.

"If he don't blow away himself."

So many things were hitting against the jailhouse, it sounded as if they were caught in a hailstorm, only with nails sleeting down instead of ice.

"If you went out there now," Otto said, "you would not make it to the Palace without being injured."

"I made it back here."

As if in answer to his statement, the wind blew hard enough to rattle the jailhouse's foundation.

"I think the worst just arrived," Otto said.

"The least y'all can do is unlock the door in case something happens and we need to get out of this cell," one of the cowboys said.

Sheriff Mack Armstrong tapped the key ring on his belt and smiled. "Hey, that sounds like a great idea. Maybe we could all start up a card game or maybe sing songs around the stove."

His smile turned to a scowl as he turned his back on the prisoners.

Branch had his eyes on the door as it thumped in its frame. "If I'm stuck here, I'll spend the entire time worrying. I don't like to worry."

"Sitting still was never your strong suit," Mack said. "But if you step outside, that'll leave us worrying about *you*."

Branch opened the door a crack. Water ran down the center of Main Street like a newly born creek. An untethered buggy rolled down the road, teetered, and then flipped onto its side. The sky had gone from gray to black. In the sudden darkness, they all heard a tremendous crack and crash. Branch couldn't see where it was coming from. It sounded as if an entire building had just been turned to kindling.

Otto gently closed the door. He looked to Whiskey. "Good. You left some for us. For now, all we can do is drink and wait." He grabbed the bottle and tilted it back to take a long swallow, then handed it back to Whiskey.

"I don't drink when I'm on the job," the deputy said. "Or much any other time."

"You should consider making an exception." The pounding of something tumbling over the roof stole their attention. "This might be your last chance to ever have a stiff drink."

Mack broke the ice by knocking one back. "Boy, do I hope you're wrong."

Branch refused a drink, opting to pace by the front door. He wouldn't be good company until he knew Kate was okay.

Young Archibald Gibbons was nestled in the crook of Gloria Amaryllis's arm, frightened of the storm. The hotel manager had urged everyone to come downstairs to the first floor and congregate in the dining hall. That way, should something happen, the hotel's patrons were close to the hotel's exits.

Of course, if that should happen, they would be exiting into a killer storm. Kate Armstrong thought this was the very definition of "out of the frying pan and into the fire."

Waiters nervously brought out drinks and food in an attempt to take people's minds off the storm outside, which was clearly an impossibility. Kate and Gloria were offered another glass of Old Crow.

"I think we should make sure we have our wits about us," Kate said to the waiter, a well-coiffed gentleman who went by the monicker, Handy. "To that end, we should probably have something to eat. What would you like, Mrs. Amaryllis?"

The schoolteacher patted Archibald on his upper arm and pulled him closer. "I'll just have some toast. What about you, Archibald?"

The boy's eyes flicked about the packed dining room, flinching slightly with every gust of wind. "I'm not hungry."

Kate's heart broke for him. It was bad enough he'd had to watch his father's murder and know he was an orphan. Having to ride out the storm of a lifetime was simply too much to ask of the boy.

The waiter asked, "Sure you can't think of something?"

Archibald shook his head.

Kate knew the boy needed a distraction. Busy hands kept the mind from wandering. To that, she proposed to Handy, "Would it be a bother if you enlisted the help of this capable young man? It looks like you have your hands full."

For a moment, Handy looked confused, and was about to say no. Kate arrested his attention and he quickly caught on.

"I think that's a great idea. Another set of hands will go a long way until everything blows over." He leaned closer to Archibald. "How about it? I can show you the kitchen, and while you're there, if your stomach is up to it, you can sample anything you like. You can help me bring out food and drinks. Do a good enough job, you might even make a little money."

Archibald looked up at Mrs. Amaryllis, waiting for permission.

"Sounds like fun to me," she said. "Go along. I'll be right here."

Before they departed, Handy asked Kate if she wanted anything. "I'll have a steak, rare, with boiled potatoes." She got up and whispered in the waiter's ear, "Thank you for understanding."

"My pleasure. I was orphaned around his age, so I understand."

Kate wasn't surprised that the man knew about what had happened to Archibald. Pine Lick may have been growing, but it still retained its small-town sensibility and closeness.

While they waited for their food, Kate and Gloria made small talk. Kate was impressed, but not surprised, by the teacher's intelligence and wit. She was a good person to jaw with. It had been a while since Kate had been to town to socialize. She just wished it had been under better circumstances.

The rafters groaned, catching most people's attention. Some were too drunk to notice if a talking buffalo came waltzing into the dining room.

"I do hope your husband and son are okay," Gloria said.

"I married a smart man and raised a smart boy. I'm sure they're hunkered down at the jailhouse." Deep down, there was a small ember of worry, but Kate meant what she said. The Armstrong men were more than capable of holding their own, even when the wrath of God was raging all around them. Changing the subject slightly, Kate said, "I can see why my son has eyes for you."

Stunned speechless, the schoolteacher blushed.

"You're very pretty and smart as a whip. And from what I see with you and Archibald, very caring."

"You're too kind."

"Hard to find all those traits in one person. I know Mack is young, but he's wise for his age. You get that way when your father was sheriff and you lived every day wondering if he would ride back home again."

"That must have been difficult."

Kate nodded. "It was. And still is for me. But it makes him happy. In the end, that's all a mother wants. To see her children happy. You seem to make him happy as well."

Their food came, much to Gloria's relief. Kate tucked into her bloody steak, while Gloria nibbled at the corners of her dry toast. No wonder she was so skinny. She was sure Branch would like to fatten her up with a passel of babies. Now that they'd had a chance to get to know each other better, Kate hoped that despite the age gap, maybe there was hope for them.

At one point, Gloria set her toast down and peered at something over Kate's shoulder.

Just as Kate caught on and was about to look for what had her attention, Gloria said, "Don't turn around. But there are two men who have been looking at us just about the whole time we've been here."

Kate grinned. "Well, we are two attractive women. Can't say that I blame them. They're just lucky Branch or Mack isn't here."

"It's not just that. It's the *way* they're looking at us. And to say they look a little rough around the edges is an understatement. One of them especially gives me the shivers."

"Where are they?"

"Three tables behind you. One is young, with blondish hair and eyes that look like they see something that's not there. The other is older, with a thick black mustache."

Unable to resist, Kate intentionally dropped a fork and turned back in her chair to get it. She cast a sideways glance behind her and spotted the men right way. They looked to be halfway through drying, fresh off a considerable time out in the country. Between them was a bottle, though only the older man had a glass. She'd seen plenty of men like them before. Most were harmless wanderers, men in search of a way to make a dollar or find a woman for a quick dalliance. Men who traveled, whether on the range or searching for a place to settle, had very little contact with the fairer sex and were easily beguiled. Others were the kind of men that her husband and son locked away to keep the town safe. When they had eyes for a woman, it meant trouble was on the horizon.

It was only a brief moment, but Kate decided those two were the latter.

"They sure don't look like hotel guests," Kate said. "More like drifters that came in from the storm."

"Well, I don't like them looking at us that way."

"If you like, we can switch seats. I'll give it right back at them."

Gloria looked down at her toast. "No, I'll be fine. Just being silly, I guess."

"We women have to be smarter than men to keep ourselves safe," Kate said. "You're not silly. Just bright enough to know men like that could be trouble. The one saving grace is that we're surrounded by dozens of people."

Kate saw the blacksmith, Elmer Mizner, sitting by the bar. He'd been known to frequent the Palace ever since his wife had passed. She'd died after being thrown from her horse while he was tying a few on at the Sawdust. Ever since then, he drank even more to mask his misery and avoided the Sawdust out of guilt.

Branch had helped Elmer out of a few pickles when he'd been in his cups and was grateful for his understanding. Kate excused herself and walked over to the bar.

"Mr. Mizner, good to see you're keeping dry." On the outside, at least. His eyes were as glassy as his forearms were huge.

He looked over at her, slightly startled. He got to his feet, tottering just a tiny bit. "Mrs. Armstrong, very nice to see you. What brings you all the way out here?"

"It's a long story. I wanted to know if I can ask a favor of you."

He puffed up a bit. "Of course."

"See those men over there?" She casually pointed at the two men who were attempting to steal surreptitious glances her way—and failing.

Elmer nodded.

"I wonder if you might keep an eye on them for me. They've been giving us the eye, if you know what I mean, and I'm not familiar with either of them."

Scratching at his dark stubble, Elmer said, "Neither am I. You want me to show them the door?"

"Oh no. Nothing like that." The last thing she needed was Elmer causing a kerfuffle in the center of the dining room. "I'm with Mrs. Amaryllis, and I would appreciate it if you made sure they don't follow us when we're finally permitted to leave."

He flexed his fingers until the knuckles popped. "It would be my pleasure. Don't you worry a thing about them, Mrs. Armstrong."

"Thank you. It's much appreciated." She patted his arm and walked back to the table, but not before hearing Elmer ask for a pot of coffee.

"What was all that about?" Gloria asked when Kate took her seat.

"Just a little insurance. One thing my husband taught me is that you can never be too careful."

The old man watched Kate Armstrong weave her way through the seated guests and talk to the drunken mountain of a man at the bar. He didn't like the way the man looked over at him and Slip.

It was now a source of potential trouble, which was the last thing he needed.

"Keep an eye on that big feller," he told Slip.

"Already am. You sure I can't have a drink?"

"I'm more sure than ever. Have some peanuts." He nudged the bowl of shelled nuts toward his nephew.

They'd happened upon Armstrong's wife by pure luck. The old man had heard a waiter talking to another about corking the bottle of Old Crow because Mrs. Armstrong was no longer asking for it.

Seeing the beautiful woman made his blood boil.

How dare the fates allow that murderer to find a woman like that to share his life with, when the old man's brother was nothing but bits of bone six feet in the dirt!

He had stolen a few quick glances at her as they sat amid the rabble in the dining hall. He should have never told Slip about her. The wild boy couldn't help staring at her or her companion. It had obviously spooked them enough for the Armstrong woman to enlist the help of the biggest man in the room.

Not that size mattered. The man could be the size of Goliath himself. When faced with the old man's pistol, he'd be just as small as anyone else who had stood on the wrong side of a barrel.

A normal man wouldn't consider doing something that brash when surrounded by so many people.

But the old man wasn't normal. He was also tired and angry and anxious that he was so close to finishing business that needed closing. Personal consequences meant nothing to him. And if by some twist of fate it was his time to go, Slip would have to go with him. The boy wasn't fit to be on his own, not that he'd last long anyway.

Barely paying any mind to the storm, the old man said, "Slip, if I catch your eyes rolling to either of those women, I'll cut them out myself."

To emphasize his point, he removed his heavy blade from the scabbard on his gun belt and ran his thumb along its edge, as if to inspect its sharpness. He quickly put it back before calling any undue attention. "Do I make myself clear?"

Slip immediately cast his gaze at the table, looking like a scolded child. "You didn't hafta threaten me like that."

Oh, yes I did, the old man thought. *Violence is all you really know.*

The question now was how to best utilize this knowledge that Armstrong's wife was near enough to draw the man to them. The fact that she was with another woman did give him pause.

Was she really with the same Armstrong he'd been searching for? Or was she a widow and he'd been too late? If he was alive, why wasn't he here?

The only way to find out was to get ahold of the pretty woman.

And now, to do that, they'd have to contend with the hulk at the bar who was draining cups of coffee and making no bones that he was fixed on them. He'd be a challenge for Slip, for sure, but the old man knew that will often times trumped physicality.

They just needed this damn storm to blow itself out. No sense putting things in motion if Armstrong wasn't able to get to the hotel. If Armstrong was even still alive. And if this woman was married to the actual man he sought.

He checked his pocket watch, then settled in his chair, making it a point not to look anywhere near the two women.

The time would come soon enough when they would be closer than skin to bones.

Chapter 21

The storm got angrier and angrier. Mayor Tibbs watched pieces of the town fly in every direction. A window upstairs shattered. Something crashed in the back of the house.

He wished his sons still lived with them to help him keep the entire place from falling apart. But they were long gone, Franklin in Oklahoma, and Ned settling down in North Carolina.

Tibbs hurried up the stairs. First he checked their bedroom to make sure the windows were intact. Eleanor was sound asleep, lulled into her personal dreamworld, thanks to the dose of laudanum he'd given her a couple of hours earlier.

Then he went to the guest bedroom and was immediately hit in the face with a spray of pelting rain. A broken tree branch lay gnarled on the floor. Kicking it aside, he put his shoulder against the armoire and pushed with all his might. He should have emptied it first, but there was no time. Stopping the rain from pouring in was the top priority.

The clunky piece of furniture scraped against the wood floor as Tibbs grunted and cursed. When he finally shifted it to seal up the broken square of window, he slid down to the floor and wiped the sweat from his brow with the handkerchief he always kept in his pants pocket.

With the wind whipping wildly, it sounded like the house was under assault.

He could only imagine what was happening to other houses and businesses across Pine Lick. This was surely a hurricane, something they were not prepared for. How far back would this set all the progress that had been made?

If anything catastrophic happened to the sawmill, Pine Lick could become a memory literally overnight.

No, he had to believe that Smits and Knoop would do whatever it took to rebuild. If they had any thoughts of picking up stakes and cutting their losses, he would have to find a way to convince them otherwise.

Something else hit him. How many people would perish before it was all over? He remembered his father telling him of one that happened in his home state of North Carolina back in '45 that claimed close to fifteen lives. And that small town had nothing on Pine Lick.

Normally, he would condemn himself for this kind of negative thinking. It was borrowing trouble on a grand scale. Though perhaps it was only rational to assume the worst when a storm from hell was battering your town.

No matter what, tomorrow would be a long and arduous day. The first, he was sure, of many to come.

Checking on Eleanor one more time before heading downstairs, Tibbs felt a sharp pain in his chest. It knocked the wind out of him and set his rear end on the stairs so he could catch his breath.

While willing the pain to go away, more glass shattered somewhere downstairs.

Sweat spilled from his forehead into his eyes. Eli Tibbs winced from the salty sting and ache in his chest, wondering when the madness would end.

The jailhouse was swamped with water as rain poured through cracks in the roof and through the shattered windows. Sheriff Mack Armstrong kept his eyes glued to the ceiling, waiting for the whole kit and caboodle to either come crashing down or blow away like a bird's nest in a high branch.

No one was in the mood for talking in the crowded building. The prisoners looked all about as parts of the structure groaned and creaked. A steady stream of water had soaked the lone bunk, as well as the men inside the cell.

Whiskey busied himself with cleaning his pistol just to try to take his mind off things. He whistled a tuneless tune, his wide eyes occasionally glancing out the window to watch some piece of the town proper go flying by.

Otto sat in a dry corner, puffing away at his cigar. He was the only one who appeared unafraid. He said he'd been in worse storms, and out in the open plain, to boot.

Meanwhile, Mack's father looked ready to be hog-tied. He couldn't stop stalking around the jailhouse, going to the window every thirty seconds. Mack felt just as anxious, but he forced himself to remain still. He could only hope that the men who had built the Palace Hotel had done the best job of their lives, and the three-story building was still standing.

Branch Armstrong spun on his heel and went to the broken window. Rain splashed his face. He suddenly recoiled, his hand slapping over his left cheek.

"What happened?" Mack asked, rising from his chair.

"It's nothing. Got hit with something." When his father pulled his hand away, there was a jagged rent across his cheek. Blood trickled down to his jawline. He took out a bandana from his back pocket and pressed it to the wound.

"Doc is gonna be awful busy later," Whiskey commented. "Probably the undertaker, too."

The deputy was right. Just going outside was like walking through a firing range. How many people had been hurt or worse when their damaged shelter forced them outside into the thick of it?

"You should keep your face out of the window," Otto said. "It will not make the storm go away."

"Thanks for the advice," Branch replied with irritation.

Mack saw a sliver of wood embedded in his father's cheek. "Just hold still while I get this out."

He plucked it out quickly. His father didn't even flinch. Fresh blood seeped from the hole. This time, Branch didn't even try to stanch the flow with the bandana. Instead, he stepped to one of the flowing leaks from the roof and let the rain wash it semi-clean.

"This has to slow down some and soon," Branch said. "I've been in plenty of storms, and the bigger they blow, the quicker they die."

"That's probably what Noah thought, too," Whiskey said.

The former sheriff shot his former deputy a look that got him concentrating on his gun again.

The tension in the jailhouse was thicker than a steer's hide. They were getting on one another's nerves too easily.

"I have to check on your mother."

"We're still okay, and this place ain't half as sturdy as the Palace."

"You don't get it. The jailhouse is squat, like a turtle. Wind is having a hard time finding it. That's not the case with the hotel. I should have let her stay at home. I should be there with her." He punched the wall.

"You did what you had to do," Otto said. His face was obscured by a cloud of smoke. "Pretty soon, you can go to Kate."

"How do you know that?"

"You forget I am old and wise," Otto replied with a grin.

For a moment, it looked as if Branch Armstrong would smile.

Instead, he looked to the window again. The wind blew hard enough to make the rain shoot sideways across the street.

"Empty your desk," he said to Mack.

"Empty my desk? Why?"

"I need it."

"For what?"

"Protection. Here, I'll help you."

Branch opened the top drawer, pulling everything out and depositing it on Whiskey's desk. Mack gave him some space, unsure of what his father planned to do with it. Once everything was cleared out, he tipped it over with his boot.

"Dad, maybe you . . ."

Branch proceeded to kick all four legs off the desk. He then grabbed it by the sides and strode to the door. "Somebody open this door for me."

"You can't go out there," Mack said.

"I beg to differ. Otto, would you mind?"

The old Indian slowly got up from his chair and put his hand on the door handle. "This is not one of your better ideas."

"Yeah, well, it's all I've got at the moment."

"At least let me go with you," Mack said.

"No, you need to stay here. You have a full house to keep an eye on."

"A full leaky house," Whiskey said.

"It is at that. Okay, boys, wish me luck."

"You will need more than that," Otto said as he opened the door.

Branch Armstrong thrust himself headlong into the storm, using the broken desk as a shield. He fought the wind every faltering, limping step. The steady thump of debris smashing into the desktop was immediately drowned out by the wailing winds.

Chapter 22

There was a commotion coming from the Palace lobby. Kate Armstrong heard voices calling out and someone asking, "How bad is he hurt?"

She pushed away from the table and got to her feet. "You should stay here," she said to Gloria Amaryllis. "I'll see what's going on."

As she rushed to the lobby, along with a few men from other tables, she passed by Handy the waiter and Archibald, who was helping clear a table of dirty plates. The boy looked at her with frightened eyes.

"Keep up the great work," she said to him before turning to the lobby.

Several men were crowded around the foyer. She saw a man lying prone on the floor. The open front door slammed against the building, over and over, as the wind attempted to reduce it to splinters.

"He scared the life outta me," one of the men who manned the front desk exclaimed. "I wasn't expecting anyone to still be out in that storm."

Kate's heartbeat quickened.

She knew her husband. For the past hour, she kept expecting to see him waltz into the hotel to make sure she was okay. The man couldn't sit still to save his life.

With the way things were being scattered by the wind, she knew it was downright dangerous and foolhardy to even take one step outside.

"He's bleeding. Someone get me a towel," Sam Snodgrass, the hotel manager, barked. "And give him some room to breathe!"

Kate saw the blood on the carpet. She pushed her way through the throng of people.

The man on the ground looked up at her with a nose that had been mashed like a potato. His eyes were black and blue, and blood poured from his nostrils into his mouth, some of it absorbed by the fibers of his bushy beard.

Bear O'Hanlon looked like he'd been hit by a stagecoach. The big man's clothes, in rough shape on a good day, were tattered and torn. Wherever dirty flesh showed through, there was blood.

"Bear? What on earth were you doing out there?" Kate asked. She'd met the mountain man several times over the years, and was especially appreciative for the time he'd helped Branch put up a new corral. He was handy, but flighty. She recalled how Mack had said he'd been a witness to the murder of Archibald's father by Tony Cheever. But ever since that day, he'd gone missing, which was not unusual for him.

"Howdy, Mrs. Armstrong." He smeared the blood on his face with the back of his sleeve and got to his feet. "I was hunkered down in that equipment shack at the sawmill, but the wind blew it right to kingdom come. Been looking for a safe place to stay ever since."

One of the maître d's came back with two fresh white towels. Kate took one and applied it to Bear's squashed nose. To his credit, he didn't complain when she touched it, even though she knew it had to hurt like blazes.

"Let's get you to a chair," she said.

Snodgrass helped her guide the big man to a settee. His bulk made the dainty piece of furniture protest loudly.

"You're a right mess, but you're lucky to be alive. Mr. Snodgrass, maybe you can get him a drink?"

The hotel manager snapped his fingers, and a young man rushed out of the room.

"You don't have to tend to me. I'll be fine," Bear said as he attempted to take the towel from her. "Just needed a place out of that hellacious wind."

"What you need is a doctor," Snodgrass said. "When the winds start to die down, I'll send for him."

I'll bet the doc will have plenty of work to do when this is all over, Kate thought. *By the time he gets here, Bear will be gone.*

A bottle of what she noted was cheap whiskey and a glass were brought to them by the breathless hotel worker. Kate poured until the glass was full and then dipped the tip of the towel in the whiskey. She dabbed Bear's wounds with the alcohol, saving the deep cut on the bridge of his nose for last. By that time, everyone but Snodgrass had dispersed.

"Is there anything else I can get you?" Snodgrass asked them both. Unlike other hotel managers Kate had met, Sam Snodgrass was a genuine human being who cared about people, even those who weren't paying customers.

"Maybe some food," Kate said. "When's the last time you ate?"

Bear patted his belly. "I was on a fishing trip with some fellas. Ate enough fish to keep me until Christmas."

Just then, there were heavy booted footsteps in the lobby. Kate turned her head and saw the two men who had been leering at her and Gloria.

Bear sat up straight on the settee when he eyeballed them.

"Please thank your friend again for the fish," the older man said. "It was much appreciated on the long ride."

Out of the corner of his mouth, Bear said to Kate, "They come across us on our fishing trip. I didn't like the look of them. Heard they was coming to Pine Lick, so I thought I should make my way, too. You know them?"

Kate shook her head. Then she whispered, "I feel the same as you. They've been looking at me and the schoolteacher oddly ever since we came down here."

The two men took a step forward in a way that Kate felt was menacing.

A massive gust of wind pounded the hotel. Loud crashing came from above. Plaster rained down from the ceiling as glass shattered and wood crackled all around them.

There was a tremendous crash and the sounds of people screaming and running about the dining room. The chandelier over Kate and Bear swung wildly before slamming to the ground.

In an instant, chaos had broken out at the Palace. Kate's immediate thoughts went to Gloria and Archibald. She was about to sprint to the dining room when a wave of terrified humanity came spilling out.

They knocked the two men down, trampling over them as if they weren't there. Snodgrass wrapped Kate in his arms and pushed her against the wall. Bear jumped from the settee to jostle anyone who came near.

The first people to burst through the front doors, nearly taking them off their hinges, were swallowed up by the wind and swept out of sight.

That led to more screaming. A woman who had tried to escape the collapsing hotel was struck in the face by something. A man caught her before she hit the ground. He bullied his way through the crowd with her in his arms. Kate's stomach flipped when she saw there wasn't much of the woman's face left. Just a bloody smear with no discernible features.

Now everyone stopped, realizing there was nowhere to go. They were tightly packed in the lobby, with men shouting above the din, "Y'all need to get away from the doors! Step back! Step back!"

Kate wriggled free, searching desperately for the boy and schoolteacher. She couldn't find them in the mass of panicked humanity. She did spot Elmer Mizner, who was pushing people aside. When their eyes met from across the lobby, Kate shouted to him, "Do you see Mrs. Amaryllis? Or the boy we were with?"

The burly blacksmith looked all around, though she noticed he wouldn't take his eyes off her for more than a second or two.

He must have seen those two men leave the dining room just before the upper floors were breached.

Sheets of rainwater began to spill from the zigzag cracks in the ceiling, adding to the growing unease.

Kate headed into the crowd. Folks pushed and shoved with no place to go, just a need to try to find any safe space.

"You need to stay here," Bear implored. "You'll get crushed."

"I have to find them."

He reached for her, but she was too fast. She wedged herself between two men and smashed her forehead into the back of another.

"Gloria! Archibald!"

She was sure her cries wouldn't be heard above the rising voices all around her, but it was worth a try. Wending her way through the crowd, searching for Gloria and Archibald, took her mind off thoughts of the entire hotel collapsing on top of them or the deadly storm that dared anyone to flee the carnage.

"Move!" she huffed, pressing her entire body weight against a corpulent man who had his arms raised and was shouting holy hell for air.

She felt a pair of hard, strong hands grab her by the waist. Kate whipped around and came face-to-face with the young man who had been staring at her. She chopped at his wrists with her forearms. He only tightened his grip.

The older man appeared beside him as if by magic.

"Get your hands off me!" she spat.

The young man's lips stretched into a madman's grin. He pulled her closer, bent down, and threw her over his shoulder. She pounded on his back with her fists. The older man acted as a cattle catcher, thrusting people aside so the younger man could drag her deeper into the crumbling hotel.

Chapter 23

Something blunt, but not exceptionally heavy, hit Branch Armstrong square on the shin. It staggered him for a moment, but no more so than the buffeting wind. There was a steady staccato of objects bouncing off the desk. His hands had gone numb from the constant reverberation.

With his head low and pressed against the wood, he willed his hands and arms not to falter. If he should drop the desk for even a second, it might be his last.

Armstrong scanned the shops to either side of him to gauge his progress.

His boots squelched in mud that fought to stop him cold.

All the glass at Daisy's Eatery had been blown out. He saw tables and chairs thrown all about. The entire place was flooded. Food baskets and empty bottles flowed out of it like flotsam down a raging river.

Almost there. Just one step at a time.

The muscles in his arms twitched and his nerves were on fire.

All around him, storefronts were being dismantled bit by bit. When he wasn't deep in a mud puddle, he was calf-deep in running water. The nearby Angelina had broken free of its banks and was sweeping the town clean.

He saw a horse, wild-eyed and bleeding in more places than he could count, gallop past him, running with the wind to God knows where.

Thank the Lord he didn't run into me, Armstrong thought.

He'd never been so frightened or bone weary in his life. Even the Union assault on Fort Fisher, where he and his fellow Confederates fought valiantly despite being surrounded and outmanned, paled in comparison. For what was the power of man compared to the unleashed and indifferent wrath of nature itself?

Fighting forward the best he could, he realized the foolishness of his endeavor. What good would he be to Kate if he ended up dead in the mud? Mack was right, the Palace was more than likely sturdy enough to withstand the storm. But that wasn't enough reassurance for Branch.

The desk cracked down the middle when something hit it. Branch held on for dear life, trying to keep the shield from splitting entirely and leaving him exposed.

The Palace wasn't far. He would make it.

He heard the roar of wind escalate to an earsplitting crescendo. It funneled down the street, coming straight for him. The cacophony of disintegrating buildings added to the terror.

When the gust hit him, he was sent sprawling backward, still clinging to the desk. He hit the ground hard. It knocked the wind out of him. He saw stars, but still his hands clutched the sides of the desk.

There was no way he could fight the wind and rise up. Trying to stand only netted him a few inches out of the mud and rushing water.

Water flowed into his nostrils, drowned his vision. Branch choked and gasped. Opening his mouth just invited more of the murky water to invade his throat, lungs, and stomach. He coughed violently, clutching for air in between harsh barks. All the while, the wind did its damnedest to rip the wood shield from his grasp. Objects thumped across it, widening the crack.

He had to get up. If he didn't, he would drown right there in the middle of the street! Struggling to lift himself up, Branch vomited down his shirt from the strain. The desk shuddered as he forced it up and against the wind. His arms trembled and his fingers ached something fierce.

The crackling of wood drew his eyes to the splitting desk.

No!

There was nothing he could do to hold it together. It separated into two jagged pieces. He turned his head and ended up back in the mud to protect himself.

To his amazement, the wind began to dissipate. The rain dialed back from pounding sheets to a simple downpour.

Slipping out from under the broken halves of the desk, Branch Armstrong struggled to his feet.

The street was strewn with debris in every direction. Whole businesses had collapsed upon themselves, while most others were under a foot or more of water.

But the air was no longer rife with deadly projectiles.

He saw the Palace and his heart stopped.

The third floor was in shambles, having fallen into the second floor. Windows were busted out and the roof was at an angle, tilted toward the street. Great sheets of rain spilled from the roof, forming a waterfall that concealed the front entrance.

"Kate!"

He ran to the hotel, his wounded leg barking at him with every step. Just as he passed through the soaking waterfall and grabbed the knob to the front door, it pushed outward, knocking him aside.

Seeing that the worst of the storm had suddenly passed, the hotel patrons hustled out of the sagging structure as if the devil himself was on their heels. They fled in droves like spooked cattle. All he could do was stand aside and watch them go by, searching for Kate among them.

A slat of wood fell from the roof and slammed to the ground just a foot away from Branch. It nearly clipped the head of a woman who was running with tears streaming down her face.

Once outside, people scattered in every direction, their only goal was getting away from the hotel before it completely fell apart.

After a minute or so, there was no one left. Or at least no one heading out the door.

Branch went inside to the pitch-black lobby. A handful of workers, looking worse for wear, was searching for candles.

"Don't bother," Sam Snodgrass said. "You need to get out of here, now."

They didn't need to be told twice.

Armstrong approached the hotel manager, who had a fat lip and whose clothes, normally impeccable, were in utter disarray. "That goes for you, too, Mr. Armstrong. There's no telling how much longcr this placc will stand."

As he hurried past, Armstrong grabbed his arm. "Have you seen my wife?"

"I was with her before the roof collapsed. Bear had made it through the storm, but he was in bad shape. She was tending to him when all hell broke loose."

Armstrong's jaw flexed as tension coiled every muscle in his body. "Do you know where she is now?"

"I assumed she left with everybody else."

"She didn't."

Snodgrass put his hand over his mouth. "Oh, my, are you sure? It would be easy for her to be lost in that crowd."

"I'm positive."

"Then I don't know where she could be."

Both men looked down the dark hallway leading deeper into the wounded hotel.

"I'll look for her," Armstrong said. "You go save your skin."

The ceiling cracked wider, letting in more water from above. "I'd make it quick if I were you," Snodgrass said. "I'll wait outside. If anything happens, I'll get as many people as I can to search for you."

Armstrong patted his shoulder. "Hopefully, it won't come to that."

The hotel manager scurried out of the building, while Branch strode down the hallway. "Kate! Kate, can you hear me?"

The dining room looked as if it had been rolled down a hill. In their panic, folks had overturned every table and chair, smashed plates and glassware, and scattered food, which floated atop the standing water.

Where would Kate have gone? And if she was tending to Bear, where was he?

"Kate? Bear? Just make a sound and I'll come to you."

The only reply was running water as it splashed onto the flooded floor.

He looked around for a lantern, but quickly realized the matches he had in his pocket would be too wet to ignite. The farther he went into the hotel, the darker it became.

There was a chance his wife had smartly avoided the stampeding masses and left the hotel from a different door. Branch wasn't normally a praying man, but he offered a prayer now.

The water in this section of the hotel was above his ankles and rising as more collected rain fell from the upper floors. He sloshed through it, calling out for Kate and Bear with each step.

He was near the back end of the first floor, right where the kitchen was located, when he heard a muffled cry.

"Kate?"

It sounded as if it came from the kitchen. He double-timed it, barging his way through the double swinging doors.

With the twin windows at the back of the kitchen blown out, he was able to see in the gray light. The stoves and countertops were laden with pots and pans and plates filled with food.

A man's voice said, "Well, lookit that. Hand delivered right to us."

Branch immediately went for his gun.

"I wouldn't do that, mister," another voice said.

Two men stepped out from the shadow of a large pantry. They dragged three people along with them—Kate, Mrs. Amaryllis, and the boy who had been orphaned by Tony Cheever. The older man had a gun at Kate's temple and his other hand clamped over her mouth. The younger one kept the barrel of his gun jammed in the boy's ear. The schoolteacher was pale as death, with tears streaming down her face.

The younger one flicked a match to life, alighting their faces better.

In an instant, Branch Armstrong knew, and the blood in his veins turned to ice.

Chapter 24

Elmira Prison Camp, Elmira, New York
Late February 1865

The freezing rain pelted the canvas tent with relentless abandon. It was cold as the grave inside, and the clouds of mist with each exhalation made it difficult for Branch Armstrong to see what he was doing.

"Turn the other way, Jimmy," he said to his toothless companion. "I don't want to accidentally hack my thumb off."

"Let me help."

"We only have the one spoon. If I get tired, you can take over for a spell."

"Sure thing, Branch. Sure thing. I'll keep an eye out, see if that old cuss Bragg is sneaking around."

Branch labored at the gnarled tree root with the sharpened spoon he'd nicked from suppertime two weeks ago. His fingers were numb, but the wood was beginning to fray. A splinter stuck out of his right index finger, but there was no pain. He didn't have time to go plucking it out.

One place their guard and personal tormentor wasn't going to be was within a stone's throw of their tent. Not in this weather. The tent was outside the twelve-foot stockade wall at the rear of the camp, with the icy Chemung River roiling just beyond the flap. Branch and Jimmy were being punished for talking back to the guards. At worst, Corporal Henry Bragg would be in the guard tower directly above them, making sure they didn't do what they were about to do. More likely, he was in the officers' barracks, sitting beside the woodstove with his pipe, not giving a second thought about Branch and Jimmy, other than hoping they died before morning from exposure to the cold.

Sergeant Sebastian Bragg, younger brother to the hardest jailer in Elmira, was far too lazy to come out in this weather. If anything, he was making someone's life hell in the warmish barracks.

The Bragg brothers were the stuff of nightmares for the captured Confederates. Yes, war was hell, but it took a different kind of man to revel in the worst parts of it.

The jagged end of the spoon slid off the wet root and sliced into Branch's hand. A thin line of blood was drawn, but again, the oppressive cold shielded him from feeling a thing. Branch kept on sawing at the root. It was just big enough to suit his purposes. What remained in question was whether he could extract it from the frozen ground before Corporal Bragg, who had forced them to be in this tent, or any of the other guards checked in on them.

As much as Branch cursed the foul New York weather, he had to give it a nod of thanks for keeping the guards away.

"You al-al-almost done?" Jimmy asked, keeping his face turned away from the work at hand. He shivered so hard, Branch thought he could hear the man's bones rattling. His gums smacked together wetly, like whacking a rolling pin against raw red meat. It made

Branch sick to his stomach. Not the fact that the young man, just turned twenty-two, had no teeth, but the reason why.

"Not by a long shot. You just keep watching."

Jimmy had been lucky to survive the cutting of rations by the prison camp's commandant, Colonel Benjamin Tracy, and resulting malnutrition. In his year at Elmira, he'd managed to avoid the waves of dysentery, typhoid, and smallpox that had taken too many prisoners of war to an early and undeserved grave.

What had gotten Jimmy in its clutches was a miserable case of scurvy, which took his teeth and swelled his joints like an old-timer. He also was a tad soft in the brain. There was no telling if it was from his time at Elmira or if something had happened to him on the battlefield. There wasn't anyone around who knew Jimmy before the war to set the matter straight.

Branch had only been in Elmira a month, after having been captured at Fort Fisher in North Carolina, but in that time, he'd taken a liking to the man and vowed to get them out of Hellmira, which was what their fellow POWs had nicknamed their prison. Someone had to look after the Jimmys of the world. It was what Branch's wife, Kate, would have told him to do.

Thinking of Kate brought a dull ache to his heart.

I'll come home to you, he thought as he pictured her that last day on the farm before he went off to fight. A few stray auburn curls had slipped out from her bonnet, and her cheeks glowed as she did her best to hold back her tears. One hand rested on her flat belly, their unborn child nestled within. He or she would be a few months old by now. *I'll come home to you both.*

A savage gust of wind caved in one side of the tent. Branch dropped the spoon and threw his body against the tent before it pulled up stakes. Jimmy shook even more and covered his ears like a frightened child.

"It's all right," Branch said, getting back to work. "Just a quick thump by the Lord to make sure we know He's there."

"Do you m-m-mean that?"

"I never say things I don't mean."

After several more minutes of hacking away, Branch got through the end of the root. There was no time to celebrate. Dusk had turned to night. He'd have to work the other end in complete darkness.

"I reckon my hands are gonna look like a steak that's been dragged behind a stagecoach by the time I get through," he said as he got back to work on the root.

"What I wouldn't give for a s-s-steak."

Branch thought he should let Jimmy take over, if just to keep his blood flowing so he didn't freeze up. He tapped Jimmy on the leg with the spoon. "I'm tuckered for the moment. You good to give it a go?"

"Just show me where to cut," Jimmy said as he swiped the spoon from Branch's grasp. Branch had to guide Jimmy like a blind man to find the portion of the partially exposed root that needed attention.

While Jimmy got to work, Branch popped his head out of the tent. Flickering candlelight emanated from the guard tower's lone window. The Chemung River had swollen up good. Branch wondered if it would slip on up the narrow bank and just rip the tent free, sweeping them into an icy grave during the night. He was sure that's exactly what Bragg would want to happen. Either that, or freeze to death. Two less mouths to feed and vivid examples of what happened when you opened your mouth.

All the more reason to double-time and get this root free. It would only take ten or fifteen minutes to whittle one end to a fine, deadly point.

"Faster, Jimmy," Branch said. He could tell just from the sound of things that his friend was having a hard time of it. Branch cupped his hands and blew on them, getting ready to take over.

Jimmy grunted. The spoon clattered against the hard-packed ground. "I think I can just . . . just . . ."

There was a loud crack a second before Jimmy crashed into Branch. They both tumbled to the ground.

"I got it!" Jimmy shouted.

Branch covered Jimmy's mouth with his hand. "You gotta keep quiet," he whispered in the man's ear.

"Yeah. Yeah. You're right, Branch. You're always right."

Branch patted his hand on the ground until he palmed the freed tree root. He then scuttled to the tent flap and flipped it open to make sure Jimmy's bit of excitement hadn't alerted the guard.

The wind howled across the river. It sent a chill to his bone marrow, but it also masked any sounds he and Jimmy would make.

"Hand me the spoon."

Jimmy had to blindly search the ground for a moment.

"And hold the tent flap open just a bit to let some light in."

What little moonlight that made it through the storm clouds was as meager as a mouse's appetite, but just enough for Branch to whittle the end of the root without taking off several layers of skin. A few times, bursts of wind barreled into the tent, stealing the breath from them. He coughed, quickly shook it off, and got back at it.

"We're really gonna do this," Jimmy said.

"Too late to turn back now," Branch said while he worked on the point of the root. "If you're afraid, you can always stay here. You can tell them I've escaped, after giving me a little head start. They might even reward you for alerting them and not running."

Despite the cold, a bead of sweat dropped from the tip of Branch's nose.

"I'm coming with you," Jimmy said. "There ain't no rewards in this place."

Fighting a coughing fit as the icy air seeped into his lungs, Branch tapped his index finger on the tip of the branch. Pretty sharp. It would have to do. "You sure are right about that."

Jimmy threw the tent flap wide. "Let's go!"

"Wait. We need the tent, remember? It's the only thing that'll maybe keep us from freezing to death."

They bolted from the tent and went about pulling up the stakes, looping the ropes around their shoulders. The freezing rain had turned to snow.

Branch cursed Mother Nature.

Snow meant footprints. And footprints could easily be followed.

He cast a glance at the guard tower.

Was that a shadow by the window?

There was no time to wonder.

Branch gathered the canvas tent under his arm and started running perpendicular to the Chemung River, with Jimmy hot on his heels. He thought he heard a man shout, but whatever was said was swallowed up by the bitter wind.

Each deep breath felt like sucking in the cold fires of hell. It was slow going at first, with his knees practically frozen in place while working that gnarled root. Now that his blood was flowing, Branch outpaced his feeble friend.

He turned back and shouted, "Keep up, Jimmy!"

There was a sharp crack behind them.

Damn it!

They'd been spotted. It was only a matter of time before every available gun was pointed at them. Elmira had an excellent reputation for keeping its prisoners right where they belonged. Commandant Tracy would upend all of New York to drag them back, dead or alive.

"Branch! Wait up!"

Fighting every survival instinct, Branch slowed so Jimmy could catch up to him. Jimmy was breathing hard, and his face was paler than fresh milk. They had a long way to go and he already looked just about done in.

"We have to keep running," Branch exclaimed against the wind and shouts and rifle fire. "Run as fast as you can. Faster than you've ever run in your whole life!"

He grabbed his friend's jacket sleeve and propelled him forward.

It wouldn't be long before they made it past the stockade wall. Flicking his eyes to the top of the wall, Branch saw guards bearing their rifles down on them. Lucky for him, they were bad shots.

He wondered how long they'd give chase in this bad weather. He was gambling on them giving up quickly, choosing a warm bed over freezing to death chasing a couple of Confederate privates, who would more than likely be found frozen stiffer than a bull's horn by morning.

Snow and mud kicked up from the ground right beside Branch. Adrenaline gave his legs a little more gallop, even with having to drag Jimmy along.

They made it past the outer wall of the fort. Ahead of them was a hell of a lot of open space, and if they were very lucky, freedom.

That is if a bullet didn't part their skull right down the middle.

"I can't . . . I can't . . ." Jimmy said, puffing hard while his arms pinwheeled.

"Yes you can!"

"I think my chest is about to burst."

Branch gave him a hard tug. "No such thing ever happened to a man while running. We're getting out of here and going home, even if I have to carry you all the . . ."

A dark shape sprang from behind a pile of rocks.

The shape wore the cap of a Union soldier and lifted a rifle with a bayonet secured at the end to face them.

Branch dropped to the ground, pulling Jimmy with him. The slick ice and snow only sped up their momentum. When they slammed into the soldier's legs, Branch absorbed the shocking blow with the side of his ribs.

All three ended up in a tangle.

Branch saw the man reach for his knife. No words were said as the cold ripped the words from their throats. The hand with the knife jabbed forward, right at Jimmy's thigh. Jimmy yowled in agony.

Yanking the sharpened root from his belt, Branch struck as hard as he could, feeling the slick wood push through something soft and yielding. The soldier grabbed for the root with shaking, desperate hands. Branch put all his weight into the improvised weapon. Snow pelted Branch's watering eyes, making it difficult to see the man's face or where the sharpened root had pierced his body.

He heard wet gurgling. The hands dropped away.

Branch had killed men during his time defending Fort Fisher. At the fort, he had been part of a crew manning the massive seven-inch Brooke rifle. The cannon had taken down its share of men and ships filled with Union Navy men as they choked the harbor.

Never had he killed a man by hand, close enough to smell his dying breath.

Scrambling to his feet, he reached out for Jimmy. His wounded friend had his hand pressed to the side of the blade in his thigh. Tears ran down his cheeks.

"I'm hurt! I'm hurt really bad!" Jimmy wailed against the howling wind and the closer and closer gunshots.

"You'll be hurt a lot worse if we don't get moving. Give me your hands."

"I can't!"

"You can!"

Fast-approaching shapes were emerging from the curtains of snow. Branch ducked as more shots were fired.

"Just leave me. Just leave me. I can't move."

"We promised we'd do this together. I don't break my promises."

Branch made a quick decision. If he couldn't get Jimmy back on his feet and running, he would stay with his POW brother and suffer the consequences. It would be this side of heaven to leave Hellmira behind and be with his wife and child, but how could he face Kate knowing he'd let a man down when he needed him most?

Grabbing Jimmy by both forearms, he pulled him to his feet. Jimmy cried out in agony.

"Can you walk?"

Jimmy took a faltering step and sagged against Branch.

"Dear Jesus, it hurts so bad."

They were running out of time. Branch would have to remove the knife from Jimmy's thigh if they were to have any chance at all of escaping.

"What's the name of your sweetheart back home again?" Branch asked.

"What?"

With Jimmy distracted by the question, Branch gripped the blade's handle and ripped it free from his thigh.

Jimmy's head tipped back and he screeched like one of those Irish banshees Branch had heard about.

His agonized cry didn't last long.

One moment, he was in Branch's arms, his body rigid with pain.

The next, the top half of his skull disappeared in a mist of blood and flesh and bone.

Branch's mouth was filled with his friend's blood and brains. His entire world had been tinted by the taste of copper.

Another shot came so close to his ear, he heard it pierce the air with a high whistle.

Instinct took over. Branch let Jimmy's lifeless body slip from his hands. He gathered up the tent and ran, spitting out what he could to lessen the revulsion that threatened to drop him to his knees.

He ran faster than before, both to escape this nightmare he'd gotten himself and Jimmy into, and to find his way home.

The snow, the cold, the ice, the biting wind, all disappeared as his mind focused inward while willing his legs to move as if Satan was nipping at his heels.

I'm not going to die in this godforsaken northern hellhole.

Branch repeated it to himself with each step, while the taste of his friend's blood seeped into his tongue until it found its way to his soul.

Chapter 25

Pine Lick, East Texas
Late summer 1888

Belle Dupree sensed the calming of the storm. She asked Tiny Ed to go outside and see if she was right.

"Calm as can be. Just some drizzle now," the bouncer said, much to the delight of Belle and her ladies.

"Thank heaven," Belle said. She patted the parlor wall. "And praise to the men who built this house."

"You want me to take the boards off the windows?" Tiny Ed asked.

"By all means. I've never heard of back-to-back hurricanes before. We're in the calm after the storm, at least weatherwise."

She stepped outside, with her ladies following close behind. Belle's place was on a hill overlooking the town proper. Some of the house's siding was strewn about the yard, but that was an easy repair. A tree was down and there were leaves everywhere.

But it was the view of downtown that took her breath away.

Pine Lick was in shambles. It seemed as if every other building was either in a pile of lumber or about to collapse into one. People walked about in a daze. A whole new river had been birthed, and it ran down the center of the street. She could see where the waters had completely broken from the confines of the Angelina and snaked their way into town.

It was bad. Really bad.

Belle turned to her ladies. "All right, everyone, go put on your knockabout clothes. We're going to have a lot of work to do. People need help. Delilah, you might as well bring your nursing kit. I think you'll be the busiest of all."

Pretty, full-lipped Delilah nodded and hurried to her room. Her mother had been a nurse at a hospital after the Civil War and had taught Delilah everything she knew, hoping she would become a nurse as well. Turned out nursing wasn't in the cards for the young woman, but she had retained a lot and used those skills whenever anyone in the house fell ill or was injured.

"Ed, grab as many pairs of leather gloves as you can find. We're going to be rummaging through woodpiles, I suppose."

The brothel was a hive of activity as everyone got ready to lend a hand in getting Pine Lick back on its feet. Belle had a feeling it would take a good, long while.

Mayor Eli Tibbs felt the house grow suddenly calm. He was slumped in a chair next to Eleanor, who had slumbered through the worst of it in her drugged state.

The pain in his chest had subsided after imbibing several glasses of brandy to settle his nerves. He rose on unsteady legs, bent down to kiss Ellie's forehead, and headed for the stairs. It was a slow process, with him clinging to the handrail to make sure he didn't take a drunken tumble.

Being drunk was only half of his problem. He was also weak as a newborn lamb as the adrenaline rush subsided and left him spent.

When he opened the front door and stepped onto the porch, he had to grab the rail to keep himself upright.

With his view of the sawmill, the lifeblood of the town, it was quickly apparent that Pine Lick was in dire straits. Half of the structures of the sawmill were underwater. Heavy logs had been tossed about, along with equipment, and had formed a makeshift dam. Water slammed against it, and then diverted to the shore, rushing into the town streets.

Tibbs felt sick. He dry-heaved for a spell, all the while calculating how long it would take to rebuild the sawmill and what the cost might be. When he asked himself if Smits and Knoop would even want to rebuild, he vomited on the wet porch and felt the pain in his chest return.

Pull yourself together, Eli. Tears streamed down his face. *The town needs you, now more than ever.*

He would have to make his way to his broken town and show strength in the face of adversity. The only problem was, he wasn't sure if he could even stand upright without swooning.

"It's gone," Reverend Jake Smiley said aloud to himself, sitting on his porch with the remains of the rain dripping down. He stared at what was left of the church. Half of it still stood, looking over the ruined half that was nothing but a pile of splintered wood. He openly drank from the bottle, no longer concealing it from Matilda. His nerves were frayed, and he felt as if he were watching everything from outside his body.

He didn't even feel Matilda's hand when she grasped his shoulder and removed the bottle from his hand. "That is the last thing you need."

"I would sincerely beg to differ," he replied. He swiped at her hand to get the bottle back, but his reflexes were dulled and Matilda was determined.

"What you should be doing first is getting on your knees and thanking God that neither of us was hurt. And when you're done being grateful, we need to get in our wagon and see who needs help."

Even though they were on a slightly higher elevation from the center of town, the ground was saturated. If he got the wagon out of the barn, it would make it maybe ten feet before the wheels got stuck in the mud.

Besides that, he wasn't in an especially grateful mood. It may have been a sin to even think that way, but so be it. The truth was the truth, and there was no sense trying to hide it from Matilda or God.

If there was any silver lining in this mess, it was the retreating of the oppressive heat that had lain over Pine Lick for days. A light, cool breeze touched his sweaty face.

"Wagon won't make it far," he said, slurring slightly.

"Then we'll have to saddle up the horses. Come on, you can't just sit here staring at the church. The real Church is out there, needing our help!"

"What use would I be to them? I can't even bring comfort to my wife. If anything, you should go. They all look to you anyway."

Matilda grabbed him by his collar and lifted him from his seat. "I am *not* the reverend, *you* are. If you want to quit the Church and be a lost soul, that's your prerogative. And you know as well as I do that I'll try to stop you. But that's for a later time. There are people out there who are hurt, lost, afraid, and worse. They need to know that despite all this, God is with them. So quit sulking and get to saddling our horses."

She stood before him with her hands on her hips. Her words were stern, but there was love and concern in her eyes that pierced the fog in Smiley's brain.

Slowly he rose from the chair, waited for the world to stop spinning, and headed for the barn.

Chapter 26

Mack Armstrong stepped out of the jailhouse as soon as the wind and rain died down. It was as if the storm had been snuffed out like a candle—a terrifying tempest one moment, and gone the next, heading north to terrorize the neighboring towns.

Just ten minutes earlier, a good chunk of the roof had been ripped away. They'd been forced into a corner of the building to avoid being drenched to their underclothes. The roof above the cell had stayed intact, though with a few holes poked through.

Surveying the damage, Mack felt his stomach drop.

Everything was in shambles. The street was still a running river, though now one choked with scraps of wood, glass, clothes, and household items. A dead cat floated by.

What made him cringe were the rats swimming through the water as if this were the greatest day ever made. For them, he guessed, it was. They didn't need to hide in the darkness, and there was more than a hatful of easy pickings per varmint out there.

"God almighty, what we done to deserve this?" Whiskey said at his side. The deputy made the sign of the cross.

"Nature doesn't care what men do. It just is."

"Do you think your pop made it to the hotel?"

The first thing Mack had been looking for was any sign of his father. It was impossible to tell with all the debris scattered everywhere. "I have to hope so."

Otto came out, saw what had become of the town, and pitched his smoldering cigar into the water. He pointed at the slanted, sagging roof of Maxel's across the street. There was a body up there, chest down with the head impossibly facing the sky. "Do you know who that is?"

Mack nervously scratched at his chin. "Can't say I do."

"You, Whiskey?"

Whiskey squinted, trying to get a better look at the dead man who had been given a free ride by the hurricane before being unceremoniously deposited on the roof. "Doesn't look familiar."

"We have to get him down from there," Mack said.

Otto patted his back. "Go find your father and mother first. That body is not going anywhere."

What he didn't say was what they were all thinking. The three of them definitely knew everyone in Pine Lick by face and name. That dead stranger would most likely have been staying at the Palace. If he had been blown clear of it by the storm, there was no telling what Mack would find when he got there.

Mack hurried to the Palace, ignoring the pleas of townsfolk who were out wandering the waterlogged street in a daze. Some were bleeding, all were soaked to the bone. On any other day, Mack would have dropped everything to help anyone who came or called to him.

Not so at this moment. All he had on his mind was finding his mother and father.

"Sheriff!" a woman cried out, her voice pleading, desperate. He knew that if he glanced her way, he would stop and help.

Instead, he shouted, "My deputy will be around to help!"

Whiskey may have been taken aback by the damage wrought by the storm, but he would shake it off quickly and seek out those in need.

The crowds were thicker the closer he got to the Palace. Great slabs of the boardwalk that lined both sides of the main street floated down the newly minted river. When Mack saw the state of the hotel, his legs pumped even faster, kicking up great splashes of brown water.

The guests were milling about, pestering Sam Snodgrass with questions the man couldn't answer. Mack angled his way through thc crowd until they were face-to-face.

"Where's my mother?"

Snodgrass looked as if he'd aged five years in the span of an afternoon. "I don't know, Mack. Your father came to the hotel looking for her. I thought maybe she'd run out when the building was compromised, but I'm not sure. He's in there now looking for her. I told him I'd keep an eye out in case anything worse happens and he needs rescuing."

Mack eyed the crumpling hotel. The way the wood was creaking, the whole thing would tumble to the ground any minute. If that happened, there wasn't a damn thing Snodgrass could do.

At least he'd confirmed Mack's father had made the treacherous walk to the hotel. That was one question answered.

Mack patted Snodgrass on the chest and headed inside.

"Wait! Don't go in there!"

The walls of the lobby were tilted. The ceiling sagged and water poured through numerous jagged cracks. If he thought too much about how long it would be until it all went to hell, he'd paralyze himself.

He cupped his hands around his mouth and called out, "Mom! Dad! Where are you?"

The Palace wasn't an enormous building. It appeared to Mack that the top floor had caved in, so there were limited places for them to be. If they were conscious, they would have been able to hear him and respond.

Slogging through the water, Mack crossed the lobby and peeked into the dining room. It was pure chaos in there, but devoid of any people.

"Mom! Where are you? Dad!"

His heart thrummed in his ears. With every step, he expected to stumble across his worst nightmare.

One look at the staircase told him there was no chance of him getting to the second floor. The railing was gone and water sluiced down what steps remained like a waterfall.

If his mother had been in her room when the hotel started falling apart, she could be up there now, hurt or worse. Had his father managed to make his way up there and was now in a similar situation?

Mack pressed on. He had to explore the entire first floor before tackling the issue of getting to the second floor. And if he managed that, would it be more of a suicide than a rescue?

Down the dark hallway was the kitchen, which was the last place to check, besides Snodgrass's office, and that was behind the front desk.

Using the tip of his boot, Mack pushed one of the swinging doors open. The water on the other side made it harder to swing.

What he saw had him reaching for his pistol.

"Hands at your side," the man holding his mother said. "Unless you want me to plug a hole through your momma's head. She is your momma, right? At least that's what I assumed when I heard you crying out for your mommy and daddy just a few seconds ago."

Tony Cheever stepped onto the porch of the main house and walked to the side where he could see the state of the bungalows. Only one was still standing, though it looked like it was about to fall as well.

Several trees had been uprooted, one of them blocking the main path to the house. His shoes clomped on the slick steps. Walking a dozen or so feet into the muddy yard, he inspected the state of the main house. The roof was intact, but some tiles were missing. There was damage to the sides of the house he could see, no doubt caused by objects being flung at it by the hurricane winds.

All in all, it could have been far worse.

Day one and they're socked with a hurricane! Thank goodness, he had enough liquor on hand to keep his guests happy and sedated. Even now, they were passed out on couches in the main house, unaware that the storm was over.

All except one.

Armand Gloucester was striding his way across the yard. He looked extremely worried.

"Do you have a horse?" the wealthy businessman asked.

"Of course. Why would you need a horse?"

"There's no time to discuss the matter. You need to ride into town and warn them about the dam."

Cheever had been so concerned about the Arcadian, he hadn't thought about the dam, even though Gloucester had warned him about it just hours ago.

"Has it . . . burst?" Cheever asked.

Gloucester shook his head. "Not at the moment, but it won't stand for much longer. Go now! There are lives at stake!"

The man's panic was infectious. Cheever looked at the barn and saw it was still erect. One of his horses whinnied.

"They'll never listen to me," he said.

"Nonsense! After that storm, they would surely know the dam giving way is a possibility."

There was no sense telling him how he was reviled by the people of Pine Lick. The last person they'd believe was Tony Cheever.

"I would go myself, but I don't know the way." Gloucester snapped his fingers. "I know what! We'll go together. I've heard how much Pine Lick has grown, thanks to its sawmill. Place that size will need more than one town crier if we're to avoid a complete catastrophe." He headed for the barn, stopped, and waved Cheever on. "Come on, man. We don't have a minute to waste!"

Cheever hurried after him, feeling numb and knowing there was no way to refuse the man's orders. As indifferent as he was to the people of Pine Lick, he realized that without the town, the Arcadian would cease to be a favored destination.

They saddled two of Cheever's best horses, sturdy Appaloosa that were still spooked by the storm. Soon they were riding hard, the hooves kicking up great gouts of mud and water.

As they passed the Stanton Dam, Cheever realized why Gloucester was so concerned.

The water had risen above the top of the dam, spilling over the edge and creeping along the banks. It was almost as if the dam had disappeared under the swell of water.

As they rode on, he looked back to see the façade of the dam on the other side of the lake. Great spouts of water had broken out all along its face.

The dam was crumbling. Of that, there was no doubt.

Cheever swallowed, dry and hard, as fear gripped him by the spine. He was riding right into danger. If the dam exploded now, he and Gloucester would be swept away, the first casualties of what would bc a historic flood.

Chapter 27

Belle Dupree had changed from her usual fancy dress to men's long pants, a denim shirt, and black leather gloves. The madam was deep in the thick of things, helping to remove shattered slats of wood because a woman's voice had been heard beneath the pile crying for help.

Also gone was any French affectation. For the moment, she was back to being her true self, and that included a slight Louisiana drawl.

Her ladies worked alongside the townsmen, making quick work and recovering the wounded woman. She had a gash on her forehead and one of her arms was clearly broken.

Dupree ushered the men away as soon as they'd extracted her from the wrecked building and laid her down on a plank of wood set between two barrels to keep her out of the water.

"Trixie, fetch one of those blankets we brought! Cora, keep hold of her by her shoulders so she doesn't roll off! Delilah, you got your kit?"

The women snapped to Belle Dupree's barked orders, and soon

the shivering woman was wrapped in a dry blanket and was having her wounds tended to. Word was that the town doc was nowhere to be seen. If anyone here needed medical attention, they would have to rely on Delilah.

There were shouts and a gang of men sprinted to another wreck of a building. Belle steeled herself and said, "Bonnie, Lenora, Maribel, go help."

Tiny Ed, his bare hands bleeding, led the ladies across the street, where they began anew, digging for survivors.

Belle looked down at the wounded woman and stroked her hair from her face. "You're gonna be all right, sugar. You're in good hands. Now just rest."

A half smile broke on the woman's face and her eyes rolled to the top of her head before closing. Poor thing was in shock. "You need help setting her arm?"

Delilah shook her head. "I'll be fine. I just hope the pain doesn't wake her up."

Belle hoped as well. She'd broken her leg as a little girl and still remembered the white-hot agony when the local sawbones set it into place.

"What's going on here?"

Dupree looked to where the woman's voice was coming from. She turned all the way around to come face-to-face with a man and woman, covered in mud, atop their two equally filthy horses. It took her a moment to recognize the Baptist minister, Smiley. He'd never even come close to her establishment, which gave her a glimmer of hope for men of the cloth. His wife, she'd heard, could be kind one moment, then full of fire and brimstone the next. What Dupree saw in the woman's eyes told her she'd caught her on one of her fire-and-brimstone days.

"Beg your pardon?" Dupree said.

Smiley's wife hopped off her horse and stormed over to Delilah, who was about to set the bone. She nudged her aside brusquely and said, "The last thing this woman needs is a sinner making things worse!"

"Are you out of your mind?" Delilah said.

Smiley's wife slapped Trixie's and Cora's hands away. "I'll see to her until a proper doctor gets here."

Suddenly furious, Belle Dupree said, "Then she'll be waiting a very long time. I don't know if you've noticed, but there are enough wounded people to keep the doc busy until your rapture comes to pass." She moved toward the reverend's wife and glared at her. It was disgusting that this woman's version of Christian kindness didn't allow for someone she deemed immoral to help a fellow human being in need. Normally, she would grab the woman by the hair and toss her aside. However, Mrs. Smiley had the woman's broken arm in her hands, and Dupree didn't want to exacerbate the damage. "Miss Delilah is a trained nurse and knows what she's doing. With a break like that, you have to set it quick, especially now when she's asleep and might not feel a thing."

"Save her arm, but damn her soul?"

Reverend Smiley had tied the horses to a broken hitching post and tried to intervene.

"If the woman is a nurse, she has a point," he said to his wife.

Now that the reverend was close, Dupree smelled booze on his breath. His wife shot daggers at him.

"There are too many people in need of help to deny folks who want to lend a helping hand," he said to his wife, practically pleading.

The unconscious woman groaned.

"Enough of all this palaver," Delilah said. "I need to set that arm, and quick."

When she moved toward the woman, the reverend's wife bumped her with her hip, sending her falling into a deep puddle.

Delilah was not amused. Rising from the tainted water, she wiped her face with the back of her hand and snarled, "Let's see if you turn the other cheek."

Belle Dupree had to be held back by Reverend Smiley before she joined the fray.

He blurted out, "Everyone! We need to be reasonable."

Mrs. Smiley stood her ground as the soiled dove reared her fist back. A second before it connected with the woman's face, it was snatched by a powerful hand.

"Don't y'all think we have enough to worry about without you getting into a brawl?"

Sheriff's Deputy Whiskey held Delilah by the wrist. Dupree shook herself loose from Reverend Smiley's grasp.

"He's right," Dupree said. "Save your damnation for another day. Today we've all been damned, and we need to pick each other up."

Mrs. Smiley reluctantly took two steps away from the unconscious woman. Delilah motioned for Cora and Trixie to help her.

"You'll have to excuse us," Smiley said to Whiskey. "Our church was destroyed and, well, we're a mite upset."

Whiskey waved his arm around. "I guess you can take comfort knowing you ain't the only ones upset. Fact, I'd be surprised if you found anyone in all of Pine Lick ain't upset." His eyes flicked from Dupree to Mrs. Smiley. "Now, can I count on you not to cause any more of a ruckus?" He looked directly at Mrs. Smiley.

"We came here to help," she replied sheepishly.

"There's no shortage of need, for sure. Now let's not be fightin' and get to helpin'. And I'm sorry about your church. I expect a lot of folks will be needin' some Church comfort in the coming days."

"I suspect you're right," Reverend Smiley said.

Belle Dupree kept an eye on Mrs. Smiley when the deputy walked away, just to make sure she wouldn't start up again. When she moved on with her husband to talk to a man and woman who were walking in a daze, Dupree headed to where folks were digging through the wreckage.

She paused when she heard the pounding of hooves heading her way and heard the first frenzied shouting.

* * *

More than half of the sawmill was underwater. The Angelina had risen like a beast from the depths, wiping out everything it touched.

As soon as the storm had abated, Henrik Smits had ridden down to assess the damage. It was worse than he thought. He could only imagine what state the town itself was in, if it was even still there.

"It's a hell of a thing," a man said behind him. He turned to spy his partner, Jens Knoop, trudging through thigh-high water. "I suppose your house is okay?"

"A tree hit the side of it, but there was no damage. Not like . . . like this."

Knoop clucked his tongue and shook his head. Lumber had been scattered everywhere, as if a giant hand had scooped up the entire sawmill and unceremoniously dumped everything. The dam of wood, machines, and material grew by the second as more and more detritus washed along the river. "If we don't clear that soon, we'll be swimming on the roof."

Smits looked around. It was just the two of them. "It will take a lot of men. And it will be dangerous."

"Yes, it will."

Neither man spoke for a beat. They simply surveyed the intense damage to their property and business.

"How is your house?" Smits asked.

"What house?"

There wasn't a need to discuss the matter further. Smits had warned him about building so close to the river. Even mild storms would affect the Angelina. And this had been no minor storm.

But Knoop was cut from a different cloth. He was a shrewd and successful businessman who hadn't a care in the world for his own personal belongings. It didn't shock Smits that he was so nonchalant about losing his home.

"We'll figure out what to do next after we clear the river," Knoop said.

Smits had known other men who would cut and run.

Not so with either of them. They felt an obligation to the men who worked for them. If they somehow couldn't resurrect the sawmill, Pine Lick would become just another ghost town.

A man and a woman rocked from side to side as their wagon rolled as close to the sawmill as they could get without being dragged underwater. Smits recognized Pat "Bull" McManus. His face was covered in blood. His wife was beside him, staring straight ahead, though appearing to see nothing.

Smits and Knoop ran to them.

"Bull, are you all right?" Knoop asked.

The big Irishman reined his horse and looked down at him. "Yes," he replied dreamily. "We got away from it, we did. The storm was after us, but we got away."

Maureen McManus remained silent.

Smits said, "You're bleeding. Where are you hurt?"

Bull's eyes focused. "Bleeding?"

"Yes. Considerably."

Knoop pulled himself up into the wagon and wiped some of the blood away with his shirt. Bull was quiet and compliant, like a small child having his face washed by his mother after a meal. "He must have hit his head on something." Knoop removed his shirt, balled it up, and pressed it into the seeping wound. "I wouldn't be surprised if he has a concussion."

Of that, Smits had no doubt. For Bull McManus to sit there so dumbfounded, his brain had surely been hurt. It was Maureen McManus who concerned him more. She was clearly in shock.

"Let's get you two inside someplace to dry off," Smits said.

Knoop took the reins and drove the wagon to one of the sawmill's smaller buildings that wasn't submerged.

Smits took another glance at the expanding dam. He wondered

how many of the men who worked at the sawmill were in the same condition as Bull. Would they find enough capable hands in time to address the problem?

A trickle of doubt wormed through his mind as he followed the wagon.

When he saw the suit-wearing man riding his horse hell-bent for leather, he stopped. The man was shouting something, but he was too far away to hear.

Despite the distance, Smits could tell whatever he was saying wasn't good news.

Chapter 28

Branch Armstrong eyed the man holding his wife captive. His was a face Branch never thought he'd see again, other than in the occasional nightmare about his short but hellish spell in the Elmira Prison Camp.

Sebastian Bragg had been a low-down, sadistic rat, along with his brother, Henry. They were the prison guards the men feared most, and for good reason.

Seeing Bragg and the twin flames of hatred in his eyes, Branch finally knew the identity of the man he had killed during his escape from Elmira. How the younger brother found him to exact his revenge was a tale he particularly didn't care about. All that mattered was that he was here and had Kate hostage and a gun trained on his son.

"Kick your pistol over here," Bragg said to Mack.

Mack hesitated for a moment, only dropping the gun when Bragg locked his arm across Kate's throat. The gun was swallowed up by the floodwater.

"I would if I could see it," Mack said.

"Don't get smart with me!"

"Let the women and boy go," Mack said with steel in his tone. "You have an issue with me, let's settle it."

Gloria opened her mouth to speak and was slapped across the face by the young man, who looked like an escapee from a madhouse. Mack took a hurried step toward the younger man, but was stopped when he cocked the hammer back on his pistol, which was jammed into the crying boy's ear. "I wouldn't come any closer unless you want to see his brains."

"This is not about you, son," Branch said.

Branch clenched and unclenched his fists. He noticed the older man hadn't taken his eyes off him the entire time.

"You recognize me, prisoner?" Bragg asked.

As much as Branch wanted to throw caution to the wind and throttle both men, he knew he had to keep them talking, buy some time to find a way out of the situation.

"Hard to forget a face that plumb ugly," Branch replied with ice in his voice.

The man made a wolfish smile. "I haven't forgotten your face. No, sir. Not a day since you up and left us. Been looking forward to this little reunion. I'd say it's long overdue."

Even when Bragg worked for the military, where there were rules and expectations, he and his brother were wild cards. They took great delight in making the prisoners' lives miserable, doling out punishments and abuse as if they were drops of sugar candy to children.

Now, with over two decades of hate fomenting in his dark soul, and no one to control him at all, there was no telling what he was capable of doing.

Kate looked at Branch with wide, pleading eyes. She didn't make a move to break free, which was smart of her. Branch was sure that Bragg wouldn't hesitate to put a bullet in her, simply for the pleasure of watching him suffer.

"You've got a score to settle, Bragg, it's with me. Leave everyone else out of it."

"You know this man?" Mack said.

Branch stared hard at Sebastian Bragg. "From another time, in another life."

"Your daddy ever tell you how he was taken prisoner in the war? And that he's a murderer?" Bragg said to Mack.

"He killed my father," the younger man said, his eyes cold and dark and dead.

Branch felt Mack's gaze shift to him, but he wasn't going to take his eyes off Bragg.

"He killed my father, and now we're gonna kill him. Ain't that right, Uncle Sebastian?"

Branch used to carry tremendous guilt for the men he had killed during the war. All were nameless and faceless, men who had gotten too close to the fort and were shot or drowned in the bay. Taking Henry Bragg's life was Armstrong's final act of wartime self-preservation. He'd been proud to fight for the Confederacy, but never proud of the killing that was a necessity of war.

It took ten years for Kate to convince him to confess his sins to a priest and finally receive the absolution he clearly needed to properly move on with his life. He'd gone unwillingly, and had come back a changed man. Setting himself right with God, he dedicated his life to helping others, protecting them when they needed it most.

Now, with his buried past unearthed before him, he thought that old guilt would bubble up again.

It didn't. Instead, Branch was overcome with anger at this demon who had risen from the pit of hell, twisted with bloodlust, threatening his family.

Bragg's deep-set eyes slid from Branch to Mack, from Kate to the paralyzed schoolteacher. "Maybe not right away, Slip," he said. "Might serve him good to suffer the way we have."

A dull, evil light sprang in Slip's eyes. He gripped the boy harder until he yelped. "That could be a lot of fun."

Bragg smiled at Branch. "Yes, that's right, prisoner Armstrong. You thought you could get away with cold-blooded murder. My brother sends his regards." He stuck his pistol in Kate's ribs.

Mack jerked forward, but Branch shouted, "Stop!"

Kate gripped the arm across her throat, but she did not cry out. Branch knew his wife well. She would refuse to play the helpless, terrified victim for Bragg, even if that's exactly how she felt.

"Do whatever you want with me, then," Branch said. "You want to make me pay for what was done during the war, so be it. I could have spent my life looking for the Union soldiers who murdered my comrades when they stormed Fort Fisher. But I moved on. Of course, I saw actual war. I wasn't some entitled officer living far from the front lines, getting to act out his sadistic little fantasies on men who couldn't fight back."

"You shut your mouth!" Sebastian Bragg said, waving his pistol at Branch.

Slip grew visibly excited, giggling as he put his hand around Gloria's throat.

Branch took a tentative step toward Bragg. "You were a coward then, and you still are now. Back then, you hid behind your rank. Now you're hiding behind a defenseless woman."

"Don't push me, you—"

"I'm just speaking the truth. You're not man enough to take me on, so you surround yourself with women and a child. I've spent a good part of my life facing down criminals and miscreants, and you two have to be about the yellowest pair of cusses who ever darkened my doorstep."

Branch could feel Mack's questioning gaze, wondering why he

was riling Bragg and Slip up. What Mack didn't see was a shifting of shadows behind Bragg and Slip.

"You don't get to talk to me that way," Bragg said, seething.

"I think I just did."

There was a long, uncomfortable pause. No one moved, much less spoke. Branch wasn't even sure he was breathing.

"You just bought yourself a whole lot of suffering," Bragg said barely above a whisper, so great was his anger.

He shifted his pistol so it was once again pointing at Kate's side. She remained stoic, but Branch saw the flash of panic in her eyes. He captured her gaze, hoping he could convey that it was now or never to make their move. Kate blinked once, slowly, and took as deep a breath as she could under Bragg's arm lock.

Bragg sucked on his teeth, and his face broke into a sinister smile. "You remember your dim-witted friend, Jimmy?"

A cold block of ice settled in the pit of Branch's stomach. His only regret of the night he'd escaped was not being able to take care of Jimmy. The poor boy's death had stayed with him all these years later as if it had just happened. Branch saw the satisfaction his reaction gave Sebastian Bragg.

"Yes, sir, that Jimmy was about as dull as they came. But he sure liked you. It was touching, seeing you take him under your wing. To be honest, I was surprised that you left him behind that night. Sure, he was dead and all, but to run like a scared jackrabbit when your friend lay dead in the snow. Hoo-boy. That takes a special streak of yellow. If you'd stuck around, you would have been there to see him hanging on the end of a noose the next day. Call it a symbolic gesture for the rest of the inmates to see, so as they didn't get any bright ideas to follow your yellow ass into the cold." Bragg barked a short laugh. "We left him up there until the crows pecked his eyes out and ate his tongue. Gruesome stuff. But necessary."

Branch blinked hard to wash the red from his vision. He had to maintain control. Bragg was baiting him and he knew it.

Bragg jostled Kate and licked the side of her face, eliciting a scowl of disgust. "I assume you have a mite more affection for this lovely woman than that stuttering fool. I wonder what it'll feel like for you if I string her up and let the buzzards have a feast." He shoved the gun underneath one of her breasts. Kate struggled to break free. "No one escapes me, Armstrong. And no one kills my kin and gets away with it. Why don't we slowly walk on out of here and find us some sturdy rope?"

Slip giggled like a hyena, egging Bragg on.

Branch locked eyes with Kate. It was now or never.

Kate reared back with her boot, aiming for Bragg's groin, the exact same moment Branch darted forward, arms outstretched, hoping to grab ahold of the scoundrel's gun. He closed the distance between them in a flash. Kate's bootheel hit home, and Bragg let out a great whoosh of air. He loosened his grip as he doubled over.

Before Branch could get to Bragg and wrestle the gun from his grip, he saw two figures rise out of the darkness behind Bragg and Slip.

Bear O'Hanlon made for Bragg. Elmer Mizner wrapped his mighty arms around the younger man's waist, breaking his hold on the teacher and boy.

No sooner had all parties converged on one another in a tussling pile than there was a loud gunshot. Slip had extracted himself from the tussle and fired a warning shot in the air.

"The next bullet is gonna find flesh," he shouted.

A ragged spider's web of cracks zigzagged from the fresh bullet hole.

"Ah, hell," Slip groaned.

A moment later, the ceiling's water-strained wood collapsed around them.

Chapter 29

Otto was tending to a young girl who was shivering and bleeding from a cut on her arm when he saw the man on horseback tearing into town. The man wasn't paying attention and was on a collision course with them.

Sweeping the girl into his arms, Otto swung her out of the way. The horse galloped past, splattering them with mud.

"Are you all right?" Otto asked the girl.

She nodded her head rapidly, but there were fresh tears in her eyes. After being separated from her parents and surviving a hurricane, the last thing she needed was a brush with death from a careless rider. Otto finished tying a rag on the cut on her arm, but kept his eye on the rider who had stopped and was talking to Whiskey and the lady who ran the brothel. It had been a long time since Otto had been to Belle Dupree's. A man his age no longer had the same urges, and when they did come, they seemed to occur at longer and longer intervals.

"We should find your parents. Where did you last see them?"

The girl pointed down the street. It wasn't much help.

She was a stranger to Otto, so he asked, "Were you staying at the hotel?"

"Yes," she said sheepishly. She appeared to be around ten years old, but the recent trauma had regressed her to acting much younger.

"We will go look for them. Here, take my hand."

No sooner had her tiny hand slipped into his tanned, callused hand than a woman called out, "Jessica!"

"Mommy!"

The girl rushed toward her mother, who knelt in the mud and water and opened her arms. She scooped the girl up and headed back from the direction she'd come, not bothering to acknowledge Otto. Maybe she was afraid of him, a strange Indian holding her daughter's hand. Or more likely, she was swept up with the terror and relief of losing and finding her child.

No matter the reason, it didn't concern him. What he was bothered by was the expression on Whiskey's face when the rider pulled away and headed down the street.

"Who was that?" Otto asked when he caught up to the deputy and madam. Belle Dupree still cut a fine figure, even while wearing what was close to men's clothes.

Whiskey scratched the back of his neck. "He's one of the folks staying at the Arcadian. He says the Stanton Dam is about to plumb bust."

Otto's gaze drifted to the direction of the Stanton Dam. It was too far away to see, but he felt its presence and calculated how long it would take the water to reach the town if it did indeed fall apart.

"Do you believe him?"

"If he's staying at the Arcadian, he's no loon," Belle Dupree answered. "Cheever came to me to form a partnership so we could handle guest services. He told me the type of men who had booked their stay. Rich men. Intelligent men."

"Wealth does not make a man smart," Otto said. "He could be overreacting."

"But what if he isn't?" Whiskey asked.

The three of them fell into silence as three of Dupree's girls worked on wrapping a woman's arm with a splint. Otto spied a few more helping pull a man from a pile of wood. He was alive, but dazed.

"I think we need to tell everyone," Belle Dupree said. "If he's wrong, what harm will it have done? If he's right and we don't give folks a fighting chance, that's something we'll have to live with . . . if we live."

Whiskey appeared torn. He cast his eyes down the street, as if hopeful to find Sheriff Armstrong making his way back, so he could make the decision.

"Where can people go?" Whiskey said. "The whole dang place is a wreck?"

"Higher ground. Away from the river," Otto said.

They looked at the people milling about, either walking around with their eyes to the sky, savoring the passing of the dark clouds, or staring at the ruins of their places or belongings floating along the street.

"I don't think folks is in a mind to listen right about now."

Belle Dupree called her girls, who had been digging through the rubble alongside Tiny Ed, to come over. "Whether they listen or not is on them. What we need to do is at least warn them."

"She is right," Otto said. "Storm like that would have swole Stanton Lake mighty bad. I think I will ride there and see for myself."

"If it breaks, you'd be riding straight into them waters," Whiskey said.

"I have done more foolish things and I am still here. Go spread the word. I am sure you will come across the Armstrongs. Folks will listen to them."

Dupree and her team were already storming down the street, telling everyone to evacuate.

Otto headed for the livery stable, hoping it was still in one piece and his horse was there. He lit a fresh cigar, nervously puffing on it.

He had lied to Whiskey.

Yes, he had done many crazy things in his life, but nothing as danged pigheaded as potentially riding into a wall of water. But he was a man who needed to see things for himself. With any luck, the rich white man was mistaken.

And if the man was right, this could be his last cigar.

Tony Cheever was wild-eyed and disheveled.

Henrik Smits and Jens Knoop listened intently as he told them about the state of the Stanton Dam.

Knoop ran through a flood scenario in his mind, picturing the hammer of water as it smashed into the debris dam beside the sunken sawmill. It would go off like a bomb, sending dangerous shrapnel in every direction seconds before the waters converged and swept the town of Pine Lick clean. He was sure even Noah's ark wouldn't have been able to withstand that kind of catastrophic event.

Breathing hard, Cheever said, "Please pass this along to anyone you come across."

"We will," Knoop said. "You saw the dam. How much longer do you think it'll hold?"

Cheever shook his head. "I have no idea. I'm no engineer. But it's already been breached. Maybe an hour. Maybe a day. Maybe more. Maybe less."

His answer was not reassuring.

"The smart thing is to assume that it will break any minute," Henrik Smits said. "Jens, you should take Bull and Maureen and find some higher ground. I'll find a horse and help Cheever spread the word."

Jens Knoop had spotted several horses running wild when he made his way to the sawmill. None were saddled. All were wild with fear. Smits was no expert horseman.

He was about to tell his partner that it would be better if he rode on, when several men approached the sawmill. They were workers come to inspect the damage to the place that put a roof over their heads and food on their tables. There had to be at least a dozen, with more coming in the distance.

Tony Cheever took off, his horse separating the men.

Jens waved them over.

"You're not going to ask them to break up that dam, are you?" Smits asked.

"If the Stanton Dam is going to collapse, it would be akin to my signing their death warrants. No, there's nothing to be done here, not without knowing how much time we have. I'm going to ask them to fan out and spread the word, and then get themselves to safety as quickly as possible."

Smits said to Bull, "Do you think you can get to Sand Hill?"

Sand Hill was the nearest thing Pine Lick had to higher ground. It marked the end of Pine Lick proper and was made up of a chain of hills lush with trees. There were some areas of Sand Hill that rose pretty high, though getting to the top wouldn't be easy. It was too steep and treacherous for horses. Scaling it would be a hand-and-foot scrabble through soft, muddy terrain.

Bull's dull eyes lazily shifted in the direction of Sand Hill in the distance. "I can get us there."

"Good. You need to get you and your wife to the highest peak as fast as you can."

The semi-slack look on Bull's face didn't give Smits much confidence—although the man had managed to get him and his wife here through the worst of the storm.

"Aye. Let's hope that Cheever is wrong," Bull said before snapping the reins. His wife looped her arm through his and laid her head against his shoulder.

Knoop watched the husband and wife leave, then turned to face their workers, most of them single, from what he remembered, as they gathered around them.

"As you can see, the sawmill is in dire straits," Knoop said to them. "But the worst may not be over. What we need now are volunteers to possibly save the townspeople. We've just gotten word that the Stanton Dam is about to burst. If it does, the devastation to Pine Lick will make what happened during the storm look like a late-spring sun-shower. We need to tell as many people as possible to get to Sand Hill. All the while, we need to be heading in that direction as well. I'm in no way ordering any of you to do this. If you proceeded straight to Sand Hill right this minute, I wouldn't blame you."

More than two dozen men in all remained locked onto Knoop. Most of them were transients who had come to the sawmill to fill their pockets for a few months before moving on. They had no allegiance to Pine Lick. Seeing them willing to risk their lives filled his heart with hope for humanity.

Jens Knoop clapped his hands. "Okay. Here's what we need to do."

Chapter 30

Sheriff Mack Armstrong was momentarily dazed when a chunk of the ceiling clipped the side of his head just as he was reaching for Gloria Amaryllis. The blow had sent him spiraling, saving him from the deluge of wood that smashed into the very spot he'd been standing a second before.

Plaster and wood dust filled the room, but not for long as the rush of rainwater absorbed it all.

Regaining his focus, he looked for his mother, Gloria, and the boy amid the destruction.

He saw the boy first. Archibald Gibbons had managed to get out of the way as well. He sat in a deep puddle of water to Armstrong's right, with his arms wrapped around his knees, his head buried in his arms.

Mack rushed to him and lifted his head. The boy's eyes were wet with tears. "Are you hurt, son?"

He shook his head.

After helping the boy to his feet, Mack moved him to the lobby and pointed to the slanted front doors. "Run on outside. I'll be with you after I find everyone."

At first, Archibald didn't move. Mack put a little steel in his voice and barked, "Go on! Git!"

That startled the boy, and he turned and ran.

Good, Mack thought. *I didn't want to scare him, but I need him out of here before the rest of the place comes down.*

He ran back to the kitchen. It was an absolute disaster area. Where was his family? Where was Gloria?

Prying up wet boards, he started digging, hoping that the men who had the women and boy at gunpoint were buried deep. His heart hammered and his hands bled as he searched for survivors.

Flipping a hunk of plaster away, he saw a hand twitching. "I've got you," he said loudly so the trapped person could hear. He dropped to his knees and dug like a dog looking to hide a bone.

The hand became an arm, and soon he was lifting his mother out of the rubble. She used the water all around them to wipe her face clean, then doubled over, coughing. Mack scooped her into his arms and rushed her outside, barking at the people milling about to move the wood bench that was always in front of the Palace to the street. There, he set his mother down, looking for any visible wounds. She had a knot on her forehead and a tear in her shirtsleeve, but other than that, she appeared to be okay.

"Where's your father?" Kate croaked, still coughing.

"I don't know yet. I'm going back."

"Find them all, Mack."

"Archibald is already safe." He nodded toward the boy, who was staring at Kate. She opened her arms and he melted into them.

Mack turned and scooted back into the hotel. The floor vibrated as the great structure shuddered. He stood still, arms outstretched, waiting to see if he needed to turn tail and head for safety.

When everything settled, he continued on.

Stepping into the kitchen, he spotted Elmer Mizner swaying

slightly on his feet. His face was covered in blood and his shirt was ripped down the middle, revealing several deep cuts on his chest and stomach.

"You all right to get out on your own?" Mack asked him.

Mizner wiped the blood from his eyes. "You find everyone else?"

"Just my mother and the boy."

"Then I'll help you."

Being a blacksmith, Mizner had arms like tree trunks. He made quick work, pulling aside beams and splintered two-by-fours with relative ease.

The younger gunman, Slip, was found next, face down in the water, unconscious but alive. Mack was tempted to cover him back up. Instead, he and Mizner dragged him to the hallway, making sure he had no weapons on him.

Just as they got back to the kitchen, another section of ceiling caved in. This time, it was farther back in the kitchen, but the rumbling caused more of the previous hole to expand.

A slab of wood thunked into the pile of debris. A man grunted. Mack saw his father trying to pull himself out from under a heavy pile of wood.

"There!" He pointed out to Mizner. They rushed to get Mack's father free. The water falling through the hole in the ceiling had been reduced to a trickle. Branch Armstrong had his arms out, and he was trying to push a beam of wood off his lower chest.

"Hold on, Dad, we've got you."

Mack tugged on the wood, but it wouldn't budge.

Mizner grasped it in his meaty hands and, with an angry howl, lifted it up three feet. Mack grabbed his father by his shirt and pulled him before Mizner lost his grip or his arms gave out.

Branch Armstrong kicked his way out as best he could while clinging to Mack.

The second Mizner saw he was free, he let the beam go with a booming crash.

Branch's shirt and pants were in tatters. He looked to be peppered with more cuts and abrasions than Mack could count.

"Your mother?" Branch said when he was on his feet.

"Outside. She'll be okay."

"Who's left?"

"Bear, the man who had the gun on Mom, and Gloria."

The hotel made a collective groan that gave them pause; their eyes darted above. It sounded as if the entire thing was about to give way.

Trying to remember where Bear and Gloria had last been standing, Mack attacked the rubble with a burst of adrenaline. From the sound of things, time was running out. Pretty soon, they would all be buried again, and there would be no second chances.

"Hey," a muffled voice called out.

"Over here," Mizner said, ripping away wood and flipping a love seat, end over end, as if it weighed no more than a wood crate.

He single-handedly yanked Bragg out of the wreckage. The man was stunned for a moment, but his eyes became crystal clear when he spotted Branch Armstrong.

"I was afraid I'd be robbed of my chance to kill you," the man said with a bloody sneer.

Branch Armstrong coldcocked him with a savage right. The man's eyelids fluttered, and he passed out. They dragged him over to his sleeping cohort. Branch patted him down and headed back to the kitchen.

Mizner was already pulling Bear to his feet. Bear looked in need of a hospital. His eyes were practically crossed, and he was cut just about everywhere. His left wrist looked like it might be broken.

"Get him outside," Mack said to Mizner.

He and his father desperately searched for the schoolteacher—Branch realizing that Mack hoped one day to make her his wife.

The sounds of other parts of the hotel coming undone made them flinch while they dug.

Time. Time. Running out of time.

"Gloria! Gloria, can you hear me?"

Mack couldn't remember the last time he'd ever called her just by her first name. Maybe never.

His father heaved a part of the upstairs floor aside and shouted, "I found her!"

Mack hustled over, got on his hands and knees, and tore away at the debris around her, calling her name soothingly, over and over. She didn't respond. Her face was pale, at least the parts of flesh that weren't covered in filth.

"Help me get her legs free, son!"

Mack reluctantly tore himself away from her face and grabbed one end of a slab of flooring. With much grunting, father and son moved it aside. Mack slipped his arms under Gloria's still body. She felt . . . broken.

The back half of the kitchen was covered by an avalanche of debris. The Palace seemed to sway.

"Go! Go! Go!" Branch Armstrong shouted, pushing Mack on the back of his shoulder.

The two men sprinted out of the building as best they could. Gloria was deadweight in Mack's arms, but he felt he could carry her clear to Dallas if need be.

Sam Snodgrass was outside with Kate and Archibald, wiping blood and dirt from them with a handkerchief. Bear was on his rear end in the running water in the middle of the street, cradling his head.

Kate jumped from her seat and told her son to set Gloria down.

Mack saw Elmer Mizner emerge from the hotel with his hands full, dragging both unconscious men by the collars of their shirts. He unceremoniously dropped them into the muck.

"Figured you'd rather see them hang," Mizner said, huffing, with his hands on his hips.

Mack nodded his approval. He still needed to process everything that Bragg had said to his father before the ceiling caved in.

Right now, there were bigger fish to fry. Gloria was yet to show any signs of life. He checked for a pulse at her neck, but his hands were too shaky to trust.

"Back up! Back up!" Snodgrass commanded the people milling around the hotel.

No sooner had he done that than the Palace breathed its last gasp. It folded in on itself with a tremendous crash. A plume of grit spit forth like dragon's breath, temporarily blinding everyone outside.

"Where's the doc?" Mack shouted, indifferent to the hotel's demise. He had Gloria's cold hand in his and was rubbing it.

It was Whiskey who emerged from the cloud of debris billowing through the street. He was shouting, "Y'all have to get out of here! The Stanton Dam is about to give way! Everybody move!"

Chapter 31

Otto rode toward the Stanton Dam as fast as the hoof-sucking mud would allow. At one point, he came across a fella on a horse waving his arms.

"You need to head back! The dam's givin' way!"

"Have you seen it?" Otto asked.

"No, and you'd be foolish to keep ridin' just to get a gander."

The man continued on, heading toward the eastern edge of town. Otto thought he recognized him as one of the sawmill workers. He'd spotted him at the Sawdust quite a few times after his shift. He liked to play cards, but had no poker face. That face now was flooded with fear.

Otto was of a mind to follow the terrible cardplayer. What did he have to gain by going there? If it broke apart, he was likely to get swept up in the tide and float his way to the next world. And if it managed to hold up after the storm, then what? Word was being spread, and he was sure there'd be a mix of panic and apathy, depending on whose ears the warning fell upon.

It all came down to curiosity. During his long life, it had been both his savior and downfall on numerous occasions. If there was a chance that the dam would hold just long enough for him to see it and ride back to town to save his friends and as many people in Pine Lick who would listen, it was worth the risk.

The least he could do was go about his curious pursuit logically. There was slightly higher ground to be found to the right and left of him. If the dam burst, the waters of the man-made lake would flow and swell the Angelina River, while the other half of it would barrel toward Pine Lick through the valley like a funnel. It was best to position himself out of the center of the funnel to give himself a slight chance of not being swept away.

The rain had finally stopped and a few scant rays of sun speared their way out of the lightening clouds.

Funny how that light seemed to be falling on the dam just a few miles ahead. A Christian man might see that as a good sign.

Otto was not a Christian. He saw it for what it was. Sunlight after a storm. Plain and simple.

In the distance, he heard a rumble of thunder.

His horse suddenly reared up, her front legs frantically kicking the air. Otto tightened his grip on the reins and locked his fingers around the horn, hanging on for dear life.

Between the animal's desperate whinnying, he realized the thunder wasn't dying away. It built and built upon itself.

Gaining control of his horse, Otto could now feel a vibration coming up from the ground. The rumbling sound became a dull throb in his chest.

This was not thunder.

"Heyah!"

Otto turned his horse around and headed for town. This time, there was no taking it slow for fear of the horse spraining or breaking its leg in the mud. They were either going to make it or die trying.

He didn't need to see the Stanton Dam to realize all hell had broken loose.

Now all he needed to do was survive his cursed curiosity one more time.

Branch Armstrong felt as if he'd been run over by a stagecoach. He guessed having a hotel fall on you was a pretty fair equivalent.

The first thing he did when he saw Kate was pull her into his arms. For a moment back there, he thought Bragg was going to kill her. And then he thought she had been crushed by the collapsed ceiling. Nearly losing her twice in the blink of an eye was almost too much to bear. He'd never felt so relieved in his life.

"Are you hurt?" he asked her.

"Not so bad," she replied with tears in her eyes. "The fact we're still standing is a miracle."

They had about ten seconds of a reunion before Whiskey came running over yelling about the dam bursting.

Mack was preoccupied with getting Gloria Amaryllis to wake up, if she indeed was just passed out and not deceased. The color of her skin worried him that she'd never open her eyes again.

Branch grabbed his former deputy by the shoulders. "Take a breath. What's this about the dam?"

"Ain't no time to take a breath. Got word that thc storm damaged the dam. It started springing leaks and running over the top. Man from the Arcadian says it's about to go."

Kate's fingers pressed hard into Branch's arm. A few of the people around them had started running in every which direction.

"What man from the Arcadian? Was it Cheever?" Branch asked.

"Not Cheever. A man who is a guest there. Otto said he was going up there to take a look for hisself." Whiskey's eyes darted from Branch to Kate, then to Mack and Gloria, and finally the two unconscious men, with Mizner standing over them. "What happened to y'all?"

"It's a long story," Branch replied. He cast a quick glance at Bragg and Slip.

Sebastian Bragg—a nightmare from the past he'd give anything to forget. He was going to tie Bragg and Slip up and haul them to the jailhouse. To make room, he intended to talk to Mack about letting the cowpunchers free, as long as they agreed to pay for the damage to the Sawdust.

Now, if the dam was really about to blow . . .

"Mack," Branch called over to his son. When he didn't respond, he said his name again, louder.

"Yeah?" Mack replied, his eyes still on Gloria. "We need a doctor."

Branch looked around at the wind-whipped town and figured most folks were in need of one. "If the dam is going to burst, we can't leave those men in the jail to die."

"I can't tell if she's breathing," Mack said in a shaky voice.

Kate brushed their son aside and put a hand on Gloria's wrist and neck.

While she was administering to the schoolteacher, Branch said, "I'm not the sheriff. You need to make the call, son."

Mack Armstrong looked down the street, and then again at Gloria. Archibald stood next to Kate, quietly whimpering. "Could be just another false alarm. How many times have we been told the dam wasn't gonna hold up over the years?"

"And how many times did we get socked in the jaw by a storm like that?"

"Where should we even go?" Sam Snodgrass said. Quite a number of the hotel guests had gathered around the manager, unsure what to do next.

"The highest ground possible that's the closest," Branch said. He wished to hell there could be a way for him to know how much time they had. The town didn't have enough horses to bring everyone quickly to Sand Hill, which seemed the most likely place to find a measure of safety. Across the street was a carriage on its side, one of the wheels badly damaged. He supposed any decent mode of transportation was in similar condition.

“I assume you’re thinking of Sand Hill?”

“Yep. The former mayor was drawing up proper evacuation plans that he would distribute all throughout the town, but when he lost to Tibbs, the plans went with him. I do remember him showing me an evacuation route with Sand Hill as the safest location.”

Snodgrass nodded and turned to face his remaining guests. Clapping his hands, he said, “Everyone follow me. It’s going to be a long walk and a bit of a climb. Stop for nothing. Don’t wander from the group. If you’re hurt or need any kind of assistance, my staff will help you.”

Everyone looked wet and bewildered, but there didn’t seem to be too many injuries among the hotel guests. They had gotten out just in time. Branch did see potential issues with several of the older and younger folks in the crowd. Sam hired good people, and he was sure they would do their best to make sure the guests made it to the top of Sand Hill.

Naturally, there was some grumbling, and a few people voiced their opposition, refusing to go on a hike through the waterlogged streets.

“How do we know this dam is actually going to break?”

“Who’s to say the water from the dam will even make it here?”

“First you nearly kill us with your shoddy hotel. Now you want us to evacuate based on what *this man* is telling you?”

Several sets of eyes slid to Whiskey.

Branch Armstrong knew exactly what they meant when they said “this man.”

Amid the protests, Kate turned to their son with a worried smile. “She’s alive.”

Despite all that had happened and what they were potentially facing, a weight seemed to fall off Mack's shoulders. He took hold of Gloria's hand, set it gently on her chest, and addressed the crowd.

"That man is my deputy, and I would take his word above just about anyone else's."

Whiskey, who had been looking cowed, lifted his head and beamed.

"If you want to wait until the waters get here, it's a free country. Just know that if you see the water making its way to you, you're already dead. That dam is holding back a deep, deep lake that has nowhere else to go but right here. If you enjoy being this side of the grass, I suggest you hurry up and follow everyone else."

Then to Whiskey, he said, "Any chance we can scare up some horses and carts? We have three folks here who won't be walking, and I don't want to task anyone with carrying them and putting multiple lives at risk."

"I'll see what I can find." Whiskey dashed off, passing a pair of sawmill workers who were sounding the alarm about the dam. He conscripted them to help find horses and wagons.

"I'm heading to the jailhouse to let the men out," Mack said. "I'll keep that rapist thief, Kelly, with me. Don't want him getting completely loose. The others, let them head for the hills and never come back, as far as I'm concerned."

"I'll come with you," Branch said.

"No. Like you said before, you're not the sheriff anymore. They're my prisoners and I'll take care of it. You have more important people to watch over. I'll meet you at Sand Hill."

Mack ran toward the jailhouse. Branch was terrified for his son, but also proud of the man he had become.

"We should leave them lashed to a hitching post," Kate said, glowering at Sebastian and Slip.

What Branch had done to escape Elmira was no secret between them. He rarely spoke about it, and not once since his absolution from the priest. The past was the past. Men did horrible things during the war. The only time he thought of the Braggs was in the occasional nightmare he kept to himself.

And now the man of his nightmares was just ten feet away, having nearly killed his entire family. Elmer Mizner stood over the men, keeping a close eye on them.

Kate's suggestion was mighty appealing.

Chapter 32

One of the Arcadian's wealthy guests awoke before the others, who were passed out on velvet couches and chairs in the study. His head pounded something fierce, and it felt as if someone had stuffed his mouth with cotton.

It had been a long while since he'd indulged in fine cigars and even finer hooch. Back home in Chicago, there was no time to give yield to his minor vices, much less suffer the consequences the next day.

Staggering out of the study, because his head still spun like a wobbly top, he closed the door behind him and called out, "Hello? Cheever?"

He checked his pocket watch and saw it was going on late morning. Surely, there should be someone up and about, waiting to see to his needs. What was the point of paying all this money only to be left to his own devices?

Walking down the hallway, he looked out the window and saw that the storm had mercifully passed. Why, there was even a sliver of sun out.

"Fresh air. I need fresh air," he mumbled, thinking a tumbler of water would be nice as well.

Outside, the air was still, but damp. The front lawn had been turned into a swamp overnight.

Cupping his hands over his mouth, he called out for Cheever again.

Nothing.

"What kind of a business is this dolt running? Who up and leaves his guests with no one around to assist them?"

Stepping into the grass, his feet sank in the mud. He loudly lamented the damage it was doing to his shoes and swore he would make Cheever reimburse him for them. He trudged through ankle-deep mud, heading for his cabin.

To his horror, where the cabin had stood the night before, there was just a pile of smashed wood. Two other cabins had suffered the same fate.

The pain in his head intensified. What a disaster. This trip was supposed to give him the respite his doctor had urged him to take before he had a stroke or worse. Well, this wasn't helping things. Not one bit.

Walk.

He'd begun taking walks, at his doctor's insistence, to both clear his head and get his blood flowing properly. With his shoes and pants already destroyed, there was no sense complaining about his circumstances. Just walk. Maybe he'd come across Cheever and give him a piece of his mind, if not a sock in the jaw.

With each step, there was a loud squelch and plop as he broke from the ground's greedy embrace. He decided to walk to the lake and see if there was a chance he could maybe do some fishing later. A storm like that probably drove all the fish into hiding. No matter. A pole in hand and some hair of the dog could be the only things to salvage this disastrous trip.

Having not paid attention to the surrounding area when he'd

arrived by carriage, he found himself quickly lost and sliding haphazardly down a grassy hill. The main house of the Arcadian slipped out of sight. His arms pinwheeled as he struggled to stay upright.

He came to a rest at the bottom of the hill, just before falling into a roaring brook.

"That was close."

His headache was instantly forgotten when he realized this was no brook.

Looking up, he saw that he was at the base of the Stanton Dam. Water ran like a pair of raging rivers along both sides of what was clearly a crumbling structure. He had a feeling that if he took just one step forward, he would be up to his chest and swept away.

Backing up as best he could, he swallowed hard to keep the panic from clogging his throat.

The earth beneath his feet rumbled. Or was that just the rushing water?

Geysers of water spilled from breaks in the dam's surface, shooting through the thin waterfall as the lake behind it crested the top.

He thought he saw the center of the dam bow outward. There followed a tremendous cracking sound, rising above the roaring water.

Desperate to get as far away from the dam as humanly possible, he scrabbled up the slope and lost his footing. His face splashed into the mud. He flopped about, accidentally sucking in a lungful of water.

By the time he rolled onto his back, the entirety of the dam gave way with an explosion the likes he'd never heard before, even having fought in the war and surviving several cannon bombardments.

There was just enough time to raise his arms to cover his face in futility before the wall of liberated water came crashing through. It hit the man head-on, obliterating him in an instant, crushing his bones to dust, before barreling down the valley.

* * *

Otto pushed his horse as hard and fast as it would go, desperate to climb away from the natural slope of the land between the dam and downtown Pine Lick. The pressure in the air had changed, becoming fuller than a ripe tick. He opened his mouth wide to make his ears pop.

He heard the contents of Stanton Lake set loose, and it scared the living hell out of him.

Many times in his life, he had been faced with death. But being on the wrong end of a gun or knife was nothing compared to the wrath of nature breaking free from its bonds.

He could feel this in the marrow of his bones. The sound was like that ringing of the end of the world the old preacher he'd followed out of curiosity over in Jolene used to speak about, spittle on his lips like a frothing rabid dog. Otto never cared much for the white man's religion, especially their desire for an end of times. He thought it all foolish nonsense.

The ground rumbled just like it had when he'd been in that earthquake out in San Francisco twenty years back. There hadn't been much in the way of damage, but feeling the solid earth move under one's feet had a way of setting a man back and making him realize how insignificant he was in the grand scheme of things.

Whipping his head back to see if the water was upon him yet, Otto spotted several other people on horseback below and to his left. He waved his hat, urging them to head his way. He didn't know if his vantage point was any safer, but anything was better than lower ground.

They didn't see him, or maybe they were too panicked to care.

Otto's cigar had long gone out, but he clamped down hard on it with his teeth. Mud spattered his face, sometimes in great clots. He wiped it away as best he could, all the while putting the spurs to his horse. He realized there'd been no need to do so, since the horse had the good sense to know death was coming for them.

On one of his sojourns to California, he'd been beside the mighty Pacific when a massive storm had advanced from the unseeable expanse of the ocean. It kicked up the salty water mightily, creating incredible waves that bashed and churned on the rocks.

The sounds the ocean made that day had burned a permanent imprint on Otto's brain. He swore he'd never encounter anything quite as horrific ever again, even counting the intensity of lightning storms that sent bolts of death from above.

He was wrong.

Out of the corner of his eye, he saw the wall of water tearing through the valley. The thundering it made felt as if it would shake his heart from its place in his chest.

Trees were smashed and swallowed up in less than a second. They joined the brown churning mass of water and debris, helping it grow as it advanced.

His horse whinnied pitiably.

He wished he could comfort her.

Instead, he would have to ride her until she had nothing left—if either of them managed to survive.

Between his position and the center of town were plenty of homes and many pine trees that would only fuel the liquid fire. He couldn't see anything or anyone withstanding the killer wave.

He looked into the valley again and saw the roaring tide swallow up the folks trying to get away. One moment, they were there; the next, they were gone, soundlessly getting sucked into the forty-foot-high wall of death.

Otto was glad he couldn't hear their screams.

"Come on, you old nag!"

The horse pushed itself even harder. Otto no longer thought about the potential disaster if it made a misstep. He existed in pure survival mode. How long that survival would last seemed fleeting at best.

* * *

Mack Armstrong ran to the jail, his boots sloshing through the river that had erupted down the center of Main Street. He forced himself to ignore the many folks calling for him as he passed scene after scene of devastation. There were walking wounded, groups of people trying to dig folks out from the rubble, and broken, bloody bodies.

The worst was when he passed by a dead horse lying atop a pair of broken legs. Small broken legs. He didn't want to think about what child could be under there.

Whenever he heard his name, he shouted back, "Get to Sand Hill as fast as you can!"

A few heeded his warning.

Most kept about their business, paying him no mind. Those who ignored him most were Pine Lick townsfolk who had heard the song and dance before.

He wanted to shake them and remind them that all those past false alarms had not come after a dang hurricane!

The jailhouse was miraculously still standing, though the roof was shot to hell. The moment he stepped inside, the prisoners all spoke at once, with wet hands clinging to the bars trying to shake them.

"Pipe down!" Mack spat.

"I overheard someone saying the dam is gonna break," one of the cowboys said. "You can't leave us in here to die, Sheriff."

The others loudly asserted their support.

Mack waved for them to shut their mouths.

"I heard the same thing, which is why I'm letting you go."

Cheers erupted from the cell. It was the only place in all of Pine Lick that resonated with the sounds of revelry.

Before he inserted the key in the lock, Mack said, "I'm advising you to head straight to Sand Hill. It's the highest ground around and just about the only place you'll be safe."

"I'm heading back to Arkansas," one of the men said.

"I doubt you'll even find your horse. Or any horse, for that matter," Mack said. "No telling how much time we have before the water makes its way here, so I'd skedaddle like the devil himself is hot on your heels. Now take a step back, all of you."

The next few moments were going to be precarious. Once he opened that door, the men could easily rush and overtake him, maybe give him a little payback. Even lock him up in the cell and leave him to die.

He eyeballed Kelly the thief, whose gaze was fixed on the keys in his hand. He was the one he really had to worry about. Mack slipped his gun out of its holster, inserted the key, gave it a turn, and took two quick steps back while his gun was aimed at the cell.

Three of the cowboys fought to get out at the same time, practically wedging themselves between the bars. Another pushed them from behind and they popped out like a champagne cork. They rushed out the door, paying him no mind.

The last cowpoke emerged, tipping his hat to Mack. "Much obliged, Sheriff. Not everyone would give a bother about a bunch of prisoners, considering all that's happened and might happen next."

Mack still kept his gun at the ready. "Well, it's not as if you were in here for a hanging offense. I'm not of a mind to let men die just for being inconsiderate and reckless."

The cowboy grinned. "And the grub wasn't bad, neither. Good luck."

"You too. I think we're all going to need it."

The cowboys left the building, which left the thief and almost rapist. This was a man Mack would gladly see swinging from the end of a rope. Before Kelly took one step out of the cell, Mack said, "You're staying with me. The law ain't done with you yet."

As he opened his mouth to protest, Mack stopped him short. "Or I could just lock you back up and let you drown."

"No, sir," Kelly replied, bowing his head. "I never learned to swim."

Mack didn't know many men who could swim. Fear of drowning

was a very common thing. Judging by the terrified look in the man's eyes, he sensed it might be the worst of ways to die.

"That's not my concern. But if I let the water take you, I'd deprive the Maxel family the pleasure of seeing you swing. Turn around and put your hands behind your back."

Mack roughly slapped a pair of handcuffs on the man and spun him around to face him. With his gun jammed under Kelly's chin, he said, "You try anything and I'll shoot your kneecaps off and leave you for the flood. *Comprende?*"

He nodded.

Mack roughly grabbed him by an arm and led him out the door.

That's when he heard what sounded like a bomb going off in the distance. The earth and sky quaked. Everyone on the street stopped what they were doing and cast their eyes in the direction of the Stanton Dam in the unseen distance.

Mack's heart skipped a beat.

The dam really did break.

He had no idea how long it would take the waters of Stanton Lake to reach town, but of one thing he was sure.

They were all doomed.

Chapter 33

Mayor Eli Tibbs thought there was an earthquake. He'd passed out in a chair on the front porch and was woken up by a deep bass rumbling. His house seemed to sway from side to side, and glass exploded out of just about every window.

The frightful start brought a fresh wave of pain to his chest. He bolted upright and looked at the ground of the front yard, expecting a massive hole to appear and swallow everything up.

It didn't, but the rumbling persisted.

Sweat broke out all over his head as he fought against the stabbing pain in the center of his chest.

Ellie!

How long had he been out? All he could remember was stepping outside, feeling as if lightning had struck him, and then waking up to a fresh new hell.

He struggled to get up from the chair, heading back inside.

Tibbs knew he was having a heart attack. On Christmas morning when he was just a boy, he'd watched his own father die of one.

All he could do now was pray that his own wasn't fatal. If something happened to him now, what would become of his wife? The townsfolk would be concerned about their own well-being as they recovered from the storm. How long would it be until someone decided to check on him and Ellie?

Tibbs needed both hands on the handrail to pull himself from step to step. He winced when the stabbing pain radiated from his chest to his arm. His left hand went completely numb. His lungs clawed for each breath.

Have to get to Ellie.

The house continued to rock, making navigating the stairs even more difficult. Wood cracked and snapped. At one point, he lost his footing and would have tumbled to the bottom if he hadn't had the rail in a death grip.

"Ellie!"

He wasn't sure if he wanted her to know he was coming, or crying out to her for help. Not that she was in any position to help him. But he was scared and wanted only the comfort of his wife.

Huffing with each step, Tibbs swallowed the pain and fear and made it to the landing. His knees almost gave out, and he slumped against the wall. Using the wall as a kind of crutch, he staggered down the hall and into Eleanor's room.

In two faltering steps, he reached for the bedpost, missed, and flopped onto the bed.

Eleanor's eyes fluttered open. She looked about dreamily until she saw him on his side, next to her.

"What . . ." she croaked.

Tibbs shakily lifted his arm and took her cool, dry hand within his moist, clammy one. "I'm . . . here, Ellie. I'm here," he wheezed.

There was confusion in his wife's gaze. She parted her dry lips, but no other words came out.

A hot wind blew from one of the shattered windows, billowing the heavy drapes. Tibbs knew they weren't safe in the house if the earthquake persisted.

Unfortunately, there was no way he was going to be able to carry Eleanor down the stairs and outside.

All he could do was hold her hand and reassure her that everything was going to be all right. The illness and the drugs kept her from comprehending what was going on around them.

He just hoped she understood deep down that he was with her, and wouldn't leave her side.

And despite his reputation among a faction of the citizens of Pine Lick, he *did* care about them, never more so than now. He knew there had to be folks in as bad or even worse shape than he and Eleanor were. If the ground didn't stop shaking, it would only get worse for Pine Lick.

All that hard work, brought down by acts of nature as oblivious and uncaring of the human condition as a bull to a fly on its hide.

Plates crashed downstairs. He could picture Eleanor's hutch falling down, spilling all her fine china onto the floor. If she knew that, her heart would break. She so loved her china, which had been handed down from her mother.

Eleanor closed her eyes and her hand slipped from his own and she lapsed back into sleep.

It was so tempting to do just the same. The pain in his chest had lessened somewhat, though he was not going to delude himself into believing that his heart's protestations were over.

The painting of flowers in a vase fell off the wall opposite the bed.

Eli Tibbs gritted his teeth and pushed himself off the bed. He took small, shaky steps to the window. If he was going to die, he wanted to take one last look at his next-to-greatest achievement, other than marrying Eleanor. He realized what he might see would haunt him beyond death, but a man never flinched from his duty.

He had to grip the window frame for a moment and catch his breath. His goal had been to make his way across the room to the window that overlooked the sawmill and pathway to town.

What he now saw stopped his heart cold.

A massive wall of water, taller than the house itself, taller than anything he'd ever seen, was barreling their way. He saw entire trees churning in the frothing mass. Great clods of earth and shattered structures flipped in and out of the deadly wave. For a brief moment, a huge boulder, which would have taken a hundred men to simply move it, slipped in and out of the roiling water.

With his eyes wide with wonder and terror, the fact that he could no longer draw a breath didn't so much as dawn on him.

He turned to his wife, sleeping so peacefully.

As he reached for her, his legs gave way. His mouth opened and closed, desperate for air, to tell Eleanor one last time he loved her. To let her know that her suffering was at an end.

He felt not a thing as the wave demolished the house with a hammer strike that would frighten the devil himself.

Branch Armstrong didn't need to see the waters of Stanton Lake to know it was coming their way. There was something in the air, a heaviness that he had felt seconds before Fort Fisher was pounded by cannon fire.

Whiskey had managed to round up a dilapidated cart and one terrified horse. They loaded Sebastian Bragg and his young accomplice, but not before tying them up well. The younger man awoke with a start when Elmer Mizner dropped him on the hard wood planking of the cart.

"Wait? What the hell are you doing?" he protested, twisting back and forth to loosen the rope tied around his wrists and ankles.

"Saving your life," Branch said. "Which is more than you deserve."

When Slip spotted Bragg next to him, still out like a light, he said, "If you killed him, you might as well kiss that pretty wife of yours goodbye."

When his eyes slid to Kate, who was busy helping Bear O'Hanlon lift the teacher up, a wicked grin spread on his mud-caked face. Branch's hand went for his gun. He fought mightily with himself not to put the man down like a rabid dog.

Instead, he flipped the gun in his hand and struck the man on the side of the head, knocking him out again. "That's more like it."

As they delicately set Gloria Amaryllis in the cart, Kate said, "I don't like the idea of her riding right next to the likes of them."

Branch immediately pulled the horse along. "Unfortunately, we're out of options. Hopefully, she wakes up at some point and is able to walk the rest of the way to Sand Hill. Until then, I'm more than happy to keep those two quiet as church mice."

The gravity of the moment masked the fact that Branch's limp was nonexistent at the moment. He was too worried to register the usual pain and discomfort.

People rushed past them, some carrying heavy suitcases and dragging children along. A man without any legs—his name was Aaron Beauregard and he'd lost his limbs in the war—used his wooden crutches expertly, picking his way through the mud, crowds, and debris scattered everywhere. He'd always been fiercely independent, working odd jobs to keep his room paid for and whiskey flowing. There were quite a few others in town, victims of the war, who were not quite as fortunate or able. Branch wondered what would happen to them, coming to the quick and sad conclusion that unless someone lent a hand, they would perish.

He wished he could save them all, but he had his family to think about.

And speaking of family, Mack should have been back by now. Kate kept flicking glances behind them, waiting for their son to catch up.

"He'll be here," Branch reassured her.

The sun parted the clouds above them, providing an odd juxtaposition to their situation. All around them was destruction, with more to come. If they could block all that out, they would swear it was a beautiful summer afternoon, one where the heat and humidity had finally broken.

"I know," Kate said.

"I could go back for him," Whiskey said.

"He knows the way. There's only one direction we all need to be heading, and it's that way," he said, pointing toward the distant hills.

Bear and Mizner walked on either side of the cart. They had taken it upon themselves to keep an eye on the prisoners. Branch sure appreciated it. He'd given them both permission to use force if Sebastian or Slip woke up and started jawing.

People sped past them, anxious to reach Sand Hill. The impending sense of doom was palpable. Branch tugged on the reins, urging the horse to pick up the pace.

"What about them?" Kate asked. "If the dam breaks, they'll be lucky to make it out alive."

He turned to where she was looking. A group of people milled about the tannery. They shook their heads at the crowd walking down the street. One of them even called out, "What, you ain't had enough for one day? The sky already fell!"

"If the dam breaks, they won't make it out alive."

Branch recognized the man. It was Albert Whimple, retired from the sawmill on account of losing one too many fingers to be useful. He was a notorious gossip who had something to say about everyone and everything. He wasn't exactly a bad man. The hand he'd been dealt had been far from four kings. But he'd also been around long enough to have endured the passel of false alarms that had riled up the townsfolk for nothing.

"It's not the sky that's falling," Branch said. "It's the dam. You all best follow us."

One of the men held up a jug. "Maybe after we finish this."

That got a round of laughs from his friends.

Branch continued speaking. "One thing I learned is you can't help a fool."

The one person he wished he could help was Otto. Hearing that his old friend had gone to check on the dam, he worried mightily. Otto may have had more lives than a cat, but sooner or later, man and feline were sure to run out.

More and more people were jamming the main road, wading through water and mud, desperate to get out of town. Even so, Branch figured maybe a fourth of the town would refuse to evacuate, either out of stubbornness, apathy, or inability.

There was heavy splashing behind them. Branch and Kate turned around to see Mack towing a cuffed prisoner.

"Guess you didn't see it fit to set him loose," Branch said, doing his best to hide his relief.

"After what he did to Lana Maxel? I've got bigger plans for him."

The thief stopped walking. Mack tugged at his arm.

"What if I refuse to go along with you?" Kelly said defiantly.

Mack said, "I could do one of two things. Tie you up to that tree over there and see if you make it through the flood." He unholstered his pistol and aimed it at the man's crotch. "Or I can just blow your business off and leave you here to bleed out. Your choice."

The man's Adam's apple bobbed. He cast his eyes to the ground and resumed walking.

"Good choice," Mack said. He then saw Gloria in the cart and rushed to her, brushing a lock of hair from her forehead. "She hasn't woken up yet?"

"Not yet," Kate said. "But she will. We just need to keep her safe."

What sounded like rolling thunder emanated from the west.

Except unlike thunder, it didn't dissipate. Instead, it grew louder . . . and stronger.

"It's coming!" someone in the crowd yelled.

That was enough to bring about a chorus of panicked cries. People who were walking started to run, and those who were running began to sprint.

The horse whinnied as men, women, and children piled along either side of the cart. It reared up, and Branch had to put all his weight to bring it under control.

It had been many years since Branch had been in the middle of a stampede. And that's exactly what this had become—except with people, not livestock.

Kate suddenly peeled away from his side. "Get away from her!"

She bullied her way through the throng, and for a heart-stopping moment, Branch lost sight of her. When she reemerged, she was carrying a tiny girl, who had curled herself up into a ball.

"They were going to trample the poor thing to death!"

Branch wondered where the girl's parents were. Probably the first to walk over her.

"Do you want me to take her?"

"You have enough to deal with the horse. She's about as heavy as a bird." Kate cooed into the girl's ear, reassuring her that she was going to be all right.

"I have to get folks to settle down and get to Sand Hill orderly, before more people get killed," Mack said.

"You don't stand a chance," Branch said over the yammering crowd.

Whiskey was bowled into by a pair of fleeing men. He pushed them off and clung to the side of the wagon. "These people have lost their minds!"

The "thunder" had gotten so bad, Branch could feel it in the center of his chest. No, they hadn't lost their minds. They just wanted to make sure they didn't lose their lives.

And with the slow time Branch was making, he worried that they'd never make it to Sand Hill in time.

Bear and Mizner squared their shoulders and defended their position from the manic crowd. It would be easy to lose one's footing and get stomped to death in this madness.

Then Branch heard something he hadn't since his days in the army.

Waves.

Only this time, it wasn't the Atlantic Ocean lulling him to sleep.

It was the call of a wall of certain death, announcing its presence in Pine Lick.

"Run!" Branch barked.

His small band followed his lead, careful not to trample over anyone who had succumbed to the crowd. Of that, there were too many. Branch spotted too many broken legs and arms to count, mixed with cries for help.

All he could do was keep repeating one solitary word.

"Run!"

Chapter 34

"We have to go!"

"There could be others that need our help."

Reverend Jake Smiley tugged at his wife's arm. Everyone around them had left, either to the other side of town for Sand Hill, or stubbornly back to their homes. That madam had gathered her working girls to follow her lead and find higher ground. The giant of a man who looked over them had carried the still-unconscious woman in his arms as if she weighed no more than a raccoon.

Matilda fought against him, insisting on inspecting the collapsed houses and businesses, searching for survivors. With the departure of the working girls, the one who seemed to know something about nursing had also gone. The best he or Matilda could do would be to pray over someone who'd been hurt.

He could feel and hear the oncoming flood. Even the air smelled different. It had that bottom-of-the-pond stink that reeked of deep, dark mud and still water.

Though the water heading their way was anything but still.

"There's no time," he insisted. "If we're here when the floodwaters come, we won't be any good to anyone."

"Need I remind you we were put on this earth to serve?" Her words cut him deeply, and the scowl on her face rocked him. It wasn't just the anger in her eyes. It was clear she had lost her faith . . . in him.

The sad thing was, he'd lost faith in himself. Fear had taken him in its cold, inexorable grip. He found it impossible to think of anything but finding a way to keep himself alive. He did not think God was going to save them. If anything, Pine Lick on this day was the very definition of the word "godforsaken." Maybe if they'd had more parishioners. Maybe if the town hadn't been built on the promises of something as ungodly as fortune.

God had turned His back on Pine Lick today, and had let the devil have his way.

And Jake Smiley, still haunted by his childhood trauma, was not up for the task of battling the devil, much less tending to any possible faithful who needed comfort and healing.

He steeled himself and said to his wife, "And need I remind you, if we're dead, we cannot serve anyone!"

The rumbling beneath their feet matched the wild beating of his heart. Matilda locked her fiery gaze at him. No words were spoken. No words needed to be. No matter what he said, no matter how much he insisted, she was not going to leave.

Which left him with a choice.

An almost-Abrahamic choice.

He swore he could now actually hear the rush of water in the shortening distance. His head swooned and his mouth went dry. Though his hand held on to his wife's arm, he couldn't feel a thing.

Any moment now, he was going to pass out. Even on the precipice of fainting, he knew that to do so would spell his certain death.

Move, damn you! Move!

Reverend Smiley shook his head violently and refocused his eyes. "I'm not asking you to come with me. I'm telling you."

Matilda cocked her head, hearing the rampaging waters of Stanton Lake as well. But unlike him, it didn't send her into a spiral of terror.

They both turned when they heard a hoarse voice cry out for help. It came from the ruins of the barbershop, to their right. The only thing still standing was the red, white, and blue–striped pole.

"Help . . . me. I'm hurt. Hello?"

Matilda's lips tightened into a grim line. Her eyes dared him to continue asking her to leave.

Smiley willed his fingers to relax their numb grip on her arm.

"You can't save him," he said quietly.

"Then the least I can do is make sure he doesn't die alone."

Matilda turned her back on him and hurried to the pile of wood that was the barbershop.

The reverend bowed his head until he was staring at the new river that had formed down the main road. He then looked eastward, seeing the backs of the last row of people on their evacuation march.

With the sky charged with the reverberation of the pounding waters, he wearily cast his eyes in the direction of the Stanton Dam, and their demise.

Wood thunked as Matilda tossed pieces aside, assuring the buried man that she was going to find him, to be calm, to know that he was going to be all right. She asked him if he knew his prayers. The man said yes.

"Pray out loud, for God, and for me, so I can focus on your voice and find you."

The man began to recite a Hail Mary. Matilda doubled her effort to pull him free from the wreckage.

Smiley's heart, in danger of running completely off the tracks, miraculously fell into an almost-normal, steady rhythm. He felt a warmth spread from his chest to his extremities.

In place of his mind-bending panic, there was now a sense of awe of his wife's faith, courage, and devotion. And peace. Despite everything, for the first time since the storm had begun the day before, Jake Smiley was at peace.

He ran to his wife's side, grabbed a block of wood, and tossed it aside.

They caught each other's eye, and for a flicker, they smiled.

The man beneath the ruins began another Hail Mary.

Husband and wife pulled at shattered planks of wood until their hands bled and dozens of splinters were embedded in their flesh. All the while, they spoke words of comfort to the suffering man.

They no longer heard the approaching flood.

Nor did they feel it, even when the first cold spray tickled the backs of their necks.

While Jens Knoop had told his men to spread the word of the dam's imminent collapse while making their own way to higher ground, he thought about all the people who lived in the direction of the dam. Would they know what was coming? Had the two men who had warned them taken the time to seek out those homesteads that were off the beaten path?

He had to assume there were plenty of people who, at this moment, were assessing damage to their homes, livestock, and land, appreciative that the worst had come to pass.

Knoop was with Sean Clarke, who maintained the steam engines that were the heart of the sawmill. Sean was a lithe Irishman, with a keen mind for anything mechanical. He could sense when things were about to break, and was quick with devising a way to repair them. Sean was single, barely in his twenties, and tireless.

When Knoop suddenly stopped and looked behind him, Sean said, "What? Is it comin'?"

"No, not yet. You go on ahead. There's something I need to do."

"I'll come wit' you."

"It's best you go on. It will give me one less thing to worry about. Okay?"

The young man was silent, his eyes furtive. Clarke had always been loyal, working long hours without complaint when the great steam engines became bothersome. Knoop appreciated the young man's devotion, though now he didn't want his loyalty to cost him his life.

"Now go. I'll meet you and everyone at Sand Hill."

Clarke turned, took several steps, and spun around. "I'm sure I can help you."

Knoop gave him a fatherly smile. "I'm sure you could. But I need to do this alone. Go on. There are people in need of saving."

Once Sean Clarke was out of sight, Knoop started running. He tried to map out the various homes he remembered seeing during his many rambles around Pine Lick. The first place he came upon was a farm. The barn had collapsed, and half of the house's roof had been blown away. A trio of cows chewed at the muddy grass by the wooden fence.

Knoop hopped the fence and hurried to the farmhouse. The people who lived there—he remembered a family consisting of a husband, wife, and two teenage girls—were nowhere to be seen. There was an open door to a root cellar. They must have survived the storm down there and left when it passed.

The whinny of a horse lifted his spirits. He found it tied to a tree at the back of the house. There was no saddle to be found, and there wasn't time to pick through the wreck of the barn.

It took some careful coaxing, but Knoop was eventually able to slip onto the horse's back.

Riding bareback at a steady gallop, Jens Knoop went about the outskirts of town, urgently telling people to find higher ground. He came across a myriad of folks, some dazed and wounded, but most having weathered the storm without issue. Not everyone heeded his warning. As much as he wanted to plead with the doubters, he knew he had to move on and hope to find others who would believe him.

Fortunately, quite a few of the people worked in the sawmill and expressed their thanks to him for taking the time to alert them. They were quick to gather their family and possessions and head for the hills.

He'd been forty minutes or so into his mission to save as many people as he could when he heard the heavy explosion in the distance. The horse reared back and threw him, tearing off in the direction from which they'd come.

Sharp bolts of agony raced up Knoop's leg.

Writhing on the wet ground, he reached for his ankle, knowing it had snapped in half. He didn't dare take his boot off. It was the only thing holding the damn joint together.

Bright rays of sun lit his face. He looked up at the blue sky and said, "Now what am I expected to do?"

Lying as he was on the ground, he felt the deep rumbling rising up from the earth. There was no one in sight to help him.

To his left was a tall tree. He clawed at the ground, dragging himself to the tree. If he could somehow make it there and climb to the top, maybe he'd manage to stay above the water *if* it came this way.

Of course, it will come this way, you fool, he thought as salty sweat dripped into his eyes, and his shoulder muscles quivered with exertion. *You're in a bowl in a valley that leads right to the dam. If you don't move faster, you might as well start holding your breath now and pray.*

The going was slow, no matter how much he cajoled himself. At one point, he tried to stand. The second he put any pressure on his damaged leg, it went out from under him, and he was back in the damp.

With the pain increasing so much he thought he might pass out, Knoop unlooped his leather belt and stuck it in his mouth. Biting down so hard he thought his teeth might saw it in half, he screamed as he scrabbled for the tree.

Now he could hear the rush of water.

It would be here any moment.

His shaky fingers gripped the thick bark. Bright sparks flashed before his eyes as he pulled himself up, desperate to take a moment to catch his breath, but there wasn't even a second to spare. The leaves above him shook and a sharp breeze chilled the sweat on his flesh.

Using his arms and one good leg, he reached for a limb and climbed. His peal of agony was so extreme at one point, the belt fell from his mouth.

All the while he climbed, his eyes flicked to the west, waiting to see the flood of water rolling toward him.

Knoop climbed higher and higher, the branches getting thinner to the point where he wondered if the next level would be able to support his weight. When he was near the top, he lashed both arms around the trunk, pressed his face to the rough bark, and closed his eyes while trying to catch his breath.

There was nowhere to go. Somehow, he'd made it. The question now was, did he want to remain like this, or open his eyes and face his fate?

The water was so close now, the tree began to sway.

His eyes snapped open. Knoop offered a quick prayer that the roots were deep and would hold.

Then he saw the massive wall of water.

It was worse than he could have imagined.

The crest of the wave was twice the height of the tree. He may as well have just tucked himself into a ball at the base of the tree and counted the seconds left to his life.

His mouth opened in a silent O.

There were no words to say, much less think, when faced with such a gargantuan representation of nature's fury.

Roiling within the water were huge trees that had been easily uprooted as the water carved its deadly path to the center of Pine Lick.

It was an absolutely amazing . . . and horrifying sight to behold.

Jens Knoop doubted anyone would survive this flood.

Seconds before the wall of water overcame him, an enormous boulder spit from the sheer wall of water. It rocketed at the tree, snapping it in half.

Knoop lost his grip, but he never hit the ground.

The water grabbed him first, pulverizing his bones to dust until he was a lifeless sack tumbling in the ever-growing wall of destruction.

Chapter 35

Otto spotted a trio of grizzly bears ahead. They were fleeing the incoming flood as well, and they didn't need someone to tell them it was coming.

He was always amazed, but never surprised, by the intelligence of animals. White men were too ignorant to appreciate the higher levels of nature. He supposed that ignorance is what shielded them from shame and regret while they plundered the land.

His horse, who was normally skittish of bears, even when she managed to get downwind of one, plowed straight for them without a care. Soon they were galloping right alongside them.

The grizzlies paid them no mind. For a brief moment, man, horse, and bear were all united in attempting to outrun death. Their heavy musk assaulted Otto's nose. They grunted each time their front paws crashed into the soft ground.

Bears were fast as all get-out when they needed to be. That being said, his horse was faster, and soon the grizzlies were behind them. Otto was sure that if he was somehow thrown from his horse, the bears would pass him right on by without a second look.

The air literally vibrated with the flood of water at their backs. Every now and again, he cast a wary glance behind him, but so far, it was still too far away to see.

That was a very good thing. Otto was sure that once the water was within his sight, so was the end of his life.

He'd been around spontaneous floods in narrow arroyos and near rivers pregnant from sudden rainstorms. Otto knew the danger that unchecked water could wreak. He'd seen a man drown as a wave swept him off his mount and dragged him to the dark depths.

In all his years and all his wild experience, he'd never *felt* an oncoming calamity like this. Without seeing a thing, he knew this flood was on an entirely different level. He could feel the pulsing of it in his heart and bones, smell the foul water riding the air. His ears rang with its unbridled roar.

He thought of the Armstrongs, and Whiskey, and the many good people of Pine Lick. His time here had been the longest he'd spent in any one place his entire life. Part of it was concession to age. There came a point where a man got tired of roaming untamed land, coiled for the worst at every turn.

But Pine Lick had been a good place. It wasn't just a white man's land. Folks from other tribes, Mexico, and other countries had all converged there to make a life for themselves. Normally a loner, Otto had been drawn to Branch Armstrong and that pretty wife of his. He felt that even though their lives had been markedly different, they were also brothers in a way.

With any luck, they would find a way to make it through the flood. If there was any goodness left in this world, the Armstrongs would live to see another day.

The sun had parted the clouds, indifferent to the chaos below.

Otto thought he felt rain pattering on the back of his neck. He looked up and saw blue sky dotted with a few puffy white clouds.

Then he looked back, and down into the valley.

The flood was right there, a monstrous wave that was the biggest thing he'd ever seen, aside from the mountains he'd ridden past in his youth. It sounded as if it were alive and filled with unmitigated anger.

Despite his having ridden to the top of the valley's slope, the wave was higher.

Behind him, he heard the bears howl in surprise and agony, and then their voices were cut off.

"Come on, girl!" he urged his horse.

There was no way they could outride or escape the wave.

But if he was going to die, he would do it while riding as he had in his younger years, flat out while his heart thrummed to the pounding of hooves.

James Winston, owner of the Lady B Livery, had crawled atop his house, waiting for the inevitable. The storm had knocked the doors off the livery, and try as he might, he hadn't been able to keep the spooked horses from breaking loose and heading for Lord knows where.

One of the panicked horses had run right into him, cracking several of James's ribs and sending him flying into the wall. The back of his head thwacked against the wood and all went black.

When he came to, the stable had become a rushing river. All the horses were gone.

Kneading the knot in his head, he staggered to his feet and walked in a daze to the wet roads, unsure where he was going. The sun was blinding, and it hurt to keep his eyes open. What he wanted to do was lie down and sleep.

A man stopped him at one point and said the dam was about to give.

"You need to hightail it to Sand Hill, Mr. Winston!"

James gave him a nod and thanked him. As soon as the man left, he was unsure what had just transpired. He'd prided himself on knowing most people in Pine Lick. The town crier clearly knew him, but James couldn't put a name with the face.

Plodding through at times thigh-deep water and sucking mud, he walked seemingly without purpose. It wasn't until he came to his modest home that he realized his body was in better working condition than his mind.

He'd built his cabin away from the Angelina River and at the top of a small hill. Having grown up in a Kentucky holler that flooded all the time, James was not about to repeat those mistakes in Texas. He preferred things high and dry. The dampness of his childhood still haunted his bones.

As he stumbled onto his porch, a man on horseback a little ways off was shouting his fool head off about the dam. He waved his arms frantically at James, who gave a simple wave back.

As soon as his hand touched the knob, a thunderous rumbling sounded from where he couldn't tell. All he knew was that it frightened him.

There'd been talk for years about the Stanton Dam falling apart, and how dangerous the flooding would be for the town. He'd been around long enough for the drills that eventually, and mercifully, stopped.

Was this a drill?

James wasn't even sure the men he'd seen had been real or in his head. Even now, it kind of felt like he was dreaming. Only the dull throbbing in his skull grounded him to reality. There'd be no reason to dream about this kind of pain.

The timbers of his cabin vibrated, and he walked inside in time to see his favorite coffee mug dance across the table and shatter on the floor.

"I'll be."

There was his chair to his left, beside the cast-iron Franklin stove.

Sit down. Yes, need to sit down. Just close my eyes for a bit.

As he squatted over the chair, he thought about the flood.

Flood!

No, it couldn't flood here. He'd made sure of that.

Hadn't he?

The room swam out of focus, and he dropped into the chair hard enough to make the pain in his head explode like Fourth of July fireworks. He winced and bit his tongue. Blood sluiced down his throat. His hands gripped the chair's arms as if he intended to turn them to splinters.

For a while, everything went black and the pain slipped away.

Then he awoke with a start, hearing the man urging him to make it to Sand Hill. His heart hammered and the house shook.

Then all went black again.

When he came to, he was somehow on the roof of his house. James Winston patted himself from his shoulders to his legs, wondering how in the hell he'd gotten there. The thudding in his skull came roaring back.

Though when he lifted his gaze and saw straight ahead, he realized the thudding was coming from *outside* his head.

A massive wave of water, brown as the muck at the bottom of a stagnant pond and stinking just as foul, loomed over everything in its way.

His body went rigid when he spotted a horse galloping for its life, the wave just a few yards behind it and gaining ground quickly.

Suddenly the horse's back legs were snatched by the water. It lifted the horse off the ground, and the whinnying animal was sucked into the maelstrom.

Just like that, it was dead and consumed by the wave.

James had always been partial to horses over people. He didn't think of his own safety as the wave slammed into his house. Wood planking from the roof broke apart. He grabbed a plank, feeling sharp shards of wood pierce his palms.

Cold, filthy water stung his eyes, fought to tunnel into his nostrils and mouth.

Tumbling, end over end, he refused to let go of the roof, to take that desperate breath, as the roiling waters dragged him toward town.

Henrik Smits and two other men had circled back to the sawmill. So many people they had come across expressed their disbelief that anything was going to happen to the dam that Smits had started to doubt himself.

The waters of the Angelina on the other side of the dam of debris had recessed some over the past thirty minutes. More and more lumber and equipment had piled up, and it was now too high for the water to crest. How long that would be the case, Smits didn't know.

The sun was out, the infernal humidity was gone, and there were even birds chirping in the trees. Any songbirds typically around the sawmill at this time of day were drowned out by the cacophony of industry.

"Maybe they were wrong," Gustav Svenson said, wringing his callused hands. "I mean about the Stanton Dam. The one that popped up here will be a problem if we don't take care of it."

Smits nodded. "The question now is, how?"

Most of the men who worked at the sawmill were either at Sand Hill or heading there. How long would they wait until they realized all was well and they could focus on the real problem at hand?

"I don't think it's wise to stay so close to it, Mr. Smits," advised Jacob Smurls. He'd been with Smits and Knoop for five years and rarely spoke. "If something happens, we don't want to be caught up in the rushing water. We might end up in the Gulf."

Smits watched spouts of water peppering the dam of wreckage. That some water was getting through was a good thing. It helped release some of the pressure. But Smurls was right. They could wait things out right here, but farther away from the bulging shore.

"At least the sun will dry us off," Smits said with some nervous laughter. Not much of a drinking man, he wished had had a bottle of something strong tucked away in his office.

Svenson and Smurls followed him to a stack of unprocessed lumber. They climbed to the top, which was only ten feet high, and let the sun warm their faces. From their vantage point, they could get a full assessment of the damage to the sawmill.

"It sure is a shame about the sawmill," Smurls said, twirling one end of his mustache.

Much of it was underwater. Great sections of the roofing were gone. As was a goodly portion of the equipment.

Smits's chest felt heavy, but he wasn't defeated. "We can rebuild. When Mr. Knoop and I first arrived here, there was nothing but trees. At least this time around, we have a foundation. And plenty of men to help us get it back."

He smiled at his men and hoped they would feel the same sense of hope he did.

But that buildup of wreckage in the Angelina worried him greatly. He tried to calculate how much time they had before the water had its way and went on to destroy everything in its path. It didn't take him long to give up, realizing there was no way to quantify it.

He wondered where Jens was at that moment. The man always threw himself headlong into any endeavor.

When the explosion rocked the very air around them, Smits tottered on his seat and almost rolled down the heavy logs, if not for the quick and strong hands of Gustav Svenson.

"I've got you."

He held on until Smits was situated.

The three turned their heads to the west, where the Stanton Dam lay.

"You don't think . . ." Smurls said barely above a whisper.

The ground shook and there was a change in the air pressure.

Henrik Smits paled. His hands went cold.

Cheever and that other man had been right.

He looked at the direction of Sand Hill. It was too far away to reach before the flood made its way to them. Smits had no idea how large a flood it would be. If the dam had experienced a partial collapse, they would be spared from having the entirety of Stanton Lake come spilling down the valley.

But from the sound of it, there had to be nothing left. It was like being near the dynamiting of a mine, except one where they needed to blow apart the entire side of a mountain.

"I think it's safe to say our goose is cooked," Svenson said. They had missed their chance at salvation. Now all they could do was wait for the inevitable.

Smits jumped to his feet and looked around.

The dam was too far away to see, but the vibrations all around them told him a massive flood was on its way.

Where could they go that might have a chance of surviving the impact of the water? Pine Lick was built by and with fine lumber. Quite a bit of that lumber was in shards and pieces.

When his eyes alighted on St. Peter's Church, he pointed and exclaimed, "The church! We have to get to the church!"

There was one thing that made St. Peter's stand out from just about any structure in Pine Lick, save for the bank.

It was made of heavy stone.

St. Peter's was quite possibly the sturdiest building in the entire county. It had been here before the sawmill, a testament to the missionaries who had come here before the arrival of any industry.

Smits scrambled down the woodpile, nearly snapping his ankle in the process. His men were close behind.

"I think we're past saying a prayer," Svenson said as they sprinted up the street to the town's sole Catholic church.

"As long as you have breath on your lips, you can pray," Smits replied.

A strong wind brought with it a stench of moist decay.

They had to run faster.

And hope the door wasn't locked.

Smurls lost his footing and face-planted in an enormous mud puddle. Smits and Svenson turned back to lift him up, running while each held an arm, before Smurls had his feet properly under him.

They made it to the great oak door, panting and terrified. Smits grabbed the handle and pulled.

The church door swung open.

Smits yanked the door wide and came face-to-face with Father Abernathy. The elderly priest's jowls shook with surprise. His nose and cheeks were bright red, and his hair went in every which direction.

"Are you alone?" Smits asked him.

It took the priest a moment to gather his thoughts. "Why, yes, yes . . . I . . . I was going outside to see what the new commotion was about."

Smits would wonder how the man hadn't heard the urgent warnings about the dam if he didn't detect the odor and sight of a man in his cups.

"We need to get to the bell tower," Smits said.

He pushed the priest down the aisle, explaining about the Stanton Dam falling and the need to get to the highest point possible in the old church. Father Abernathy had trouble keeping up with the trio, asking to rest as they ascended the stairs.

Svenson grabbed the man of the cloth by the back of his pants and collar, lifting him off his feet to wrangle him up the stairs. Candles were lit in sconces in the wall. The end of the narrow passageway ended with a locked door.

"Do you have the key?" Smits asked, wheezing slightly.

He couldn't be stuck in the tower like this. It was like being stuffed in a coffin.

Father Abernathy fumbled through his pockets, mercifully pulling out a large brass key.

Smits looked to Smurls and Svenson. "There are things such as miracles!"

He took the key from the priest, got it into the lock on the third try, and put his shoulder to the door.

They spilled into the bell tower, the large bell silently taking up the center space. Smits had never noticed before that the face of the bell was a spiderweb of cracks.

But there was no time to worry about the bell.

They looked across from the church and beheld hell on earth.

"Dear sweet Jesus," Svenson said haltingly as he made the sign of the cross.

Smurls was silent and Father Abernathy made a high-pitched yelp before clambering back down the stairwell.

"Jesus has nothing to do with this," Smits said, transfixed by the mountain of churning water and other unidentifiable things.

The wave was so wide, part of it rode along the Angelina River, while the other half chewed up ground like a herd of starving sheep. Everything in its path was devoured, adding to the turbulent mass.

With only a few seconds until the wave smashed into the church, Smits took in a great lungful of air and held it. Balling his hands into fists, he faced nature's demon with his eyes wide open.

Water shot through the opening of the bell tower like a sledgehammer.

The power of the water was only bested by the soul-shattering noise it made.

Smits, Svenson, and Smurls were hurled into the back wall of the bell tower.

Anything after that was an endless sea of numb black.

Tony Cheever had had enough. Most folks he told about the dam barely paid him any mind, and those who did heed his warning did so without so much as a thank-you.

"Why am I doing this?" he said.

Because that Armand Gloucester bullied me into it. And where is he now? It's one thing to placate a customer so you retain his business. It's another to keep running around the countryside like a town crier for a town I couldn't care less about.

Yes, the Stanton Dam had looked to be in very bad shape when they left the Arcadian. But it seemed to still be holding. And with a day as beautiful as this, it's not as if there would be more rain to strain the damn thing.

He had to get back to the Arcadian. At least it was on high ground and out of the path where the waters of Stanton Lake would run free *if* the dam truly did break. He'd done his bit for Gloucester. Maybe he even helped turn his reputation around with the citizens of Pine Lick who saw him try to save them.

Or maybe the ones who disregarded him would think he was just another loon.

"To hell with them."

Cheever turned his horse around. With any luck, he could be back at the Arcadian to check on his other guests and collapse in his bed for a spell.

He'd made it a quarter mile when the ground shook and his horse reared up, nearly throwing him from the saddle.

A deafening explosion followed the tremor.

Cheever knew then that Gloucester had been right, and he'd been wrong to follow the man on this fool's errand. If he'd ignored the wealthy guest, he'd have a bird's-eye view of the coming disaster. A *safe* bird's-eye view.

The horse spun in circles, whinnying. There was nothing Cheever could do to get her under control. Suddenly the sky flipped, end over end, and he landed on his back, his breath coming in short hitches.

He watched his horse sprint away.

The ground beneath him rattled. He could feel the flood rushing his way.

Blinking the stars from his vision, he got up and looked for the nearest, tallest structure. When he spotted the solid bank, he sprinted to it. It was short and squat, but made of concrete.

When he was just a dozen yards away, he felt the need to turn around.

A massive brown wave towered above the town. Within the roiling waters were trees, shattered houses, and, to his utter horror, the spinning bodies of the dead.

He made it to the other side of the bank just as the wall of water slammed into the center of town. The impact stole the oxygen from the air and made his heart and lungs rattle.

Cheever pushed his back against the bank wall and let out a long, terrified scream as water cascaded over the squat structure.

The four cowboys who had been freed from jail spent too much time searching for and rounding up terrified horses. Far more proficient on horseback than their own two feet, they were finally up and riding, hoping to put Pine Lick and the impending disaster long behind them.

Riding as hard as their mounts would allow through dangerously wet terrain, one of them pointed ahead of them and shouted, "Look!"

A wall of logs, uprooted trees, heavy machinery, and everything else that made up the town spanned the width of the Angelina River. The water on one side was getting dangerously high. Massive waterspouts that had wormed their way through the wreckage spit out brown water in a deafening roar.

Straddling atop that makeshift dam was a trio of children—two boys and one girl, none of them older than ten. Their arms were outstretched as they fought to maintain their balance. The youngest boy and the girl were both crying with each tentative step.

"They're gonna get themselves killed!"

One wrong step would find them getting wedged in the deadly debris, or pitching into the roaring river, where they would surely drown.

"Hey, you!" one of the cowboys shouted. He waved his arms to get their attention. "Stay right there. We're gonna come get you."

The children looked their way, but kept walking, out of fear of being stranded atop the dam.

"Well, kids never did listen to me none."

Three of them dismounted, handing their reins to the fourth. Again, they got the children's attention and motioned for them to stay still. Tying a single rope around their waists, the first two cowboys picked their way up the dam, while the third played out the rope and remained on the soggy ground. They reached the oldest boy first.

"Okay, son. You just hold on to this rope and follow it to the other side. My partner will be there to make sure you're all right."

The boy nodded and grabbed the rope. "Mister, make sure you save my brother and sister."

"That's the plan. Now git."

The cowboy took a tentative step and almost took a tumble when the wood beneath his boot shifted. He lurched forward and snatched the crying girl by the waist. There was no time to calm her down. He told her what to do and sent her in the direction of his partner. The youngest boy didn't wait for him to come to him. Instead, he ran and leapt into his arms, wrapping his arms around the man's neck like a vise.

There was no way he was going to let go. The cowboy walked unsteadily with the boy clinging to him. His pal helped him get to the shore.

"What do we do with them now?" the cowboy who had been holding the horses asked.

"Well, we can't just leave them here."

"And we can't cross the river. Maybe we need to get to that Sand Hill everyone's been talking about. I can't see us riding anywhere safely, right about now."

"I guess Pine Lick ain't done with us yet."

The children, all of them crying and exhausted, were divided among three riders.

The dam of wreckage shifted, making a sound like some great beast bellowing across a valley.

The cowboys put their spurs to the horses, hanging tightly to the children.

With less than twenty yards of distance between them and the dam, it exploded with the power of a ton of TNT. Water and shrapnel shot from the dam faster than a bullet from a gun.

The cowboys and the young children they had saved were obliterated without having even a second to realize what had happened. In a second, their bodies were blown to pieces and those pieces swept up in the angry tide.

Chapter 36

Gloria Amaryllis came to, with a start, just before they got to the heavily wooded base of Sand Hill. Bragg and his companion had awakened earlier and shouted a nonstop litany of threats, no doubt bringing her back from her wounded slumber.

She turned her body so she could face the men and exclaimed, “It’s them!”

Mack Armstrong quickly scooped her in his arms and removed her from the cart and their proximity. He could feel her heart beating fast as a bird’s wings at her back.

“They tried to kill us!” Her eyes were clear and her terror palpable.

“It’s okay, Mrs. Amaryllis. You don’t need to fret over them. Their days of harassing women and children are over.”

“That’s what you think,” Sebastian Bragg’s partner said, sneering.

Bear O’Hanlon raised his fist and shut the man up.

Gloria threw her arms around Mack’s neck and buried her head in his chest, quietly sobbing. Mack carried her without complaint, even though the much bigger Elmer Mizner offered to spell him.

When Archibald saw that she was awake, he broke free from Kate's grasp and ran back to them. He gently touched the hem of her dress and asked her if she was hurt. Gloria sniffled and tried to compose herself. She ran her fingers through his damp hair.

"Yes, I'm going to be fine. I'm so glad to see you." To Mack, she said, "I think I'm good enough to walk." As soon as he set her down, Archibald wrapped her in a bear hug. She looked around at everyone making their way to Sand Hill and those already climbing up and through the trees. "What's happening?" In all, it looked like a swarm of ants frantically clambering up a hill.

Archibald said, "Are we going to die?"

Mack patted the boy on the shoulder. "No, son. We just need to keep walking." To clear up Gloria's confusion, he filled her in about the Stanton Dam breaking. Even through the loud procession of refugees, there was the unmistakable grumbling of something terrible headed their way.

"And who is that man?" the schoolteacher asked Mack when she saw the handcuffed thief.

"Someone I need to keep an eye on until this passes. Don't pay him no mind."

A good number of people had gotten to the top of Sand Hill. Mack heard their cries and saw them pointing. He turned around, but couldn't see anything other than the hurricane-whipped remains of the town.

"We have to hurry!" Branch Armstrong said. "They see the wave. It's close. The cart won't be able to go any farther. Everyone make your way up on all fours if it helps you. The key is speed!"

Whiskey pushed Kelly, their prisoner, ahead of him. "Don't try anything funny. I ain't taking my gun off you."

"I'm not worried about your gun. Just keep up with me." Even with his hands cuffed in front of him, Kelly proved to be nimble as a squirrel as he made his way up the hill. Mack hoped his agility was more born of fear than an attempt to escape. Then again, to where would he hope to escape?

The people at the top of the hill were wailing. It sounded as if Mack and everyone were ascending to the gates of hell, which, if the dam had burst, were in reality right behind them.

Mack urged Gloria and Archibald to join his mother.

"Stay close," Kate said to them, holding out her hand.

Looking at Sebastian Bragg and Slip, Mack said, "We should leave them here. Let nature decide their fate."

Branch extracted the knife from his belt and sawed the bindings on their legs. "Nature may be doing that for all of us. But I'd rather make it through this to see these two given proper justice."

Slip spat on Branch's boots as soon as he got to his feet.

"Show some respect, Slip," his uncle said as his legs were cut free. "Or at least wait until you can spit on the man's corpse."

Mack wanted to wipe the grins right off the men's faces. Slip cackled like a lunatic.

"Move," Branch growled, shoving Bragg hard in the back.

The men dragged their feet, slowing their escape down.

They were flanked by Mack, Branch, Mizner, and Bear.

The ground shook violently. The treetops swayed. That wet, earthy smell was so strong, it was enough to make a man gag.

In the distance, they heard structures being torn apart, trees uprooted, water rushing, and worst of all, terrified screams that were quickly cut short, only to be picked up by a fresh, short-lived chorus.

Mack and his father pushed the men. "If you don't move faster, I'll tie you to a damn tree and let nature take its course!"

The men didn't need his threats. The fast-approaching flood got them running fast as a pair of jackrabbits. Nothing like the sound of impending doom to urge a man onward.

Weaving their way through the trees, sometimes having to use their hands to claw their way, the four of them were just about the last to make the climb. Anyone who had been later or slower to flee the town was most likely already consumed by the flood.

Mack's blood had turned to ice just by hearing the anguished cries of those above who had a perfect vantage point to see what was happening. He hoped his mother, Gloria, and Archibald were already at the top, or at least close.

Mack's back was turned, so he didn't see the wave when it pummeled Sand Hill. There was a tremendous thump that rattled his bones, followed by the snapping of tree trunks, and most of all, the angry gurgling of water.

A thick spray doused them as Sand Hill vibrated from the impact. It took Mack's breath away. He glanced back and saw the water, a brown wall of filth and debris, rapidly rising as it ate up Sand Hill. Great, round trees cracked into pieces. It sounded like unrelenting cannon fire.

Fueled by a fresh injection of adrenaline, Mack picked up his pace, but lost his footing and pinwheeled his arms, knowing he was about to fall backward and get swallowed up by the flood. His father grabbed him by the forearm and pulled him hard enough to almost dislocate his shoulder.

"Don't look back! Just move!"

Sebastian Bragg and Slip were having a hard time of it because of the handcuffs. Elmer Mizner grabbed them both by their shirts and pushed them up.

They ran and dug into the earth with their hands. Mack felt as if his lungs were about to burst. His muscles burned and jittered, threatening with each step to simply give out.

His father hadn't let go of him.

People on top of Sand Hill cried out for them to run faster. Mack wished that were possible.

As the floodwaters lapped against the hill, they were doused by waves of foul water. Something in those waves was heavy and sharp, and it crashed into Mack's back. It felt like being shot. There was no time to acknowledge the pain.

The crest of Sand Hill was finally in sight. Some waved their arms, encouraging them. Others covered their mouths to stifle their screams, their eyes locked on the horror of the flood.

"Bear, look out!" someone shouted.

Mack turned around.

Bear, who had already been hurt, lagged behind them by about ten feet.

A curling wave made its way at him. Within that wave, Mack saw more solid material than water.

"Bear!" he yelled.

The burly loner waved at him. "I'm com—"

When the wave hit him, he was instantly crushed by the heavy debris the flood had picked up along the way. Mack saw a hunk of metal slice into the man, a fraction of a second before he disappeared in the swell.

The lip of the wave caught Mack's legs. For a heart-stopping moment, he thought it was going to pull him under. But his father still had a mighty grip on him, refusing to let go.

The water level rose higher and higher, hot on their heels and gaining ground.

Someone tumbled, end over end, to their left, disappearing into the murky water without so much as a cry for help.

With the water churning and chewing at the hillside, Mack couldn't help but think there was no saving anyone. Soon enough, the wave would sweep everyone off the top of Sand Hill and either consume them or send them crashing to their doom on the other side.

"Almost there!" his father shouted.

A woman who had been climbing the hill by herself shrieked as she slipped and fell backward into the water. Mack looked for her, wondering if there was a way to pull her out, but she never resurfaced.

Nearly at the top of the hill, he spotted his mother and Gloria, arms outstretched. He and his father made it to the top, dropping to their bottoms with exhaustion.

"That . . . was . . . too close," his father said, panting.

Mack looked down and saw the water had found its high point, which was roughly twenty or so feet below them. He didn't even feel Gloria Amaryllis's arms around him until her lips were close to his cheek, thanking God for saving them.

When Mack looked across at what was once the town, he wondered if all the memories of Pine Lick were just a dream.

Like the Great Flood in the Bible, Pine Lick had been completely swept away. Somewhere underneath those raging waters lay the shops, bank, hotel, and houses of friends and acquaintances.

But what was atop those angry waters was enough to shake any man or woman's faith in what was right or wrong.

"Oh no, oh no, oh no," Mack's mother said, sobbing.

There were people down below. People clinging to rooftops, trees, anything they could get ahold of, the raging waters of Lake Stanton thrusting them toward Sand Hill with the speed of the very winds that first tormented Pine Lick.

Horses struggled to stay afloat, braying with terror and confusion. Livestock from every corner of the town was either already dead, their bodies rolling with the wave, submerging and popping back up like corks, or fighting for their lives. Pigs, cows, dogs, chickens, and more succumbed to their fate.

A family of five—Mack instantly recognized them as the Sullivans—huddled close together on what remained of a roof. It spun crazily as it rode the tide.

"We have to save them!" someone on the hill shouted.

Mack's guts soured.

There was no saving them.

Ben Sullivan looked up and Mack swore they locked gazes for the briefest of moments. He saw where the flood was driving them. Sullivan pulled his three girls and wife closer, forcing them to bow their heads.

When the roof they were on hit into the side of Sand Hill, the five Sullivans flew into the air, spinning in five different directions. Everyone heard the horrified cries of the young girls as they were forced from the embrace of their parents. One by one, their bodies bashed into the hill before being sucked into the umber water.

Men, women, and children gasped and cried, some falling to their knees and beseeching an end to the madness. Others stared in mute horror as more people and animals were dashed against the hill and sucked into the watery depths.

A man held tightly to a young girl, his legs straddling a log that must have come from the sawmill. He waved one arm wildly, trying to get the attention of those on the hill. As the log sliced atop the turbulent floodwaters, he managed to get to his feet, holding the girl to his chest.

"What on earth is he doing?" Gloria said.

Mack thought he knew the man's hopeful plan. The question was if there was enough time to make it work.

Without saying a word, he headed down from the momentary safety of the hilltop.

"What the hell do you think you're doing?" his father blurted out.

"He's gonna try to toss her to safety!" Mack said.

His shoulder smashed into a tree, and he spun for a moment, but at least he was still making his way downhill. The log was getting closer by the second. Mack had to alter his course, zagging to his left so he could be in line with the log when it hit the hillside.

Above him, voices shouted for him to stop.

With his heart banging against his ribs, he willed his already-tuckered body to move faster. At least going down was easier than climbing up. He just had to hope he didn't stumble on a root or unseen ditch and end up diving into the water.

Faster, faster!

He was almost close enough to see the horrified expression on the little girl's face.

Just a dozen or so feet to go.

But the log was moving faster than his legs could carry him. The man atop it lost his balance, and for a breathtaking moment, it looked as if he was going to fall into the drink with the girl.

Somehow, he managed to keep his feet under him. His eyes were wide as boiled eggs when he saw how close they were to impact.

Instead of running, Mack leapt, letting gravity assist in covering the shortening distance. He knew what he was doing was insane. For it to work, the man would have to toss the girl at the last possible moment. And then Mack would have to be just at the waterline *and* have the good fortune of catching the child.

Remembering he'd left his lucky rabbit's foot back in his desk at the jailhouse, he figured the spirit of the totem that Otto had given him when he was just a boy would have to suffice.

He cut diagonally as the log's trajectory shifted. The girl was crying. The man saw Mack and nodded solemnly. Mack wondered if the girl was his daughter or just a stranger who had ended up as the last person he would ever be near.

The water boiled just below him as it snarled against the hill. The spray doused him instantly from head to toe.

Just a few more seconds.

Mack made it to as far as he could go without getting sucked under. The water was up to the tops of his boots.

The log came at him like a runaway train.

Mack startled when he felt something grab him by the back of his belt. He had no time to see what it was, because at that very moment, the man on the log heaved the little girl and threw her up and away as hard as he could.

Her screams were swallowed up by the bellicose floodwaters.

She kicked her legs and clawed at the air, reaching for Mack.

He threw open his arms and braced for impact.

What if he did catch her and she knocked him off balance? She'd have been saved for a mere second before being pitched into the water.

Don't think. Just catch the girl.

The instant his fingertips touched her arms, the log slammed into the hill. Mack didn't see what happened to the man, but he heard his short scream and the crunch of bones when he made impact.

Mack wasn't prepared for the full weight of the small girl. She felt as if she weighed more than a full bag of horse feed. Their chests collided and the wind was knocked out of him. He instinctively clasped his arms around her. His legs started to give. The slick ground beneath him gave way. The girl was silent.

Knowing he was about to fall, Mack threw himself backward, hoping to keep himself out of the water.

A heavy tug at his back almost made him drop the girl.

He did a quick turn of his head and saw his father, bootheels dug into the mud, pulling at Mack's belt until his face was redder than a hot poker, every vein in his face and neck bulging.

Mack pedaled his feet, mud and water reluctant to let him go.

It felt like an eternity, but it only took a few seconds to pull him and the girl to safety.

Father and son collapsed on their behinds, breathing heavily, muscles dancing like fresh-caught eels on a simmering skillet.

The little girl gasped, drawing in air with a loud gulp. Mack cupped her face and looked into her wet blue eyes. She was no more than five, a tiny doll of a thing.

For a moment, it was all she could do to draw air.

And then she began to wail.

"You're okay," he said to her, over and over, smoothing her hair as he pulled her face to his chest. "You're okay."

They sat like that until his father pointed at the rising water and said, "We better get back."

Mack took his hand and got to his feet on rubbery legs. The thought of walking back up the hill was overwhelming.

It was a slow go. His father kept his arm around Mack's shoulders.

"That was a hell of a thing you did," Branch said.

"I know you would have done the same thing."

"If I had, I would have beat you to it."

Behind them, they heard more cries for help, more bodies being dashed against Sand Hill. Ahead of them was the lamenting of those who survived to witness hell on earth as family, friends, and strangers lost their lives.

Many hands reached for them, pulling them those last few feet to the top of the hill. Mack tried to let his mother take the young girl, but she wouldn't let go of him.

Their small victory was short-lived, as everyone's attention went back to the horror below.

"We need to get some people near the waterline," Branch said. "There will be others who'll make it, but they'll need help."

Mack agreed, but at the moment, he didn't have a lick of strength left in him. Gloria was on her knees, rubbing a hand on the girl's back and looking at Mack with tears in her eyes. "That was the bravest thing I've ever seen," she whispered to him.

"If we're going to get through the day, I'm sure it won't be the last." Mack's head swooned, and for a moment, he thought he might pass out. When the weeping young girl finally let Gloria take hold of her, Whiskey gave Mack a hand.

"That was just about the wildest thing I ever did see. Please do me a favor and don't do that again. Not sure my old heart could take it."

Mack clapped his deputy on the shoulder. "You think you could handle getting some men and heading to the waterline to search for survivors and bring them up here?"

"That, I can do." Whiskey tapped Mizner on the chest and said, "Come on. Let's get us a rescue team."

Kate pulled Mack in for a powerful hug, her eyes tinged with sadness and pride.

Behind her, a man sang out, "Praise the Lord, for He is good!"

Mack pulled away from his mother to stare down Sebastian Bragg. The man wore a coldhearted grin. He looked to Mack's father and said, "When I saw you rush down there, I was sure you weren't coming back. But you did. And I know why."

Slip looked confused, but smiled like an idiot just the same.

Branch wiped dirt from his face with the back of his hand and approached Bragg. In a deep, threatening voice, he said, "Why's that?"

Bragg's eyes narrowed and his smile disappeared. "It's so *I'm* the one who gets to kill you and set things right."

Mack rushed Sebastian and doubled him over with a hammer punch to his gut. He dropped to his knees, gasping for breath, with spittle dripping from his mouth. When Slip made a move toward his uncle, Mack stepped between them and said, "Give me one reason to throw you down this damn hill!"

Chapter 37

It took one impossible moment for Reverend Jake Smiley to cast away any doubts he had in the miraculous power of God.

As he and Matilda worked to pry the desperate, praying man from the rubble of a collapsed house, the full force of Lake Stanton plowed into the ground just a few feet behind them before continuing its deadly sweep through Pine Lick. The power behind the flood burst both of his eardrums and shook every molecule of his body so mightily, he thought for a moment he would surely explode.

Before he could finish registering the shock of it, he found himself borne aloft on the water, lying on his back on what appeared to be the side of a building. Numb as an anesthetized patient, he beheld the blue sky and brilliant, glowing sun, the few clouds strung along the Creator's canvas zipping by with incredible speed.

He was content to just lie there and watch the sky roll by. He should be dead. Maybe he *was* dead. Maybe this was all part of his passage to heaven. There was a peace and fullness in his heart that he had never known before.

The desperate churning of the water was just a muffled bit of background noise. Smiley felt buoyed by the hand of one greater than he, greater than all mankind. He would have given thanks if he could think straight enough to pray.

The reverend basked in this cocoon of glory, riding the tides to the hereafter.

Until the first twinge of pain stabbed at his back.

That was strange. He shouldn't feel pain in a body that was no longer corporeal.

The great slab of wood he rested upon spun, then smashed into something that sent a frantic flutter through the very timber.

That small pinprick of pain blossomed into a knot of agony.

Smiley arched his back, suddenly feeling something long and sharp not just poking his back, but piercing it, just like the nails that had been hammered into the hands and feet of Jesus. He flopped onto his side with a cry, his hand clawing for the wound, feeling the hot wetness of fresh blood.

He was not alone.

Before he could focus his pain-glazed eyes, a bilious wave swept over him, almost pulling him into the seething water.

Blinking his eyes clear, he saw it was his wife, naked from the waist up, flat on her back with her arms splayed.

"Matilda?"

She didn't respond or move, save for the swaying of her body as the raft rode the wild current.

Smiley used his wounded hands to pull himself to her side. He cradled her cheek and called her name. When she didn't wake up, he pushed on her shoulder, saying her name louder, his voice shaking with fear and desperation.

Suddenly her eyelids fluttered. She winced from the sun, turned her head, then saw him.

"Jake?"

Her voice was dull and muffled to his wounded ears, but it was joyous to hear her speaking at all. "We've been saved," he said to her, kissing the tip of her nose. His vision blurred once again, but with tears.

Matilda didn't appear to grasp what had happened, or where she was at the moment. The poor dear was in shock. When her eyes wandered down to her naked chest, she gasped and covered herself with her arm.

Then she looked at him, really looked at him, and her consternation rose. "Where are your clothes?"

Smiley lifted his head and saw he hadn't a stitch on.

Where he should have been alarmed, he found himself laughing. He laughed until his ribs ached and his belly was sore.

Matilda stared at him in mute horror.

When he settled down, he said, "The force of the flood must have ripped the clothes from our bodies." He pulled her close. "We came into this world naked. We've been reborn just the same, my dear. Don't you see?"

But Matilda, the woman who had been his rock, broke down screaming. No matter what he said, she would not stop. Around them, the water churned and spun the life raft they had been given. There were others speeding alongside them, most clinging to anything that floated, crying for help.

There were also bodies, of both man and beast, face down in the turbulent tide.

He couldn't tell where they were because all remnants of the town had been washed away. Partially sitting up, for that was as far as he could go before the pain in his back overwhelmed him, he had a feeling they might have been channeled into a swollen Angelina River. That could explain all the lumber around them. Amid the cut lumber were trees, their roots and all, spinning and dipping in the cool water.

It was strange how his entire life had been dominated by the loss of his family in a tornado. He'd grown up, made something of himself, but that day had never left him, instead leaving an indelible mark on his soul.

Now here he was, decades later, caught in a far worse calamity, and he felt . . . free.

"Reverend, help me!"

The voice was muffled, seeming to come from a great distance. Craning his neck, Smiley saw Abigail Knepf hanging on to one of those lengths of lumber. A ragged red gash bisected her forehead, and just like them, she had been stripped bare. Abigail was a widow who had been a regular at church, always the first to volunteer and help a person in need.

"It's Mrs. Knepf," he said to his sobbing wife. "We need to help her."

Matilda was incapable of regaining her senses. When he tried to move away from her, she dug her fingers into his flesh and pulled him tight.

The log Abigail Knepf was on turned and she slipped under the water. Reverend Smiley's heart leapt into his throat. He only breathed again when she popped back up, spitting out water and gasping for air.

It took great effort to extract himself from his wife's embrace.

Crawling on all fours, losing his balance several times as the raft spun, he made it to the edge, flopped onto his belly, and thrust out his hand. Abigail reached out, but was too far away.

"Can you swim to me?" he asked over the roaring water.

She shook her head violently. Her teeth chattered. The whites of her eyes dominated her face.

"I know you're scared. But I need you to take a leap of faith. You are still here—*we* are still here—for a greater reason. I will get hold of you."

He inched farther off the raft. Water sliced at his outstretched arm.

The woman wept as she desperately tried to keep her hold on the log.

"Abigail."

Smiley curled his fingers. "Come to me."

Abigail bit her bottom lip, closed her eyes, and pushed away from the log. The current immediately took hold of her frail body and pulled it away from Smiley. Her eyes flashed open, and her arms flailed as she tried to stay afloat. Smiley took a deep breath and pulled himself farther off the raft.

For a moment, it looked as if she would be lost to him for good.

Neither saw the carcass of the calf until it careened into Abigail. The force of the impact knocked her unconscious.

But it also redirected her body, so she was now headed straight for him.

Smiley snatched her wrist and tightened his fingers around her slick flesh. The floodwater fought to tear her away from him.

With his back screaming in white-hot agony, he got hold of her arm with his other hand and pulled until white sparks writhed at the corners of his vision. Never a particularly strong man, the reverend managed to pull her onto the raft with relative ease.

He collapsed onto his back, his chest heaving, with Abigail Knepf's head resting on his bare stomach.

"I did it, Matilda!" His wife looked at him, but there was no comprehension in her gaze. Then he looked above. "No, God did it. Praise be."

He struggled to sit up and rest Abigail's body between them. Matilda gasped when he turned his back to her.

"You . . . you have a shard of wood in your back!" she said.

He probed his back with his pruned hand and felt the sharp splinter of wood. He also felt a fresh, hot gush of blood seep from the wound.

"Can you pull it from me?"

Matilda stared at his wound with mute terror.

"Don't you worry none. I've got it."

Smiley was surprised by how little pain he felt when he pulled the wood from his back. It was close to eight inches long and jagged, four inches of it covered in blood. He cast the wood into the water and lay on his numb back. A small pool of blood began to form under him. Patting his wife's hand, he assured her they would be all right. Matilda wept, shivering in her nakedness.

Abigail awoke shortly after, also shivering uncontrollably.

The three huddled together, Matilda silent and whimpering, Abigail weeping, while chaos reigned around them. Many asked for help, but whatever stores of strength Smiley had were depleted. All he could do was pray for them.

And wonder where this hell on earth was taking them.

Chapter 38

Even though Otto had managed to find some of the higher ground in the valley between the dam and town, the flood still managed to find him and his horse. One second, he was riding as fast as the old mare had ever gone; the next, he found himself swept off the saddle and paddling his arms and legs to keep from being dragged under.

His horse disappeared without a sound. He'd had her for over ten years and would miss her fiercely.

The question now was, how long would he be around to miss her?

Otto had always been a good swimmer, having grown up near both a lake and a series of rapids. Riding along the flood felt just like navigating those rapids when he was a younger man. Except then, he had a canoe. And the strength of a young man.

First things first, he needed to get out of his clothes before they dragged him under. They were instantly waterlogged and heavy. It was like being tied to a boulder. Holding his breath, he slipped underwater and removed his shirt, boots, and pants. It was very difficult, as the tide spun him this way and that. There was a moment when he was no longer sure which way was up. Thankfully, a shaft of sunlight guided his way.

He bumped his head on something heavy, but made it to the surface, lighter than before and hungry for air.

The current had him racing toward town. He sped past the top of a tree, realizing that if he'd hit it, he would have been snapped in half.

This was far from the rapids of his youth.

For in this water were the remains of everything and everyone that made up Pine Lick.

The bloated body of a man, who Otto thought might be the pig farmer Johnathan Malfi, spun in lazy circles as it passed him on his right. His shirt was in tatters, revealing a grievous wound on his chest, his pale ribs exposed to the air. In the distance to his left, he spotted a woman with her arms flung over what he thought was a chunk of wood, but turned out to be another corpse. He waved to get her attention, but could see in her eyes that she had descended into madness.

He wondered if he, too, would lose his senses.

In all his many years, he'd never seen such devastation. And though he'd managed to survive up to this point, there was no telling what more was in store for him, or the crazed woman, and where this would end.

Something heavy bludgeoned his back. He slipped under the water, fighting the pain and struggling with the impulse to take a deep breath. When he resurfaced, he found himself going in circles, as if caught by a whirlpool. Whatever had caused the current spit him out, driving him into the carcass of a dead pig. Otto pushed it away and kept pedaling his legs to stay afloat.

The water was colder than he'd thought it would be. His toes and fingers were starting to go numb. It should have been a relief after all the oppressive heat. For Otto, it was a bad omen. The numbness of the grave was calling to him.

Every time he tried to swim to the edge of the pounding flood, his body was yanked by the current, sending him right back to where he'd started.

He moved faster than many of the heavier objects around him. Up ahead, he saw something that startled him, even in the middle of such a catastrophe.

The unmoored roof of a barn floated by, as if it were a great ship.

On the roof were two wet grizzly bears.

He wondered if they were two of the three that had run past him earlier.

On the other side of the roof was a man, woman, and young boy. Their clothes were in shreds, and their exposed skin was rife with slashes.

The grizzlies paid the humans no mind, and vice versa for the humans. Everything had boiled down to a simple matter of survival.

Otto thought about trying to make his way to the large roof. There was plenty of room for him.

Then he thought of the grizzlies he'd killed over the course of his life. One time was to defend himself. The others were to provide food and warm clothing. His arrival on the roof might upset the balance and draw the ire of the grizzlies. For the sake of the family clinging to life, he didn't want to chance it.

A dog paddled by him, snapping at his hand before moving on.

That was when he noticed the floodwater dividing into two streams about a half mile away. If he judged things correctly, he was being dragged down the left side of the fork. And that fork would most likely take him to the Angelina River. Which meant he might find himself borne all the way to the ports of Louisiana.

There was no way his old heart would last that long.

Maybe it was a sign that his time had come, and he should just succumb to the water and let it take him to the beyond. There were many people he had known waiting for him there. His father had been a cruel man, but he missed his mother, as well as his sisters and brothers. How many had gone before him, he didn't know. But being the youngest, he assumed they would all be there to welcome him.

Then he spotted a way out. And the stubborn coot that he was, he realized he wasn't ready to end his time on earth.

The wide branches of a tree loomed ahead. Somehow, the tree had managed to stay rooted to the ground, defying the angry water. The woman clinging to the corpse was on a collision course with the tree. Part of its trunk was still above water.

When they collided with the trunk, the corpse exploded in a plume of blood and gore.

The woman didn't so much as make a sound. She just raised her arms and disappeared under the water.

Otto found himself about to suffer the same fate.

He had the advantage of having his wits about him. Using long strokes, he knifed through the tide, trying to set his own course.

Stay away from the trunk, he silently ordered himself.

Somehow, he would have to rely on hands with frozen knuckles to grab hold of what he hoped was a sturdy branch. The tree came at him faster than he expected. He reached out with both hands, grasping for anything that would stop his progress. The branch he snagged with his left hand snapped, causing him to spin and lose his bearing. His right hand flailed at the air, and he felt himself being pulled under. Kicking his legs upward, he rose a foot above the water and managed to find another branch.

This one did not break. Otto's fingers screamed in pain as he hoisted one hand over the other, pulling himself farther along the branch and out of the water. The water beat at his back, the cold seeped into the marrow of his bones, and he struggled to keep his grip, even though his hands couldn't feel a thing.

By sheer force of will, Otto managed to claw and pull and kick his way to the massive trunk, using the branches as a ladder to climb out of the water.

With his arms wrapped around the trunk in a lifesaving hug, Otto felt the vibration of the heavy flood as it rushed past the tree. He rested his forehead against the tree, catching his breath.

There was no telling if the tree itself would maintain its stoic stand against the flood, but all that mattered was that for now, he could rest.

When his heart no longer felt as if it were going to gallop out of his mouth, Otto looked down the valley. Where there used to be the expansive sawmill on the banks of the Angelina, there was only water. The only structure visible was one made by the storm. A dam made of rubble from the sawmill and countryside had managed to clog up the Angelina. The flood pushed against it, but it held. Instead, the water rushed around each side, rejoining the Angelina and increasing its width four-fold. All the houses that had been built around its banks had been washed away.

When he looked to the other side of the fork, his stomach soured.

The floodwaters had slammed into the Pine Lick Cemetery, uprooting not just the several hundred crosses and grave markers, but also causing the corpses below to resurface. Their emaciated bodies bobbed on the surface, headed for town in a ghastly, watery parade of the dead.

Otto had never seen or heard of anything so gruesome. The bodies spun and bumped into one another, often times causing limbs to separate and float away.

He shut his eyes against the horror, wondering if anyone would be left alive when the floodwaters receded. And those who did manage the miraculous, would they ever be the same again?

While everyone else was either in shock or standing witness to the horrors piling up against Sand Hill, Whiskey knew he had to keep himself busy in order not to go stark raving mad. Elmer Mizner, younger and stronger by a country mile, had pulled some capable men together to try to save folks being led by the floodwaters to Sand Hill. Whiskey had helped at first, but had to take a break after pulling up his sixth corpse. The muscles in his arms shook so much, he could barely lift them.

What he could do now was walk among the survivors and keep a mental tally of their numbers. Even at a cursory glance, they weren't good. Pine Lick as a town was done for.

Sadly enough, so were some of the folks who had managed to make their way to the top of Sand Hill. A woman cradled a child, his lips blue, eyes unseeing, while she wept and told him she wasn't going to let anything hurt him.

There were exclamations from a group of people. Whiskey hurried over and saw an elderly man flat on his back with his hand clutching his chest. Someone said, "He was fine just a second ago, and then he kinda keeled right over."

"Does anyone know where Doc is?" Whiskey asked.

In reply, he saw several headshakes.

He looked around, but didn't see hide nor hair of the town's doctor. His gaze drifted to the water-swamped town below and he figured ol' Doc was somewhere down there, lost to this world.

"Deputy!"

He spun on his heels and saw the town madam, Belle Dupree. Her ladies surrounded her, along with Tiny Ed, who was nursing his arm.

"Miss Dupree, I'm happy to see y'all made it."

He meant it. With a calamity such as this, there was no need for distinguishing between perceived moral and immoral, good and bad.

Well, maybe except for Sebastian Bragg, Slip, and the thief Kelly. Bragg looked like the fires of hell burned in his eyes for Branch Armstrong. There was a man so full of evil, he was impervious to the machinations of God and nature.

Belle Dupree, normally larger than life, had been reduced somewhat in her journey to Sand Hill. But she still was a commanding presence with the people she employed. "The doctor is dead.

When we were running here, I saw him in a heap on the street. My girl Delilah here even took time to check on him. It looked like he'd had his head staved in by a horse or a mule. Must have gotten in its way when it was scared and running."

That was terrible news. From what Whiskey could see, almost half the people on the hill were in need of some medical attention.

"Maybe someone staying at the hotel has medical experience," he mused.

Dupree gave a gentle push to move Delilah ahead of her. "She's done some nursing in her time. She can help."

Whiskey pointed his chin toward the old man on the ground. "What about him?"

Delilah shook her head. "I'm afraid it's too late for him. He won't be the last to suffer from an ailing heart today. Sometimes it just takes a bit to grip them."

Since he was a man of the law, others had started to gather around as they spoke. He addressed the crowd, something he would normally never do, deferring to the sheriff. At the moment, Mack Armstrong needed to gather himself.

"Pass the word around that if you need some doctorin', Miss Delilah here can see what she can do. Unfortunately, the doc didn't make it. Best form a line and keep it orderly."

"Looks like they need reinforcements," Butch Nathans, the Sawdust's owner, said, pointing to the pileup below them. Most of his britches had been torn away and he had only one sleeve on his shirt. He spoke with a nasal whistle because his nose had been busted.

Whiskey rubbed the back of his neck, suddenly feeling too weary to go on. He shook it off and said, "I'm sure they do. Find anyone you can and head down, but be careful. You don't want to end up adding to the problem."

Butch nodded and grabbed Wilbur Wilson, the chemist. Both men disappeared into the crowd.

Action was good. For him and everyone else.

The most pressing thing now was separating the wounded from the dead, the capable from the incapable.

Whiskey looked back down the hill.

The water was still rising, though it looked more like a pileup of timber and everything that was once solid in Pine Lick. The frothy brown water bubbled beneath it all, seeping through gaps in the mound of debris.

Weak, desperate voices could be heard within the chaos below.

It felt as if everyone and everything were running out of time. The only problem was, none of them knew just how much time was left for them.

Chapter 39

When Mack Armstrong asked Branch if he should uncuff the thief, the ex-sheriff said, "Maybe he can lend a hand. Lord knows, we need it. I'd just say to keep him close."

"I might tie myself to him, just to be safe."

The same could not be said for Sebastian Bragg and Slip. Branch caught both men studying him out of the corner of their eyes, assessing the situation and biding their time until they found a chance to come for him. He'd seen that look before. The hard truth was that he'd worn that same expression back when he was a prisoner of war. When he finally saw an opportunity to escape, he took it. Now his actions decades ago had come back to haunt him.

But for the moment, that would have to take a back seat.

The town and the people he had called his home and friends were decimated. The shock and grief were palpable. The weight of it was almost crushing enough to root him to the spot.

"We're gonna see who's alive and bring them on up, give the others a spell," Whiskey announced. He had a dozen or more men with him, all but one familiar to Branch.

In the time they'd been on the hilltop, the waters of Lake Stanton, unable to scale its heights, had navigated around Sand Hill. It was collecting in the basin on the other side—preventing a mass escape, should it sweep over the top. Men had been mostly dragging dead bodies out of the water and laying them on the side of the hill. But a few survivors had made it as well, so there was more work to be done.

"That's a good idea," Branch said, eyeing the volunteers. All looked worse for wear, some of them bearing bruises and cuts, clothes ragged and torn. Tiny Ed clearly had a broken arm, which he'd tied up in a sling made from his shirt. Even a one-armed Tiny Ed was better than most with both arms. "Any chance we have some rope?"

"First thing I looked for," Whiskey replied. "There may be some washed up against the hill."

Mack, who had been talking softly with Gloria, joined the group. "Until then, we'll have to just form a human chain. Best to get going."

First thing he did was uncuff Kelly. The thief eyed him suspiciously.

"You've been drafted to help," Mack said to him. "By the time we're done, you'll wish I kept you cuffed. Now move!" He grabbed the back of Kelly's shirt and shoved him toward the edge of the hill. "And don't think of leaving my sight."

Kelly grunted, turned, and was about to say something, but thought better of it.

Mack led the way, though this time he was much more careful picking his way down the hill.

"You know, Slip and I could lend a hand," Bragg said, leering at Branch.

"All you hafta do is take these cuffs off," Slip added.

Branch strode over to them. "I'd sooner lay down with a dozen rattlers." He pulled his gun from his holster. "This is for Jimmy."

Bragg opened his mouth, but the butt of the pistol crashed into the side of his skull before words could escape. The man slumped to his side.

"Try that with me, old man, and I'll wear your wife's skin when I kill you," Slip said. The look in his eyes said he meant every word of it.

Branch hit him extra hard.

Then he went about tying them to a tree, triple testing his knots to make sure they couldn't break free. To Gloria, he said, "If they so much as look to squirm out of that, you call down to me and I'll be right back up."

"I'll keep a close eye on them, Sheriff," Archibald said.

"I'd rather you not be anywhere near those two. You hear me? Maybe someday, when you're older, we can deputize you. But for today, I need you to stay away. Am I clear?"

Archibald cast his eyes to the ground. "Yes, sir."

The young girl Mack had saved clung to the schoolteacher's dress. "Any chance you knocked some sense into them?" Gloria asked.

"I'm afraid not. But hopefully, I hit them hard enough to sleep right through to Sunday."

"I'll come with you," Kate said to her husband, grabbing him by the upper arm.

"It's best you stay here with Mrs. Amaryllis and the kids. See if there's anyone else you can help here. I'm sure Dupree's girl Delilah, the nurse, would appreciate having you around."

She gave her husband a look that spoke volumes. "You can save the 'spare the women and children' nonsense for another time. Those people need all the help they can get, and I'm coming."

Branch knew there was no sense arguing. "Fine. But stay close to me."

The volunteers went down the hill in a zigzagging line, careful to avoid any pitfalls along the way. Just below them was bedlam.

People who had somehow survived being ripped along the water's current and being thrown against the hillside were now being crushed by the heavy logs and other materials that had been uprooted, smashed, and carried away.

Bent and broken bodies were littered everywhere.

"Fingers!"

Butch Nathans hurried his pace, breaking the ranks. The slim piano player lay with his back across an uprooted tree. Just from a quick look, Branch saw the man's spine and neck had been broken.

Even though he was dead, Nathans and Tiny Ed pulled his body from the carnage, dragging it until it was clear of the water and debris line.

Others had been luckier than Fingers.

A man and woman had managed to extricate themselves from the water and sat on the hill, naked and purpling with bruises from head to toe. Branch recognized them as Roger and Anna Abercrombie. They had called Pine Lick home practically since it had become a town. Neither seemed to be aware that anyone was around them, nor that they had no clothes on. Branch was grateful that Kate had come with him. He gave her his shirt and she covered Anna, helping her to her feet. She led the dazed woman up the hill, with her husband stumbling behind her as if walking in his sleep.

With Mack taking the lead, he called for everyone to link hands so he could reach precariously over the waterline to pull out a man who was being crushed between a pair of logs. At first, the man couldn't be budged an inch. Then Tiny Ed, who couldn't be part of the chain on account of only having the one working arm, dropped to his rear and used his massive legs to push the logs apart.

The man, who had been babbling incoherently the entire time, a stranger to Pine Lick, wriggled free. He carried something under his arm. When he tried to stand, he lost his grip and it thumped onto the wet earth.

"Dear God, it's Timmy Cuthbert," Whiskey said, making the sign of the cross.

The young, spirited boy was blue and bloated, having been under the water for who knew how long. Branch hadn't seen Timmy's family on the hilltop. As the boy's limp body was passed among them, he wondered if any of the Cuthberts had made it through the storm and flood. Timmy's mother, a frail woman who had already lost four children and had a delicate grip on reality, would most likely be lost for good if she saw the state of her son. It almost might be a blessing if she hadn't survived.

Timmy Cuthbert was far from the last corpse they'd fish out of the water.

The undertaker, Woodrow Paulson, was found impaled on what looked to be a hitching post. Both of his legs were also missing. It was a gruesome sight, just one of many that would haunt them for the rest of their lives.

As they came across the corpses of more strangers, it dawned on Branch that a good number of the patrons at the Palace Hotel had not heeded the warning. Or, in the cases of those who were elderly, were just not physically able to get themselves to safety.

The men worked tirelessly, sifting through the wreckage and cold, cold waters, plucking out the dead, near-dead, and wounded. No one yet had gotten this far unscathed. The ranks of the volunteers grew as more men, and some women, came down from the hilltop to help.

Occasionally there were valuable supplies that were fished out of the water. Bottles of liquor, cans of food, even clothes, though none of them were unscathed. No matter. The survivors were desperate and there was no telling how long they'd be stranded atop Sand Hill.

Branch was surprised to see Lana Maxel, the teen who had been assaulted in her father's mercantile, with her dress hitched up and sleeves pulled back. She was on her hands and knees by the waterline, reaching for another teenage girl, who had swum up from between the logs. The girl was MaryBeth Walbash, a friend of Lana's. Their tearful reunion gave everyone pause, but just for a moment before the pained cries for help from others brought them back to the task at hand.

MaryBeth had also been stripped of her clothes, now only wearing ripped knickers. Whiskey gave the girl the shirt off his back before she was helped up top by Lana.

"Lana!" Branch called out.

The girl wiped tears from her face and replied, "Yes, Sheriff?"

"When you see my wife, ask her to gather some shirts and things to cover folks up. They've been through enough without further indignity."

She solemnly nodded as her friend rested her head on her shoulder.

"How's your poppa?"

The look in her dark gray eyes told him all he needed.

Branch looked at his son, who was staring daggers at Kelly. The prisoner couldn't hide the fact that he'd been staring at Lana Maxel.

"You low-down son of a . . ." Mack hissed through gritted teeth.

"What? I ain't done nothin'," Kelly pleaded.

"Only because you can't at the moment," Mack said.

It was dirty business, being so desperate they needed the help of a thief and a pervert. Mack gripped Kelly by his upper arm and marched him close to the waterline, where the footing was slippery. "You move from there and I'll drown you myself."

Kelly balled his fists, but being a coward, he turned from Mack and reached into the water to fetch a floating trunk. Elmer Mizner helped him pull it out of the muck.

"I found one!" someone shouted.

"Got two more here!"

It was seemingly endless. Branch was more than dog-tired, but there was no time to rest. He and everyone else searching for the living and the dead would keep on until they dropped.

But even as he worked, he felt the intentions of Bragg and Slip hovering just behind him.

Branch's concern was the increasing chaos going on at the top of Sand Hill as more wounded joined the ranks. There was no doubt they would try something if given the chance. They'd already put women and a child in danger, just to lure him in.

Even though Gloria hadn't called out, he thought of going up to check on them. With any luck, they were still sawing wood. There were enough volunteers now. He'd feel better keeping a personal watch over them.

Or I can throw them in the damn water and let the Lord sort them out, he thought.

His musings were derailed when another body was passed along. This time, it was the postmaster, Clifford Mintel. Branch bit back bile as he gazed down at the man's ruined face and body before passing him to the man next to him, where he would be laid next to a growing stack of corpses.

The sun, which had been burning bright, had begun to wane. Branch wondered how they would manage to continue once darkness fell. If he remembered correctly, the best they could expect was a quarter moon.

They would tackle that problem when it arrived.

Until then, he had to ignore the ripening stench of the dead and pray they'd recover more of the living.

The ragged rooftop carried Reverend Smiley, his wife, and Abigail Knepf to a pileup of detritus jammed against Sand Hill. They hit into a jumble of logs with a jarring impact that set his wife wailing and almost spilled them into the drink.

Smiley held tightly on to the women and gave a quick look behind them to see what was coming their way.

The stiff bodies of several drowned cattle smashed into the back of their roof-turned-raft.

Abigail didn't so much as react. Smiley looked down at her and realized somewhere along their turbulent journey, she'd quietly passed on. He put his hand on her forehead and said a prayer for her soul.

More trees and logs slammed into the rest of the dead cattle, bursting them open with such force, their blood poured down on Smiley and his wife like the devil's rain.

Helping Matilda up, he said, "Come, dear, we have to go."

She looked around them with wild, wide eyes. "Go? Go where?"

Smiley pointed to Sand Hill. "You see? There are people there. We need to get to Sand Hill. Once we're close, they'll help us the rest of the way."

"But how?"

Reverend Smiley eyed the mass of material that had gathered around them. Underneath, the water boiled with rabid intensity, splashing up between any gaps, always undulating. Despite that, Smiley saw a way they could walk across the wreckage of the town, not unlike Jesus when He trod upon the Sea of Galilee.

"We can't!" Matilda let go of his hand and backed away. The roof-raft was nudged, and she would have fallen into the water, had Smiley not grabbed her waving arms.

He turned her around to look him in the eye and said, "Yes we can! Do you think the Lord let us get this far, only to let us drown or be crushed like those beasts? We've been given the gift of life. We can't be ungrateful now."

A shade of clarity parted the clouds of panic and doubt in Matilda's eyes.

"I've always been envious of your faith," Smiley said. "Now

I need you to have faith in me. Just hold my hand and walk where I walk. Can you do that?"

She nodded her head because fear had hold of her tongue.

"All right, then. Just follow me and walk like we would from our home to the church. Don't look down. Most of all, don't let go."

Reverend Smiley took the first step off the roof-raft without trepidation. There were so many logs, trees, and sections of houses and buildings packed tightly together, he felt in his heart he could make it to Sand Hill without so much as getting his bare feet wet.

He put his full trust in God to deliver them to the safety of Sand Hill. There were people there who would need a man of faith to get them through not only this day, but many, many more to come. He prayed he would find many of their congregants there. Even if Pine Lick was wiped off the map entirely, they could rebuild elsewhere.

Keeping his head high and his eyes focused on the rising shore of Sand Hill, the reverend walked with the casual air of a man set out for an amble on a calm, temperate day. Matilda's grip ground the bones in his hand together, but he didn't complain.

Someone on the shoreline saw them and waved them on.

"We're so close, dear. Not much farther now."

Smiley chanced a look down and saw the dozens of dead around them, bodies in such a state, it was difficult to remember they had once been human. Matilda must have done the same, because she cried out, stopping and holding him back.

"I can't," she said. "I can't. I can't."

Her body had gone still as stone. He'd never seen her so frightened before. In fact, Smiley wasn't sure he'd ever seen his wife frightened at all.

"I'll carry you."

She looked at him as if he'd just said he would part the waters. "You can't!"

"You've carried me for how many years? And not once did you complain. I think I can handle a dozen yards."

Before she could protest, he scooped her into his arms.

"Now just close your eyes and you'll be safe and on solid ground before you know it."

Matilda buried her face in his neck.

The sheriff and his deputy angled along the shoreline so they would be there to pull them the last step onto terra firma.

"Just keep walking straight," the young sheriff called over to them. The deputy waved for someone to hand him what looked to be a couple of shirts.

Reverend Smiley wondered what kind of sight he and Matilda must be—a man of the cloth and his beloved, bare and rising from the violent sea. Physical appearances no longer mattered. It was the opposite of Eve eating of the forbidden fruit, where she and Adam became aware of their nakedness.

All that mattered was getting Matilda to safety, and then tending to those whose own faith had been battered and broken by the tempest that had befallen Pine Lick.

Out of the corner of his eye, he witnessed a young woman being pulled from the water. He couldn't tell if she was alive or dead. Someone to his left shrieked in pain, begging for someone to come help him.

The reverend decided he would do just that, once he'd delivered Matilda safely.

"Almost there," he said to her.

The deputy leaned as far as he could with outstretched arms.

Smiley hefted his wife's weight, preparing to hand her over.

And then his foot slipped.

His leg plunged into the water up to his knee. The logs that had separated to devour it immediately rammed together. Jake Smiley felt the bones of his calf turn to dust. The pain was blinding.

Matilda hollered with surprise, snaking her arms tighter around his neck.

Instead of crying out or stopping, he pitched himself forward.

"You have to let go of my neck and let the deputy take you."

Matilda breathed rapidly; her arms were stronger than a constrictor. Smiley fought through the white-hot agony in his leg and depletion of oxygen to his brain.

"We've got you, Mrs. Smiley," Sheriff Armstrong said.

Smiley couldn't tell if night had suddenly fallen or if he was losing his vision. Matilda shouted something close to his ear, and then her weight was suddenly gone.

Sucking in a great lungful of air, he saw his wife between the deputy and sheriff. The former sheriff's wife—Kate, yes, her name was Kate—wrapped a man's shirt around Matilda.

"You think you can pull your leg loose?" a large man with an arm in a sling asked with his baritone voice.

Smiley looked down at the ruin of his leg. "I . . . I . . . I . . ."

Just as he was going to try, the logs spread apart once more. This time, his entire body plunged into the horrid water.

The shock to his system stopped his heart for a beat or two.

He sank like a stone.

With only one leg to kick, he paddled his arms, heading for the rectangle of light above.

It closed quickly, taking with it the light, enshrouding him in utter darkness.

Still, he swam upward, until his head knocked against the unyielding roof of ruin.

With his raw and ragged fingers, he tried to pry even the smallest of spaces between the logs for air.

There was no give.

No light.

And then, no air.

His last thought was of Matilda, safe now. She would recover, and she would once again be a rock to those who needed strength and comfort.

Reverend Jake Smiley sank to the bottom with a smile on his face.

Chapter 40

As more and more people were saved from the flood, almost all badly hurt and dazed, Archibald Gibbons fell deeper and deeper into himself. The young boy had reached the limits of what his mind could handle, though he'd never be able to give voice to it.

Mrs. Amaryllis had been trying to settle down the girl the sheriff had saved. The girl was prone to fits of screaming her head off while her body trembled uncontrollably. Seeing another child act that way didn't bother Archibald so much. He'd had sisters, and sometimes they threw tantrums for no reason other than to get him in trouble or gain his mother's attention.

It was the adults behaving in just the same way that unmoored him.

There was mayhem above and mayhem below.

Night was falling fast. Since his father's murder, Archibald had found himself afraid of the dark. At the moment, the coming darkness didn't affect him. He felt as if he'd been dipped in ice water, the numb feeling seeping into his skin, his bones, even his brain.

"I've got you, hon. Shh-shh. I won't let you go," Mrs. Amaryllis cooed into the girl's ear. Every now and then, she gave Archibald a look, as if to remind him that she was there for him, too. The teacher was a very kind lady, and he'd liked being taken under her care. She was softer than his mother had been, more patient and doting. Of course, she only had him, where Archibald's mother had had to look after eight kids, not to mention the house and farm.

"It's going to be okay," Archibald said to the girl in a faraway voice. When he tried to pat her bare shoulder, she smacked his hand away and fell into high keening that hurt his ears.

A man staggered up the hill naked as a jaybird. He had a ragged gash along his cheek, and bleeding wounds on his chest and legs. His eyes showed just the whites, and he shouted things no one could understand.

He dropped at Archibald's feet and reached for one of his legs.

"The son . . . the son is my absolution!"

When the man looked Archibald in the eye, he felt the numbness break.

"Come here, Archibald," Mrs. Amaryllis said.

Instead, he ran, weaving around the growing throng of the walking wounded and mad. Mrs. Amaryllis called out after him, but his legs didn't have ears and didn't care. He had to get away from that man.

Sprinting as he did, he didn't see the body in his path until he tripped over it and fell face down in the mud. He quickly spun around to regain his footing and saw the bluish pallor of a half-naked woman, her eyes gray and staring at the purple sky.

The shriek he heard could have been from anyone, though he had a suspicion he was the source.

"Are you all right?" a woman asked.

Archibald set to running again. He had no destination in mind, though he thought if he could find someplace, anyplace, to crawl into and shut the world out forever, that would be just fine with him.

More cautious of where he stepped, he found only more misery.

He stopped to catch his breath, stooped over with his hands on his knees. Where could he go?

He should go back to Mrs. Amaryllis. Back to the warmth and safety of her.

Now walking with his eyes focused on the ground, with blinders to everything around him, he didn't even register the sun dipping in the western sky, and the stars and moon coming to life. Before he and his father had ever stepped foot in Pine Lick, Archibald liked to set up his tent outside their house, lie on his bedroll, and count stars. He bet there wasn't a person alive who could ever come to the final and definitive number.

When he came upon a large rock on the side of the hill, away from everyone else, he sat on its cool surface and stared into what he could see of the rolling water below. He assumed it was water, because from his vantage point, it just looked like an endless sea of wreckage—like the shore of some Pacific island after an armada of pirate ships had been destroyed by cannons.

The smell coming off the water was pungent, to say the least. It reminded him of the muck at the bottom of the swimming hole by their old farmhouse, before a drought dried it all up.

There was something else mingled with it, too—a kind of chemical smell, much like what billowed from the exhaust of the machines at the sawmill. Normally, such a thing would send him seeking a better place upwind, but this was not a normal day.

He could still hear the frantic and tired voices of the surviving townsfolk, but it was as if they were on another hill.

What he missed was the sound of crickets. The night bugs must have been just like him, too scared to come out tonight.

Archibald looked to the sky, hoping to count the stars and take his mind off his predicament.

What he saw, instead, were the dark striations of incoming clouds. A light mist started to fall, coating his face and clothes. The mist turned to a drizzle, then rain. Soon he was soaked, just like most everyone else.

Something about the rain made him get up from his rocky perch and decide it was time to go back to Mrs. Amaryllis, who was probably worried to death. He shouldn't have run away—but he knew he had to.

A streak of lightning slammed into the mass below him, immediately followed by a thunderclap that made even the wet hair on his head stand on end.

Below him, a man cried out in pain, begging for help.

Archibald's first instinct was to run. He'd been taught well to get inside when lightning hit.

There was no inside to go to.

Hadn't his father said lightning never struck the same place twice?

Archibald took a few tentative steps down the hill, toward the sound of the man's voice.

"Dear God, help me! I'm stuck!"

The naked terror in the man's voice, an adult's voice, rooted Archibald to the spot. He was just a boy. What possible help could he be?

Maybe if I see what kind of trouble he's in, I can get someone to help.

Archibald carefully threaded his way down the dark hill, worried about his feet getting caught in an upraised root. The man's voice grew louder. There was splashing and moaning and pleading with God.

It should have terrified the boy, but the numbness was creeping back in.

Grabbing hold of a low-hanging tree branch, he leaned forward and saw the man. His legs were pinned in the floating wreckage.

Even in the meager moonlight, Archibald clearly saw the rivers of blood running down the man's face.

There was something else of concern not far from the trapped man.

Fire.

The lightning must have hit nearby and caught on those fumes. The man kept turning his head to the fire, each time spurning him to frantically try again to extricate himself with great verbal fanfare.

Archibald's foot slipped and he had to use both hands to hold on to the branch to keep from falling.

That got the attention of the man.

"You there! Help me!"

"I . . . I . . ."

There came a soft *whup* as the flame jumped to another section of floating wood. In the orange glow of the firelight, Archibald was able to clearly see the man's face.

It belonged to Tony Cheever, the man who had killed his father.

Cheever couldn't see him because he was hidden in shadow. But that didn't stop Cheever from shouting at him. "You! Are you deaf? I . . . need . . . help! Get someone if you can't do it yourself!"

The fire's glow danced in Archibald's glazed eyes. "That fire is moving awful fast."

"Don't you think I know that? Stop standing there and help me!"

Archibald didn't move. He was surprised he'd even spoken, though it was more to himself than Cheever.

While Cheever struggled and cursed, the boy's attention was solely fixed on the growing fire. It advanced on the resort owner steadily, like mosquitoes to sweaty skin.

When the log next to Cheever lit up, the man's voice screeched so loud and high, Archibald wondered if he'd somehow broken his throat.

“Why won’t you help me? Why?” Cheever pleaded with his shadowy form.

“You killed my poppa,” Archibald said.

Cheever stopped his wriggling and shouting, peering into the darkness.

Archibald waited until the flame jumped to the log resting against Cheever’s left side. In no time, it would catch on his clothes, on his hair. He didn’t want to see that. Knowing it was going to happen was enough.

While Tony Cheever burned alive, Archibald turned away and headed back up the hill.

He wasn’t sorry he’d left Mrs. Amaryllis.

Chapter 41

The sudden rain didn't last long, but it brought with it a barrage of lightning that seemed hell-bent to add to the misery of the surviving townspeople of Pine Lick. A ripple of flame danced over the floating mound of wreckage as lightning touched on the oil and kerosene that had been swept up with the flood.

On the one hand, it added much needed light so the volunteers could see what they were doing as they continued to fish people out of the water. The injuries they were encountering now were even greater than those they'd found earlier. Limbs were smashed to a pulp, if not entirely gone. A young woman was found alive, but with half of her skull caved in. An elderly man and women were pulled from the water, their flesh blackened from flames. The couple would not last the next hour. They found James Winston, who owned the livery, passed out atop a section of roof. Somewhere during his nightmarish journey, his nose had been shaved clean off, along with part of his right cheek. The rest of him from the neck down wasn't in much better shape. He was carried to the top of the hill to be looked after, though Mack was damn sure Winston wouldn't live to see the morning.

And maybe that was a blessing.

There was a riot of commotion when a group of men Mack recognized as workers from the sawmill made their way to the hill, clinging to a ten-foot log. One of the men had had his hair catch fire when they barreled through the flames. He was in a state of panic and agony. The three men with him became frantic as well as the line of rescuers hustled to drag them out of the water.

Kelly, Mack's prisoner, recoiled when the man on fire reached for him. As he flinched, he slipped in the mud. One of the other men leapt to the undulating shore and got hold of Kelly's leg and tried to claw his way up it.

"Get off my damn leg!" Kelly shouted. He kicked at the man's hands, but missed.

The sawmill worker was desperate to get out of the water and away from the man whose face was now completely enshrouded by flame. In his desperation, he managed to pull Kelly into the water. The thief was pushed under as the man used him as support to cling to the shore. The other two men did as well, while the man on fire went instantly silent before slipping away.

Mack and some men managed to extract the sawmill workers while holding their ground. It wasn't easy work.

Kelly's hand split the water. Mack reached for it. Two massive pieces of lumber slammed together, demolishing Kelly's hand as if it were an overripe tomato. More detritus pushed against the lumber, forming an impenetrable wall between the surface and the water.

"He's gone," Branch said as he pulled Mack back before he lost his own limb to the thumping lumber.

Mack stared at the spot where he'd seen Kelly's hand. Now there was just a red stain on the shaved wood surface. He should have felt relieved that nature had taken care of such a bad man.

Instead, he felt failure. A life was a life. If Kelly was going to get his due, it should have been within the constraints of the law.

They continued the work of rescuing anyone they could—with soaked and delirious bodies either walking with assistance to the top of the hill, or being carried to the growing collection of the dead.

The wounded were left with Belle Dupree's girls to look after them.

Belle was a force of nature, gathering any supplies she could from the survivors, as well as making trips to the waterline to see what had washed up. Her girl Delilah was doing the best she could, though even a handful of trained, experienced doctors would have cracked under the sheer enormity of it all.

As much as a little light was appreciated at first, the danger made itself quickly known as it touched upon bodies that had looked dead and broken, reviving them to flail and scream their voices raw. Those trapped within the floating wreckage or too wounded and too far away to be saved burned alive. The stench of it washed over Mack and everyone on the hill, turning stomachs and plunging their already-broken spirits into depths unknown.

The worst part was there was nothing they could do for them. It wasn't like running into a burning building and scooping up a crying child, then running out a hero.

Walking atop the debris could very well end with someone being dragged under, set aflame, or both.

The fire spread rapidly, the heat of it searing Mack's exposed chest and face. It felt as if his hair was being singed off.

"Come on, don't stop now!" he shouted at the volunteers. They doubled their efforts to pull people to shore as the fire spread in every direction.

It became rapidly apparent that they had indeed managed to retrieve everyone they could.

At one point, Mack felt the vise grip of a hand on his shoulder, pulling him back from trying to shove a log aside so he could see if anyone alive or dead was underneath it.

"We have to call it, son."

Branch was covered in a sheen of sweat. He looked pale as death in the wan moonlight and orange glow of the fire.

"There could be more people," Mack protested.

The cries of those who were burning left an indelible mark on Mack's soul. Of all the horrors and indignities the people of Pine Lick had suffered, listening to their brethren burning alive was by far the worst.

Branch didn't let go of Mack's shoulder. "We've done all we can. Now we just have to pray that fire doesn't make it to the hill."

Mack's heart sank. "What if it does?"

"The waterline's been lowering the past hour, what with it finding its way around the hill. We have to hope the ground is saturated enough to form a line of defense."

"And if it doesn't?"

All Mack could see in his head was the total annihilation of his family, friends, and everyone he'd ever known.

"We're just going to have to pray it does. Come on."

All the volunteers took their lead and halted their exhausting rescue efforts.

All but one.

"I think I see someone," Tiny Ed said.

"Where?" Mack asked.

The big man pointed a blunt, meaty finger to a point where the fire was raging the most. "Looks like a woman."

The panicked and pained wails of men and women had all blended into one high-pitched plea for mercy. Mack squinted and could just make out a shadow against the flames waving its arms.

"I can get her," Tiny Ed said.

"She's too far out, and too close to the fire," Branch said.

"Don't matter. I can do it."

Tiny Ed stepped onto the trunk of a tree. Mack tried to stop him, reaching out, but his fingers closed on air.

"Ed, don't!" Mack said.

The bouncer proceeded walking along the debris without casting a single look back.

"He is one crazy fella," Whiskey said.

"Just crazy enough to save that lady," Wilbur Wilson said.

Everyone watched Ed make his way to the flailing woman. Not a word was said between them. Barely a breath was taken.

There were a few heart-stopping moments when Ed just about lost his footing. Each time, he managed to settle down and straighten himself out. He plodded at a steady pace as the fire got closer and closer to the woman.

The waves of heat rising from the detritus made it hard to make things out when Tiny Ed finally got to the woman and bent down, working to free her. Their shadows merged, becoming indeterminate.

Somehow, even with just one arm, Tiny Ed pulled the woman to safety. No sooner was she on her feet than the fire descended on them in a blooming ball of death. The audience of volunteers cried out. Mack felt a knot form in his gut.

"Look!" Whiskey said.

The small shadow of the woman jumped off whatever she was on and proceeded to pick her way to the hill.

All while the fire touched upon Tiny Ed and rapidly consumed him. He fell to his knees as his body was encased by flames. A few moments later, he fell face down as black smoke snaked from his burning corpse.

Several minutes later, the woman made it to the shoreline and was scooped up by Whiskey and Butch Nathans. She was bloodied and bruised, but still had some clothes on and nothing appeared to be broken. The two men put an arm over her shoulders and walked the weeping woman to the hilltop.

"What the hell were you thinking, Ed?" Mack whispered.

"He spent a lot of years looking after women. Guess he felt he had one more to protect," Branch said.

Volunteers began to drift back up the hill.

"I'll stay to keep watch, just in case the fire spreads here," Mack said.

"We can see that just as easily up top," his father said.

Mack had to be dragged away by Branch—the young sheriff haunted by the desperate pleas for help still coming from within the conflagration.

Kate was waiting for them when they crested the hill. She pulled them both in for an embrace, then bade them to sit down on the dirt while she draped somewhat-dry shirts over them.

Mack looked over at Bragg and Slip, who watched the horror below without expression. He wondered how black their souls were to behold such a thing and not show the least amount of sympathy.

Elmer Mizner towered over them with his arms folded. Mack thought he saw a tear in the man's eye.

"I feel like we're looking straight into hell," Mack said.

No one attempted to tell him he was wrong.

A wave of exhaustion washed through his bones. It was hard to keep his head up, much less his eyes open.

Gloria's sharp shouting snapped him fully awake for a moment. "Archibald! Where have you been? I've been worried half to death!"

He saw the young boy run into her arms. There was something about his blank expression that worried Mack.

But Mack was beyond worrying too deeply at the moment.

As the fire raged and the floodwaters receded, Mack Armstrong drifted into a fitful sleep to the sounds of tortured humans.

Chapter 42

By daybreak, the fires had burned themselves out, the rising smoke blackening the sky and leaving a bitter scent and taste in the air. Branch watched over Bragg and Slip, who were still lashed to the tree, with their chins on their chests.

The screaming below had stopped a couple of hours ago. Branch was sick knowing it meant there were no more survivors. Whiskey had done a quick count of everyone on the hilltop about an hour ago because he couldn't sleep. All told, there were just over three hundred people, out of a town that had boasted two thousand. Yes, there would be other survivors, who by some stroke of luck or miracle had managed to ride it out, but when all was said and done, the final death toll would be staggering, something that would become the stuff of history.

A burst of sun made it through the smoke, causing him to squint.

He felt weak as a newborn calf and his spirits were lower than the ocean floor.

"Hey, buddy," he said, patting Elmer Mizner on the shoulder.

The blacksmith had finally taken some time to sleep during the night. He'd done it in an upright, sitting position. Branch had never seen anything like it. When Mizner's eyes opened, Branch said, "You mind keeping an eye on them for a few minutes?"

"Happy to."

Mizner sniffed the air, and his face crinkled. They looked at each other with no need for words.

Kate and Mack were still asleep, lying on their sides, with Gloria, Archibald, and the little girl Mack had saved all bunched up on the wet ground. Branch gave a silent prayer of thanks for sparing his family. He wasn't naïve enough to think the mental stress of the past twenty-four hours wouldn't forever change their lives, the horror coming back to them in dreams and quiet moments. But at least they'd have a life to spend trying to rise up from this incredible tragedy.

He walked to the hill's edge, seeing other early risers who shuffled about, lost in their own worlds. The water had gone down considerably. The sky beyond the patches of smoke was blue and clear. That was good. They couldn't afford another storm. A few of the taller buildings in Pine Lick poked out of the water like the fingers of a drowning man grasping for help.

Staring off into the distance and the utter ruin of Pine Lick, he didn't hear Whiskey pull up alongside him until he spoke.

"Our trouble is just beginning."

It was as difficult to hear as it was to acknowledge.

"Water and food are going to be a problem," Branch said. "And we need real medical attention. That Delilah girl did a hell of a job, but too many of these people need a hospital. I don't know what we'll do about shelter. And all those dead, especially the ones in the water, will turn rotten and start killing off the rest of us."

"I never seen nothing like this."

"I don't think anyone has."

From their vantage point, Branch could see areas of the countryside that were now passable as the waters leveled off or were sucked downstream into the Angelina River.

"We need to assume no one was able to get out to get help. If we can find some horses this morning, we need to ride out."

"Any horses we find might be too spooked to ride."

"We'll just have to figure it out. If we can't get some horses, we walk. I say the sooner, the better."

"I can get a few men together."

"Much appreciated. After you do, it's probably best you stay here, help Mack, and keep things in order."

Whiskey looked at him for a beat, and resignation clouded his eyes. They both knew that a Black man, even one wearing a deputy star on his chest, might not be taken seriously if he walked into a strange town with a tale too enormously horrendous to sound real. And at this time, they couldn't afford any delays when it came to help.

"We also need to round up some folks to look for food and water and anything remotely resembling medical supplies." Branch snapped his fingers. "And tents, if any wash up."

"I'll go down and see what's left," a man said from behind them. It was Pat "Bull" McManus from the sawmill. Branch remembered seeing him on the hill yesterday, staring off into nowhere and covered in blood. He looked much more coherent now. Someone had washed most of the blood from his face.

"Are you sure you're up to it?"

"Aye. My wife is out like a light, poor thing, and Belle Dupree said they would keep an eye on her. If I don't get up and do something, I think I'll go mad."

Branch knew how he felt. "All right, then. You and Whiskey, see who you can round up. I want to talk to my son before I head out."

Whiskey gave a sharp nod and tapped Bull on the arm. They headed into the crowd, shaking people awake. Branch didn't know how many folks on this morning were both able-bodied and of sound mind, but they had to think ahead before matters got worse.

Mack was already awake by the time he got back. So was Kate.

"I just saw Whiskey and Bull looking like they were on a mission," Mack said. "What's the plan?"

Branch told him, all the while keeping Sebastian Bragg and Slip in his peripheral. He could tell they were awake and listening to every word, even though they pretended they were asleep.

"It's best we get going, then," Mack said.

"Not so fast, son. You're going to be needed here. As far as I can tell, you're the person with the highest authority now. Folks are going to get restless. Especially once they get over the shock and start getting thirsty and hungry. I told Whiskey the same thing."

"I'm a grown man. You can't make a decision like that for me."

Branch gripped his son's upper arms and smiled for the first time in days. "It's the right thing to do, and if you take a moment, you'll agree with me. There's plenty of people you need to look after." He turned his gaze to Kate, then Gloria and the boy and girl. Mack nodded his understanding.

"I never knew what hell on earth truly meant," Kate said as she stared at the remains of Pine Lick. Charred bodies lay about the slowly rolling swells. Everything in Pine Lick had been wiped clean. "When I woke up, I had hoped for a moment that it had all just been a nightmare."

Branch took her hand. "It is a nightmare. Worse than anything I even saw in the war. But we're still here, and people are going to need us."

Kate hugged him. Her hair smelled of smoke and damp earth.

"Elmer, you up for coming with me to Nacogdoches to get help?"

"What about them?" the blacksmith asked about Bragg and Slip.

"We're taking them with us. We need to make sure they're behind bars, where they belong."

Now Bragg opened an eye.

"Time to rise and shine, Bragg. I believe back in Elmira, you used to shout at us, 'Wake up, scum!' We have some traveling to do now."

Slip opened his eyes as well. Both men stared daggers at Branch, but neither said a word.

"Should we get someone else to come with us?" Elmer Mizner asked. "Strength in numbers?"

A smile jerked at the corner of Branch's mouth. He removed his gun from its holder and said, "Between this and you, I think we're on the good side of the odds."

Otto wondered why any luck would continue to shine on an old man like him. Just before dawn, as he was dozing in the tree, something thumped against the trunk. He slowly opened his eyes and saw a canoe pushed against the tree, somehow defying the current that should have sent it around the tree and out of sight.

The water was lower than it had been when he latched on to the tree the day before. Stanton Lake must have exhausted itself clear out.

His bones and muscles were stiff as boards. It took a bit to undo the knot at his waist. All the while, he kept expecting the canoe to float away.

It didn't. The dang thing waited patiently for him to pick his way down the tree and make the final leap into it. The canoe rocked precariously for a moment, then steadied.

Otto looked for a paddle.

When there was none to be found, he shrugged and said, "Sometimes you expect too much, old man."

The canoe lazily made its way down the new river that had sprung up the day before. Otto had his pick of shafts of wood to choose from, as the surface was anything but clear. He plucked a two-by-four out of the water and used it to paddle into town.

There was a cloud of ominous black smoke in the distance, shrouding Sand Hill. That was where he would go. If anyone had survived the flood, it would be there, even though that smoke was a bad omen.

It was impossible to gauge his progress because the landscape had either been destroyed and washed away or was under the muddy water. Birds flew overhead; their songs not as gay as they would be on an ordinary day.

Otto dipped the two-by-four in the water, switching sides, keeping the canoe on a steady course toward Sand Hill. There was no need to rush. By all means, he shouldn't even be alive.

He spotted a jacket floating on the water and used the tip of the board to fish it out. He slipped it on to cover at least some of his nakedness. The jacket was heavy with water and uncomfortable. The morning sun would help dry it out.

With great surprise, he came across the stone tower of St. Peter's Church. Most of it was submerged, but it had managed to stand in the face of the powerful flood. A body hung out of one of the ledges on its broken back. Otto steered the canoe closer to see if there were any survivors.

As the canoe bumped against the bell tower, he recognized the face of the dead man. It was Henrik Smits, the co-owner of the sawmill. It looked like his chest had been caved in, as well as his spine snapped. A look of agony was etched on his lifeless face.

"Hello!" Otto called out.

A head of white hair popped up. It was the priest. Otto had seen him at the Sawdust a time or two.

Father Abernathy looked dazed, but unhurt.

"Can you make it down to me?" Otto asked.

The priest looked at Otto, then the canoe, and then off into the distance. "I don't think so."

Otto remembered him being a portly man and possibly older than himself. Climbing down the stone surface of the bell tower would not end well for him.

"The water is going down," Otto said. "But you should stay there. I will get help to come to you."

The man's jowls shook as he nodded his head. "Th-thank you."

"Is there anyone else with you?"

"Yes, but they're all . . . dead. Men from the sawmill."

The priest did not look like he would fare well being trapped in the bell tower with corpses for long. "Do not leave the tower. Someone will come for you."

The gray head slipped back out of sight. Otto dug into the water with the two-by-four. Now there was a need to rush.

As he got closer to town, the number of bodies, both human and animal, increased, as did the awful stench of their decay. The canoe nudged aside a dog with most of its hair stripped right off. A swollen-bellied pig thumped the canoe from behind, a cloud of black flies hungrily buzzing over the carcass.

Most of the human bodies were face down in the water, arms and legs splayed. On the back of one was a buzzard, pecking with its hard beak for its morning breakfast.

"Get out!" Otto yelled, splashing water on the buzzard. He knew it was a futile gesture. The buzzard flapped its wings, but refused to yield its meal.

Other bodies were on their backs, gray eyes glazed over, mouths hanging open, filled with filthy water. Death, in all its forms, was an ugly thing. He recognized the bald pate of the town barber, Sam Redmond, who hadn't a stitch of clothing on.

Otto paddled for another half hour, the priest being the only survivor he'd come across.

Every time he thought he'd had his fill of death, there was more to come.

Chapter 43

Sebastian Bragg had been forced into a sitting position by the mountain of a man who had been their babysitter. He inched closer to Slip so he could whisper in his ear.

"We can't let them take us to another town. I'm not gonna be hanged while Armstrong still lives."

Everyone around them was busy at the moment, talking about who had died during the night, what was needed for those who hadn't, and dividing the able-bodied men between who would look for help and who would forage for supplies. The young sheriff had taken charge, trying to listen to the rabble that was all talking at once. It was giving Sebastian a headache.

"I know that," Slip said. "But I don't see what we can do with these cuffs on and no weapons."

"We might not have weapons, but I can see plenty of them around. We just need to get our hands on them."

"That's kinda hard to do with our hands cuffed behind our backs."

"Way I see it, we didn't make it all this way just to be waltzed into a jail cell, where we can wait for the hangman to free up his schedule. If we don't do something now, Slip, we're gonna die like whipped dogs."

The man called Mizner had stepped away from them to talk to a woman streaked with mud.

A wild, untamable animal lived inside his nephew. Bragg needed to find a way to bring it out.

"What do you think of Armstrong's wife?" he asked the boy.

"She's pretty, for an older lady. She has a nice body."

"Would you like to take her?"

That wolf-smile spread on Slip's face. "I sure would."

"She's yours then. Or any of the women around. We just need to get a gun."

Mizner cast a wary glance their way. Bragg kicked at the dirt with his heel and kept his mouth shut.

Bragg had been using a sharp stone he'd found at the base of the tree to saw away at the rope around them for the past hour. It was just a few strokes from giving way.

Slip finally noticed and whispered, "You sly dog."

"Act like nothing's happened. Do not, and I mean it, do not free yourself from the rope until I tell you. We clear?"

"Crystal."

The rope parted with a soft snap. Uncle and nephew sat perfectly still.

When Mizner looked away, Bragg said, "I'm going to rush Armstrong's wife. Get people focused on her. When I do that, I need you to grab the sheriff's gun. You think you can do that?"

Slip's eyes burned. "With my hands tied behind my back."

"Good. Now get ready."

Bragg waited until the crowd around the sheriff thinned. The search and forage parties departed, leaving only a few women to talk about the sick and wounded. Branch Armstrong's wife was deep in conversation with one of the women.

With a quick check to make sure Mizner was still distracted, Bragg jumped to his feet more nimbly than he'd moved in many a year. Another testament to knowing his destiny was at hand.

Lowering his shoulder, he ran straight for Kate Armstrong. He closed the gap between them quickly, catching her in the ribs and using his weight to sweep her off her feet and drive her hard into the ground. He felt a satisfying crack of bone and heard every ounce of wind being expelled from her lungs.

A frenzied commotion immediately followed. Hands reached for Bragg, grabbing and clawing to get him off the woman.

Kate made desperate, choking sounds as she fought for air. He nudged her broken ribs with his shoulder until only the whites of her eyes were visible.

Someone grabbed him by the hair and jerked his head back. His neck cracked and his shoulders burned as someone else grabbed him by his bound arms. As they lifted him off, he managed to deliver a final kick to the woman's side. She went into a fetal position, her mouth opening and closing, desperate for air.

Branch Armstrong stepped before Bragg and punched him in the stomach. Bragg felt the blow all the way to his toes.

"Damn you!" Branch shouted as he drove his fist into Bragg's cheek. The old man tasted the flow of copper in his mouth.

As Bragg took a knee, Armstrong went to his wife's side, lifting her head up and telling her to breathe. Others took his place, kicking and punching Bragg as if he were the one who had sent the storm and floodwaters to demolish their precious little dung heap of a town.

Bragg thought he was going to black out when a shot rang out. Suddenly everyone stepped away from him.

He craned his head and saw Slip holding a smoking gun at his side. He was still cuffed, but he'd managed to pinch the pistol and get off a shot.

Bragg couldn't help but smile when he saw the man on the ground.

It was the young sheriff.

A red hole was on the upper right side of his chest, and getting redder by the second.

Slip had his boot on a little girl's back and the gun pointed at her head.

"Back away or I'll splatter her brains all over this godforsaken hill!"

Branch cradled his wife, upset with himself for first pummeling Bragg before seeing to her. It was a spur-of-the-moment thing, and though it felt good to hammer at Bragg, he knew Kate should have been his top priority.

Kate gasped like a frog. He saw the panic in her eyes. He reassured her that she'd be able to breathe. She just needed to calm down.

Then the shot went off.

And he saw Mack on the ground.

Gloria shrieked. The girl they had saved was now under Slip's bootheel. Gloria dropped to her knees, her eyes bouncing between Mack and the girl.

Branch set Kate down and drew his pistol.

"I wouldn't do that if I were you," Bragg said, spitting out blood and teeth. "He won't stop at the girl. And he won't hesitate. In fact, nothing would give him greater joy than you giving him a reason to end her life."

Branch cast a glance at his son. Mack didn't appear to be breathing. The bloodstain spread out across his shirt.

In all his years, he'd never felt the red-hot hatred that was consuming him from his body to his soul. These twisted men who rode in with the storm, true harbingers of evil, had hurt his wife and possibly killed his only child. He not only wanted them to die, he wanted to ride atop them as they descended to hell, happy to spend his eternity there knowing they were where they belonged.

Bragg began to laugh. "I know my brother is looking down at us now and having himself a good old time."

"Where your brother is, there's no such thing as a good old time."

That wiped the smirk from Bragg's face. He struggled to get up.

"First thing you're gonna do is set that there pistol on the ground, real slow. Then you're gonna get these cuffs off me and Slip. And if you don't want anyone else to die, you're gonna take your punishment like a man. It won't be quick. A gut shot to make you suffer. But at least your death won't be in vain. You're the big hero, right? Well, be a hero and save that girl and plenty of others from joining your son there."

Slip jammed the gun against the wailing girl's temple. "You got three seconds, big fella."

Armstrong had no doubt that Slip would relish killing the girl.

"All right!"

He dropped his pistol in the mud. Bragg rushed over to cover it with his boot.

"Cuffs."

Armstrong stared hard at Bragg.

"Cuffs!" Slip shouted.

Mack had the keys in his pocket.

"I should have killed you and your brother that night," Branch growled. "Saved the world from a couple of pieces of trash."

Bragg sneered. "Maybe you should have. You have the whole of the afterlife to think about it."

Kate was on her side, breathing raggedly now. When she saw Mack, she screamed.

"Don't you move, pretty lady," Bragg said to her. "Your husband has orders."

"You're insane," Armstrong said.

"Oh, not me. Him, yes. I'm just a man who likes to see things through. Now get the keys and keep your hands where we can see them."

Armstrong slowly approached his son. He knelt on one knee, briefly touching Mack's chest. There was no movement. Branch bit his lower lip until he drew blood. Trying to keep his hand from shaking, he reached into Mack's pocket for the keys.

"Don't!" someone yelled.

Elmer Mizner, who was less than ten feet away from Slip, lunged at him. Quick as a cat, Slip lifted the gun from the girl and blew a neat hole in Mizner's forehead. The big man's head snapped back, and he dropped, landing at Slip's feet. Slip moved the pistol back to the poor girl.

Adding insult to injury, Slip spit on Mizner. "Man, that felt good!"

Armstrong looked over at a grinning Bragg. "I told you. My boy loves to kill, and he's very good at it."

Kate tried to scrabble toward Mack. Slip fired a warning shot into the dirt, just inches from her face.

Branch found the keys and looped his finger into the ring. He pulled his hand out of Mack's pocket to show he had the keys.

"Good boy," Bragg said. "Now undo my cuffs first."

Of all the people who had suffered and died in the past day, Branch couldn't understand how these two scum of the earth had managed to live.

It's your fault, he thought. *You should have left them to the flood. But your sense of justice got in the way of doing what was necessary.*

Once he uncuffed Bragg and Slip, he couldn't see a way out of the situation.

"You going to make me count to three again?" Slip asked with his maniacal face.

Branch got behind Bragg on legs that had no feeling. He inserted the key and undid the handcuffs. As soon as they hit the ground, Bragg pulled Branch's gun from under his boot and jabbed it at the center of his chest.

"You really think killing me, after everything that has happened here, is going to give you peace?"

"I don't give a spit about your town, Armstrong. I'm just here to set things right. I resolved not to have peace in my life a long time ago."

"No, please!" Kate struggled to shout.

Bragg swiveled the gun in her direction. "Stay where you are!"

Branch reached for Bragg's gun hand, latching his fingers over the man's wrist. There was a struggle for control, and Bragg flexed on the trigger, the shot going just wide of Gloria Amaryllis.

"Slip!" Bragg shouted.

"Say goodbye to the little witch," Slip cackled.

The little girl's cries were piercing.

There was a dull *thwack*.

Slip's knees buckled and he collapsed face down.

His arm went limp. The gun slipped from his fingers.

Otto stood over Slip, brandishing a wet two-by-four. He wore a ripped black jacket and no pants. He picked up the gun and didn't hesitate to shoot Slip in the back of his head. Slip's body jerked once, and his legs and arms jittered for a spell before going still.

Branch's strength was renewed.

He butted his head into Bragg's chin, relishing the clacking of his teeth. While Bragg was wobbly, Branch kneed his wrist, snapping it. The gun flew from Bragg's hand.

Branch Armstrong felt all his fury enter his hands. He punched

Sebastian Bragg square in the nose, flattening it. He then delivered a left uppercut, which shattered his already-fragile front teeth.

Blow after blow rained down on Bragg until Branch could no longer feel his hands.

What he did feel was a satisfaction that he never realized was possible.

Even when Sebastian's eyes rolled up into his head and he fell flat on his back, Branch got to his knee and continued to batter him from his face to his stomach. Bragg spit up gouts of blood with each blow.

He would have kept punching Bragg if Otto hadn't dragged him away.

"He is done," Otto said.

Huffing, Branch looked down at Bragg's battered and bloody body. His swollen and crimson hands fell to his sides.

Bragg rocked his head back and forth, his breathing raspy. His eyes were swollen shut and his nose was flat as a pancake.

"No, he's not done," Kate said.

She stood over Bragg, brandishing Mack's pistol. She pulled the trigger, shooting Sebastian Bragg in the neck at point-blank range.

Spatters of blood streaked her unflinching face.

Before Branch could take the gun away, she emptied it in Bragg's body.

When she was done, she tossed the gun aside and melted into Branch's embrace.

He held his wife, looking over her shoulder at his son's body.

"I am sorry I could not get here sooner," Otto said, staring down at Bragg's bullet-riddled corpse. "At least now I know why I survived."

Everything around them was blurred by Branch's tears. Kate wept fiercely against his chest. He felt as if his heart would break in half.

There was a loud gasp.

Gloria yelped with surprise. "He's alive!" she shouted.

The schoolteacher lifted Mack's head into her lap. Mack coughed, managed to open one eye, and said, "What did I miss?"

Belle Dupree and Delilah had come running over as soon as they heard the gunshot. Delilah dropped to her knees to pull at Mack's shirt to examine the wound.

It seemed all the survivors had gathered around them. The hotel manager, Sam Snodgrass, did what he could to give the Armstrongs some breathing room.

"He's going to be all right. Looks like the bullet didn't hit anything major," Delilah said.

"Wait, did someone shoot me?" Mack asked.

Branch's vision blurred with relief. Mack's sweaty head was flanked by Kate and Gloria. Both women spoke encouragingly to him, while stroking his hair, as Delilah cleaned the wound with some alcohol that had been fished out of the water.

Otto put his hand on Branch's shoulder. "That is one tough kid you made. Takes after his father."

"I remember you saving my bacon a time or two," Branch said, "so I guess we are alike. Thank you, my friend."

"I would say you could thank me with a dry cigar, but I think that is not to be."

Branch looked Otto over. The man had clearly been through hell, but God was merciful, guiding him back to them like a guardian angel.

"What I can do," Branch said, "is rustle you up a pair of pants."

Otto seemed to just realize that he was bottomless. He tugged his coat down. "That is a wise idea. I do not want to excite the ladies too much."

The sound of bells rang across the valley, carrying all the way to the top of Sand Hill. An instant hush fell over the survivors.

"That Father Abernathy is alive and trapped in the bell tower of St. Peter's," Otto said. "I promised I would send someone to get him."

Hundreds of exhausted souls listened in rapt attention to the bells.

They rang for an end to the horror that had befallen them.

They rang for hope.

TURN THE PAGE FOR AN EXCITING PREVIEW!

JOHNSTONE COUNTRY.
WHERE TEXANS FIGHT FOR FREEDOM,
HONOR—AND WHISKEY.

Welcome to the Whiskey Capital of Texas,
where a proud family of distillers faces off with a ruthless rival,
who's trading shots of liquor with hot lead . . .

The small but lively town of Glen Rose, Texas,
is famous for its home-brewed whiskey—thanks to the
Stark family's secret recipe. Over the years, Civil War veteran
Jed Stark and his tough-as-nails mom, Minnie,
have managed to turn their small family distillery
into a highly successful business.
But whiskey's not the only thing that's brewing in Glen Rose.
There's plenty of trouble, too—namely, Merlin Sheldrake,
a rival distiller who's got the money, power, and connections
to swallow the Starks' operation in a single gulp.
Sure, his rancid brand of rotgut whiskey is no match
for their smooth Texas blend. But this is more than friendly
competition. This is nasty, all-out war . . .

First Sheldrake sends a couple of goons to the Stark ranch
to steal their family recipe—but they get a load of buckshot
from Minnie instead. Then he sets fire to the Stark distillery,
burning everything to the ground.
Thankfully, Jed has a stash of stills hidden in a cave
and no intention of backing down.
But then the whiskey wars take an even darker turn—when
Minnie is kidnapped by Sheldrake's hired guns.
Now Jed has no choice but to fight this fight to the bitter end.
Even if the blood flows faster than whiskey, Jed is prepared
to teach these lowlifes a lesson: Don't mess with Texas.
Especially when there's family, honor, and whiskey involved . . .

Chapter 1

Jedediah Stark, a lean, whip-hard man in a sweat-stained faded-blue shirt beneath worn leather braces, leaned back from raking a steel poker over a bed of hardwood coals.

He watched them for a moment as they pulsed and glowed beneath a wide steel pan. This, as very few folks knew, was one of the tricks the Stark family had used for generations of making whiskey, first back in Tennessee, then there at Whiskey Woods, the longtime family ranch outside of Glen Rose, Texas.

Stark stood up straight, stretching his back and letting out a long pent-up sigh, sounding like steam from a worn valve. He rubbed the small of his back and squinted at the drops of sweat sliding down his forehead.

Jed, third-generation Stark to live most of his days and nights on this land, was a tall, broad-shouldered fellow with a gaze difficult to look away from if you were a lady, and dare to meet eye to eye if you were a man.

He tugged free a rumpled red kerchief from a trouser pocket, mopped at his sweat-stippled brow, and thought about how fine a nice, long, cool drink of water would taste then. Movement to his right, below the long eave of the open entrance to his still, caught his eye.

He shifted his gaze and squinted out into the hot midafternoon sun cooking the dooryard. There lay his old, droop-eared, long-boned red hound named Redeye. The dog was a solid, if lazy beast, but performed admirably the only real task asked of him—to lend a cold eye and a gruff bark of warning to strangers.

So far as Jed knew, Redeye was past the ten-year-old mark, but it didn't really matter. The beast had been born old, as if he had had no youth or prime middle years. For a whole long time, for as long as Jed had known him, which was most of the beast's life, Redeye had acted as if each movement cost him an incredible amount of effort. It seemed only by the grace of good fortune was he able to perform the task of rising, walking slowly to his water bowl or his grub. Once sated and filled, it was all the hound could do to drop, as if clubbed on the head with a sledge, into another of his lengthy, snore-filled snooze sessions.

That it had turned out to be another hot day, especially for April, was not a surprise to Jed, but this hot this early in the season only meant more of the same, in his experience, born of roving this spot all his days thus far.

All—save for three years during the cursed war when he was called away and was nearly killed every moment of it, or so it had felt. And at the end of it, or at least of his time in it, never had a man been more relieved to return to his place of birth.

From then on, he vowed to never roam farther than thirty or so miles from it again. Glen Rose was as good a town to live near as any other, in his experience, and Whiskey Woods an ideal home-place.

The one-thousand-acre ranch had been established long years

before by his grandpappy Hawcliffe Stark on reaching the region and deciding to sink roots after he arrived from Tennessee.

Jed cast his gaze once more on ol' Redeye, who had roused himself enough from his usual slumberous pose to raise his head from the dirt, droopy hound-dog eyes taking in whatever it was he had first heard.

Normally, on a steaming day such as this, the old dog would slump, slow-walking, from shade spot to shade spot, only to collapse once more as if shot. It never failed to elicit a chuckle from Jed.

As the whiskey maker wiped sweat from his trim beard, he saw the dog not drop his head back to the earth, but do the opposite and force himself to sit up. Must indeed be something out of the ordinary, thought Jed. He looked again, visoring his eyes against the day as he walked closer toward the sunlight from where he had been toiling before the fire at his still.

Jed looked up the long, winding lane that led from the plateau above the ranch toward the road that led to the town of Glen Rose. He had learned as a boy to always trust a beast's attention, no matter a dog, a cat, a cow, or a horse. They sensed disturbances, differences, far sooner than humans could.

He continued to squint up the road, glancing back once at Redeye, whose flopping ears now showed slight boldness, as if they had sprouted a little dignity. He saw the first possibilities of telltale puffs of someone, or something, approaching the ranch along the dusty roadway. He adjusted the angle of his big, visoring hand against his forehead.

"It's likely Loud," said Jed, not looking over again at his silent conversation pard, ol' Redeye.

Loudon Paley was his newspaperman friend, a chubby Easterner who had made his way West some years before, seeking the woolly and the raw, grist for his story mill, revenge tales resulting in foolish gunplay and unnecessary mayhem.

What the man had found instead was a town, one Glen Rose, Texas, pretty enough, and sizable enough with 216 residents and another couple of hundred in the immediate surrounding area.

What he also found was that Glen Rose had need of a newspaper. In fact, it had never had one, and as the self-proclaimed "Whiskey Making Capital of Texas . . . and maybe the world," Glen Rose seemed ripe and ready, at least to the residents and to the puffed-up mayor, Fendall Hawkins, to welcome the services of a back-East educated journalist.

Much to Loudon Paley's lasting regret, he had, in a fit of whiskey-fueled pique, agreed to be that man and to fulfill that role for Glen Rose. Regret because nothing much ever happened in Glen Rose.

And as Paley was a chatty type and not prone to sitting in the shadows and listening for news, he found himself knowing lots of people, but not having all that many friends.

Somehow, Jed wasn't quite certain how it came to be, he and Paley had become friends. For Jed's part, being with Loud was simple enough. Jed was inclined toward quietness, and as Loud was, well, *loud*, they struck a perfect balance.

Many afternoons, practically year-round, Loud could be counted on to visit Whiskey Woods on foot or more often to ride his old flop-eared mule, Alice, out to the ranch for conversation and a sip of whiskey from the shop bottle.

But as Jed continued to watch the clouds of dust puff up and grow, closer and larger, he noticed that whoever it was, for it surely wasn't Loud, was neither a single man afoot nor a rider on horseback—or muleback.

As Jed continued to watch and sip tepid water from a canning jar, he saw steady plumes of dust rise up, closer, ever closer on this hot day. It was someone in a buggy. A small two-wheel buggy. And this was no person intent on doing anything but getting to the end of the long, winding lane quick.

It wouldn't be his sweetheart, Lilly, because she would be busy at the diner. Besides, he'd seen her the night before and hoped to do so again this night.

Of course, Jed received visits from folks every few days, and sometimes with more frequency than that, but he knew well the schedules of all the saloon owners and others who made regular trips to Whiskey Woods to buy whiskey.

This was not one of those days and, from the approaching look of this buggy, it was not one of his regular visitors. But within another half a minute, Jed Stark knew who this visitor was. And despite his predilection for calmness, level thinking, and even acting in his life, Jed felt his guts tighten a smidgen. For he realized that this visitor was one Merlin Sheldrake.

And while Sheldrake had only been to the ranch two previous times, he had been there for the same reason each time. Jed didn't think this time would be any different. The man would once again make him an offer that most other folks in the region, or perhaps the state, would be hard-pressed to refuse. Sheldrake wanted to buy Stark's distillery, his whiskey, the recipe—everything about it.

For certain, the land would never belong to anyone but a Stark, at least not while Jed lived. And with even more certainty, he knew that they would never sell the distillery and certainly not their family recipe for Whiskey Woods whiskey. Never ever, even if he was killed defending it. He would take it to his grave.

And if Jed was that certain about that point, then his mother, Minerva Florabelle Stark, known as Minnie, or by Jed as Mama, or to folks who knew the family well enough, Mother Stark, was doubly certain. For they were the only surviving Starks of their line in the world, and that coveted recipe was not written down anywhere. Never had been, no sir. It now resided in his head and in his mother's head and that was it, that was all.

It would die with them. And then where would his so-called rivals be—the folks such as Sheldrake, and other whiskey makers who thought they could make a golden liquid half as good as Whiskey Woods brew?

Jed sighed and rubbed a hand over his weary face. This was not something he had suspected was going to happen yet again, and it was certainly not an encounter he was looking forward to. For he would have two knobheaded folks to deal with. Sheldrake and Mama. The thought that they were similar in so many ways made Jed chuckle. And doubly so when Jed mused on Mama's reaction, should such a proclamation ever crawl out of Jed's mouth.

Life in Glen Rose had been fine before Sheldrake came to town four years earlier. He recognized that this area of the country was growing as more folks moved in and settled.

With that fact in mind, Sheldrake reasoned rightly that Glen Rose, famous for its whiskey-making traditions and culture, would be an ideal place to set up operations for the whiskey production and distribution arm of his business holdings, of which booze was the fastest growing and most lucrative.

Jed knew that the man had made much money as an industrialist and railroad man in the upper Midwest and had been slowly broadening his empire. The rangy whiskey maker sighed in silence and walked into the sunlight from the darkened, albeit hotter interior of the whiskey shed. It was a largely open-sided affair with long, low overhangs of roof, which in the infrequent wet times kept the rain from soaking him while he worked.

The cooler months were such that Jed was plenty warm, even without the protection of much in the way of walls, as he spent much of his time tending the fire and receiving plenty of heat.

In fact, the winter months were about the only time when Jed felt about right, not too hot and not too cold. The ever-present urge to make another successful, consistently Stark-tasting whiskey kept the man from caring all that much about his own comforts.

"What are you thinking, eh, dog?" said Jed, barely glancing at Redeye, who sat erect now and was working up a growl deep in his old chest. That didn't bother Jed much. Redeye looked to be more of a menace than he was.

Despite Sheldrake having met the dog on two previous occasions, the rangy hound remained unimpressed with the rich, fat man, something for which Jed approved. It was an attitude, to Jed's relief, that his dear, surly mama shared with the dog.

As if his very thoughts cued her, Mother Stark strode on down from beneath the shade porch of the house. She looked, as Jed knew she would, tight and hard and working up a case of mean. And she was toting Ol' Shredder, a single-barrel shotgun that had been in the Stark family, according to Mama, "since Methuselah was in knee pants."

The gun, so named because it had been known to make a ribboned mess out of whatever it was that it was aimed at and trigger squeezed at, was now aimed and ready.

This was due in part to the fact that the shells Mama used were nasty things brimming with lead nuggets the size of a child's fingertips. And when she gave that trigger a tug, Ol' Shredder spoke like a dragon that had been kept shut up in a dark place for far too long.

It would roar and growl and cough and belch flame and smoke, and it would spit those maiming nuggets as if for the pure enjoyment of it.

Jed also noted, with mild relief, that she had not yet cocked the vicious, barking thing, which, with Mama as the wielder, didn't mean all that much.

The woman was adept at ratcheting back that hammer and sending a dose of "Mother Stark's spicy mix!" at anything or anyone she deemed in need of her attention.

"Mama," said Jed in a low, even voice. "You don't even know what he wants yet."

She swung her gaze from the fast-approaching, dust-clouded buggy and fixed her big son with a hard eye. "I know and you know what that thieving brute wants. And you know and I know he ain't about to get it. But I do know what he's going to get. Held my trigger finger at bay for far too long where that fat rascal's concerned. No more, I say!"

Jed sighed. "Mama, don't kill him. Stark or no, the local law, as you well know, is no friend of ours. Marshal Chiswick will lock you up on murder charges quick as a wink."

"I'd like to see him try!" she said, cackling and squaring off.

Sheldrake's buggy, driven by the man himself, slowed and turned so that all he had to do was stay seated and address them from there, as he had done on his two previous forays out to Whiskey Woods. But then, Jed noted that Sheldrake set the brake and looped the lines. It looked as if the fat man in the fine but dusty suit was about to step down.

Yep, he was, and it was not a pretty sight.

"What in tarnation do you think you are doing, Sheldrake?" said Mama.

The man did not reply until he grunted himself down half backward, out of the buggy.

In a none-too-quiet voice, Mama said to Jed, "That backside of his looks like two pigs fighting under a blanket!"

Red-faced, out of breath, and now facing them, Merlin Sheldrake once more stood on the firm earth of the Starks' dooryard. "Well, now, it is nice to see you both again, I'm sure."

Redeye hadn't yet moved, but Jed noticed the dog was tense all over, every muscle tight and set to hurtle his lean form into a lunge. The growling sound he'd made earlier had only increased in volume.

The hound's floppy ears were angled back, as if he were already darting forward at tremendous speed—something that Jed had never considered would be possible for the beast. All it would take is one step from where Sheldrake stood and that dog would be on him like stink on dung, thought Jed.

And if it happened, he didn't think he would work too hard to stop the beast. He would come to Sheldrake's aid, but Jed didn't think he would hurry himself at it. Time might tell, he thought, getting small pleasure from watching everybody work through their various stances.

He regarded the smile on the rich man's fleshy face, pink and clean-shaven, save for a thin, fancy-man mustache that always looked to Jed to require more effort than it was worth, given its meager showing.

Sheldrake turned to Mama, with what Jed had to assume was intended to be a winning, ingratiating smile. "Mother Stark, I must say it is lovely to see you. Why, you look younger with each week that passes, I do declare!"

As Jed watched, doing his best but not succeeding in suppressing a wincing smile, he was about to say something to help suppress the ruckus that he knew was on its way. He was too late.

"First off," growled Mama from somewhere down deep in her throat, the sound she was making matching that steady, menacing gurgle that Redeye had maintained all the while Sheldrake had been there, "you didn't answer my question, curse you!"

Sheldrake's smile began to slip, but he yanked it back up again and began to splutter, but the old woman cut him off because she kept right on talking.

"You great, greasy-joweled, slop-bellied fool! What makes you think you can set foot on Stark land?" Even as she said this, she raised Ol' Shredder from the near-waist height she lugged the heavy thing at, taking her time and seeming to enjoy the fact that Sheldrake's beady eyes were locked on the thing, the brows rising with the gun.

"Why, my dear lady," he said, offering a slight bow, his derby shucked and clutched tight to his chest. His gleaming bald head was pink and Jed saw the sweat stippling the thing.

On anyone else, he might think the man was sweating extra out of nervousness, but with Sheldrake, Jed didn't think so, not given the bold, swaggering way Sheldrake normally carried himself in life.

The fat man held up his free hand, palm out, and wagged it, as if waving bye-bye to them, which Jed wished he would do, and soon.

"My dear, dear Mother Stark!"

Jed winced again.

"And that's another thing, you pathetic mess! What in the name of all that is kind and decent in the world gives you the right to address me as anything other than Mrs. Stark? Huh? I ain't dear or sweet to you, and I certainly ain't your mama, and for that, I count myself among the luckiest of folks."

Mama certainly was on a roll today, thought the whiskey maker. Speaking of, he had things to do and this unexpected and annoying visit had best get to its inevitable end. Jed cleared his throat and Sheldrake looked over at him, with what Jed thought was a begging look, as if Jed might rescue him from the hole he'd dug for himself.

Nothing doing, Jed thought. "See here, Sheldrake. I have things to do and standing here listening to you jaw and seeing you sweat and stammer and not get to the point is nothing but annoying. Hop to the game, man, or get gone."

"Right, yes, sir, Jed, eh, Mr. Stark." Here Sheldrake glanced quickly at the old woman toting the shotgun before looking back to Jed. "The reason why I am here"—he straightened and stiffened his back, seeming to remember that he was not a mewling, pathetic man, but a wealthy, confrontational businessman, who always got what he wanted—"I came here today with nothing but the best of intentions."

The old woman snorted and spat at the dusty earth before her boots.

"Mama," said Jed. "Let's let the man speak his piece."

She mumbled something, but didn't commit to a yes or no.

"Yes, yes," said Sheldrake. "You see, I know my previous offers to purchase your fine whiskey recipe fell short of the mark you have in mind, and I respect that. I really do! That is why, on reflection and consideration of the fact that you have been an established presence here in the Glen Rose region for a good many years—"

"None longer!" howled Mama.

"Yes, well, I drove all the way out here on this stifling day to make you a third and final offer." Here he had to once again hold up his hands because he saw on Mrs. Stark's face what was coming. "No, no, please, ma'am, please let me finish."

He glanced at Jed, who nodded.

"Thank you, sir. Now my final offer effectively doubles"—here Sheldrake's voice faltered, as if the words were causing him no small amount of grief to utter—"I . . . I offer you double the amount of my last offer. I daresay you recall that figure, Mr. Stark?"

Jed eyed the man through squinted eyes, his arms folded over his chest. He didn't really recall the specifics of that offer, aside from recalling that the amount was substantial even then, and double that was nothing but a foolish figure, to be sure. But it was no use, never would be. But how to convince the man of it? Sheldrake was a hard learner.

"Look here, Mr. Sheldrake, we both appreciate—"

"Ha! Curse your hide, Sheldrake!"

Jed sighed and glared at Mama, then back to the visitor. "We both appreciate your coming out here on this fine day, prettier than a picture if you ask me," said Jed, digging a little at the fat man's complaint about the day being sweltering.

"But as we told you last time, and the time before that, the Stark whiskey recipe is not for sale. We like it here fine and we like what we do, making whiskey. That's it, that's all, man. I'm sorry you wasted your time."

Jed wasn't really sorry. The man was a grown fellow—overgrown, more like. Sheldrake made his choice and so did Jed, a whole lot of them on this day alone.

"But I don't think you understand me, Mr. Stark!"

Sheldrake's tone, Jed sensed, had shifted, changing from soft and placating to something with a harder edge. Not much, but it was there. "What I am offering you is twice the amount of cash. And for that, all I want is a piece of paper with the recipe written on it. Naturally, too, for that amount of money, I have to ask that you both not share that recipe with anyone else for a period of, say, a dozen years. But"—here Sheldrake held up a thick pink index finger, as if prodding the underbelly of the air itself—"since we are, shall we say, friends, and since we are both men of the world and seem to know one another's mind, I am prepared to make certain, albeit limited, concessions."

Sheldrake tapped his chin and pooched his lips a moment, as if deciding between pie or cake at a diner. Finally a smile broadened on his face and he nodded. "Yes, here is what I am prepared to do: I will allow you both to retain ownership of this pretty homestead the Starks have carved for themselves here.

"You will not, of course, be allowed to make whiskey yourselves for another dozen years, it's true, but with money such as that, only a fool would wish to continue working like a galley slave, eh?"

He chuckled and regarded them.

Jed wanted to ask the man if he was funning them, but he knew the answer. He was surprised that his mother hadn't jumped down the fat man's throat almost at once. He glanced at the old woman and saw a rare sight, indeed.

Mama Stark was staring at the fat stranger, her shotgun halfway poised to deliver, the hammer uncocked. But it was her mouth that surprised Jed. It was sagged open and her eyebrows were raised high. He knew about what she was feeling. He himself could hardly believe what he'd heard.

Jed cleared his throat. "Sheldrake, you have to be joshing me." He advanced a half step on the man, Redeye tight to his right knee, advancing with him with steady dog half steps.

"As long as Starks are on this land, we will make whiskey. With our recipe. And we will sell our whiskey. That will never change, and we aren't going anywhere," said Jed, advancing. He paused when he was within a foot and a half of the red-faced, sweating man.

He'd only come this close because he was not a little worried that after all that insulting blather, Mama was about to twitch on that trigger and turn the richest man in these parts into a slopped, oozing, bloodied heap of dying fat man.

A sheen of oil, likely grease oozing from Sheldrake's pores, slicked the fellow's features, a look that made even the normally placid Jed want to punch the man. It smacked of laziness and overindulgence and craven cowardice in the face of life's everyday challenges. None of these were something Jedediah Stark tolerated in himself, and barely so in others.

He made exceptions, of course, for folks who were good at heart, such as his chubby pal, the newsman Loudon Paley. Loud liked his pie, perhaps a pinch too much, but he was intelligent, challenging, and worried about the plight of the less fortunate in life. And Loud woke up each day, Jed was convinced, with an earnest desire to help other folks. A good man.

On the other hand, given what Jed knew of Merlin Sheldrake, he had to say that there was very little kindness or good-hearted intention to the man. He was a loudmouthed, brazen braggart with one urge, and one urge only—to own everything he desired.

The closer he drew to Sheldrake, the more Jed realized the fat man also had an awful stink wafting off him, like a ditch critter gone bloated in the sun. Time to get him gone.

"Look here, Sheldrake, I'm not your friend, I don't know your mind—a freakish thought at best—so I will tell you now for the last time, we don't want to sell our whiskey recipe. The only thing we sell is the whiskey itself, to folks we know and folks we like. Now we didn't ask you to come here once, let alone three times, each time with the same unwanted offer. Stop it and go. Now."

As Jed spoke, he straightened and knew his face was growing redder with the heat of the moment. His right arm assumed a long, straight point to it that whiskered by the fat man's head and aimed at one thing—the fool's silly little buggy.

For one, two, three gulps, all Sheldrake could do was work his thick, wet lips like a banked fish, his eyes round and wide.

He was about to speak when Jed, in a lowered tone, said, "If you don't do as I say, and do it right now, Mr. Sheldrake, I will have no choice but to turn Mother Stark loose on you."

As if to slam the point in place, like a well-smacked nail, from slightly behind and off to Jed's right rose up the deadly, oiled, throaty cold clicking of a shotgun hammer knocking back all the way to the deadliest position of all.

"And I ain't never, not once, failed to hit my target, mister. Keep that in mind, you great, sloppy oaf. Now do as my son says and get gone!"

Standing less than an arm's length from Jed—a head taller and a good deal fitter, leaner, and more muscled than Sheldrake—the rich man looked up at him, then over at Mother Stark, his newly narrowed eyes locked on her sneering face. And he did something that once more surprised the two Starks.

Sheldrake spoke, this time in a low, cold, grating voice that rivaled the steely ratcheting of the shotgun's hammer in menace. "And I have never, not once, failed to get what I want in life, woman." The words curled from his mouth like smoke on the slightest of breezes. "I will have your recipe. Or I will see you both barking in the netherworld, begging for my forgiveness. Keep that in mind."

He turned and walked to his buggy and climbed up into it with a smoothness and speed that Jed thought impossible by the fat fellow, considering his bumbling entrance and descent from the same buggy not long before.

Sheldrake gathered up the reins and looked over at them. "Keep it in mind, but not too long. Merlin Sheldrake won't be kept waiting." With that, he smacked the lines hard on the horse's rump and the buggy lurched forward.

Mama walked over and stood beside Jed and they both watched him maneuver the buggy in no hurry out toward the end of their wide yard.

For one of the very few times in his life, Jed found himself wondering if what he was doing was worth risking the lives of those he cared for, namely his mother. And sure, the Stark recipe and name and home, too. Not to mention his own life.

More to the point, he wondered why it was that, when backed right up to the wall, he and Mama didn't do anything more than stand there like turtles sunning on a log and listen to the great, blustering fellow.

He looked down at Mama and to his surprise he saw a smirk on her face as she watched the slow, low cloud of dust that was Sheldrake's buggy roll away from them.

The old woman raised the shotgun the last few inches to her shoulder, snugged her cheek down, and touched off the trigger.

The shot whipped forward, parting the air like a clot of kill-crazy bees.

Jed saw that she had aimed a pinch high, no doubt in hopes of having the pellets arc down on the retreating buggy. Nothing sounded as if it met with its half-hearted-intended target.

Neither one spoke for a time. Then Jed said, "I will hand it to Sheldrake, he isn't one to give up on a thing."

"It's because what we do, we do better than anybody in these parts. Heck, in the entire country. Maybe even the world!"

Jed smiled. "I think the Scots might have something to say about that."

"Bah," she said. "They're always whining and yowling about how great their whisky is. I don't see it myself."

"You don't drink the stuff, Mama," said Jed, smirking as he tidied up for the night.

"That doesn't matter a whit. I know what I know."

Jed did not respond, knowing after a lifetime of such traded comments, there was no arguing with Minnie Stark and coming out on top. She would not, could not, be bested.